C0054 02533

Formerly a television and film producer, Carol McKellen now spends her time writing fun, impassioned and emotive romance with an undercurrent of sensual tension. When she's

After Hours...

CHRISTY McKELLEN
THERESE BEHARRIE
BELLA BUCANNON

MILLS & BOON

First Published in Great Britain 2019
by Mills & Boon, an imprint of HarperCollins*Publishers*
1 London Bridge Street, London, SE1 9GF

AFTER HOURS... © 2019 Harlequin Books S. A.

Unlocking Her Boss's Heart © 2016 Christy McKellen
The Tycoon's Reluctant Cinderella © 2016 Therese Beharrie
A Bride for the Brooding Boss © 2017 Harriet Nichola Jarvis

ISBN: 978-0-263-27005-1

0519

MIX
Paper from
responsible sources
FSC™ C007454

FSC
www.fsc.org

This book is produced from independently certified FSC™ paper to ensure responsible forest management.

For more information visit: www.harpercollins.co.uk/green

Printed and bound in Spain
by CPI, Barcelona

UNLOCKING HER BOSS'S HEART

CHRISTY McKELLEN

This one is for Babs and Phil, the most generous,
loving and supportive parents in the world.
You've seen me through all my ups and downs
(and there have been a few), and always picked me up,
dusted me off and cheered me on.

I love you. I hope you know that.

CHAPTER ONE

CARA WINSTONE CLIMBED the smooth slate steps to the shiny black front door of the town house in South Kensington and tried hard not to be awed by its imposing elegance.

This place was exactly the sort of house she'd dreamed about living in during her naïve but hopeful youth. In her fantasies, the four-storey Victorian house would be alive with happy, mischievous children, whom she and her handsome husband would firmly but lovingly keep in line and laugh about in the evenings once they'd gone to bed. Each room would have a beautiful display of fresh seasonal flowers and light would pour in through the large picture windows, reflecting off the tasteful but comfortable furnishings.

Back in real life, her topsy-turvy one-bed flat in Islington was a million miles away from this grand goddess of a mansion.

Not that it was going to be her flat for much longer if she didn't make good on this opportunity today.

The triple espresso she'd had for breakfast lurched around in her stomach as she thought about how close she was to being evicted from the place she'd called home for the past six years by her greedy landlord. If she didn't find another job soon she was going to have to slink back to Cornwall, to the village that time forgot, and beg to share her parents' box room with the dogs until she got back on her feet.

She loved her parents dearly, but the thought of them all bumping elbows again in their tiny isolated house made her shudder. Especially after they'd been so excited when she'd called six months ago to tell them about landing her dream job as Executive Assistant to the CEO of one of the largest conglomerates in the country. Thanks to her mother's prodigious grapevine, word had quickly spread through both the family and her parents' local community and she'd been inundated with texts and emails of congratulations.

The thought of having to call them again now and explain why she'd been forced to hand in her notice after only three months made her queasy with shame. She couldn't do it. Not after the sacrifices they'd made in order to pay for her expensive private education, so she'd have the opportunities they'd never had. No, she owed them more than that.

But, with any luck, she'd never be forced to have that humiliating conversation because this chance today could be the ideal opportunity to get her feet back under the table. If she could secure this job, she was sure that everything else would fall into place.

Shifting the folder that contained her CV and the glowing references she'd accumulated over the years under her arm, she pressed the shiny brass bell next to the door and waited to be greeted by the owner of the house.

And waited.

Tapping her foot, she smoothed down her hair again, then straightened the skirt of her best suit, wanting to look her most professional and together self when the door finally swung open.

Except that it didn't.

Perhaps the occupier hadn't heard her ring.

Fighting the urge to chew on the nails she'd only just grown out, she rang again, for longer this time and was just about to give up and come back later when the door swung open to reveal a tall, shockingly handsome man with a long-limbed, powerful physique and the kind of self-possessed air that made her heart beat a little faster. His chocolate-brown hair looked as though it could do with a cut, but it fell across his forehead into his striking gold-shot hazel eyes in the most becoming manner. If she had to sum him up in one word it would be *dashing*—an old-fashioned-sounding term, but somehow it suited him down to the ground.

His disgruntled gaze dropped from her face to the folder under her arm.

'Yes?' he barked, his tone so fierce she took a pace backwards and nearly fell off the top step.

'Max Firebrace?' To her chagrin, her voice came out a little wobbly in the face of his unexpected hostility.

His frown deepened. 'I don't donate to charities at the door.'

Taking a deep breath, she plastered an assertive smile

onto her face and said in her most patient voice, 'I'm not working for a charity. I'm here for the job.'

His antagonism seemed to crackle like a brooding lightning storm between them. 'What are you talking about? I'm not hiring for a job.'

Prickly heat rushed across her skin as she blinked at him in panicky confusion. 'Really? But my cousin Poppy said you needed a personal assistant because you're snowed under with work.'

He crossed his arms and shook his head as an expression of beleaguered understanding flashed across his face.

'I only told Poppy I'd look into hiring someone to get her off my back,' he said irritably.

She frowned at him in confusion, fighting the sinking feeling in her gut. 'So you don't need a PA?'

Closing his eyes, he rubbed a hand across his face and let out a short, sharp sigh. 'I'm very busy, yes, but I don't have time to even interview for a PA right now, let alone train them up, so if you'll excuse me—'

He made as if to shut the door, but before he could get it halfway closed she dashed forwards, throwing up both hands in a desperate attempt to stall him and dropping her folder onto the floor with a loud clatter. 'Wait! Please!'

A look of agitated surprise crossed his face at the cacophony, but at least he paused, then opened the door a precious few inches again.

Taking that as a sign from the gods of perseverance, Cara scooped up her folder from the floor, threw back her shoulders and launched into the sales pitch she'd been practising since Poppy's email had landed in her inbox last night, letting her know about this golden opportunity.

'I'm *very* good at what I do and I'm a quick learner—I have six years of experience as a PA so you won't need to show me much at all.' Her voice had taken on an embarrassing squeaky quality, but she soldiered on regardless.

'I'm excellent at working on my own initiative and I'm precise and thorough. You'll see when you hire me,' she said, forcing a confidence she didn't feel any more into her voice.

He continued to scowl at her, his hand still gripping the door as if he was seriously contemplating shutting it in her face, but she was not about to leave this doorstep without a fight. She'd had *enough* of feeling like a failure.

'Give me a chance to show you what I can do, free of charge, today, then if you like what you see I can start properly tomorrow.' Her forced smile was beginning to make her cheeks ache now.

His eyes narrowed as he appeared to consider her proposal.

After a few tense seconds of silence, where she thought her heart might beat its way out of her chest, he nodded towards the folder she was still clutching in her hand.

'Is that your CV?' he asked.

'Yes.' She handed it to him and watched with bated breath as he flipped through it.

'Okay,' he said finally, sighing hard and shoving the

folder back towards her. 'Show me what you can do today, then if I'm satisfied I'll offer you a paid one-month trial period. After *that* I'll decide whether it's going to work out as a full-time position or not.'

'Done.' She stuck out a hand, which he looked at with a bemused expression, before enveloping it in his own large, warm one.

Relief, chased by an unnerving hot tingle, rushed through her as he squeezed her fingers, causing every nerve-ending on her body to spring to life.

'You'd better come in,' he said, dropping the hand-shake and turning his broad back on her to disappear into the house.

Judging by his abrupt manner, it seemed she had her work cut out if she was going to impress him. Still, she was up for the challenge—even if the man did make her stomach flip in the most disconcerting way.

Shaking off her nerves, she hurried inside after him, closing the heavy door behind her and swivelling back just in time to see him march into a doorway at the end of the hall.

And what a hall. It had more square footage than her entire flat put together. The high, pale cream walls were lined with abstract works of art on real canvases, not clip-framed prints like she had at her place, and the colourful mosaic-tiled floor ran for what must have been a good fifty metres before it joined the bottom of a wide oak staircase which led up to a similarly grand stairwell, where soft light flooded in through a huge stained-glass window.

Stopping by a marble-topped hall table, which, she

noted, was sadly devoid of flowers, she took a deep calming breath before striding down the hallway to the room he'd vanished into.

Okay, she could do this. She could be impressive. Because she *was* impressive.

Right, Cara? *Right?*

The room she entered was just as spacious as the hall, but this time the walls were painted a soft duck-egg blue below the picture rail and a crisp, fresh white above it, which made the corniced ceiling feel as if it was a million miles above her and that she was very small indeed in comparison.

Max was standing in the middle of the polished parquet floor with a look of distracted impatience on his face. Despite her nerves, Cara couldn't help but be aware of how dauntingly charismatic he was. The man seemed to give off waves of pure sexual energy.

'My name's Cara, by the way,' she said, swallowing her apprehension and giving him a friendly smile.

He just nodded and held out a laptop. 'This is a spare. You can use it today. Once you've set it up, you can get started on scanning and filing those documents over there,' he said, pointing to a teetering pile of paper on a table by the window. 'There's the filing cabinet—' he swung his finger to point at it '—there's the scanner.' Another swing of his finger. 'The filing system should be self-explanatory,' he concluded with barely concealed agitation in his voice.

So he wasn't a people person then.

'Okay, thank you,' she said, taking the laptop from him and going to sit on a long, low sofa that was pushed up against the wall on the opposite side of the room to a large oak desk with a computer and huge monitor on top of it.

Tamping down on the nervous tension that had plagued her ever since she'd walked away from her last job, she booted up the laptop, opened the internet browser and set up her email account and a folder called 'Firebrace Management Solutions' in a remote file-saving app. Spotting a stack of business cards on the coffee table next to the sofa, she swiped one and programmed Max's mobile number into her phone, then added his email address to her contacts.

Throughout all this, he sat at his desk with his back to her, deeply absorbed in writing the document she must have stopped him from working on when she'd knocked on his door.

Okay. The first thing she was going to do was make them both a hot drink, then she'd make a start on the mountain of paperwork to be digitally backed up and filed.

Not wanting to speak up and disturb him with questions at this point, she decided to do a bit of investigative work. Placing the laptop carefully onto the sofa, she stood up and made for the door, intent on searching out the kitchen.

He didn't stir from his computer screen as she walked past him.

Well, if nothing else, at least this was going to be a very different experience to her last job. By the end of her time there she could barely move without feeling a set of judging eyes burning into her.

The kitchen was in the room directly opposite and she stood for a moment to survey the lie of it. There was a big glass-topped table in the middle with six chairs pushed in around it and an expanse of cream-coloured marble work surface, which ran the length of two sides of the room. The whole place was sleek and new-looking, with not a thing out of place.

Opening up the dishwasher, she peered inside and saw one mug and one cereal bowl sitting in the rack. *Hmm.* So it was just Max living here? Unless his partner was away at the moment. Glancing round, she scanned the place for photographs, but there weren't any, not even one stuck to the enormous American fridge. In fact, this place was so devoid of personalised knick-knacks it could have been a kitchen in a show home.

Lifting the mug out of the dishwasher, she checked it for remnants of his last drink, noting from the smell that it was coffee, no sugar, and from the colour that he took it without milk. There was a technical-looking coffee maker on the counter which flummoxed her for a moment or two, but she soon figured out how to set it up and went about finding coffee grounds in the sparsely filled fridge and making them both a drink, adding plenty of milk to hers.

Walking back into the room, she saw that Max hadn't budged a centimetre since she'd left and was still busy tapping away on the keyboard.

After placing his drink carefully onto the desk, which he acknowledged with a grunt, she took a look through the filing cabinet till she figured out which system he was using, then squared up to the mountain of paperwork on the sideboard, took a breath and dived in.

Well, she was certainly the most *determined* woman he'd met in a long time.

Max Firebrace watched Cara out of the corner of his eye as she manhandled the pile of documents over to the sofa and heard her put them down with a thump on the floor.

Glancing at the drink she'd brought him, he noticed she'd made him a black coffee without even asking what he wanted.

Huh. He wasn't expecting that. The PAs he'd had in the past had asked a lot of questions when they'd first started working with him, but Cara seemed content to use her initiative and just get on with things.

Perhaps this wasn't going to be as much of a trial as he'd assumed when he'd agreed to their bargain on the doorstep.

It was typical of Poppy to send someone over here without letting him know. His friend was a shrewd operator all right. She'd known he was blowing her off when he promised to get someone in to help him and had clearly taken it upon herself to make it happen anyway.

Irritation made his skin prickle.

He was busy, sure, but, as he'd told Poppy at the time, it wasn't anything he couldn't handle. He'd allow Cara to work her one-month trial period to placate his friend, but then he'd let her go. He wasn't ready to hire someone else full-time yet; there wasn't enough for her to do day-to-day, and he didn't need someone hanging around, distracting him.

Leaning back into the leather swivel chair that had practically become his home in the past few months, he rubbed the heels of his hands across his eyes before picking up the drink and taking a sip.

He'd been working more and more at the weekends now that his management consultancy was starting to grow some roots, and he was beginning to feel it. It had been a slog since he'd set up on his own, but he'd been glad of the distraction and it was finally starting to pay dividends. If things carried on in the same vein, at some point in the future he'd be in a position to rent an office, hire some employees and start expanding. *Then* he could relax a little and things would get back to a more even keel.

The thought buoyed him. After working for other people since graduating from university, he was enjoying having full control over who he worked for and when; it seemed to bring about a modicum of peace—something that had eluded him for the past eighteen months. Ever since Jemima had gone.

No, *died*.

He really needed to allow the word into his interior monologue now. No one else had wanted to say it at the time, so he'd become used to employing all the gentler euphemisms himself, but there was no point pretending it was anything else. She'd died, so suddenly and unexpectedly it had left him reeling for months, and he still wasn't used to living in this great big empty house without her. The house Jemima had inherited from her great-aunt. The home she'd wanted to fill with children—which he'd asked her to wait for—until *he* felt ready.

Pain twisted in his stomach as he thought about all that he'd lost—his beautiful, compassionate wife and their future family. Recently he'd been waking up at night in a cold sweat, reaching out to try and save a phantom child with Jemima's eyes from a fall, or a fire—the shock and anguish of it often staying with him for the rest of the following day.

No wonder he was tired.

A movement in the corner of his eye broke his train of thought and he turned to watch Cara as she opened up the filing cabinet to the right of him and began to deftly slide documents into the manila folders inside.

Now that he looked at her properly, he could see the family resemblance to Poppy. She had the same shiny coal-black hair as his friend, which cascaded over her slim shoulders, and a very short blunt-cut fringe above bright blue almond-shaped eyes.

She was pretty. Very pretty, in fact.

Not that he had any interest in her romantically. It was purely an observation.

Cara looked round and caught him watching her, her cheeks flushing in response to his scrutiny.

Feeling uncomfortable with the atmosphere he'd created by staring at her, he sat up straighter, crossing his arms and adopting a more businesslike posture. 'So, Cara, tell me about the last place you worked. Why did you leave?'

Her rosy cheeks seemed to pale under his direct gaze.

Rocking back on her heels, she cleared her throat, her gaze skittering away from his to stare down at the papers in her hands, as if she was priming herself to give him an answer she thought he'd want to hear.

What was *that* about? The incongruity made him frown.

'Or were you fired?'

Her gaze snapped back to his. 'No, no, I left. At least, I opted for voluntary redundancy. The business I was working for took a big financial hit last year and, because I was the last in, it felt only right that I should be the first out. There were lots of people who worked there with families to support, whereas I'm only me—I mean I don't have anyone depending on me.'

Her voice had risen throughout that little monologue and the colour had returned to her cheeks to the point where she looked uncomfortably flushed. There was something not quite right about the way she'd delivered her answer, but he couldn't put his finger on what it was.

Perhaps she was just nervous? He knew he could come across as fierce sometimes, though usually only when someone did something to displease him.

He didn't suffer fools gladly.

But she'd been fine whilst persuading him to give her a shot at the PA job.

'That's it? You took voluntary redundancy?'

She nodded and gave him a smile that didn't quite reach her eyes. 'That's it.'

'So why come begging for this job? Surely, with your six years of experience, you could snap up a senior position in another blue-chip firm and earn a lot more money.'

Crossing her arms, she pulled her posture up straighter, as if preparing to face off with him. 'I wouldn't say I *begged* you for this job—'

He widened his eyes, taken aback by the defensiveness in her tone.

Noting this, she sank back into her former posture and swept a conciliatory hand towards him. '—but I take your point. To be honest, I've been looking for a change of scene from the corporate workplace and when Poppy mailed me about this opportunity it seemed to fit with exactly what I was looking for. I like the idea of working in a small, dedicated team and being an intrinsic part of the growth of a new business. Poppy says you're brilliant at what you do and I like working for brilliant people.' She flashed him another smile, this time with a lot more warmth in it.

He narrowed his eyes and gave her an approving nod. 'Okay. Good answer. You're an excellent ambassador for yourself and that's a skill I rate highly.'

Her eyes seemed to take on an odd shine in the bright mid-morning light, as if they'd welled up with tears.

Surely not.

Breaking eye contact, she looked down at the papers in her hand and blinked a couple of times, giving the floor a small nod. 'Well, that's good to hear.' When she looked back up, her eyes were clear again and the bravado in her expression made him wonder what was going on in her head.

Not that he should concern himself with such things.

An odd moment passed between them as their gazes caught and he became uncomfortably aware of the silence in the room. He'd been on his own in this house for longer than he wanted to think about, and having her here was evidently messing with his head. Which was exactly what he didn't need.

Cara looked away first, turning to open one of the lower filing cabinet drawers. After dropping the documents into it, she turned back to face him with a bright smile. 'Okay, well, it won't take me too much longer to finish this so I'll nip out in a bit and get us some lunch from the café a couple of streets away. When I walked past earlier there was an amazing smell of fresh bread wafting out of there, and they had a fantastic selection of deli meats and cheeses and some delicious-looking salads.'

Max's stomach rumbled as he pictured the scene she'd so artfully drawn in his mind. He was always too busy to go out and fetch lunch for himself, so ended up eating whatever he could forage from the kitchen, which usually wasn't much.

'Then, if you have a spare minute later on, you can give me access to your online diary,' Cara continued, not waiting for his response. 'I'll take a look through it and organise any transport and overnight stays you need booking.'

'Okay. That would be useful,' he said, giving her a nod. It would be great to have the small daily inconveniences taken care of so he could concentrate on getting this report knocked into shape today.

Hmm. Perhaps it would prove more advantageous than he'd thought to have her around for a while.

He'd have to make sure he fully reaped the benefit of her time here before letting her go.

CHAPTER TWO

SHE WAS A terrible liar.

The expression on Max's face had been sceptical at best when she'd reeled out the line about leaving her last job, but Cara thought she'd pulled it off. At least he hadn't told her to sling her hook.

Yet.

She got the impression he was the type of person who wouldn't tolerate any kind of emotional weakness—something she was particularly sensitive to after her last boyfriend, Ewan, left her three months ago because he was fed up with her 'moaning and mood swings'. So she was going to have to be careful not to let any more momentary wobbles show on her face. It was going to be happy, happy, joy, joy! from here on in.

After slipping the last document into the filing cabinet, taking care not to let him see how much her hands were still shaking, she grabbed her coat and bag and, after taking a great gulp of crisp city air into her lungs, went to the café to pick up some lunch for them both, leaving the door off the latch so she wouldn't have to disturb Max by ringing the bell on her return.

Inevitably, she bought a much bigger selection of deli wares than the two of them could possibly eat in one session, but she told herself that Max could finish off whatever remained for his supper. Judging by the emptiness of his cavernous fridge, he'd probably be glad of it later.

This made her wonder again about his personal situation. Poppy had told her very little in the email—which she'd sent in a rare five minutes off from her crazy-sounding filming schedule in the African desert. Cara didn't want to bother her cousin with those kinds of questions when she was so busy, so it was up to her to find out the answers herself. For purely professional reasons, of course. It would make her working life much easier if she knew whether she needed to take a partner's feelings into consideration when making bookings away from the office.

Surprisingly, Max didn't put up much resistance to being dragged away from his computer with the promise of lunch and came into the kitchen just as she'd finished laying out the last small pot of pimento-stuffed olives, which she hadn't been able to resist buying.

'Good timing,' she said as he sat down. 'That deli is incredible. I wasn't sure what you'd prefer so I got just about everything they had—hopefully, there'll be something you like—and there should be plenty left over for tomorrow, or this evening if you don't already have dinner plans.'

Good grief—could she jabber more?

Clearly, this had occurred to Max too because he raised his eyebrows, but didn't say a word.

Trying not to let his silence intimidate her, Cara passed him a plate, which he took with an abrupt nod of thanks, and she watched him load it up with food before tucking in.

'So, Max,' she said, taking a plate for herself and filling it with small triangular-cut sandwiches stuffed with soft cheese and prosciutto and a spoonful of fluffy couscous speckled with herbs and tiny pieces of red pepper. 'How do you know Poppy? She didn't tell me anything about you—other than that you're friends.'

He gave a small shrug. 'We met at university.'

Cara waited for him to elaborate.

He didn't. He just kept on eating.

Okay, so he wasn't the sort to offer up personal details about himself and liked to keep things super professional with colleagues, but perhaps she'd be able to get more out of him once they'd built up a rapport between them.

That was okay. It was early days yet. She could bide her time.

At least she had some company for lunch, even if he wasn't interested in talking much. She'd spent all her lunchtimes at her last place of work alone, either sitting in the local park or eating a sandwich at her desk, forcing the food past her constricted throat, trying not to care about being excluded from the raucous group of PAs who regularly lunched together. The Cobra Clique, she'd called them in her head.

Not to their faces.

Never to their faces.

Because, after making the mistake of assuming she'd

be welcomed into their group when she'd first started working there—still riding on a wave of pride and excitement about landing such a coveted job—she'd soon realised that she'd stepped right into the middle of a viper's nest. Especially after the backlash began to snap its tail a couple of days into her first week.

Fighting the roll of nausea that always assaulted her when she thought about it, she took a large bite of sandwich and chewed hard, forcing herself to swallow, determined not to let what had happened bother her any more. They'd won and she was not going to let them keep on winning.

'It's a beautiful house you have, Max,' she said, to distract herself from the memories still determinedly circling her head. 'Have you been here long?'

His gaze shot to hers and she was alarmed to see him frown. 'Three years,' he said, with a clip of finality to his voice, as if wanting to make it clear he didn't want to discuss the subject any more.

Okay then.

From the atmosphere that now hummed between them, you'd have thought she'd asked him how much cold hard cash he'd laid down for the place. Perhaps people did ask him that regularly and he was fed up with answering it. Or maybe he thought she'd ask for a bigger wage if she thought he was loaded.

Whatever the reason, his frostiness had now totally destroyed her appetite, so she was pushing the couscous around her plate when Max stood up, making her jump in her seat.

'Let me know how much I owe you for lunch and I'll

get it out of petty cash before you leave,' he said, turning abruptly on the spot and heading over to the dishwasher to load his empty plate into it.

His movements were jerky and fast, as if he was really irritated about something now.

It couldn't be her, could it?

No.

Could it?

He must just be keen to get back to work.

As soon as he left the room, she let out the breath she'd been holding, feeling the tension in her neck muscles release a little.

The words *frying pan* and *fire* flitted through her head, but she dismissed them. If he was a friend of Poppy's he couldn't be that bad. She must have just caught him on a bad day. And, as her friend Sarah had pointed out after she'd cried on her shoulder about making a mess of her recent job interviews, she was bound to be prone to paranoia after her last experience.

Once she'd cleared up in the kitchen, Cara got straight back to work, using the link Max gave her to log in to his online diary and work through his travel requirements for the next month. His former ire seemed to have abated somewhat and their interaction from that point onwards was more relaxed, but still very professional. Blessedly, concentrating on the work soothed her and the headache that had started at the end of lunch began to lift as she worked methodically through her tasks.

Mid-afternoon, Max broke off from writing his document for a couple of minutes to outline some research he wanted her to do on a few businesses he was considering targeting. To her frustration, she had to throw every molecule of energy into making scrupulous notes in order to keep focused on the task in hand and not on the way Max's masculine scent made her senses reel and her skin heat with awareness every time he leaned closer to point something out on the computer they were huddled around.

That was something she was going to have to conquer if they continued to work together, which hopefully they would. She definitely couldn't afford a crush on her boss to get in the way of her recuperating future.

After finally being released from the duress of his unnerving presence, she spent the remainder of the day happily surfing the internet and collating the information into a handy crib sheet for him, revelling in the relief of getting back into a mindset she'd taken for granted until about six months ago, before her whole working life had been turned inside out.

At five-thirty she both printed out the document and emailed it to him, then gathered up her coat and bag, feeling as though she'd done her first good day's work in a long time.

Approaching his desk, she cleared her throat and laid the printout onto it, trying not to stare at the way his muscles moved beneath his slim-fitting shirt while she waited for him to finish what he was typing. Tearing her eyes away from his broad back, she took the opportunity to look at his hands instead, noting with a strange satisfaction that he wasn't wearing a wedding ring on his long, strong-looking fingers.

Okay, not married then. But surely he must have a girlfriend. She couldn't imagine someone as attractive as Max being single.

He stopped typing and swivelled round in his chair to face her, startling her out of her musings and triggering a strange throb, low in her body.

'You've done well today; I'm impressed,' he said, giving her a slow nod.

She couldn't stop her mouth from springing up into a full-on grin. It had been a long while since she'd been complimented on her work and it felt ridiculously good.

'Thank you—I've really enjoyed it.'

His raised eyebrow told her she'd been a bit over-effusive with that statement, but he unfolded his arms and dipped his head thoughtfully.

'If you're still interested, I'm willing to go ahead with the one-month trial.'

Her squeak of delight made him blink. 'I can't promise there'll be a full-time job at the end of it, though,' he added quickly.

She nodded. 'Okay, I understand.' She'd just have to make sure she'd made herself indispensable by the end of the month.

He then named a weekly wage that made her heart leap with excitement. With money like that she could afford to stay in London and keep on renting her flat.

'I'll see you here at nine tomorrow then,' he concluded, turning back to his computer screen.

'Great. Nine o'clock tomorrow,' she repeated, smiling at the back of his head and retreating out of the room.

She floated out of the house on a cloud of joy, desperate to get home so she could phone her landlord and tell him she was going to be able to make next month's rent so he didn't need to find a new tenant for her flat.

It was all going to be okay now; she could feel it.

Back in her flat, she dialled her landlord's number and he answered with a brusque, 'Yes.'

'Dominic—it's Cara Winstone. I'm calling with good news. I've just started at a new job so I'll be able to renew my lease on your property in Islington.'

There was a silence at the end of the phone, followed by a long sigh. 'Sorry, Cara, but I've already promised my nephew he can move in at the end of the week. I got the impression you wouldn't be able to afford the rent any more and I've kept it pitifully low for the last couple of years already. I can't afford to sub you any more.'

Fear and anger made her stomach sink and a suffocating heat race over her skin as she fully took in what he'd just said. He was such a liar. He'd been hiking the rent up year on year until she'd felt as if she was being totally fleeced, but she hadn't wanted the hassle of moving out of her comfortable little flat so she'd sucked it up. Until she wasn't able to any more.

'Can't you tell your nephew that your current tenant has changed her mind?' Even as she said it she knew what his answer was going to be.

'No. I can't. You had your chance to renew. I couldn't wait any longer and my nephew was having trouble finding somewhere suitable to live. It's a cut-throat rental market in London at the moment.'

That was something she was about to find out herself, she felt sure of it.

'Do you have anywhere else available to rent at the moment?' she asked, desperately grasping for some glimmer of a solution.

'No. Sorry.'

He didn't sound sorry, she noted with another sting of anger.

'You've got till the end of the week, then I want you out,' he continued. 'Make sure the place is in a good state when you leave or I'll have to withhold your damage deposit.' And, with that, he put the phone down on her.

It took a few minutes of hanging her head between her knees for the dizziness to abate and for her erratic heartbeat to return to normal.

Okay, this was just a setback. She could handle it.

Just because it would be hard to find a decent flat to rent in London at short notice didn't mean she wouldn't find somewhere else. She'd have to be proactive though and make sure to put all her feelers out, then respond quickly to any leads.

That could prove tricky now that she was working so closely with Max and she was going to have to be very careful not to mess up on the job, because it looked as though she was going to need things to work out there more than ever now.

The rest of the week flew by for Max, with Cara turning up exactly when she said she would and working diligently and efficiently through the tasks he gave her.

Whilst it was useful having her around to take care of some of the more mundane jobs that he'd been ignoring for far too long, he also found her presence was disrupting his ability to lose himself in his work, which he'd come to rely on in order to get through the fiercely busy days.

She was just so *jolly* all the time.

And she was making the place smell different. Every morning when he came downstairs for his breakfast he noticed her light floral perfume in the air. It was as though she was beginning to permeate the walls of his house and even the furniture with her scent.

It made him uncomfortable.

He knew he'd been rude during their first lunch together when Cara had asked him about the house and that he'd been unforthcoming about anything of a personal nature ever since—preferring to spend his lunchtimes in companionable silence—but he was concerned that any questions about himself would inevitably lead on to him having to talk about Jemima.

Work was supposed to be sanctuary from thinking about what had happened and he really didn't want to discuss it with Cara.

He also didn't want them to become too sociable because it would only make it harder for him to let her go after the promised month of employment.

Clearly she was very good at her job, so he had no concerns about her finding another position quickly after her time was up, but it might still prove awkward when it came down to saying no to full-time employment if they were on friendly terms. He suspected Cara's story about taking voluntary redundancy wasn't entirely based on truth and that she and Poppy had cooked up the story to play on his sympathy in order to get him to agree to take her on. While he was fine with allowing his errant friend to push him into a temporary arrangement to appease her mollycoddling nature, he wasn't going to allow her to bully him into keeping Cara on full-time.

He didn't need her.

After waking late on Friday morning and having to let an ebullient Cara in whilst still not yet ready to face the day, he had to rush his shower and hustle down to the kitchen with a pounding headache from not sleeping well the night before. Opening the fridge, he found that Cara had stocked it with all sorts of alien-looking food—things he would never have picked out himself. He knew he was bad at getting round to food shopping, but Cara's choices were clearly suggesting he wasn't looking after himself properly. There were superfoods galore in there.

He slammed the fridge door shut in disgust.

The damn woman was taking over the place.

Cara was in the hallway when he came out of the kitchen a few minutes later with a cup of coffee so strong he could have stood his spoon up in it. She waved a cheery hello, then gestured to a vase of brightly coloured flowers that she'd put onto the hall table, giving him a jaunty smile as if to say, *That's better, right?* which really set his teeth on edge. How was it possible for her to be so damn happy all the time? Did the woman live with her head permanently in the clouds?

They'd never had fresh flowers in the house when Jemima was alive because she'd suffered with bad hay fever from the pollen, and he was just about to tell Cara that when he caught himself and clamped his mouth shut. It wasn't a discussion he wanted to have this morning, with a head that felt as if it was about to explode. The very last thing he needed right now was Cara's fervent pity.

'I thought it would be nice to have a bit of colour in here,' she said brightly, oblivious to his displeasure. 'I walked past the most amazing florist's on my way over here and I just couldn't resist popping in. Flowers are so good for lifting your mood.'

'That's fine,' he said through gritted teeth, hoping she wasn't going to be this chipper all day. He didn't think his head could stand it.

'I'll just grab myself a cup of tea, then I'll be in,' she said.

Only managing to summon a grunt in response, he walked into the morning room that he'd turned into an office. He'd chosen it because it was away from the distractions of the street and in the odd moment of pause he found that staring out into the neatly laid garden soothed him. There was a particular brightly coloured bird that came back day after day and hopped about on the lawn, looking for worms, which captivated him. It wasn't there today, though.

After going through his ever-growing inbox and dealing with the quick and easy things, he opened up his diary to check what was going on that day. He had a conference call starting in ten minutes that would probably last till lunchtime, which meant he'd need to brief Cara now about what he wanted her to get on with.

Where was she, anyway?

She'd only been going to make herself a hot drink. Surely she must have done that by now?

Getting up from his chair with a sigh of irritation, he walked through to the kitchen to find her. The last thing he needed was to have to chase his PA down. It was going to be a demanding day which required some intense concentration and he needed her to be on the ball and ready to knuckle down.

She was leaning against the table with her back to the door when he walked into the kitchen, her head cocked to one side as if she was fascinated by something on the other side of the room.

He frowned at her back, wondering what in the heck could be so absorbing, until she spoke in a hushed tone and he realised she was on the phone.

'I don't know whether I'll be able to get away at lunchtime. I have to fetch my boss's lunch and there's a ton of other stuff I have to wade through. His systems are a mess. Unfortunately, Max isn't the type you can ask for a favour either; he's not exactly approachable. I could make it over for about six o'clock, though,' she muttered into the phone.

The hairs rose on the back of his neck. She was making arrangements to see her friends on his time?

He cleared his throat loudly, acutely aware of the rough harshness of his tone in the quiet of the room.

Spinning around at the noise, Cara gave him a look of horror, plainly embarrassed to be caught out.

Definitely a personal call then.

Frustration rattled through him, heating his blood.

How could he have been so gullible as to think it would be easy having her as an employee? Apparently she was going to be just as hard work to manage as all the other PAs he'd had.

'Are you sure you took redundancy at your last place? Or did they let you go for taking liberties on the job?' he said, unable to keep the angry disappointment out of his voice.

She swallowed hard and he found his gaze drawn to the long column of her throat, its smooth elegance distracting him for a second. Shaking off his momentary befuddlement, he snapped his gaze back to hers, annoyed with himself for losing concentration.

'I do not expect behaviour like this from someone with six years of experience as a personal assistant. This isn't the canteen where you waste time gossiping with your mates instead of doing the job you're being paid to do. Things like this make you look stupid and amateurish.'

She nodded jerkily but didn't say anything as her cheeks flushed with colour and a tight little frown appeared in the centre of her forehead.

Fighting a twist of unease, he took another step forwards and pointed a finger at her. 'You do not take personal phone calls on my time. Is that understood? Otherwise, you and I are going to have a problem, and problems are the last thing I need right now. I took a chance on you because you came recommended by Poppy. Do not make a fool out of my friend. Or out of me.'

'I'm sorry—it won't ever happen again. I promise,' she said, her voice barely above a whisper.

The look in her eyes disturbed him. It was such a change from her usual cheery countenance that it sat uncomfortably with him. In fact, to witness her reaction you'd have thought he'd just slapped her around the face, not given her a dressing-down.

'See that it doesn't,' he concluded with a curt nod, an unnerving throb beginning to beat in his throat.

As he walked back into his office, he found he couldn't wipe the haunted expression in her eyes from his mind, his pace faltering as he allowed himself to reflect fully on what had just happened.

Perhaps he'd been a bit too hard on her.

Running a hand over his tired eyes, he shook his head at himself. Who was he kidding—he'd definitely overreacted. For all he knew, it could have been a sick relative on the phone whom she needed to visit urgently.

The trouble was, he'd been so careful to keep her at arm's length and not to let any of his own personal details slip he'd totally failed to ask her anything about herself.

And he was tired. So tired it was making him cranky.

Swivelling on the spot, he went back out of the room to find her, not entirely sure what he was going to say, but knowing he should probably smooth things over between them. He needed her on his side today.

Walking back towards the kitchen, he met her as she was coming out, a cup of tea in her hand.

Instead of the look of sheepish upset he'd expected to see, she gave him a bright smile.

'I know you have a conference call in a couple of

minutes, so if you can walk me through what I need to tackle today I'll get straight on it,' she said, her voice steady and true as if the past few minutes hadn't happened.

He stared at her in surprise, unnerved by the one hundred and eighty degree turn in her demeanour.

Had he imagined the look in her eyes that had disturbed him so much?

No, it had definitely been there; he was sure of it.

Still, at least this showed she wasn't one to hold grudges and let an atmosphere linger after being reprimanded. He appreciated that. He certainly couldn't work with someone who struggled to maintain a professional front when something didn't go their way.

But her level of nonchalance confused him, leaving him a little unsure of where they now stood with each other. Should he mention that he felt he'd been a bit hard on her? Or should he just leave it and sweep it under the carpet as she seemed keen to do?

What was the matter with him? This was ridiculous. He didn't have time for semantics today.

Giving her a firm nod, he turned around and walked back towards the office. 'Good, let's get started then.'

Determined to keep her hand from shaking and not slop hot tea all over herself, Cara followed Max back into the office, ready to be given instructions for the day.

She knew she couldn't afford to show any weakness right now.

Based on her experiences with Max so far, she was pretty damn sure if he thought she wasn't up to the job he'd fire her on the spot and then she'd be left with absolutely nothing.

That was not going to happen to her today.

She needed this job, with its excellent wage and the prospect of a good reference from a well-respected businessman, to be able to stay here in London. All she had to do was keep her head down and stick it out here with him until she found another permanent position somewhere else. She had CVs out at a couple more places and with any luck another opportunity might present itself soon. Until then she'd just have to make sure she didn't allow his blunt manner and sharp tongue to erode her delicate confidence any further.

The trouble was, she'd allowed herself to be lulled into a false sense of security on her first day here after Max's compliment about her being a good ambassador for herself, only for him to pull the rug out from under her regrouping confidence later with his moods and quick temper.

The very last thing she needed was to work with another bully.

Not that she could really blame him for being angry in this instance. It must have looked really bad, her taking a personal phone call at the beginning of the working day. The really frustrating thing was that she'd never done anything like that before in her life. She was a rule follower to the core and very strict with herself about not surfing the Net or making personal calls on her employer's time, even in a big office where those kinds of things could go unnoticed.

Putting her drink down carefully, she wheeled her

chair nearer to Max's desk and prepared to take notes, keeping her chin up and a benign smile fixed firmly on her face.

His own professional manner seemingly restored, Max outlined what he wanted her to do throughout the day, which she jotted down in her notebook. Once he appeared to be satisfied that he'd covered everything he leaned back in his chair and studied her, the intensity of his gaze making the hairs stand up on her arms.

'Listen, Cara, I'm finishing early for the day today,' he said, surprising her with the warmth in his voice. 'I'm meeting a friend in town for an early dinner, so feel free to leave here at four o'clock.'

She blinked at him in shock before pulling herself together. 'That would be great. Thank you.'

There was an uncomfortable pause, where he continued to look at her, his brows drawn together and his lips set in a firm line. He opened his mouth, as if he was about to tell her what was on his mind, but was rudely interrupted by the alarm going off on his phone signalling it was time for his conference call.

To her frustration, he snapped straight back into work mode, turning back to his computer and dialling a number on his phone, launching straight into his business spiel as soon as the person on the other end of the line picked up.

Despite her residual nerves, Cara still experienced the familiar little frisson of exhilaration that swept through her whenever she heard him do that. He'd set up a small desk for her next to his the day after he'd offered her the trial, which meant there was no getting away from the sound of his voice with its smooth, re-assuring intonation.

He really was a very impressive businessman, even if he was a bit of a bear to work for.

Forcing her mind away from thinking about how uplifting it would be to have someone as passionate and dedicated as Max for a boyfriend—especially after the demeaning experience of her last relationship—she fired up her laptop and started in on the work he'd given her to take care of today.

After a few minutes, her thoughts drifted back to the fateful phone call she'd taken earlier, before their confrontation, and she felt a twitch of nerves in her stomach. It had been a friend calling to let her know about a possible flat coming onto the rental market—which was why she'd broken her rule and answered the call. If she managed to get there early enough she might just be able to snag it, which was now a real possibility thanks to Max's sudden announcement about leaving work at four o'clock.

Come to think of it, she was a little surprised about him finishing early to meet a friend in town. He'd never done that before, always continuing to work as she packed up for the day and—she strongly suspected—on into the evening. That would certainly account for the dark circles under his eyes. And his irascible mood.

The man appeared to be a workaholic.

After an hour of working through some truly tedious data inputting, Cara got up to make them both a hot drink, aware that Max must be parched by now from having to talk almost continuously since he'd begun his call.

Returning with the drinks, she sat back down at her desk to see she had an email from the friend that had called her earlier about the flat for rent.

Hmm. That couldn't be a good sign; she'd already mailed the details through earlier.

With a sinking feeling, she opened it up and scanned the text, her previously restored mood slipping away.

The flat had already been let.

An irrational impulse to cry gripped her and she got up quickly and made for the bathroom before the tears came, desperate to hide her despondency from Max.

Staring into the mirror, she attempted to talk herself down from her gloom. Her friend Sarah had offered to put her up on her sofa for a few days, so she at least had somewhere to stay in the interim. The only trouble was, her friend lived in a tiny place that she shared with her party animal boyfriend and he wouldn't want her hanging around, playing gooseberry, for too long.

The mere idea of renting with strangers at the ripe old age of twenty-seven horrified her, so she was going to have to be prepared to lower her standards to be in with a chance of finding another one-bedroom flat that she could afford in central London.

That was okay; she could do that. Hopefully, something would come up soon and then she'd be able to make some positive changes and get fully back on her feet.

Surely it was time for things to start going her way now?

CHAPTER THREE

AFTER MAKING UP the excuse about seeing a friend on Friday night in order to let Cara leave early, Max decided that he might as well phone around to see if anyone was available for a pint after work and actually surprised himself by having an enjoyable night out with some friends that he hadn't seen for a while.

He'd spent the rest of the weekend working, only breaking to eat his way through the entire contents of the fridge that Cara had stocked for him. Despite his initial disdain at her choices, he found he actually rather enjoyed trying the things she'd bought. They certainly beat the mediocre takeaways he'd been living on for the past few months.

Perhaps it *was* useful for him to have someone else around the house for a while, as Poppy had suggested the last time they'd seen each other. He'd baulked at her proposal that he should get back out on the dating scene though—he definitely wasn't ready for that, and honestly couldn't imagine ever being ready.

He and Jemima had been a couple since meeting at the beginning of their first year at university, their initial connection so immediate and intense they'd missed lectures for three days running to stay in bed together. They'd moved in with each other directly after graduating, making a home for themselves first in Manchester, then in London. After spending so much of his youth being moved from city to city, school to school, by his bohemian mother—until he finally put his foot down and forced her to send him to boarding school—it had been a huge relief to finally feel in control of his own life. To belong somewhere, with someone who wouldn't ask him to give up the life and friends he'd painstakingly carved out for himself—just *one* more time.

Jemima had understood his need for stability and had put up with his aversion to change with sympathetic acceptance and generous bonhomie. His life had been comfortably settled and he'd been deeply content—until she'd died, leaving him marooned and devastated by grief.

The idea of finding someone he could love as much as Jem seemed ludicrous. No one could ever replace his wife and it wouldn't be fair to let them try.

No, he would be fine on his own; he had his business and his friends and that would be enough for him.

Walking past the flower arrangement that Cara had left on the hall table on his way to sort through yesterday's junk mail, he had a memory flash of the expression on her face when he'd bawled her out in the kitchen the other day.

His chest tightened uncomfortably at the memory.

He needed to stop beating himself up about that now. He'd made amends for what had happened, even if she hadn't seemed entirely back to her happy, bright-eyed self again by the time she'd left on Friday afternoon. But at least he hadn't needed to delve into the murky waters of how they were both *feeling* about what had happened. He'd had enough of that kind of thing after forcing himself through the interminable sessions with grief counsellors after Jemima's death; he certainly didn't need to put himself through that discomfort again for something as inconsequential as a spat with his employee.

Fortunately, Cara seemed as reluctant to talk about it all as he was.

Rubbing a hand over his face, he gave a snort of disbelief about where his thoughts had taken him. Again. Surely it wasn't normal to be spending his weekend thinking about his PA.

Hmm.

His initial concerns about her being an unwanted distraction seemed to be coming to fruition, which was a worry. Still, there were only a few more weeks left of the promised trial period, then he'd be free of her. Until then he was going to have to keep his head in the game, otherwise the business was going to suffer. And that wasn't something he was prepared to let happen.

Monday morning rushed around, bringing with it bright sunshine that flooded the house and warmed the still, cool air, lifting his spirits a little.

Max had just sat down at his desk with his first cup of coffee of the day when there was a ring on the doorbell.

Cara.

Swinging open the door to let her in, he was taken aback to see her looking as if she hadn't slept a wink all night. There were dark circles around her puffy eyes and her skin was pallid and dull-looking. It seemed to pain her to even raise a smile for him.

Was she hung-over?

His earlier positivity vanished, to be replaced by a feeling of disquiet.

'Did you have a good weekend?' he asked as she walked into the house and hung up her coat.

She gave him a wan smile. 'Not bad, thanks. It was certainly a busy one. I didn't get much sleep.'

Hmm. So she had been out partying, by the sound of it.

Despite his concerns, Cara appeared to work hard all day and he only caught her yawning once whilst making them both a strong cup of coffee in the kitchen, mid-afternoon.

At the end of the day, she waved her usual cheery goodbye, though there was less enthusiasm in her smile than she normally displayed at knocking-off time.

To his horror, she turned up in the same state the following day.

And the next.

In fact, on Thursday, when he opened the door, he could have sworn he caught the smell of alcohol on her as she dashed past him into the house. She certainly looked as though she could have been up drinking all night and plainly hadn't taken a shower that morning, her hair hanging greasy and limp in a severely pulled back ponytail.

Her work was beginning to suffer too, in increments. Each day he found he had to pick her up on more and more things she'd missed or got wrong, noticing that her once pristine fingernails were getting shorter and more ragged as time went on.

Clearly she was letting whatever was happening in her personal life get in the way of her work and that was unacceptable.

His previous feelings of magnanimity about having her around had all but vanished by Thursday afternoon and he was seriously considering having a word with her about her performance. The only reason he hadn't done so already was because he'd been so busy with back-to-back conference calls this week and in deference to Poppy he'd decided to give Cara the benefit of the doubt and put her slip-ups down to a couple of off days.

But he decided that enough was enough when he found her with her head propped on her arms, fast asleep, on the kitchen table when she was supposed to be making them both a hot drink.

Resentment bubbled up from his gut as he watched her peaceful form gently rise and fall as she slumbered on, totally oblivious to his incensed presence behind her. He'd been feeling guilty all weekend about how he'd spoken to her on Friday and here she was, only a few days later, turning up unfit for work.

His concern that her presence here would cause more harm than good had just been ratified.

'Wakey, wakey, Sleeping Beauty!' he said loudly, feeling a swell of angry satisfaction as she leapt up from the table and spun around to look at him, her face pink and creased on one side where it had rested against her arm.

'Oh! Whoa! Was I sleeping?' she mumbled, blinking hard.

Crossing his arms, he gave her a hard stare. 'Like a baby.'

She rubbed a hand across her eyes, smudging her make-up across her face. 'I'm so sorry—I only put my head down to rest for a moment while I was waiting for the kettle to boil and I must have drifted off.'

'Perhaps you should start going to bed at a more reasonable time then,' he ground out, his hands starting to shake as adrenaline kicked its way through his veins. 'I didn't hire you as a charity case, Cara. For the money I'm paying, I expected much more from you. You had me convinced you were up to the job in the first couple of days, but it's become clear over the last few that you're not.' He took a breath as he made peace with what he was about to say. 'I'm going to have to let you go. I can't carry someone who's going to get drunk every night and turn up unfit to work.'

Her eyes were wide now and she was mouthing at him as if her response had got stuck in her throat.

Shaking off the stab of conscience that had begun to poke him in the back, he pointed a finger at her. 'And you can hold the "It'll never happen again" routine,' he bit out. 'I'm not an idiot, though I feel like one for letting you take me in like this.'

To his surprise, instead of the tears he was readying himself for, her expression morphed into one of acute fury and she raised her own shaking finger back at him.

'I do not get drunk every night. For your information, I'm homeless at the moment and sleeping on a friend's couch, which doesn't work well for her insomniac boyfriend, who likes to party and play computer games late into the night and who came home drunk and spilled an entire can of beer over me while I was trying to sleep and who then hogged the bathroom this morning so I couldn't get in there for a shower.'

Her face had grown redder and redder throughout this speech and all he could do was stand there and stare at her, paralysed by surprise as she jabbed her finger at him with rage flashing in her eyes.

'I've worked my butt off for you, taking your irascible moods on the chin and getting on with it, but I'm not going to let you treat me like some nonentity waster. I'm a real person with real feelings, Max. I tried to make this work—you have no idea how hard I've been trying—but I guess this is just life's way of telling me that I'm done here in London.' She threw up her hands and took a deep shaky breath. 'After all the work I put into building myself a career here that I was so proud of—'

Taking in the look of utter frustration on her face, he felt his anger begin to drain away, only to be replaced with an uncomfortable twist of shame.

She was right, of course—he had been really unfriendly and probably very difficult to work with, and she was clearly dealing with some testing personal circumstances, which he'd made sure to blithely ignore.

He frowned and sighed heavily, torn about what to do next. While he could do without any extra problems at the moment, he couldn't bring himself to turn her away now he knew what she was dealing with. Because, despite it all, he admired her for standing up for herself.

Cara willed her heart to stop pounding like a pneumatic drill as she waited to see what Max would say next.

Had she really just shouted at him like that?

It was so unlike her to let her anger get the better of her, but something inside her had snapped at the unfairness of it all and she hadn't been able to hold back.

After spending the past few days using every ounce of energy keeping up the fake smile and pretending she could cope with the punishing days with Max on so little sleep, she'd hit a wall.

Hard.

The mix of panic, frustration and chronic tiredness had released something inside her and in those moments after she'd let the words fly she had the strangest sensation of the ground shifting under her feet. She was painfully aware that she'd probably just thrown away any hope of keeping this job, but at the same time she was immensely proud of herself for not allowing him to dismiss her like that. As if she was worth nothing.

Because she *wasn't*.

She deserved to be treated with more respect and she'd learnt by now that she wasn't going to get that from Max by meekly taking the insults he so callously dished out.

At her last place of work, in a fug of naïve disbelief,

she'd allowed those witches to strip her of her pride, but there was no way she was letting Max do that to her, too.

No matter what it cost her.

She could get another job—and she would, eventually—but she'd never be able to respect herself again if she didn't stand up to him now.

Her heart raced as she watched a range of expressions run across Max's face. The fact that he hadn't immediately repeated his dismissal gave her hope that there might be a slim chance he'd reverse his decision to fire her.

Moving her hands behind her back, she crossed her fingers for a miracle, feeling a bead of sweat run down her spine.

Sighing hard, Max ran a hand through the front of his hair, pushing it out of his eyes and looking at her with his usual expression of ill-concealed irritation.

'I'm guessing you became homeless on Friday, which is when the mistakes started to happen?' he asked finally.

She nodded, aware of the tension in her shoulders as she held her nerve. 'I spent all day on Sunday moving my furniture into storage. I've been staying with my friend Sarah and her boyfriend ever since.'

'But that can't carry on,' he said with finality to his voice.

Swallowing hard, she tipped up her chin. 'No. I know. I've tried to view so many places to rent in the last week, but they seem to go the second they're advertised. I can't get to them fast enough.'

He crossed his arms. 'And you have nowhere else to stay in London? No boyfriend? No family?'

Shaking her head, she straightened her posture, determined to hang on to her poise. She wouldn't look away, not now she'd been brave enough to take him on. If she was going to be fired, she was going down with her head held high. 'My parents live in Cornwall and none of my other friends in London have room to put me up.' She shifted uncomfortably on the spot and swallowed back the lingering hurt at the memory of her last disastrous relationship. 'I've been single for a few months now.'

He stared back at her, his eyes hooded and his brow drawn down.

A world of emotions rattled through her as she waited to hear his verdict.

'Okay. You can stay here until you find a flat to rent.'

She gawped at him, wondering whether her brain was playing tricks on her. 'I'm sorry—*what*?'

'I said—you can stay here,' he said slowly, enunciating every word. 'I have plenty of spare rooms. I'm on the top floor so you could have the whole middle floor to yourself.'

'Really?'

He bristled, rolling his eyes up to the ceiling and letting out a frustrated snort. 'Yes, really. I'm not just making this up to see your impression of a goldfish.'

She stared at him even harder. Had he just made a *joke*? That was definitely a first.

Unfolding his arms, he batted a hand through the air. 'I'm sure it won't take you long to find somewhere else and until then I need you turning up to work fully rested and back to your efficient, capable self.'

Her eyes were so wide now she felt sure she must look as if she was wearing a pair of those joke goggle-eye glasses.

He was admitting to her being good at her job too now? Wonders would never cease.

But she was allowing these revelations to distract her from the decision she needed to make. Could she really live in the same house as her boss? Even if it was only for a short time.

Right now, it didn't feel as though she had much of a choice. The thought of spending even one more night in Party Central made her heart sink. If she turned Max down on his offer, that was the only other viable option—save staying in a hotel she couldn't afford or renting a place a long way out and spending her life commuting in. Neither of them were appealing options.

But could she really live here with him? The mere idea of it made her insides flutter and it wasn't just because he was a bit of a difficult character. During the week and a half that she'd known him, she'd become increasingly jittery in his presence, feeling a tickle of excitement run up her spine every time she caught his scent in the air or even just watched him move around his territory like some kind of lean, mean, business machine. Not that he'd ever given her a reason to think she was in any kind of danger being there alone with him. Clearly, he had no interest in her romantically. If anything, she'd felt it had been the total opposite for him, as if he didn't think of her as a woman at all, only a phone-answering, data-sorting robot.

So she was pretty sure he didn't have an ulterior motive behind his suggestion that she should stay in his house.

Unfortunately.

Naughty, naughty Cara.

'Well, if you're sure it won't be too much of an inconvenience to you,' she said slowly.

'No. It's fine,' he answered curtly. 'We'll have to make sure to respect each other's privacy, but it's a big place so that shouldn't be a problem. All the rooms have locks on them, in case you're worried.'

Her pulse picked up as a host of X-rated images rushed through her head.

Slam a lid on that, you maniac.

'I'm not worried,' she squeaked.

He nodded.

'And your girlfriend won't mind me staying here?' she asked carefully.

'I don't have a girlfriend.'

'Or your w—?' she began to ask, just in case.

'I'm single,' he cut in with a curt snap to his voice.

Okay, so the subject of his relationships was out of bounds then.

She was surprised to hear that he wasn't attached in any way, though. Surely someone with his money, looks and smarts would have women lining up around the block for the pleasure of his company. Although, come to think of it, based on her run-ins with him so

far, she could see how his acerbic temperament might
be a problem for some people.

'Right, I may as well show you your room now,'
Max said, snapping her out of her meandering thoughts.
'Clearly, you're not in a fit state to work this afternoon,
so you may as well finish for the day.' He turned and
walked out of the room, leaving her gaping at the empty
space he'd left.

So that was it then—decision made.

'Oh! Okay.' She hustled to catch him up, feeling her
joints complain as she moved. *Crikey.* She was tired.
Her whole body ached from sleeping on a saggy sofa
and performing on so little sleep for the past few days.

She followed him up the sweeping staircase to the
next level and along the landing to the third door on
the right.

Opening it up, he motioned for her to walk past him
into the bedroom.

She tried not to breathe in his fresh, spicy scent as
she did so, her nerves already shot from the rigours of
the day.

It was, of course, the most beautifully appointed bedroom she'd ever been in.

Light flooded in through the large window, which
was framed by long French grey curtains in a heavy
silk. The rest of the furnishing was simple and elegant,
in a way Cara had never been able to achieve in her own
flat. The pieces that had been chosen clearly had heritage and fitted perfectly with the large airy room. His
interior designer must have cost a pretty penny.

Tears welled in her eyes as she took in the original

ornate fireplace, which stood proudly opposite a beautiful king-sized iron-framed bed. Fighting the urge to collapse onto it in relief and bury herself in the soft, plump-looking duvet, she blinked hard, then turned to face Max, who was hanging back by the door with a distracted frown on his face.

'This is a beautiful room—thank you,' she said, acutely aware of the tremor in her voice.

Max's frown deepened, but he didn't comment on it. 'You're welcome. You should go over to your friend's house and get your things now, then you'll have time to settle in. We'll start over again tomorrow.'

'Okay, good idea.'

'I'll leave you to it then,' he said, turning to go.

'Max?'

He turned back. 'Yes?'

'I'm really grateful—for letting me stay here.'

'No problem,' he said, turning briskly on the spot and walking away, leaving her staring after him with her heart in her mouth.

Well, she certainly hadn't expected this when she'd woken up this morning reeking of stale beer.

Sinking down gratefully onto the bed, she finally allowed her tense muscles to relax, feeling the tiredness rush back, deep into her bones.

How was she ever going to be able to drag herself away from this beautiful room when she managed to find a place of her own to rent?

More to the point, was she really going to be able to live in the same house as Max without going totally insane?

Steeling herself to make the journey over to Sarah's house and pick up her things, she rocked herself up off the bed of her dreams and onto her feet and took a deep, resolute breath.

There was only one way to find out.

CHAPTER FOUR

IF SOMEONE HAD asked Max to explain exactly what had prompted him to suggest that Cara move in, he was pretty sure he'd have been stumped for an answer.

All he knew was that he couldn't let things go on the way they were. Judging by her outburst, she was clearly struggling to cope with all that life had thrown at her recently and it was no skin off his nose to let her stay for a few nights in one of the empty bedrooms.

He had enough of them, after all.

Also, as a good friend of her cousin's he felt a responsibility to make sure that Cara was okay whilst Poppy was away and unable to help her herself. He knew from experience that good friends were essential when life decided to throw its twisted cruelty your way, and he was acutely aware that it was the support and encouragement of his friends that had helped him find his way out of the darkness after Jemima died.

Watching Cara working hard the next day, he was glad she was still around. When she was on good form, she was an asset to the business and, truthfully, it had become comforting for him to have another person around—it stopped him from *thinking* so much in the resounding silence of the house.

They hadn't talked about what had happened again, which was a relief. He just wanted everything to get back to the way it had been with the minimum of fuss. With that in mind, he was a little concerned about what it would be like having her around at the weekend. He'd probably end up working, like he always did, so he wasn't too worried about the daytime, but they'd need to make sure they gave each other enough space in the evenings so they didn't end up biting each other's heads off again.

With any luck, she'd be out a lot of the time anyway, flat-hunting or seeing friends.

At six o'clock he leant back in his chair and stretched his arms above his head, working the kinks out of his tight muscles.

'Time to finish for the day, Cara,' he said to the side of her head.

She glanced round at him, the expression in her eyes far away, as if she was in the middle of a thought.

'Um, okay. I'll just finish this.' She tapped on her keyboard for a few more seconds before closing the laptop with a flourish.

'Okay then. Bring on the weekend.' She flashed him a cheeky smile, which gave him pause.

'You're not thinking of bringing the party to this house, I hope.'

Quickly switching to a solemn expression, she gave a shake of her head. 'Of course not. That's not what I meant.'

'Hmm.'

The corner of her mouth twitched upwards. 'You seem to have a really skewed impression of me. I don't go in for heavy drinking and partying—it's really not my style.'

'Okay.' He held up both hands. 'Not that it's any of my business; you can stay out all night at the weekends, for all I care,' he said, aware of a strange plummeting sensation in his chest as images of what she might get up to out on the town flashed through his head.

Good God, man—you're not her keeper.

'As long as your work doesn't suffer,' he added quickly.

'Actually,' she said, slouching back in her seat and hooking her slender arm over the back of her chair, 'I was thinking about cooking you a meal tonight, to say thank you for letting me stay.'

He wasn't sure why, but the thought of that made him uncomfortable. Perhaps because it would blur the lines between employee and friend too much.

'That's kind, but I have plans tonight,' he lied, racking his brain to remember what his friend Dan had said about his availability this weekend. Even if he was busy he was sure he could rustle up a dinner invitation somewhere else, to let Cara off the hook without any bad feelings.

'And you don't need to thank me for letting you stay here. It's what any decent human being would have done.'

Her face seemed to fall a little and she drew her arm back in towards her body, sliding her hands between her knees so that her shoulders hunched inwards. 'Oh, okay, well, I'm just going to pop out and shop for my own dinner, so I'll see you shortly,' she said, ramping her smile back up again and wheeling her chair away from the desk with her feet.

'Actually, I'm heading out myself in a minute and I'll probably be back late, so I'll see you tomorrow.'

Her smile froze. 'Right. Well, have a good night.'

This was ridiculous. The last thing he'd wanted was for them both to feel awkward about living under the same roof.

He let out a long sigh and pushed his hair away from his face. 'Look, Cara, don't think you have to hang out with me while you're staying here. We don't need to be in each other's pockets the whole time. Feel free to do your own thing.'

Clearly he'd been a bit brusque because she recoiled a little. 'I understand,' she said, getting up and awkwardly pushing her chair back under her desk. 'Have a good night!' she said in that overly chirpy way she had, which he was beginning to learn meant he'd offended her.

Not waiting for his reply, she turned her back on him and walked straight out of the room, her shoulders stiff.

Great. This was exactly what he'd hoped to avoid.

He scrubbed a hand over his face. Maybe it had been a mistake to ask her to stay.

But he couldn't kick her out now.

All he could do was cross his fingers and hope she'd find herself another place to live soon.

* * *

To his surprise, he didn't see much of Cara over the next couple of days. She'd obviously taken his suggestion about giving each other space to heart and was avoiding being in the house with him as much as possible.

The extremity of her desertion grated on his nerves.

What was it that made it impossible for them to understand each other? They were very different in temperament, of course, which didn't help, but it was more than that. It was as if there was some kind of meaning-altering force field between them.

On Sunday, when the silence in the house got too much for him, he went out for a long walk around Hyde Park. He stopped at the café next to the water for lunch, something he and Jemima had done most Sundays, fighting against the painful undertow of nostalgia that dragged at him as he sat there alone. It was all so intensely familiar.

All except for the empty seat in front of him.

He snorted into his drink, disgusted with himself for being so pathetic. He should consider himself lucky. He was the one who got to have a future, unlike his big-hearted, selfless wife. The woman who everyone had loved. One of the few people, in his opinion, who had truly deserved a long and happy life.

Arriving home mid-afternoon, he walked in to find the undertones of Cara's perfume hanging in the air.

So she was back then.

Closing his eyes, he imagined he could actually sense her presence in the atmosphere, like a low hum of white noise.

Or was he being overly sensitive?

Probably.

From the moment she'd agreed to move in he'd experienced a strange undercurrent of apprehension and it seemed to be affecting his state of mind.

After stowing his shoes and coat in the cloakroom, he went into the living room to find that a large display of flowers had been placed on top of the grand piano. He bristled, remembering the way he'd felt the last time Cara had started to mess with his environment.

Sighing, he rubbed a hand through his hair, attempting to release the tension in his scalp. They were just flowers. He really needed to chill out or he was going to drive himself insane. Jemima would have laughed if she'd seen how strung-out he was over something so inconsequential. He could almost hear her teasing voice ringing in his ears.

A noise startled him and he whipped round to see Cara standing in the doorway to the room, dressed in worn jeans and a sloppy sweater, her face scrubbed of make-up and her bright blue eyes luminous in the soft afternoon light. To his overwrought brain, she seemed to radiate an ethereal kind of beauty, her long hair lying in soft, undulating waves around her face and her creamy skin radiant with health. He experienced a strangely intense moment of confusion, and he realised that somewhere in the depths of his screwed-up consciousness he'd half expected it to be Jemima standing there instead—which was why his, 'Hello,' came out more gruffly than he'd intended.

Her welcoming smile faltered and she glanced down

at her fingernails and frowned, as if fighting an impulse to chew on them, but when she looked back up her smile was firmly back in place.

'Isn't it a beautiful day?' She tipped her head towards the piano behind him. 'I hope you don't mind, but the spring sunshine inspired me to put fresh flowers in most of the rooms—not your bedroom, of course; I didn't go in there,' she added quickly. 'The house seemed to be crying out for a bit of life and colour and I wanted to do something to say thank you for letting me stay, even though you said I didn't need to.'

'Sure. That's fine,' was all he could muster. For some reason his blood was flying through his veins and he felt so hot he thought he might spontaneously combust at any second.

'Oh, and I stripped and remade the bed in the room next to yours,' she added casually. 'It looked like the cleaners had missed it. I gave it a good vacuum, too; it was really dusty.'

The heat was swept away by a flood of icy panic. 'You *what*?'

The ferocity in his tone obviously alarmed her because she flinched and blinked hard.

But hurting Cara's feelings was the least of his worries right then.

Not waiting for her reply, he pushed past her and raced up the stairs, aware of his heart thumping painfully in his chest as he willed it not to be so.

Please don't let her have destroyed that room.

Reaching the landing on the top floor, he flung open the door and stared into the now immaculate bedroom, the stringent scent of cleaning fluid clogging his throat and making his stomach roll.

She'd stripped it bare.

Everything he'd been protecting from the past had been torn off or wiped away. The bed, as she'd said, now had fresh linen on it.

He heard her laboured breath behind him as she made it up to the landing and whipped round to face her.

'Where are the sheets from the bed, Cara?' he demanded, well past the point of being able to conceal his anger.

Her face was drained of all colour. 'What did I do wrong?'

'The *sheets*, Cara—where are the *sheets*?'

'I washed them,' she whispered, unable to meet his eyes. 'They're in the dryer.'

That was it then. Jemima's room was ruined.

Bitterness welled in his gut as he took in her wide-eyed bewilderment. The woman was a walking disaster area and she'd caused nothing but trouble since she got here.

A rage he couldn't contain made him pace towards her.

'Why do you have to meddle with everything? Hmm? What is it with you? This need to please all the time isn't natural. In fact it's downright pathetic. Just keep your hands off my personal stuff, okay? Is that really too much to ask?'

She seemed frozen to the spot as she stared at him with glassy eyes, her jaw clamped so tight he could see the muscle flickering under the pressure, but, instead of shouting back this time, she dragged in a sharp, painful-sounding breath before turning on the spot and walking out of the room.

He listened to her heavy footsteps on the stairs and then the slam of her bedroom door, wincing as the sound reverberated through his aching head. Staring down at the soulless bed, he allowed the heat of his bitterness and anger and shame to wash through him, leaving behind an icy numbness in its wake.

Then he closed his eyes, dropped his chin to his chest and sank down onto the last place he'd been truly happy.

Oh, God, please don't let this be happening to me. Again.

Cara wrapped her arms around her middle and pressed her forehead against the cool wall of her bedroom, waiting for the dizziness and nausea to subside so she could pack up her things and leave.

What was it with her? She seemed destined to put herself in a position of weakness, where the only option left to her was to give up and run away.

Which she really didn't want to do again.

But she had to protect herself. She couldn't be around someone so toxic—someone who clearly thought so little of her. Even Ewan hadn't been that cruel to her when he'd left her after she'd failed to live up to his exacting standards. She'd never seen a look of such pure disgust on anyone's face before. The mere memory of it made the dizziness worse.

There was no way she was staying in a place where she'd be liable to see that look again. She'd rather go home and admit to her parents that she'd failed and deal with their badly concealed disappointment than stay here with Max any longer.

She'd never met anyone with such a quick temper. What was his problem, anyway? He appeared to have everything here: the security of a beautiful house in one of the most sought-after areas of London, a thriving business, friends who invited him out for dinner, and he clearly had pots of cash to cushion his easy, comfortable life. In fact, the more she thought about it, the more incensed she became.

Who was he to speak to her like that? Sure, there had been a couple of little bumps in the road when she'd not exactly been at her best, but she'd worked above and beyond the call of duty for the rest of the time. And she'd been trying to do something nice for him in making the house look good—pretty much the only thing she could think of to offer as a thank you to a man who seemed to have everything. What had been so awful about that? She knew she could be a bit over the top in trying to please people sometimes, but this hadn't been a big thing. It was just an empty guest room that had been overlooked.

Wasn't it?

The extremity of his reaction niggled at her.

Surely just giving it a quick clean didn't deserve that angry reaction.

No.

He was a control freak bully and she needed to get away from him.

As soon as she was sure the dizziness had passed,

she carefully packed up all her things and zipped them into her suitcase, fighting with all her might against the tight pressure in her throat and the itchy heat in her eyes.

She'd known this opportunity had to be too good to be true—the job, working with someone as impressive as Max and definitely being invited to stay in this amazing house.

But she wasn't going to skulk away. If she didn't face up to Max one last time with her head held high she'd regret it for the rest of her life. He wasn't going to run her out of here; she was going to leave in her time and on her terms.

Taking a deep breath, she rolled her shoulders back and fixed the bland look of calm she'd become so practised at onto her face.

Okay. Time for one last confrontation.

She found Max in the guest room where she'd left him, sitting on the bed with his head in his hands, his hunched shoulders stretching his T-shirt tight against his broad back.

As she walked into the room, he looked up at her with an expression of such torment on his face that it made her stop in her tracks.

What was going on? She'd expected him to still be angry, but instead he looked—*beaten*.

Did he regret what he'd said to her?

Giving herself a mental shake, she took another deliberate step towards him. It didn't matter; there wasn't anything he could say to make up for the cruelty of his last statement anyway. This wasn't the first time he'd treated her with such brutal disdain and she wasn't going to put up with it any longer.

Forcing back her shoulders, she took one final step closer to him, feeling her legs shaking with tension.

'This isn't going to work, Max. I can't live in a place where I'm constantly afraid of doing the wrong thing and making you angry. I don't know what I did that was so bad, or what's going on with you to make you react like that, but I'm not going to let you destroy what's left of my confidence. I'm not going to be a victim any more.' She took a deep, shuddering breath. 'So I'm leaving now. And that goes for the job, too.'

Her heart gave a lurch at the flash of contrition in his eyes, but she knew she had to be strong and walk away for her own good.

'Goodbye, Max, and good luck.'

As she turned to go, fighting against the tears that threatened to give her away, she thought she heard the bedsprings creak as if he'd stood up, but didn't turn round to find out.

She was halfway down the stairs when she heard Max's voice behind her. 'Wait, Cara!'

Spinning round, she held up a hand to stop him from coming any closer, intensely aware that, despite her anger with him, there was a small part of her that was desperate to hear him say something nice to her, to persuade her that he wasn't the monster he seemed to be. 'I can't walk on eggshells around you any more, Max; I don't think my heart will stand it.'

In any way, shape or form.

He slumped down onto the top step and put his elbows on his knees, his whole posture defeated. 'Don't go,' he said quietly.

'I have to.'

Looking up, he fixed her with a glassy stare. 'I know I've been a nightmare to be around recently—' He frowned and shook his head. 'It's not you, Cara—it's one hundred per cent me. Please, at least hear me out. I need to tell you what's going on so you don't leave thinking any of this is your fault.' He sighed and rubbed a hand through his hair. 'That's the last thing I want to happen.'

She paused. Even if she still chose to leave after hearing him out, at least she'd know *why* it hadn't worked and be able to make peace with her decision to walk away.

The silence stretched to breaking point between them. 'Okay,' she said.

He nodded. 'Thank you.' Getting up from the step, he gestured down the stairs. 'Let's go into the sitting room.'

Once there, she perched on the edge of the sofa and waited for him to take the chair opposite, but he surprised her by sitting next to her instead, sinking back into the cushions with a long guttural sigh which managed to touch every nerve-ending in her body.

'This is going to make me sound mentally unstable.'

She turned to frown at him. 'Oka-ay…' she said, failing to keep her apprehension out of her voice.

'That bed hasn't been changed since my wife, Jemima, died a year and a half ago.'

Hot horror slid through her, her skin prickling as if

she were being stabbed with a thousand needles. 'But I thought you said—' She shook her suddenly fuzzy head. 'You never said—' Words, it seemed, had totally failed her. Everything she knew about him slipped sickeningly into place: the ever-fluctuating moods, the reluctance to talk about his personal life, his anger at her meddling with things in his house.

His *wife's* house.

Looking away, he stared at the wall opposite, sitting forward with clenched fists as if he was steeling himself to get it all out in the open.

'I couldn't bring myself to change it.' He paused and she saw his shoulders rise then fall as he took a deep breath. 'The bed, I mean. It still smelled faintly like her. I let her mother take all her clothes and other personal effects—what would I have done with them?—but the bed was mine. The last place we'd been together before I lost her—' he took another breath, pushing back his hunched shoulders '—before she died.'

'Oh, God, Max… I'm so, so sorry. I had no idea.'

He huffed out a dry laugh. 'How could you? I did everything I could to avoid talking to you about it.' He grimaced. 'Because, to be honest, I've done enough talking about it to last me a lifetime. I guess, in my twisted imagination, I thought if you didn't know, I could pretend it hadn't happened when you were around. Outside of work, you're the first normal, unconnected thing I've had in my life since I lost her and I guess I was hanging on to that.'

He turned to look at her again. 'I should have told you, Cara, especially after you moved in, but I couldn't find a way to bring it up without—' He paused and swallowed hard, the look in his eyes so wretched that, without thinking, she reached out and laid a hand on his bare forearm.

He frowned down at where their bodies connected and the air seemed to crackle around them.

Disconcerted by the heat of him beneath her fingertips, she withdrew her hand and laid it back on her lap.

'It's kind of you to consider me *normal*,' she said, flipping him a grin, hoping the levity might go some way to smoothing out the sudden weird tension between them.

He gave a gentle snort, as if to acknowledge her pathetic attempt at humour.

Why had she never recognised his behaviour as grief before? Now she knew to look for it, it was starkly discernible in the deep frown lines in his face and the haunted look in his eyes.

But she'd been so caught up in her own private universe of problems she hadn't even considered *why* Max seemed so bitter all the time.

She'd thought he had everything.

How wrong she'd been.

They sat in silence for a while, the only sound in the room the soothing *tick-tock* of the carriage clock on the mantelpiece, like a steady heartbeat in the chaos.

'How did she die?' Cara asked eventually. She was pretty sure he wouldn't be keen to revisit this conversation and she wanted to have all the information from this point onwards so she could avoid any future blunders.

The familiarity of the question seemed to rouse him. 'She had a subarachnoid haemorrhage—it's where a blood vessel in the brain bursts—' he added, when she frowned at him in confusion. 'On our one-year wedding anniversary. It happened totally out of the blue. I was late for our celebration dinner and I got a phone message saying she'd collapsed in the restaurant. By the time I got to the hospital she had such extensive brain damage she didn't even recognise me. She died two weeks later. I never got to say goodbye properly.' He snorted gently. 'The last thing I said to her before it happened was "Stop being such a nag; I won't be late," when I left her in bed that morning and went to work.'

Cara had to swallow past the tightness in her throat before she could speak. 'That's why you didn't want me to leave here with us on bad terms.' She put a hand back onto his arm and gave it an ineffectual rub, feeling completely out of her depth. 'Oh, Max, I'm so sorry. What a horrible thing to happen.'

He leant back against the cushions, breaking the contact of her touch, and stared up at the ceiling. 'I often wonder whether I would have noticed some signs if I'd paid more attention to her. If I hadn't been so caught up with work—'

She couldn't think of a single thing to say to make him feel better—though maybe there wasn't anything she could say. Sometimes you didn't need answers or solutions; you just needed someone to listen and agree with you about how cruel life could be.

He turned to look at her, his mouth drawn into a tight line.

'Look, Cara, I can see that you wanting to help comes from a good place. You're a kind and decent person—much more decent than I am.' He gave her a pained smile, which she returned. 'I've been on my own here for so long I've clearly become very selfish with my personal space.' He rubbed a hand across his brow. 'And this was Jemima's house—she was the one who chose how to decorate it and made it a home for us.' He turned to make full eye contact with her again, his expression apologetic. 'It's taking a bit of adjusting to, having someone else around. Despite evidence to the contrary, I really appreciate the thoughtful gestures you've made.'

His reference to her *gestures* only made the heavy feeling in her stomach worse.

'I'm really sorry, Max. I can totally understand why you'd find it hard to see me meddling with Jemima's things. I think I was so excited by the idea of living in such a beautiful house that I got a bit carried away. I forgot I was just a visitor here and that it's your home. That was selfish of *me*.'

He shook his head. 'I don't want you to feel like that. While you're here it's your home, too.'

She frowned and turned away to stare down at the floor, distracted for a moment by how scratty and out of place her old slippers looked against the rich cream-coloured wool carpet.

That was exactly the problem. It wasn't her home and it never would be. She didn't really *fit* here.

For some reason that made her feel more depressed than she had since the day she'd left her last job.

'Have you had any luck with finding a flat to rent?' he asked, breaking the silence that had fallen like a suffocating layer of dust between them.

'Not yet, but I have an appointment to view somewhere tomorrow and there are new places coming up all the time. I'll find something soon, I'm sure of it,' she said, plastering what must have been the worst fake smile she'd ever mustered onto her face.

He nodded slowly, but didn't say anything.

Twitching with discomfort now, she stood up. 'I should go.'

He frowned at her in confusion. 'What do you mean? Where are you going?'

'Back to Sarah's. I think that would be best.'

Standing up, too, he put out a hand as if to touch her, but stopped himself and shoved it into the back pocket of his jeans instead.

'Look, don't leave. I promise to be less of an ogre. I let my anger get the better of me, which was unfair.'

'I don't know, Max—' She couldn't stay here now. Could she?

Obviously seeing the hesitation on her face, he leant forward and waited until she made eye contact. 'I like having you around.' There was a teasing lightness in his expression that made her feel as if he was finally showing her the real Max. The one who had been hiding inside layers of brusque aloofness and icy calm for the past few weeks.

Warmth pooled, deep in her body. 'Really? I feel like I've made nothing but a nuisance of myself since I got here.'

He gave another snort and the first proper smile she'd seen in a while. It made his whole face light up and the sight of it sent a rush of warm pleasure across her skin. 'It's certainly been *eventful* having you here.'

She couldn't help but return his grin, despite the feeling that she was somehow losing control of herself.

'Stay. Please.'

Her heart turned over at the expression on his face. It was something she'd never seen before. Against all the odds, he looked *hopeful*.

Despite a warning voice in the back of her head, she knew there was no way she could walk out of the door now that he'd laid himself bare. She could see that the extreme mood swings were coming from a place of deep pain and the very last thing he needed was to be left alone with just his tormenting memories for company in this big empty house.

It appeared as though they needed each other.

The levelling of the emotional stakes galvanised her.

'Okay,' she said, giving him a reassuring smile. 'I'll stay. On one condition.'

'And that is?'

'That you *talk* to me when you feel the gloom descending—like a *person*, not just an employee. And let me help if I can.' She crossed her arms and raised a challenging eyebrow.

He huffed out a laugh. 'And how do you propose to help?'

'I don't know. Perhaps I can jolly you out of your moods, if you give me the chance.'

'*Jolly.* That's a fitting word for you.'

'Yeah, well, someone has to raise the positivity levels in this house of doom.' She stilled, wondering whether she'd gone a step too far, but when she dared to peek at him he was smiling, albeit in a rather bemused way.

A sense of relief washed over her. The last thing she wanted to do was read the situation wrong now they'd had a breakthrough. In fact, she really ought to push for a treaty to make things crystal clear between them.

'Look, at the risk of micromanaging the situation, can we agree that from this point on you'll be totally straight with me, and in return I promise to be totally straight with you?'

He gave her a puzzled look. 'Why? Is there something you need to tell me?'

She considered admitting she'd lied about why she'd left her last job and dismissed it immediately. There was no point going over that right now; it had no relevance to this and it would make her sound totally pathetic compared to what he'd been through.

'No, no! Nothing! It was just a turn of phrase.'

He snorted gently, rolling his eyes upward, his mouth lifting at the corner. 'Okay then, Miss Fix-it, total honesty it is. You've got yourself a deal.'

CHAPTER FIVE

JUST AS MAX thought he'd had enough drama to last him a lifetime, things took another alarming turn, only this time it was the business that threatened to walk away from him.

Opening his email first thing on Monday morning, he found a missive from his longest standing and most profitable client, letting him know that they were considering taking their business elsewhere.

Cara walked in with their coffee just as he'd finished reading it and the concern on her face made it clear how rattled he must look.

'Max? What's wrong?'

'Our biggest client is threatening to terminate our contract with them.'

Her eyes grew larger. 'Why?'

'I'm guessing one of our competitors has been sniffing around, making eyes at them and I've been putting off going to the meetings they've been trying to arrange for a while now. I haven't had the time to give them the same level of attention as before, so their head's been turned.'

'Is it salvageable?'

'Yes. If I go up there today and show them exactly why they should stay with me.'

'Okay.' She moved swiftly over to her desk and opened up her internet browser, her nails rattling against her keyboard as she typed in an enquiry. 'There's a train to Manchester in forty minutes. You go and pack some stuff; I'll call a cab and book you a seat. You can speak to me from the train about anything that needs handling today.'

He sighed and rubbed a hand through his hair, feeling the tension mounting in his scalp. 'It's going to take more than an afternoon to get this sorted. I'll probably need to be up there for most of the week.'

'Then stay as long as you need.'

Shaking his head, he batted a hand towards his computer. 'I have that proposal to finish for the end of Thursday, not to mention the monstrous list of things to tackle for all the other clients this week.'

'Leave it with me. If you set me up with a folder of your previous proposals and give me the questions you need answering, I'll put some sections together for you, so you'll only need to check and edit them as we go. And don't worry about the other clients; I can handle the majority of enquiries and rearrange anything that isn't urgent for next week. I'll only contact you with the really important stuff.'

'Are you sure you can handle that? It's a lot to leave you with at such short notice.'

'I'll be fine.' She seemed so eager he didn't have the heart to argue.

In all honesty, it was going to be tough for him to let go of his tight grip on the business and trust that this would work out, but he knew he didn't have a choice—there was no way he was letting this contract slip through his fingers. He really couldn't afford to lose this firm's loyalty at this point in his business's infancy; it would make him look weak to competitors as well as potential new clients, and presenting a confident front was everything in this game.

'Okay.' He stood up and gathered his laptop and charger together before making for the door. 'Thanks, Cara. I'll get my stuff together and call you from the train.'

Turning back, he saw she was standing stiffly with her hands clasped in front of her, her eyes wide and her cheeks flushed.

Pausing for a moment, he wondered whether he was asking too much of her, but quickly dismissed it. She'd chosen to stay and she knew what she was getting herself into.

They were in it together now.

To his relief, Cara successfully held the fort back in London whilst he was away, routinely emailing him sections of completed work to be used in the business proposal that he wrote in the evenings in time to make the deadline. She seemed to have a real flair for picking out relevant information and had made an excellent job of copying his language style.

She also saved his hide by sending flowers and a card in his name to his mother for her birthday, which he was ashamed to discover he'd forgotten all about in his panic about losing the client.

Damaging the precarious cordiality that he and his mother had tentatively built up after working through their differences over the past few years would have been just as bad, and he was immensely grateful to Cara for her forethought and care.

She really was excellent at her job.

In fact, after receiving compliments from clients about how responsive and professional she'd been when they'd contacted her with enquiries and complications to be dealt with, he was beginning to realise that he'd actually been very fortunate to secure her services. He felt sure, if she wanted to, she could walk into a job with a much better salary with her eyes shut.

Which made him wonder again why she hadn't.

Whatever the reason, the idea of losing her excellent skill base now made him uneasy. Even though he'd been certain he'd want to let her go at the end of the trial month, he was now beginning to think that that would be a huge mistake.

He had some serious thinking to do.

If he was honest, he reflected on Thursday evening, sitting alone in the hotel's busy restaurant, having time and space away from Cara and the house had been a relief. He'd been glad of the opportunity to get his head together after their confrontation. She was the first person, outside his close circle of friends, that he'd talked to in any detail about what had happened to Jemima and it had changed the atmosphere between them. To Cara's credit, she hadn't trotted out platitudes to try and make him feel better and he was grateful to her for that, but he felt a little awkward about how much of himself he'd exposed.

Conversely, though, it also felt as though a weight that he'd not noticed carrying had been lifted from his shoulders. Not just because he'd finally told Cara about Jem—which he'd begun to feel weirdly seedy about, as if he was keeping a dirty secret from her—but also because it had got to the point where he'd become irrationally superstitious about clearing out the room, as though all his memories of Jemima would be wiped away if he touched it. Which, of course, they hadn't been—she was still firmly embedded there in his head and his heart. So, even though he'd been angry and upset with Cara at the time, in retrospect, it had been a healthy thing for that decision to be wrenched out of his hands.

It felt as though he'd taken a step further into the light.

Cara was out when he arrived back at Friday lunchtime, still buzzed with elation from keeping the client, so he went to unpack his bags upstairs, return a few phone calls and take a shower before coming back down.

Walking into the kitchen, he spotted her standing by the sink with her back to him, washing a mug. He stopped to watch her for a moment, smiling as he realised she was singing softly to herself, her slim hips swaying in time to the rhythm of the song. She had a beautiful voice, lyrical and sweet, and a strange, intense warmth wound through him as he stood there listening to her. It had been a long time since anyone had sung in this house and there was something so pure and uplifting about it a shiver ran down his spine, inexplicably chased by a deep pull of longing.

Though not for Cara, surely? But for a time when his life had fewer sharp edges. A simpler time. A happier one.

Shaking himself out of this unsettling observation, he moved quickly into the room so she wouldn't think he'd been standing there spying on her.

'Hi, Cara.'

She jumped and gasped, spinning round to face him, her hand pressed to her chest. She looked fresh and well rested, but there was a wary expression in her eyes.

'Max! I didn't hear you come in.'

'I was upstairs, taking a shower and returning some urgent calls. I got back about an hour ago.'

She nodded, her professional face quickly restored. 'How was Manchester?'

'Good. We got them back on board. How have things been here?'

'That's great! Things have been fine here. It's certainly been very quiet without you.'

By 'quiet' he suspected she actually meant less fraught with angry outbursts.

There was an uncomfortable silence while she fussed about with the tea towel, hooking it carefully over the handle of the cooker door and smoothing it until it lay perfectly straight.

Tearing his eyes away from the rather disconcerting sight of her stroking her hands slowly up and down the offending article, he walked over to where the kettle sat on the work surface and flicked it on to boil. He was unsettled to find that things still felt awkward between them when they were face to face—not that he should be surprised that they were. Their last non-work conversation had been a pretty heavy one, after all.

Evidently he needed to make more of an effort to be friendly now if he was going to be in with a chance of persuading her to stay after the month's trial was up.

The thought of going back to being alone in this house certainly wasn't a comforting one any more. If he was honest, it had been heartening to know that Cara would be here when he got back. Now that the black hole of Jemima's room had been destroyed and he'd fully opened the door to Cara, the loneliness he'd previously managed to keep at bay had walked right in.

Turning to face her again, he leant back against the counter and crossed his arms.

'I wanted to talk to you about the quality of the work you've been producing.'

Her face seemed to pale and he realised he could have phrased that better. He'd never been good at letting his colleagues know when he was pleased with their work—or Jemima when he was proud of something she'd achieved, he realised with a stab of pain—but after Cara had given it to him straight about how it affected her, he was determined to get better at it.

'What I mean is—I'm really impressed with the way you've handled the work here this week while I've been away,' he amended.

'Oh! Good. Thank you.' The pride in her wobbly smile made his breath catch.

He nodded and gave a little cough to release the peculiar tension in his throat, turning back to the counter to grab a mug for his drink and give them both a moment to regroup. There was a brightly coloured card propped up next to the mug tree and he picked it up as a distraction while he waited for the kettle to finish boiling and glanced at what was written inside.

'You didn't tell me it was your birthday,' he said, turning to face her again, feeling an unsettling mixture of surprise and dismay at her not mentioning something as important as that to him.

Colour rushed to her cheeks. 'Oh, sorry! I didn't mean to leave that lying around.' She walked over and took the card from his hand, leaning against the worktop next to him and enveloping him in her familiar floral scent. She tapped the corner of the card gently against her palm and he watched, hypnotised by the action. 'It was on Wednesday. As you were away I didn't think it was worth mentioning.' She looked up at him from under her lashes. 'Don't worry—I didn't have a wild house party here while you were away, only a couple of friends over for dinner and we made sure to tidy up afterwards.'

Fighting a strange disquiet, he flapped a dismissive hand at her. 'Cara, it's okay for you to keep some of your things in the communal areas and have friends over for your birthday, for God's sake. I don't expect the place to be pristine the whole time.'

'Still. I meant to put this up in my room with the others.'

Despite their pact to be more open with each other, it was evidently going to take a lot more time and effort to get her to relax around him.

Maybe he should present her with some kind of peace offering. In fact, thinking about it, her birthday could provide the perfect excuse.

He'd seen her reading an article about a new play in a magazine one lunchtime last week, and when he picked it up later he noticed she'd put a ring around the box office number, as if to remind herself to book tickets.

After dispatching her back to the office with a list of clients to chase up about invoices, he called the theatre, only to find the play had sold out weeks ago. Not prepared to be defeated that easily, he placed a call to his friend James, who was a long-time benefactor of the theatre.

'Hey, man, how are things?' his friend asked as soon as he picked up.

'Great. Business is booming. How about you?'

'Life's good. Penny's pregnant again,' James said with pleasure in his voice.

Max ignored the twinge of pain in his chest. 'That's great. Congratulations.'

'Thanks. Let's just hope this one's going to give us less trouble arriving into the world.'

'You're certainly owed an easy birth after the last time.'

'You could say that. Anyway, what can I do for you, my friend?'

'I wanted to get hold of tickets for that new play at the Apollo Theatre for tonight's performance. It's my PA's birthday and I wanted to treat her, but it's sold out. Can you help me with that?'

'Your PA, huh?' There was a twist of wryness in James's voice that shot a prickle straight up his spine.

'Yeah. My PA,' he repeated with added terseness born of discomfort.

His friend chuckled. 'No problem. I'll call and get them to put some tickets aside for you for the VIP box. I saw it last week—it's great—but it starts early, at five, so you'll need to get a move on.' There was a loaded pause. 'It's good to hear you're getting out again.'

Max bristled again. 'I go out.'

'But not with women. Not since Jemima passed away.'

He sighed, beginning to wish he hadn't called now. 'It's not a date. She's my *PA*.'

James chuckled again. 'Well, she's lucky to have you for an *employer*. These tickets are like gold dust.'

'Thanks, I owe you one,' Max said, fighting hard to keep the growl out of his voice. To his annoyance, he felt rattled by what his friend was insinuating. It wasn't stepping over the line to do something like this for Cara, was it?

'Don't worry about it,' James said.

Max wasn't sure for a moment whether he'd voiced his concerns out loud and James was answering that question or whether he was just talking about paying him back the favour.

'Thanks, James, I've got to go,' he muttered, wanting to end the call so he could walk around and loosen off this weird tension in his chest.

'No worries.'

Max put the phone down, wondering again whether this gesture was a step too far.

No. She'd worked hard for him, under some testing circumstances and he wanted her to know that he appreciated it. If he wanted to retain her services—and he was pretty sure now that he did—he was going to have to make sure she knew how much she was valued here so she didn't go looking for another job.

Cara was back at her desk, busily typing away on her laptop, when he walked into the room they used as an office. Leaning against the edge of her desk, he waited until she'd finished and turned to face him.

'I'm nearly done here,' she said, only holding eye contact for a moment before glancing back at her computer.

'Great, because a friend of mine just called to say he has two spare tickets to that new play at the Apollo and I was thinking I could take you as a thank you for holding the fort so effectively whilst I've been away. And for missing your birthday.'

She stared at him as if she thought she might have misheard. 'I'm sorry?'

He smiled at her baffled expression, feeling a kink of pleasure at her reaction. 'We'll need to leave in the next few minutes if we're going to make it into town in time to catch the beginning.' He stood up and she blinked in surprise.

'You and *me*? Right *now*?'

'Yes. You don't have other plans, do you?'

'Um, no.'

He nodded. 'Great.'

Gesturing up and down her body, she frowned, looking a little flustered. 'But I can't go dressed like this.'

He glanced at her jeans and T-shirt, trying not to let his eyes linger on the way they fitted her trim, slender body. 'You're going to have to change quickly then,' he said, pulling his mobile out of his pocket and dialling the number for the taxi.

Cara chattered away in the cab all the way there about how the play had been given rave reviews after its preview performance and how people were already paying crazy money on auction websites for re-sold tickets to see it. Her enthusiasm was contagious and, stepping out of the car, he was surprised to find he was actually looking forward to seeing it.

The theatre was a recently renovated grand art deco building slap-bang in the middle of Soho, a short stroll from the hectic retail circus of Oxford Street.

It had been a while since he'd made it into town on a Friday night and even longer since he'd been to see any kind of live show. When he and Jemima had moved to London they'd been full of enthusiasm about how they'd be living in the heart of the action and would be able to go out every other night to see the most cutting-edge performances and mind-expanding lectures. They were going to become paragons of good taste and spectacularly cultured to boot.

And then real life had taken over and they'd become

increasingly buried under the weight of work stress and life tiredness as the years went by and had barely made it out to anything at all. It had been fine when they'd had each other for company, but he was aware that he needed to make more of an effort to get out and be sociable now he was on his own.

Not that he'd been a total recluse since Jem had died; he'd been out with friends—Poppy being his most regular pub partner—but he'd done it in a cocoon of grief, always feeling slightly detached from what was going on around him.

Doing this with Cara meant he was having to make an effort again. Which was a good thing. It felt healthy. Perhaps that was why he was feeling more upbeat than he had in a while—as if there was life beyond the narrow world he'd been living in for the past year and a half.

After paying the taxi driver, they jogged straight to the box office for their tickets, then through the empty lobby to the auditorium to find their seats in the VIP box, the usher giving them a pointed look as she closed the doors firmly behind them. It seemed they'd only just made it. This theory was borne out by the dimming of the lights and the grand swish of the curtain opening just as they folded themselves into their seats.

Max turned to find Cara with her mouth comically open and an expression that clearly said *I can't believe we've just casually nipped into the best seats in the house.* He flashed her a quick smile, enjoying her pleasure and the sense of satisfaction at doing something good here, before settling back into his plush red velvet chair, his heart beating heavily in his chest.

A waft of her perfume hit his nose as she reached up to adjust her ponytail, which made his heart beat even harder—perhaps from the sudden sensory over-load. Taking a deep breath, he concentrated on bring-ing his breathing back to normal and focused on the action on stage, determined to put all other thoughts aside for the meantime and try to enjoy whatever this turned out to be.

Cara was immensely relieved when the play stood up to her enthusiastic anticipation. It would have been pretty embarrassing if it had been a real flop after all the fuss she'd made about it on the way there. Every time she heard Max chuckle at one of the jokes she experienced a warm flutter of pleasure in her stomach.

Max bringing her here to the theatre had thrown her for a complete loop. Even though he'd finally let her into his head last weekend, she'd expected him to go back to being distant with her again once he came back from Manchester. But instead he'd surprised her by complimenting her, then not only getting tickets to the hottest play in London, but bringing her here him-self as a reward for working hard.

Dumbfounded was not the word.

Not that she was complaining.

Sneaking a glance at him, she thought she'd never seen him looking so relaxed. She could hardly believe he was the same man who had opened the door to her on the first day they'd met. He seemed larger now somehow, as if he'd straightened up and filled out in the time since she'd last seen him. That had to be all in her head, of course, but he certainly seemed more *real* now that she knew what drove his rage. In fact it was incredible how differently she felt now she knew what sort of horror he'd been through—losing someone he loved in such a senseless way.

No wonder he was so angry at the world.

Selfishly, it was a massive relief to know that none of his dark moods had been about her performance— apart from when she'd fallen asleep on the kitchen table during business hours, of course.

After he'd left for Manchester, she'd had a minor panic attack about how she was going to cope on her own, terrified of making a mistake that would impact negatively on the business, but, after giving herself a good talking-to in the mirror, she'd pulled it together and got on with the job in hand. And she'd been fine. More than fine. In fact she'd actually started to enjoy her job again as she relaxed into the role and reasserted her working practices.

Truth be told, before she'd started working for Max, she didn't know whether she'd be able to hold her nerve in a business environment any more. He'd been a hard taskmaster but she knew she'd benefited from that, dis- covering that she had the strength to stand up for her- self when it counted. She'd been tested to her limits and she'd come through the other side and that, to her, had been her biggest achievement in a very long time.

She felt proud of herself again.

As the first half drew to a close she became increasingly conscious of the heat radiating from Max's powerful body and his arm that pressed up against hers as he leaned into the armrest. Her skin felt hot and prickly where it touched his, as if he was giving off an electric charge, and it was sending little currents of energy through the most disconcerting places in her body.

It seemed her crush on him had grown right along with her respect and she was agonisingly aware of how easy it would be to fall for him if she let herself.

Which she wasn't going to do. He was clearly still in love with his wife and there was no way she could compete with a ghost.

Only pain and heartache lay that way.

As soon as the curtain swished closed and the lights came on to signal the intermission she sprang up from her seat, eager to break their physical connection as soon as possible.

'Let's grab a drink,' Max said, leaning in close so she could hear him over the noise of audience chatter, his breath tickling the hairs around her ear.

'Good idea.' She was eager to move now to release the pent-up energy that was making her heart race.

Max gestured for her to go first, staying close behind her as they walked down the stairs towards the bar, his dominating presence like a looming shadow at her back.

They joined the rest of the audience at the bottom of the stairs and she pushed her way through the shouty crowd of people towards the shiny black-lacquered bar, which was already six people deep with waiting customers.

'Hmm, this could take a while,' she said to Max as they came to a stop at the outskirts of the throng.

'Don't worry, I'll get the drinks,' he said, walking around the perimeter of the group as if gauging the best place to make a start. 'Glass of wine?' he asked.

'Red please.'

'Okay, I'm going in,' he said, taking an audible breath and turning to the side to shoulder through a small gap between two groups of chatting people with their backs to each other.

Cara watched in fascinated awe as Max made it to the bar in record time, flipping a friendly smile as he sidled through the crowd and charming a group of women into letting him into a small gap at the counter next to them.

After making sure his newly made friends were served first, he placed his order with the barman and was back a few moments later, two glasses of red wine held aloft in a gesture of celebration.

'Wow, nice work,' Cara said, accepting a glass and trying not to grin like a loon. 'I've never seen anyone work a bar crowd like that before.'

Max shrugged and took a sip of wine, pinning a look of exaggerated nonchalance onto his face. 'I have hidden depths.'

She started to laugh, but it dried in her throat as she locked eyes with someone on the other side of the room.

Someone she thought she'd never see again.

Swallowing hard, she dragged her gaze back to Max and dredged up a smile, grasping for cool so she wouldn't have to explain her sudden change in mood.

But it was not to be. The man was too astute for his own good.

'Are you okay? You look like you've seen a ghost,' he said, his intelligent eyes flashing with concern.

Damn and blast. This was the last thing she wanted to have to deal with tonight.

'Fine,' she squeaked, her cheeks growing hot under the intensity of his gaze.

'Cara. I thought we'd agreed to be straight with each other from now on.'

Sighing, she nodded towards the other side of the bar. 'That guy over there is an old friend of mine.'

He frowned as she failed to keep the hurt out of her voice and she internally kicked herself for being so transparent.

'He can't be a very good friend if you're ignoring each other.'

She sighed and tapped at the floor with the toe of her shoe. 'It's complicated.'

He raised his eyebrows, waiting for her to go on.

After pausing for a moment, she decided there was no point in trying to gloss over it. 'The thing is—his fiancée has a problem with me.'

'Really? Why?'

'Because I'm female.'

He folded his arms. 'She's the jealous type, huh?'

'Yeah. And no matter how much Jack's tried to convince her that our friendship is purely platonic, she won't believe him. So I've been confined to the rubbish heap of Friends Lost and Passed Over.' She huffed out a sigh. 'I can't really blame him for making that choice, though. He loves her and I want him to be happy, and if that means we can't be friends any more then so be it.'

The look of bewildered outrage in Max's expression made the breath catch in her throat and she practically stopped breathing altogether as he reached out and stroked his hand down her arm in a show of solidarity, his touch sending tingles of pure pleasure through every nerve in her body.

Staring up into his handsome face, she wondered again what it would feel like to have someone like Max for a partner. To know that he was on her side and that he had her back, no matter what happened.

But she was kidding herself. He was never going to offer her the chance to find out. She was his employee and she'd do well to remember that.

Tearing her gaze away from him, she glanced back across the room to where the fiancée in question had now appeared by Jack's side. From a distance they appeared to be having a heated discussion about something, their heads close together as they gesticulated at each other. As she watched, they suddenly sprang apart and Jack turned to catch her eye again, already moving towards where she and Max were standing.

He was coming over.

Her body tensed with apprehension and she jumped in surprise as Max put his hand on her arm again, then increased his grip, as if readying himself to spirit her away from a painful confrontation.

'Cara! It's been ages,' Jack said as he came to a stop in front of her, looking just as boyishly handsome as ever, with his lopsided grin and great mop of wavy blond hair.

'It has, Jack.'

'How are you?' he asked, looking a little shame-faced now, as well he should. They'd become good friends after meeting at their first jobs after university and had been close once, spending weekends at each other's houses and standing in as 'plus ones' at weddings and parties if either of them were single and in need of support.

There had been a time when she'd wondered whether they'd end up together, but as time had passed it became obvious that wasn't meant to be. He was a great guy, but the chemistry just wasn't there for her—or for him, it seemed. But seeing him here now reminded her just how much she missed his friendship. She could have really done with his support after Ewan sauntered away from their relationship in search of someone with less emotional baggage, but it had been at that point that his fiancée had issued her ultimatum, and Cara had well and truly been the loser in that contest.

Not that she blamed him for choosing Amber. She had to respect his loyalty to the woman he loved.

'I'm great, Jack, thanks. How are you—' she paused and flicked her gaze to his fiancée, who had now appeared at his side '—both?' Somehow she managed to dredge up a smile for the woman. 'Hi, Amber.'

'Hi, Cara, we're great, thanks,' Amber said, acerbity dripping from every word as she pointedly wrapped a possessive arm around Jack's waist. Turning to look at Max, she gave him a subtle, but telling, once-over.

'And who's this?'

'This is Max…' Cara took a breath, about to say *my boss*, when Max cut her off to lean in and shake hands with Amber.

'It's lovely to meet you, Amber,' he said in the same smooth tone she'd heard him use to appease clients.

It worked just as well on Amber because her cheeks flooded with colour and she actually fluttered her lashes at him. Turning back to Cara, she gave her a cool smile, her expression puzzled, as if she was trying to work out how she'd got her hands on someone as impressive as Max.

'Did Jack tell you—our wedding's on Sunday so this evening is our last hurrah before married life?' Amber's eyes twinkled with malice. 'Jack's firm is very well reputed in the City and people practically throw invitations at him every day,' she said, her tone breezy but her eyes hard, as though she was challenging Cara to beat her with something better than that.

Which, of course, she had no hope of doing.

Pushing away the thump of humiliation, Cara forced her mouth into the shape of a smile.

'That's wonderful—congratulations! I had no idea the wedding was so soon.'

Amber leaned in and gave her a pitying smile. 'We've kept it a small affair, which is why we couldn't send you an invitation, Cara.'

Max shifted next to her, pulling her a bit tighter against him in the process and surprising her again by rubbing her arm in support. She wondered whether he could feel how fast her pulse was racing through her body with him holding her so close.

'But we had two spaces open up this week,' Jack said suddenly and a little too loudly, as if he'd finally decided to step out of his fiancée's shadow and take control. 'My cousin and her husband have had to drop out to visit sick family abroad. If you're not busy you could come in their place.'

Judging by the look on Amber's face, she obviously hadn't had this in mind when she'd agreed to be dragged over here.

'It would be great if you could make it,' Jack pressed, his expression open, almost pleading now. It seemed that he genuinely wanted her to be there. Perhaps this was his way of making things up to her after cutting her out of his life so brutally. At least that was something.

But she couldn't say yes when the invitation was for both her and Max and she hated the idea of turning up and spending the day on her own amongst all those happy couples.

Before she could open her mouth to make up an excuse and turn them down, Max leaned in and said, 'Thank you—we'd love to come.'

She swivelled her head to gape at him, almost giving herself whiplash in the process, stunned to find a look of cool certainty on his face.

'Are you sure we're not busy?' she said pointedly, raising both eyebrows at him.

'I'm sure,' he replied with a firm nod.

Turning back to Jack, she gave him what must have

been the weirdest-looking smile. 'Okay—er—' she swallowed '—then we'd love to come. Thanks.'

'That's great,' Jack said, giving her a look that both said *I'm sorry for everything* and *thank you*.

'We'd better go and get a drink before the performance starts again,' Amber said with steel in her voice, her patience clearly used up now.

'I'll text you with the details, Cara,' Jack said as Amber drew him away.

'Okay, see you on Sunday,' Cara said weakly to their disappearing figures.

As soon as they were out of earshot she turned to stare at Max, no doubt doing her impression of a goldfish again.

'He's a brave man,' was all Max said in reply.

'You realise they think we're a couple?'

He nodded, a fierce intensity in his eyes causing a delicious shiver to rush down her spine. 'I know, but I wanted to see the look on that awful woman's face when we said yes, and I have no problem pretending to be your partner if it's going to smooth the way back to a friendship with Jack for you.'

Max as her partner. Just the thought of it made her quiver right down to her toes.

'That's—' she searched for the right words '—game of you.'

'It'll be my pleasure.'

There was an odd moment where the noises around her seemed to get very loud in her ears. Tearing her gaze away from his, she gulped down the last of her wine and wrapped her hands around the glass in order to prevent herself from chewing on her nails.

Okay. Well, that happened.

Who knew that Max would turn out to be her knight in shining armour?

CHAPTER SIX

MAX HAD NO idea where this strange possessiveness towards Cara had sprung from, but he hadn't been about to let that awful woman, Amber, treat her with so little respect. She deserved more than that. Much more. And while she was working for him he was going to make sure she got it.

Which meant he was now going to be escorting her to a wedding—the kind of event he'd sworn to avoid after Jemima died. The thought of being back in a church, watching a couple with their whole lives ahead of them begin their journey together, made his stomach clench with unease.

One year—that was all he'd been allowed with his wife. One lousy year. It made him want to spit with rage at the world. Why her? Why them?

Still, at least he didn't know the happy couple and would be able to keep a low profile at the wedding, hiding his bitterness behind a bland smile. He didn't need to engage. He'd just be there to support Cara; that was all.

After the play finished they travelled home in silence, a stark contrast to their journey there, but he was glad of the quiet. Perversely, it felt as though he and Cara had grown closer during that short time, the confrontation and subsequent solidarity banding them together like teammates.

Which of course they were, he reminded himself as he opened the front door to his house and ushered her inside, at least when it came to the business.

Cara's phone beeped as she shrugged off her coat and she plucked it out of her handbag and read the message, her smile dropping by degrees as she scanned the text.

'Problem?' he asked, an uncomfortable sense of foreboding pricking at the edge of his mind. It had taken him a long time to be able to answer the phone without feeling the crush of anxiety he'd been plagued with after the call telling him his wife had collapsed and had been rushed into hospital.

He took a step closer to her, glad she was here to distract him from the lingering bad memories.

Glancing up, she gave him a sheepish look. 'It's a text from Jack with the details of the wedding.'

'Oh, right.' He stepped back, relief flowing through him, but Cara didn't appear to relax. Instead her grimace only deepened.

'Um. Apparently it's in Leicestershire. Which is a two and a half hour drive from here. So we'll need to stay overnight.' She wrinkled her nose, the apology clear on her face.

Great. Just what had he let himself in for here?

'No problem,' he forced himself to say, holding back

the irritation he felt at the news. It wasn't Cara's fault and he was the one who had pushed for this to happen.

More fool him.

'Really? You don't mind?' she asked, relief clear in her tone.

'No, it's fine,' he lied, trying not to think about all the hours he'd have to spend away from his desk so he could make nice with a bunch of strangers.

'Great, then I'll book us a couple of rooms in the B&B that Jack suggested,' she said, her smile returning.

'You do that.' He gave her a firm nod and hid a yawn behind his hand. 'I'm heading off to bed,' he said, feeling the stress of the week finally catching up with him. 'See you in the morning, Cara. And Happy Birthday.'

Cara disappeared for most of the next day, apparently going to look at potential flats to rent, then retiring to bed early, citing exhaustion from the busy, but fruitless, day.

After the tension of Friday night, Max was glad of the respite and spent most of his time working through the backlog of emails he'd accumulated after his week away.

Sunday finally rolled around and he woke early, staring into the cool empty air next to him and experiencing the usual ache of hollowness in his chest, before pulling himself together and hoisting his carcass out of bed and straight into the shower.

The wedding was at midday so at least he had a couple of hours to psych himself up before they had to head over to the Leicestershire estate where it was being held.

The sun was out and glinting off the polished windows of the houses opposite when he pulled his curtains open, momentarily blinding him with its brightness. It was definitely a day for being outdoors.

He'd barely breathed fresh air in the past week, only moving between office and hotel, and the thought of feeling the warm sun on his skin spurred him into action. He pulled on his running gear, something he'd not done for over a year and a half, and went for a long run, welcoming the numbing pain as he worked his lethargic muscles hard, followed by the rewarding rush of serotonin as it chased its way through his veins. After a while it felt as though he was flying along the pavement, the worries and stresses of the past week pushed to the very back of his mind by the punishing exercise.

For the first time in a long while he felt as if he were truly awake.

Cara appeared to be up and about when he limped back into his kitchen for a long drink of water, his senses perking up as he breathed in the comforting smell of the coffee she'd been drinking, threaded with the flowery scent of her perfume.

Glancing up at the clock as he knocked back his second glass of water, he was shocked to see it was already nearly nine o'clock, which meant he really ought to get a move on if he was going to be ready to leave for the wedding on time.

Turning back from loading his glass into the dishwasher, he was brought up short by the sight of Cara standing in the hallway just outside the kitchen door, watching him. She'd twisted her long hair up into some sort of complicated-looking hairstyle and her dark eyes sparkled with glittery make-up. The elegant silver strapless dress she wore fitted her body perfectly, moulding itself to her gentle curves and making her seem taller and—something else. More mature, perhaps? More sophisticated?

Whatever it was, she looked completely and utterly beautiful.

Realising he was standing there gawping at her like some crass teenage boy, he cleared his suddenly dry throat and dredged up a smile which he hoped didn't look as lascivious as it felt.

'Hey, you look like you're dressed for a wedding,' he said, cringing inside at how pathetic that sounded.

She smiled. 'And you don't. I hope you're not thinking of going like that because I'm pretty sure it didn't say "sports casual" on the invitation.' Her amused gaze raked up and down his body, her eyebrows rising at the sight of his sweat-soaked running gear.

He returned her grin, finding it strangely difficult to keep it natural-looking. His whole face felt as if he'd had his head stuck in the freezer. What was wrong with him? A bit of sunshine and a fancy dress and his mind was in a spin.

'I'd better go and take a shower; otherwise we're going to be late,' he said, already walking towards the door.

'Could you do me a favour before you go?' she asked, colour rising in her cheeks.

'Er…sure. As long as it's not going to cost me anything,' he joked, coming to a stop in front of her. In her heels she was nearly as tall as him, making it easier to directly meet her gaze. She had such amazing eyes: bright and clear with vitality and intellect. The make-up and hair made him think of Audrey Hepburn in *Breakfast at Tiffany's*.

'Could you do up the buttons on the back of my dress?' she asked, her voice sounding unusually breathy, as if it had taken a lot for her to ask for his help.

'Sure,' he said, waiting for her to turn around and present her back to him. His breath caught as he took in the long, elegant line of her spine as it disappeared into the base of her dress. There were three buttons that held the top half of it together, with a large piece cut out at the bottom, which would leave her creamy skin and the gentle swells of muscle at the base of her back exposed.

Heaven help him.

Hands feeling as if they'd been trapped in the freezer, too, he fiddled around with the buttons, feeling the warmth of her skin heat the tips of his fingers. Hot barbs of awareness tracked along his nerves and embedded themselves deep in his body and his breath came out in short ragged gasps, which he'd like to think was an after-effect of the hard exercise, but was more likely to be down to his close proximity to a woman's body, after his had been starved of attention for the past year and a half.

'There you go,' he said, snapping the final button into its hole with a sigh of relief. 'I'll be back down in fifteen.'

And with that he made his escape.

* * *

Wow. This felt weird, being at Jack's wedding—a friend she thought she'd never see again—with Max—her recalcitrant boss—as her escort. The whole world seemed to have flipped on its head. If someone had told her a week ago that this was going to happen she would have given them a polite smile whilst slowly backing away.

But here she was, swaying unsteadily in the only pair of high heels she owned, with Max at her side. The man who could give Hollywood's top leading men a run for their money in the charisma department.

There had been a moment in the kitchen, after he'd turned around and noticed her, when she thought she'd seen something in his eyes. Something that had never been there before. Something like desire.

And then when he'd helped her with her dress it had felt as though the air had crackled and jumped between them. The bloom of his breath on her neck had made her knees weak and her heart race. She could have sworn his voice had held a rougher undertone than she was used to hearing as he excused himself.

But she knew she was kidding herself if she thought she should read more than friendly interest into his actions.

They had Radio Four on for the entire journey up to Leicestershire, listening in rapt silence to a segment on finance, then chuckling along to a radio play. Cara was surprised by how easy it was to sit beside Max and how relaxed and drawn into their shared enjoyment of the programme she was. So much so, that it was to her great surprise that they pulled into the small car park of the church where the wedding was taking place, seemingly only a short time after leaving London.

The sunshine that had poured in through her bedroom window that morning had decided to stick around for the rest of the day, disposing of the insubstantial candyfloss clouds of the morning to reveal the most intensely blue sky she'd ever seen.

All around her, newly blooming spring flowers bopped their heads in time to the rhythm of the light spring breeze, their gaudy colours a striking counterpoint to the verdant green of the lawns surrounding them.

Taking a deep breath, she drew the sweet, fresh air deep into her lungs. This should mark a new beginning in her life, she decided. The start of the next chapter, where the foundations she'd laid in the past few weeks would hopefully prove strong enough to support her from this point onwards.

'It's nearly twelve o'clock; we should go in,' Max said with regret in his voice as he cast his gaze around their beautiful surroundings.

Attempting to keep her eyes up and off the tantalising view of his rear in the well-cut designer suit he'd chosen to wear today, she tripped into the church after him, shivering slightly at the change in temperature as they walked out of the sunshine and into the nave.

Most of the pews were already full, so they hung back for a moment to be directed to a seat by one of the ushers.

And that was when the day took a definite turn for the worse.

Her world seemed to spin on its axis, rolling her stomach along with it, as her former and current life lined up on a collision course. One of the PAs who had belonged to the Cobra Clique was standing down by the altar, her long blond hair slithering down her back as she threw her head back and laughed at something that the man standing next to her said.

Taking a deep breath, Cara willed herself not to panic, but her distress must have shown plainly on her face because Max turned to glance in the direction she was staring and said, 'Cara? What's wrong?'

'Ah…nothing.' She flapped a dismissive hand at him, feeling her cheeks flame with heat, and took a step backwards, hoping the stone pillar would shield her. But serendipity refused to smile as the woman turned towards them, catching her eye, her pupils flaring in recognition and her gaze moving, as if in slow motion, from Cara to Max and back again. And the look on her face plainly said she wasn't going to miss this golden opportunity to make more trouble for her.

Looking around her wildly, Cara's heart sank as she realised there was nowhere to run, nowhere to hide.

It was usually at this point in a film that the leading lady would pull the guy she was with towards her and kiss him hard to distract him from the oncoming danger, but she knew, as she stared with regret at Max's full, inviting mouth, that there was no way she could do that. He'd probably choke in shock, then fire her on the spot if she even attempted it. It wouldn't just put her job in jeopardy—it would blow it to smithereens.

There was only one thing left to do.

'Max, I need to tell you something.'

He frowned at her, his eyes darkening as he caught on to her worried tone.

'What's wrong?'

'I—er—'

'Cara?' He looked really alarmed now and she shook her head, trying to clear it. She needed to keep her cool or she'd end up looking even more of an idiot.

'I wasn't entirely straight with you about why I left my last job. Truth is—' she took a breath '—I didn't take redundancy.'

He blinked, then frowned. 'So you were fired?'

'No. I—'

'What did you do, Cara? What are you trying to tell me?' His voice held a tinge of the old Max now—the one who didn't suffer fools.

'Okay—' She closed her eyes and held up a hand. 'Look, just give me a minute and I'll explain. The thing is—' Locking her shaking hands together, she took a steadying breath. 'I was bullied by a gang of women there who made my life a living hell and I handed in my notice before my boss could fire me for incompetence as a result of it,' she said, mortified by the tremor in her voice.

When she opened her eyes to look at him, the expression of angry disbelief on his face made her want to melt into a puddle of shame.

'What?'

She swallowed past the tightness in her throat. 'I had no choice but to leave.'

He shook his head in confusion. 'Why didn't you tell me?'

Out of the corner of her eye she saw her nemesis approaching and felt every hair on her body stand to attention. The woman was only ten steps away, at most.

'And why are you telling me this now?' he pressed.

'Because one of the women is here at the wedding and she'll probably tell you a pack of lies to make me look bad. I didn't exactly leave graciously. There was a jug of cold coffee and some very white blouses involved.' She cringed at the desperation in her voice, but Max just turned to glare in the direction she'd been avoiding, then let out a sharp huff of breath.

'Come outside for a minute.'

Wrapping his hand around her arm, he propelled her back out through the doors of the church and down the steps, coming to a sudden halt under the looming shadow of the clock tower, where he released her. Crossing his arms, he looked down at her with an expression of such exasperation it made her quake in her stilettos.

'Why didn't you mention this to me before?' he asked, shoving back the hair that had fallen across his forehead during their short journey, only drawing more attention to his piercing gaze.

Sticking her chin in the air, she crossed her own arms, determined to stand up for herself. 'I really wanted to work with you and I thought you might not hire me if you knew the truth. It didn't exactly look good on my CV that I'd only stuck it out there for three months before admitting defeat.'

'So you thought you had to lie to me to get the job?'

She held up her hands in apology. 'I know I should have told you the truth, but I'd already messed up other job interviews because I was so nervous and ashamed of myself for being so weak.' She hugged her arms around her again. 'I didn't want you to think badly of me. Anyway, at the time you barely wanted to talk to me about the work I had to do, let alone anything of a personal nature, so I thought it best to keep it to myself.' She looked at him steadily, craving his understanding. 'You can be pretty intimidating, you know.'

She was saved from having to further explain herself by one of the ushers loudly asking the stragglers outside to please go into the church and take their seats because the bride had arrived.

From the look on Max's face she wasn't sure whether he was going to walk away and leave her standing there like a total lemon on her own or turn around and punch the wall. She didn't fancy watching either scenario play out.

To her surprise, he let out a long, frustrated sigh and looked towards the gaggle of people filing into the church.

'We can't talk about this now or we'll be walking in with the bridal party, and there's no way I'd pass for a bridesmaid,' he said stiffly.

She stared at him. 'You mean you're not going to leave?'

'No, I'm not going to leave,' he said crossly. 'We'll talk more about this after the ceremony.'

And with that he put his hand firmly against the middle of her back and ushered her inside.

Sliding into the polished wooden pew next to Max and surreptitiously wiping her damp palms on her dress, she glanced at him out of the corner of her eye. From the set of his shoulders she could tell he wasn't likely to let *this* go with a casual wave of his hand.

In fact she'd bet everything she had left that he was really going to fire her this time.

Frustration churned in her stomach. After all the progress she'd made in getting back on her feet, and persuading Max to finally trust her, was it really going to end like this?

Looking along the pews, she saw that her nemesis was sitting on the other side of the church, a wide smile on her face as she watched the ceremony unfold. At least that threat had been neutralised. There wasn't anything left that she could do to hurt her.

She hoped.

Rage unfurled within Cara at the unfairness of it all. Why did this woman get to enjoy herself when she had to sit here worrying about her future?

As she watched Amber make her stately way up the aisle towards a rather nervous-looking Jack, she could barely concentrate for wondering what Max was going to say to her once they were facing each other over their garlic mushrooms at the lunch afterwards. There was no way she was going to be able to force down a bite of food until they'd resolved this.

Oh, get a grip, Cara.

When she dared take a peek at him from the corner of her eye again, he seemed to be grimly staring straight ahead. Forcing herself to relax, she uncrossed her legs, then her arms and sat up straighter, determined not to appear anxious or pitiful. She knew what she had to do. There would be no gratuitous begging or bartering for a reprieve. She would hold her head high throughout it all and calmly state her case.

And until she had that opportunity she was going to damn well enjoy watching her friend get married.

Judging by her rigid posture and ashen complexion, Cara really didn't appear to be enjoying the ceremony, which only increased Max's discomfort at being there, too. Not that he blamed her in any way for it. He'd chosen to come here with her after all. Though, from the sound of it, she must be regretting bringing him along now.

Had he really been so unapproachable that she'd chosen to lie to his face instead of admitting to having a rough time at her last place of work?

He sighed inwardly.

She was absolutely right, though. Again. He could be intimidating. And he'd been at the peak of his remoteness when she'd first arrived on his doorstep and asked him for a job. He also knew that if she'd mentioned the personal issues that had been intrinsic to her leaving her last job when they'd first met it would have given him pause enough to turn her away. He hadn't wanted any kind of complication at that point.

But he was so glad now that he hadn't.

Somehow, in her innocent passive-aggressive way, she'd managed to push his buttons and, even though he'd fought it at the time, that was exactly what he'd needed.

She was what he'd needed.

After the ceremony finished they were immediately ushered out of the church and straight up the sweeping manicured driveway to the front of a grand Georgian house where an enormous canvas marquee had been set up next to the orangery.

A small affair, his foot.

As soon as they stepped inside they had toxic-coloured cocktails thrust upon them and were politely but firmly asked to make their way back outside again to the linen-draped tables on the terrace next to the house.

'This is like a military operation,' he muttered to Cara, who had walked quietly next to him since they'd left the church, her face pale and her expression serious. She gave him a weak smile, her eyes darting from side to side as if she was seriously contemplating making a run for it and scoping out the best means of escape.

He sighed. 'Come and sit down over here where it's quiet,' he said, looping his arm through hers and guiding her towards one of the empty tables nearest the house.

To his frustration she stiffened, then slipped out of his steadying grip and folded her arms across her chest instead, her shoulders rigid and her chin firmly up as they walked. Just as they picked their way over the last bit of gravelled path to reach the table she stumbled and on reflex he quickly moved in to catch her.

'Are you okay?' he asked, placing a hand on the exposed part of her back, feeling the heat of her body warm the palm of his hand and send an echoing sensation through his entire abdomen.

His touch seemed to undo something in her and she collapsed into the nearest chair and gave him such a fearful look his heart jumped into his throat.

'I'm sorry for lying to you, Max. Please don't fire me. If I lose this job I'll have to move back to Cornwall and I really, really don't want to leave London. It's my home and I love it. I can't imagine living anywhere else now. And I really like working for you.' Swallowing hard, she gave him a small quavering smile. 'I swear I will never lie to you again. Believe it or not, I usually have a rock-solid moral compass and if I hadn't felt backed into a corner I never would have twisted the truth. I was on the cusp of losing everything and I was desperate, Max. Totally. Desperate.' She punctuated each of the last words with a slap of her hand on the table.

'Cara, I'm not going to fire you.'

How could she think that he would? Good grief, had he done such a number on her that she'd think he'd be capable of something as heartless as that?

'You're not?' Her eyes shone in the reflected brightness thrown up by the white tablecloth and he looked away while she blinked back threatening tears.

'Of course not.' He shifted forward in his seat, closer to her. 'You well and truly proved your worth to the business last week.' He waited till she looked at him again. 'I have to admit, I'm hurt that you thought I'd fire you for admitting to being bullied.' He leaned back in his chair with a sigh. 'God, you must think I'm a real tool if you seriously believed I'd do something like that.'

'It's just—you can be a bit...fierce...sometimes. And

I didn't want to show any weakness.' She visibly cringed as she said it, and his insides plummeted.

'Tell me more about what happened at your last job,' he said quietly, wanting to get things completely straight between them, but not wanting to spook her further in the process.

Her gaze slid away. 'It's not a happy tale, or something I'm particularly proud of.'

'No. I got that impression.'

'Okay, I'll tell you, but please don't judge me too harshly. Things like this always look so simple and manageable from a distance, but when you're in the thick of it, it's incredibly difficult to think straight without letting your emotions get in the way.'

He held up his hands, palms forward, and affected a non-judgemental expression.

She nodded and sat up straighter. 'I thought I'd hit the jackpot when I was offered that position. Ugh! What an idiot,' she said, her self-conscious grimace making him want to move closer to her, to draw her towards him and smooth out the kinks of her pain. But he couldn't do that. It wasn't his place.

So he just nodded and waited for her to continue.

'When I started as Executive Assistant to the CEO of LED Software I had no idea about the office politics that were going on there. But it didn't take me long to find out. Apparently one of the other PAs had expected to be a shoo-in for my job and was *very* unimpressed when they gave it to me. She made it her mission from my first day to make my life miserable. As one of the longest-standing members of staff—and a very, er, *strong* personality—she had the allegiance of all the other PAs and a lot of the other members of staff and they ganged up on me. At first I thought I was going mad. I'd make diary appointments for my boss with other high-ranking members of staff in the company, which their PAs would claim to have no knowledge of by the time I sent him along for the meeting. Or the notes I'd print out for an important phone call with the Executive Board would go missing from his desk right before it took place and he'd have to take it unbriefed.' She tapped her fingers on the table. 'That did not go down well. My boss was a very proud guy and he expected things to be perfect.'

'I can relate to that,' Max said, forcing compassion into his smile despite the tug of disquiet in his gut. He was just as guilty when it came to perfectionism.

But, instead of admonishing him, she smiled back.

'Lots of other little things like that happened,' she continued, rubbing a hand across her forehead, 'which made me look incompetent, but I couldn't prove that someone was interfering with my work and when I mentioned it to my boss he'd wave away my concerns and suggest I was slipping up on the job and blaming others to cover my back. I let the stress of it get to me and started making real mistakes, things I never would have let slip at the last place I worked. It rattled me, to the point where I started believing I wasn't cut out for the job. I wasn't sleeping properly with the stress of it and I ended up breaking down one day in front of my boss. And that—' she clicked her fingers '—was the end of our working relationship. He seemed to lose all respect

for me after that and started giving the other PAs things
that were my job to do.'

Max snorted in frustration. 'The guy sounds like
an idiot.'

She gave him a wan smile. 'I was the idiot. I only
found out what was really going on when I overheard
a couple of the PAs laughing about it in the ladies'
bathroom.'

Her eyes were dark with an expression he couldn't
quite read now. Was it anger? Resentment? It certainly
didn't look like self-pity.

'So you left,' he prompted.

She took a sip of her drink and he did the same, grimacing at the claggy sweetness of the cocktail.

'I had to,' she said. 'My professional reputation was
at stake, not to mention my sanity. I couldn't afford to
be fired; it would have looked awful on my CV. Not
to mention how upset my parents would have been.
They're desperate for me to have a successful career.
They never had the opportunity to get a good education or well-paid job themselves so they scrimped and
saved for years to put me through private school. It's a
point of pride for my dad in particular. Apparently he
never shuts up to his friends about me working with
"the movers and shakers in the Big Smoke".' She shot
him an embarrassed grimace.

He smiled. 'You're lucky—my mother couldn't give
two hoots whether I'm successful or not. She's not what
you'd call an engaged parent.'

Her brow furrowed in sympathy. 'And your father?'

'I never met him.' He leant back with a sigh. 'My

mother fell pregnant with me when she was sixteen and still maintains that she doesn't know who he was. She was pretty wild in her youth and constantly moved us around the country. Barely a term at school would go by before she had us packing up and moving on. She couldn't bear to stay in the same place for long. Not that she's exactly settled now.'

Her gaze was sympathetic. 'That must have been tough when you were young.'

He shrugged. 'It was a bit. I never got to keep the friends I made for very long.'

He thought about how his unsettled youth had impacted on the way he liked to live now. He still didn't like change, even all these years later; it made him tetchy and short-tempered. Which was something Cara had got to know all about recently.

Keen to pull his mind away from his own shortcomings, he leaned forward in his seat and recaptured eye contact with her. 'So what happened when you handed in your notice?'

She started at the sudden flip in subject back to her and twisted the stem of her glass in her fingers, looking away from his gaze and focusing on the garish liquid as it swirled up towards the rim. 'My boss didn't even bat an eyelid, just tossed my letter of resignation onto his desk and went back to the email he was typing, which confirmed just how insignificant I was to him. I took a couple of weeks to get my head straight after that, but I needed another job. I've never earned enough to build up any savings and my landlord chose that moment to hoick my rent up. I sent my CV out everywhere and got a few interviews, but every one I attended was a washout. It was as if they could sense the cloud of failure that hung around me like a bad smell.'

'And that's when Poppy sent you to me.'

Wrinkling her nose, she gave him a rueful smile. 'I told her a bit about what had happened before she went off to shoot her latest project and she must have thought the two of us could help each other out because she emailed me to suggest I try you for a job. She made it sound as if you were desperate for help and it seemed like fate that I should work for you.'

'Desperate, huh?' He leant back in his seat and raised an eyebrow, feeling amusement tug at his mouth. That was textbook Poppy. 'Well, I have to admit it's been good for me, having you around. It's certainly kept me on my toes.'

'Yeah, there's never a dull moment when I'm around, huh?'

The air seemed to grow thick between them as their eyes met and he watched in arrested fascination as her cheeks flamed with colour.

Sliding her gaze away, she stared down at the table, clutching her glass, her chewed nails in plain view. He'd known it the whole time, of course, that she was fighting against some inner trauma, as her nerve and buoyancy deteriorated in the face of his brittle moods. Her increasingly ragged nails had been the indicator he'd been determined to ignore.

But not any more.

A string quartet suddenly started up on the terrace behind them and he winced as the sound assaulted his ears. He'd never liked the sound of violins and an instrument such as that should never be used to play soft rock covers. It was a crime against humanity.

'Come on, let's take a walk around the grounds and clear our heads,' he said, standing up and holding out his hand to help her up from the chair.

She looked at it with that little frown that always made something twist in his chest, before giving a firm nod and putting her hand in his.

CHAPTER SEVEN

A walk was exactly what Cara needed to clear her head.

She couldn't quite believe she'd just spilled her guts to Max like that, but it was a massive relief to have it all out in the open, even if she did still feel shaky with the effort of holding herself together.

Of course, seeing the concern on his handsome face had only made her ridiculous crush on him deepen, and she was beginning to worry about how she was going to cope with seeing him every day, knowing that they'd never be anything more than colleagues or, at the very most, friends.

A twinkling light in the distance danced in her peripheral vision and she stopped and turned to see what it was, feeling her heels sink into the soft earth beneath her feet. Pulling her shoes off, she hooked her fingers into the straps before running to catch up with Max, who was now a few paces ahead of her, seemingly caught up in his own world, his head dipped as a frown played across his brow.

'Hey, do you fancy walking to that lake over there?' she asked him.

'Hmm?' His eyes looked unfocused, as if his thoughts were miles away. 'Yes, okay.'

The sudden detachment worried her. 'Is everything okay?' Perhaps, now he'd had more time to reflect on what she'd told him, he was starting to regret getting involved in her messed up life.

She took a breath. 'Do you want to head back to London? I wouldn't blame you if you did.'

Turning to look her in the eye again, he blinked, as though casting away whatever was bothering him. 'No, no. I'm fine.' His gaze flicked towards the lake, then back to her again and he gave her a tense smile. 'Yeah, let's walk that way.'

It only took them a couple of minutes to get there, now that she was in bare feet, and they stopped at the lakeshore and looked out across the water to the dark, impenetrable-looking forest on the other side.

'It's a beautiful setting they've chosen,' Cara said, to fill the heavy silence that had fallen between them.

'Yes, it's lovely.' Max bent down and picked up a smooth flat stone, running his fingertips across its surface. 'This looks like a good skimmer.' He shrugged off his jacket and rolled up the sleeves of his shirt, revealing his muscular forearms.

Cara stared at them, her mouth drying at the sight. There was something so real, so virile about the image of his tanned skin, with its smattering of dark hair, in stark contrast to the crisp white cotton of his formal shirt. As if he was revealing the *man* inside the businessman.

Supressing a powerful desire to reach out and trace

her fingers across the dips and swells of his muscles, she took a step away to give him plenty of room as he drew his elbow back and bent low, then flung the stone hard across the water.

A deep, satisfied chuckle rumbled from his chest as the stone bounced three times across the still surface, spinning out rings of gentle ripples in its wake, before sinking without a trace into the middle of the lake.

He turned to face her with a grin, his eyes alive with glee, and she couldn't help but smile back.

'Impressive.'

He blew on his fingers and pretended to polish them on his shirt. 'I'm a natural. What can I say?'

Seeing his delight at the achievement, she had a strong desire to get in on the fun. Perhaps it would help distract her from thinking about how alone they were out here on the edge of the lake. 'Does your natural talent stretch to teaching me how to do that?'

'You've never skimmed a stone?' He looked so over-the-top incredulous she couldn't help but laugh.

'Never.'

'Didn't you say your parents live in Cornwall? Surely there's plenty of opportunities to be near water there.'

She snorted and took a step backwards, staring down at the muddy grass at their feet. 'Yeah, if you live near the coast, which they don't. I never learnt to drive when I was living there and my parents didn't take me to the beach that much when I was young. My dad's always suffered with a bad back from the heavy lifting he has to do at work, so he never got involved in anything of a physical nature. And my mum's a real homebody. She's suffered with agoraphobia for years.'

She heard him let out a low exhalation of breath and glanced up to find an expression of real sympathy in his eyes. 'I'm sorry to hear that. That must have been hard for you as a kid,' he said softly.

Shrugging one shoulder, she gave a nod to acknowledge his concern, remembering the feeling of being trapped inside four small walls when she was living at home, with nowhere to escape to. Going to school every day had actually been a welcome escape from it and as soon as she'd finished her studies she'd hightailed it to London.

'Yeah, it was a bit. My parents are good people, though. They threw all their energy into raising me. And they made sure to let me know how loved I was.' Which was the absolute truth, she realised with a sting of shame, because she'd distanced herself from them since leaving home in an attempt to leave her stultifying life there behind her. But she'd left them behind, too. They didn't deserve that. A visit was well overdue and she made a pact with herself to call them and arrange a date to see them as soon as she got back to London.

Max nodded, seemingly satisfied that she didn't need any more consoling, and broke eye contact to lean down and pick up another flat pebble.

She watched him weigh it in his palm, as if checking it was worth the effort of throwing it. Everything he did was measured and thorough like that, which was probably why he was such a successful businessman.

'Here, this looks like a good one. It's nice and flat

with a decent weight to it so it'll fly and not sink immediately.' He turned it over in his hand. 'You need to get it to ride the air for a while before it comes down and maintain enough lift to jump.'

He held it out to her and she took it and looked at it with a frown. 'Is there a proper way to hold it?'

'I find the best way is to pinch it between my first finger and thumb. Like this.' He picked up another stone and demonstrated.

She copied the positioning in her own hand then gave him a confident nod, drew back her arm and threw it as hard as she could.

It landed in the lake with a *plop* and sank immediately.

'Darn it! What did I do wrong?' she asked, annoyed with herself for failing so badly.

'Don't worry; it can take a bit of practice to get your technique right. You need to get lower to the ground and swing your arm in a horizontal arc. When it feels like the stone could fly straight forward and parallel with the water, loosen the grip with your thumb and let it roll, snapping your finger forwards hard.'

'Huh. You make it sound so easy.'

He grinned and raised his eyebrows. 'Try again.'

Picking up a good-looking candidate, she positioned the stone between her finger and thumb and was just about to throw it when Max said, 'Stop!'

Glancing round at him with a grimace of frustration, she saw he was frowning and shaking his head.

'You need to swing your arm at a lower angle. Like this.'

Before she could react, he'd moved to stand directly behind her, putting his left hand on her hip and wrapping his right hand around the hand she was holding the stone in. Her heart nearly leapt out of her chest at the firmness of his touch and started hammering away, forcing the blood through her body at a much higher rate than was reasonable for such low-level exercise.

As he drew their arms backwards the movement made her shoulder press against the hard wall of his chest and she was mightily glad that he couldn't see her face at that precise moment. She was pretty sure it must look a real picture.

'Okay, on three we'll throw it together.' His mouth was so close to her ear she felt his breath tickle the downy little hairs on the outer whorl.

'One…two…three!'

They moved their linked hands in a sweeping arc, Cara feeling the power of Max's body push against her as the momentum of the move forced them forwards. She was so distracted by being engulfed in his arms she nearly didn't see the stone bounce a couple of times before it sank beneath the water.

'Woo-hoo!' Max shouted, releasing her to take a step back and raise his hand, waiting for her to give him a high five.

The sudden loss of his touch left her feeling strangely light and disorientated—but now was not the time to go to pieces. Mentally pulling herself together, she swung her hand up to meet his, their palms slapping loudly as they connected, then bent down straight away, pretending to search the ground for another missile.

'Who taught you to skim stones? A brother?' she asked casually, grimacing at the quaver in her voice, before grabbing another good-looking pebble and righting herself.

He'd stooped to pick up his own stone and glanced round at her as he straightened up. 'No. I'm an only child. I think once my mother realised how much hard work it was raising me she was determined not to have any more kids.' He raised a disparaging eyebrow then turned away to fling the stone across the lake, managing five bounces this time. He nodded with satisfaction. 'I used to mountain bike over to a nearby reservoir with a friend from boarding school at the weekends and we'd have competitions to see who could get their stone the furthest,' he said, already searching the ground for another likely skimmer, his movements surprisingly lithe considering the size of his powerful body.

A sudden need to get this right overwhelmed her.

She wasn't usually a superstitious person, but she imagined she could sense the power in this one simple challenge. If she got this stone to bounce by herself, maybe, just maybe, everything would be okay.

She was throwing this for her pride and the return of her strength. To prove to Max—but mostly to herself—that she was resilient and capable and—dare she even suggest it?—brave enough to try something new, even if there was a good chance she'd fail spectacularly and end up looking foolish again.

Harnessing the power of positive thought, she drew back her hand, took a second to centre herself, then flung the stone hard across the water, snapping her finger like he'd taught her and holding her breath as she watched it sail through the air.

It dropped low about fifteen feet out and for a second she thought she'd messed it up, but her spirits soared as she saw it bounce twice before disappearing.

Spinning round to make a celebratory face at Max, she was gratified to see him nod in exaggerated approval, a smile playing about his lips.

'Good job! You're a quick study; but then we already knew that about you.'

The compliment made her insides flare with warmth and she let out a laugh of delight, elation twisting through her as she saw him grin back.

Their gazes snagged and held, his pupils dilating till his eyes looked nearly black in the bright afternoon light.

A wave of electric heat spread through her at the sight of it, but the laughter died in her throat as he turned abruptly away and stared off towards the house instead, folding his arms so tightly against his chest she could make out the shape of his muscles under his shirt.

He cleared his throat. 'You know, this place is just like the venue where Jemima and I got married,' he said, so casually she wondered how much emotion he'd had to rein in, in order to say it.

Ugh. What a selfish dolt she was. Here she'd been worrying about what he thought of her and her tales of woe, when he was doing battle with his own demons.

It had occurred to her earlier that morning, as she'd struggled to do up her dress, that attending a wedding could be problematic for him, but she'd forgotten all about it after the incident in the kitchen, her thoughts distracted by the unnerving tension that had crackled between them ever since.

Or what she'd thought was tension.

Perhaps it had been apprehension on his part.

And then, when he'd mentioned how transient and lonely his youth had been over drinks earlier, it had brought it home to her why Jemima's death had hit him so hard. It sounded as if she'd been the person anchoring his life after years of feeling adrift and insecure. And this place reminded him of everything he'd lost.

No wonder he seemed so unsettled.

He'd still come here to help her out, though, despite his discomfort at being at this kind of event, which was a decent and kind thing for him to do and way beyond the call of duty as her boss. Her heart did a slow flip in her chest as she realised exactly what it must have cost him to agree to come.

'I'm sorry for dragging you here today. I didn't think about how hard it would be for you. After losing Jemima.'

He put his hand on her arm and waited for her to look at him before speaking. 'You have nothing to apologise for. *Nothing*. I wanted to come here to support you because you've done nothing but support me for the last few weeks. It's my turn to look after you today.' He was looking directly at her now and the fierce intensity in his eyes made a delicious shiver zip down her spine.

'Honestly, I thought it would be awful coming here,' he said, casting his gaze back towards the house again, 'but it's not been the trial I thought it'd be. In fact—'

he ran a hand over his hair and let out a low breath '—it's been good for me to confront a situation like this. I've been missing out on so much life since Jem died and it's time I pulled my head out of the sand and faced the world again.'

Cara swallowed hard, ensnared in the emotion of the moment, her heart thudding against her chest and her breath rasping in her dry throat. Looking at Max now, she realised that the ever-present frown was nowhere to be seen for once. Instead, there was light in his eyes and something else…

They stood, frozen in the moment, as the gentle spring wind wrapped around them and the birds sang enthusiastically above their heads.

It would be so easy to push up onto tiptoe and slide her hands around his neck. To press her lips against his and feel the heat and masculine strength of him, to slide her tongue into his mouth and taste him. She ached to feel his breath against her skin and his hands in her hair, her whole body tingling with the sensory expectation of it.

She wanted to be the one to remind him what living could be like, if only he'd let her.

To her disappointment, Max broke eye contact with her and nodded towards the marquee behind them. 'We should probably get back before they send out a search party. We don't want to find ourselves in trouble for messing with Amber's schedule of events and being frogmarched to our seats,' he said lightly, though his voice sounded gruffer than normal.

Had he seen it in her face? The longing. She hoped

not. The thought of her infatuation putting their fragile relationship under any more strain made her insides
squirm.

Anyway, that tension-filled moment had probably
been him thinking about Jemima again.

Not her.

They walked in silence back to the marquee, the
bright sun pleasantly warm on the back of her neck and
bare shoulders, but her insides icy cold.

Despite their little detour, they weren't the last to
sit down. It was with a sigh of relief that Cara slumped
into her seat and reached for the bottle of white wine
on the table, more than ready to blot out the ache of
disappointment that had been present ever since he'd
suggested they give up their truancy from the festivities and head back into the fray.

It wasn't that she didn't want to be here exactly; it
was just that it had been so much fun hanging out with
him. Just the two of them together, like friends. Or
something.

Knocking back half a glass of wine in one go, she
refilled it before offering the bottle to Max.

He was looking at her with bemusement, one eyebrow raised. 'Thirsty?'

Heat flared across her cheeks. 'Just getting in the
party mood,' she said, forcing a nonchalant smile. 'It
looks like we have some catching up to do.'

The raucous chatter and laughter in the room suggested that people were already pretty tiddly on the
cocktails they'd been served.

'Okay, well, I'm going to stick to water if I have to

drive to the bed and breakfast place later. I think one of us should stay sober enough to find our way there at the end of the night. I don't fancy kipping in the car.'

She gave him an awkward grin as the thought of sleeping in such close proximity to him made more heat rush to her face.

Picking up her glass, she took another long sip of wine to cover her distress.

Oh, good grief. It was going to be a long night.

The meal was surprisingly tasty, considering how many people were being catered for, and Cara began to relax as the wine did its work. She quickly found herself in a conversation with the lady to her right, who turned out to be Amber's second cousin and an estate agent in Angel, about the dearth of affordable housing to rent in London. By the end of dessert, the woman had promised to give Cara first dibs on a lovely-sounding one-bedroom flat that was just about to come onto her books. And that proved to Cara, without a shadow of a doubt, that you just had to be in the right place at the right time to get lucky.

Turning to say this exact thing to Max, she was disturbed to find he'd finished his conversation with the man next to him and was frowning down at the table-cloth.

'Sorry for ignoring you,' she said, worried he was getting sucked down into dark thoughts again with all the celebrating going on around him.

He gave her a tense smile and pushed his chair away from the table. 'You weren't. I overheard your conversation about finding a flat; that's great news—you should definitely get her number and follow that up,' he said, standing and tapping the back of his chair. 'I'm going to find the bathrooms. I'll be back in a minute.'

She watched him stride away with a lump in her throat. Was he upset about the prospect of her moving out? She dismissed the notion immediately. No, he couldn't be. He must be craving his space again by now. Even though she'd loved living there, she knew it was time to move out. Especially now that her feelings for him had twisted themselves into something new. Something dangerous.

'That's a good one you've got there—very sexy,' Amber's second cousin muttered into her ear, pulling back to waggle her eyebrows suggestively, only making the lump in Cara's throat grow in size.

Unable to speak, she gave the woman what she hoped looked like a gracious smile.

'Hi, Cara.'

The voice behind her made her jump in her seat and she swivelled round, only to find herself staring into the eyes of the woman she'd been trying to avoid since spotting her in the church earlier.

Her meal rolled uncomfortably in her stomach.

'Hi, Lucy.'

Instead of the look of cool disdain Cara was expecting, she was surprised to see Lucy bite her lip, her expression wary.

'How are you?' Lucy asked falteringly, as if afraid to hear the answer.

'Fine, thank you.' Cara kept her voice deliberately

neutral, just in case this was an opening gambit to get her to admit to something she really didn't want to say.

'Can I talk to you for a moment?'

Cara swallowed her anxiety and gestured towards the chair Max had vacated, wondering what on earth this woman could have to say to her. Whatever it was, it was better to get it over with now so she didn't spend the rest of the night looking over her shoulder. Straightening her back, she steeled herself to deal with anything she could throw at her.

Lucy sat on the edge of the seat, as close as she could get to Cara without touching her, and laid her hands on her lap before taking a deep breath. 'I wanted to come over and apologise as soon as I could so there wasn't any kind of atmosphere between us today.'

Cara stared at her. 'I'm sorry? Did you say *apologise*?'

Lucy crossed her legs, then uncrossed them again, her cheeks flooding with colour. 'Yes… I'm really sorry about the way you were treated at LED. I feel awful about it. I let Michelle bully me into taking her side— because I knew she'd turn on me, too, if I stood up for you—and I was pathetic enough to let her. I want you to know that I didn't do any of those awful things to you, but I didn't stop it either.' She shook her head and let out a low sigh. 'I feel awful about it, Cara, truly.'

At that moment Cara felt a pair of hands land lightly on her shoulders. Twisting her head round, she saw that Max had returned and was standing over her like some kind of dark guardian angel.

'Everything okay, Cara?' From the cool tone in his

voice she suspected he'd be more than willing to step in and eject Lucy from her seat if she asked him to.

'Fine, thanks, Max. This is Lucy. She came over to apologise for her *unfriendliness* at the last place I worked.'

'Is that so?'

Cara couldn't see the expression on his face from that angle but, from the sound of his voice and the way Lucy seemed to shrink back in her chair, she guessed it wasn't a very friendly one.

Lucy cleared her throat awkwardly. 'Yes, I feel dreadful about the whole thing. It was horrible working there. In fact, I left the week after you did. I couldn't stand the smug look on Michelle's face any more. Although—' she leaned forward in a conspiratorial manner '—I heard from one of the other girls that she only lasted a month before he got rid of her. She couldn't hack it, apparently.' She snorted. 'That's karma in action, right there.' Clearly feeling she'd said her piece, Lucy stood up so that Max could have his chair back and took a small step away from them. 'Anyway, I'd better get back to my table; apparently there's coffee on the way and I'm desperate for some. Those cocktails were evil, weren't they?'

'Why are you here today?' Cara asked before she could turn and leave, intrigued by the coincidence.

'I'm Jack's—the groom's—new PA.'

Cara couldn't help but laugh at life's weird little twist. 'Really?'

'Yeah, he's a great boss, really lovely to work for.' She leant forward again and said in a quiet voice, 'I don't think Amber likes me very much, though; she didn't seem very pleased to see me here.'

'I wouldn't take that too personally,' Cara said, giving her a reassuring smile. 'She's an intensely protective person.' She put a hand on Lucy's arm. 'Thanks for being brave enough to come over and apologise, Lucy; I really appreciate the gesture.'

Lucy gave her one last smile, and Max a slightly terrified grimace, before retreating to her table.

Max sat back down in his chair, giving her an impressed nod. 'Nicely handled.'

Warm pleasure coursed through her as she took in the look of approval in his eyes. Feeling a little flustered by it, she picked up her glass of wine to take a big gulp, but judged the tilt badly and some escaped from the side of the rim and dribbled down her chin. Before she had time to react, Max whipped his napkin under her jaw and caught the rogue droplets with it, stopping them from splashing onto her dress.

'Smooth!' she said, laughing in surprise.

'I have moves,' he replied, his eyes twinkling and his mouth twitching into a warm smile.

A wave of heat engulfed her and her stomach did a full-on somersault.

Oh, no, what was *happening* to her?

Heart racing, she finally allowed the truth to filter through to her consciousness.

It was, of course, the very last thing she needed to happen.

She was falling in love with him.

CHAPTER EIGHT

AFTER THE MEAL and speeches, all the guests were encouraged to go through to the house, where a bar had been set up under the sweeping staircase in the hall and a DJ in the ballroom was playing ambient tunes in the hope of drawing the guests in there to sit around the tables that surrounded the dance floor.

Waiting at the bar to grab them both a caffeinated soft drink to give them some energy for the rest of the evening's events, Max allowed his thoughts to jump back over the day.

He'd had fun at the lake with Cara, which had taken him by surprise, because the last thing he'd expected when he'd got up that morning was that he would enjoy himself today.

But Cara had a way of finding the joy in things.

In fact, he'd been so caught up in the pleasure of showing her how to skim stones, he hadn't thought about what he was doing until his hand was on the soft curve of her hip and his body was pressed up close to hers, the familiar floral scent of her perfume in his nose and the heat of her warming his skin. He'd hidden his instinctive response to it well enough, he thought, using the excessive rush of adrenaline to hurl more stones across the water.

And then she'd been so delighted when she'd managed to skim that stone by herself he'd felt a mad urge to wrap his arms around her again in celebration and experience the moment with her.

But that time he'd managed to rein himself in, randomly talking about his own wedding to break the tension, only to feel a different kind of self-reproach when Cara assumed his indiscriminate jump to the subject was down to him feeling gloomy about his situation.

Which it really hadn't been.

Returning with the drinks to where he'd left Cara standing just inside the ballroom, he handed one to her and smiled when she received it with a grimace of relieved thanks. The main lights in the room were set low and a large glitter ball revolved slowly from the ceiling, scattering the floor and walls with shards of silver light. Max watched them dance over Cara's face in fascination, thinking that she looked like some kind of ethereal seraph, with her bright eyes and pale creamy skin against the glowing silver of her dress.

A strange elation twisted through him, triggering a lifting sensation throughout his whole body—as if all the things that had dragged him down in the past eighteen months were losing their weight and slowly drifting upwards. The sadness he'd expected to keep on hitting him throughout the day was still notably absent, and instead there was a weird sense of rightness about being here.

With her.

Catching her giving him a quizzical look, he was just about to ask if she wanted to take another walk outside so they could hear each other speak when Jack and Amber walked past them and onto the empty dance floor. Noticing their presence, the DJ cued up a new track as a surge of guests crowded into the room, evidently following the happy couple in to watch their first dance as husband and wife.

Max found himself jostled closer to Cara as the edges of the dance floor filled up and he instinctively put an arm around her to stop her from being shoved around, too. She turned to look at him, the expression in her eyes startled at first, but then sparking with understanding when he nodded towards a gap in the crowd a little along from them.

He guided them towards it, feeling her hips sway against his as they moved, and had to will his attention-starved body not to respond.

Once in the space, he let her go, relaxing his arm to his side, and could have sworn he saw her shoulders drop a little as if she'd been holding herself rigid.

Feeling a little disconcerted by her obvious discomfort at him touching her again, he watched the happy couple blindly as they twirled around the dance floor, going through the motions of the ballroom dance they'd plainly been practising for the past few months.

Had he overstepped the mark by manhandling her like that? He'd not meant to make her uncomfortable but they were supposed to be there as a couple, so it wasn't as though it wasn't within his remit to act that way around her.

Ugh. There was no point in beating himself up about it. He'd just have to be more careful about the way he touched her, or not, for the rest of the evening.

As soon as the dance finished, other couples joined the newlyweds on the dance floor and, spotting Cara, Jack broke away from Amber and made his way over to them.

'Cara, I'm so glad you made it!' he said, stooping down to pull her into a bear hug, making her squeal with laughter as he spun her around before placing her back down again.

Cara pulled away from him, her cheeks flushed, and rubbed his arm affectionately. 'Congratulations. And thank you for inviting us. It's a beautiful wedding.'

'I'm glad you're having a good time,' Jack replied, smiling into her eyes. 'Want to dance with me, for old times' sake?' he said, already taking her arm and leading her away from Max onto the dance floor. 'You don't mind if I steal her away for a minute, do you, Max?' he tossed over his shoulder, plainly not at all interested in Max's real opinion on the matter.

Not that Max *should* mind.

Watching Cara laugh at something that Jack whispered into her ear as he began to move her around the dance floor, Max was hit by an unreasonable surge of irritation and had to force himself to relax his arms and let them hang by his sides instead of balling them into tight fists. What the heck was going on with him today? How messed up was he to be jealous of a new groom, who was clearly infatuated with his wife, just because he was dancing with Cara? It must be because the guy seemed to have everything—a wife who loved him, a successful career with colleagues who respected him, Cara as a friend…

The track came to a close and a new, slower one started up. Before he could check himself, Max strode across to where Jack and Cara were just breaking apart.

'You don't mind if I cut in now, do you?' he said to Jack, intensely conscious that his words had come out as more of a statement than a question.

Jack's eyebrows rose infinitesimally at Max's less than gracious tone, but he smiled at Cara and swept a hand to encompass them both. 'Be my guest.' Leaning forward, he kissed Cara on the cheek before moving away from her. 'It's great to see you so happy. You know, you're actually glowing.' He slapped Max on the back. 'You're obviously good for her, Max. Look after her, okay? She's a good one,' he said. 'But watch your feet; she's a bit of a toe-stamper,' he added, ducking out of the way as Cara swiped a hand at him and walked off laughing.

Turning back, Cara fixed Max with an awkward smile, then leaned in to speak into his ear. 'Sorry about that. I didn't want to admit to the truth about us and break the mood.'

Max nodded, his shoulders suddenly stiff, surprised to find he was disappointed to hear her say that her glow was nothing to do with him.

Don't be ridiculous, you fool—how could it be?

His feelings must have shown on his face because she

took a small step away from him and said, 'You don't really need to dance with me, but thanks for the gesture.'

He shrugged. 'It's no problem. You seemed to be enjoying yourself and I was anticipating Jack being commandeered at any second by Amber or another relative wanting his attention so I thought I'd jump in,' he replied, feeling the hairs that had escaped from her up-do tickle his nose as he leaned in close to her.

She looked at him for the longest moment, something flickering behind her eyes, before giving him a small nod and a smile. 'Okay then, I'd love to dance.'

Holding her as loosely as he could in his arms, he guided her around the dance floor, leading her in a basic waltz and finding pleasure in the way she responded to his lead, copying his movements with a real sense that she trusted him not to make a false step. His blood roared through his veins as his heart worked overtime to keep him cool in the accumulated heat of the bodies that surrounded them. Or was it the feeling of her in his arms that was doing that to him?

He felt her back shift against his palm and turned to see she was waving to Lucy, the woman who had come over to apologise to her at dinner.

A sense of admiration swept thorough him as he reflected on how well she'd handled that situation. When he'd returned to the table, after needing to take a breath of air and talk himself down from a strange feeling of despondency when he heard she was likely to find a new place to live soon, and seen them talking, he'd feared the worst. An intense urge to step in and protect her had grabbed him by the throat, making him move fast and put his hands on her, to let her know he had her back if she needed him.

She hadn't, though. In fact she'd shown real strength and finesse with her response. Another example of why she was so good at her job. And why he respected her so much as a person. Why he liked her—

Halting his thoughts right there, he guided her over to the side of the dance floor as the music changed into retro pop and drew away from her, feeling oddly bereft at the loss of her warm body so close to his own.

The room was spinning.

And it wasn't from the alcohol she'd consumed earlier or even the overwhelming heat and noise—it was because of Max. Being so close to him, feeling the strength of his will as he whirled her around the dance floor had sent her senses into a nosedive.

'Max, do you mind if we go outside for a minute? I need some air.'

The look her gave her was one of pure alarm. 'Are you all right?'

'I'm fine, just a bit hot,' she said, flapping a hand ineffectually in front of her face.

Giving her a curt nod, he motioned for her to walk out of the ballroom in front of him, shadowing her closely as she pushed her way through the crowd of people in the hallway and out into the blissfully cool evening air.

Slumping down onto a cold stone bench pushed up against the front of the house, she let out a deep sigh of relief as the fresh air pricked at her hot skin.

'I'm going to fetch you a drink of water,' Max said, standing over her, his face a picture of concern. 'Stay here.'

She watched him go, her stomach sinking with embarrassment, wondering how she was ever going to explain herself if she didn't manage to pull it together.

Putting her head in her hands, she breathed in the echo of Max's scent on her skin, its musky undertones making her heart trip over itself.

'Are you okay there?'

The deep voice made her start and she looked up to see one of the male guests looking down at her, his brow creased in worry. She seemed to remember Amber's second cousin pointing him out as Amber's youngest brother and the black sheep of the family. *Womaniser* was the word she'd used.

Sitting up straighter in her seat, she gave him a friendly but dispassionate smile. 'I'm fine, thanks, just a bit hot from dancing.'

Instead of nodding and walking away, he sat down next to her and held out his hand. 'I'm Frank, Amber's black sheep of a brother,' he said with a twinkle in his eye.

She couldn't help but laugh as she shook his hand. 'I'm Cara.'

'I don't know whether anyone's told you this today, Cara, but you look beautiful in that dress,' he said, his voice smooth like melted chocolate. He wanted her. She could see it in his face.

Cara was just about to open her mouth to politely brush him off when a shadow fell across them. Looking up, she saw that Max had returned with her glass of water and was standing over them with a strange look on his face.

'Here's your drink, Cara,' he said, handing it over and giving Frank a curt nod.

Frank must have seen something in Max's expression because he got up quickly and took a step away from them both. 'Okay, well, it looks like your boyfriend's got this, so I'll say good evening. Have a good one, Cara,' he said, flashing her a disappointed smile as he backed away, then turning on his heel to disappear into the dark garden.

'Sorry,' Max said gruffly, 'I didn't mean to scare him off.' He didn't look particularly sorry, though, she noted as he sat down next to her and laid his arm across the back of the bench. In fact, if anything, he seemed pleased that the guy had gone. Turning to look him directly in the eye, her stomach gave a flutter of nerves as something flickered in his eyes. Something fierce and disconcerting.

Telling herself she must be seeing things, she forced a composed smile onto her face. 'It's okay; he wasn't my type anyway.'

Not like you.

Pushing the rogue thought away, she took a long sip of the water he'd fetched to cover her nerves. What was she doing, letting herself imagine there was something developing between them?

'Thanks for the water. I didn't mean to worry you. I'm feeling better now I'm in the fresh air.'

Despite her claims, he was still looking at her with that strange expression in his eyes.

'Why are you single?' he asked suddenly, making her blink at him in surprise.

'Oh, you know...'

He frowned. 'It's not because I've been working you too hard, is it?'

'No, no!' She shook her head. 'It's through personal choice.'

His frown deepened, as if he didn't quite believe her.

She swallowed before expanding on her answer, linking her fingers tightly together around the glass. 'I decided to take a break from dating for a while. My last relationship was a bit of a disaster.'

He relaxed back against the bench. 'How so?'

'The whole fiasco at LED pretty much ruined it. After I started having trouble coping with what was going on at work I got a bit down and it made me withdraw into myself. My ex-boyfriend, Ewan, got fed up with me being so...er...*unresponsive*.' She cringed. 'That's why I've been trying so hard to stay positive. I know how it can get boring, having people around who feel sorry for themselves all the time.'

He ran his hand through his hair, letting out a long, low sigh.

Heat rushed through her as she realised how Max might have interpreted what she'd just said. 'I didn't mean... I wasn't talking about you.'

He snorted gently and flashed her a smile. 'I didn't think you were. I was frustrated on your behalf. I can't believe the guy was stupid enough to treat you like that.'

'Yeah, well, it's in the past now. To be honest, that relationship was always doomed to fail. He was a little too self-centred for my liking. He made it pretty obvious he thought I wasn't good enough for him.'

'Not good enough! That's the most ridiculous thing I ever heard,' he snapped out, the ferocity in his tone telling her he had a lot more he wanted to say on the matter, but for the sake of propriety was keeping it to himself.

She smiled at him, her heart rising to her throat. 'It's okay. It doesn't bother me any more.' And it really didn't, she realised with a sense of satisfaction. Her experiences since breaking up with Ewan had taught her that her real self-worth came from her own actions and achievements, not pleasing someone else.

Putting the empty glass onto the ground by the bench, she tried to hide a yawn of tiredness behind her hand. It had been a long and intense day.

'Do you want to get out of here?' Max asked quietly.

Clearly she hadn't been able to hide her exhaustion from him.

Looking at him with a smile of gratitude, she nodded her head. 'I wouldn't mind. I don't think I've got the energy for any more dancing.'

He stood up. 'Okay, I'll go and fetch the car.'

'I'll just pop back in and say goodbye to Jack and Amber and I'll meet you back here,' she said, gesturing to the pull-in place at the end of the sweeping driveway.

He nodded, before turning on his heel and heading off towards where they'd left the car parked by the estate's church.

She watched him disappear into the darkness, with his

jacket slung over his arm and the white shirt stretched across his broad shoulders glowing in the moonlight, before he dipped out of sight.

After saying a hurried goodbye to the now rather inebriated newlyweds, she came out to find Max waiting for her in the car and jumped in gratefully, sinking back into the soft leather seat with a sigh. Now she knew that bed wasn't far away, she was desperate to escape to her room and finally be able to relax away from Max's unsettling presence.

It only took them five minutes to drive to the B&B she'd booked them into and as luck would have it there was a convenient parking space right outside the pretty thatched cottage.

'We're in the annexe at the back,' she said to Max as he hauled their overnight bags out of the boot. 'They gave me a key code to open the door so we won't need to disturb them.'

'Great,' Max said, hoisting the bags onto his back and following her down the path of the colourful country cottage garden towards the rear of the house. The air smelled sweetly of the honeysuckle that wound itself around a large wooden arch leading through to the back garden where their accommodation was housed, and Cara breathed it in with a great sense of pleasure. The place felt almost magical, shrouded as it was in the velvety darkness of the night.

Cara tapped the code into the keypad next to the small oak door that led directly into the annexe and flipped on the lights as soon as they were inside, illuminating a beautifully presented hallway with its simple country-style furniture and heritage-coloured décor. Two open bedroom doors stood opposite each other and there was a small bathroom at the back, which they would share.

'I hope this is okay. All the local hotels were fully booked and Jack said this was the place his cousin and her family were going to stay in, so the owners were pleased to swap the booking to us, considering it was such a last-minute cancellation.'

Max nodded, looking around at the layout, his expression neutral. 'It's great.'

The hallway was so small they were standing much closer to each other than Cara was entirely comfortable with. Max moved past her to drop his bag into one of the rooms and his musky scent hit her senses, making her whole body quiver with longing. The thought of him being just a few feet away from her was going to make it very difficult to sleep, despite how tired she was.

After dropping her bag into the other room, Max walked back into the hallway and stood in front of her, a small frown playing across his face. 'Are you feeling okay now?'

She smiled, the effort making her cheeks ache. 'I'm fine.' She took a nervous step backwards, and jumped a little as her back hit the wall behind her. 'Thank you so much for coming with me. I really appreciate it.'

He was looking at her with that fierce expression in his eyes again and a heavy, tingly heat slid from her throat, deep into her belly, sending electric currents of need to every nerve-ending in her body. For some reason she was finding it hard to breathe.

'It was my pleasure, Cara,' he said, his voice gruff as if he was having trouble with his own airways. 'You know, that guy you were talking to earlier was right. You do look beautiful in that dress.'

She stared at him, a disorientating mixture of excitement and confusion swirling around her head.

His gaze flicked away from hers for a second and when his eyes returned to hers the fierce look had gone and was replaced with a friendly twinkle. 'It occurred to me that you might have a bit of trouble getting out it—after needing my help to do it up this morning. Want me to undo the buttons for you?'

What was this?

Cara knew what she wanted it to be: for Max to want the same thing that she did—to alleviate this unbearable need to touch and kiss and hold him. To slide off all their clothes and lose themselves in each other's body.

To love him.

Did he want that, too?

Could he?

Her heart was beating so hard and fast, all she could hear and feel was the hot pulse of her blood through her body.

'That would be great. Thank you,' she managed to force past her dry throat.

She rotated on the spot until her back was to him, her whole body vibrating with tension as she felt his fingers graze her skin as he released each of the buttons in turn.

As soon as the last one popped free, she trapped the now loose dress against her body and turned to face him again, trying to summon an expression that wouldn't give her feelings away.

He looked at her for the longest time, his eyes wide and dark and his breathing shallow.

She watched him flick his tongue between his lips and something snapped inside her. Unable to stand the tension any longer, she rocked forward on her toes and tipped her head up, pressing her mouth to his. His lips were firm under hers and his scent enveloped her, wrapping round her senses, only adding to her violent pull of need to deepen the kiss.

Until she realised he wasn't kissing her back.

He hadn't moved away from her, but she could feel how tense he was under her touch. As if he was holding himself rigid.

She stilled, one hand anchoring herself against his broad shoulder, the other still holding her dress tightly against her body, and pulled away, eyes screwed shut, her stomach plummeting to her shoes at his lack of response.

What had she *done*?

When she dared open her eyes, he was looking at her with such an expression of torment that she had to close them again.

'I'm sorry. So, so sorry,' she whispered, her throat locking up and her face burning with mortification.

'Cara—' He sounded troubled. Aggrieved. Exasperated.

Stumbling away from him, her back hit the wall again and she felt her way blindly into her bedroom and slammed the door shut, leaning back on it as if it would keep out the horror of the past few seconds.

Which, of course, it wouldn't.

What must he think of her? All he'd done was offer to help her with her dress and she'd thrown herself at him. What had possessed her to do that when she knew he wasn't over losing his wife? How could she have thought he wanted anything more to develop between them?

She was a fool.

And she couldn't even blame it on alcohol because she'd been drinking soft drinks for the past couple of hours.

She jumped in fright as she felt Max knock on the door, the vibration of it echoing through her tightly strung body. She knew she had to face him. To apologise and try to find some way to make things right again.

Struggling to get her breathing under control, she stepped away from the door and opened it, forcing herself to look up into Max's face with as much cool confidence as she could muster.

Before he could say anything, she held up a hand. 'I really am sorry... I don't know what happened. It won't ever happen ag—'

But, before she could finish the sentence, he took a step towards her, the expression in his eyes wild and intense as he slid his hand into her hair, drawing her forward and pressing his lips against hers.

They stumbled into the room, off balance, as their mouths crashed together. Electric heat exploded deep within her and she heard him groan with pleasure when she pressed her body hard into his. She could feel the urgency in him as he pushed her back against the wall, his hard body trapping her there as he fervently explored her mouth with his own, his tongue sliding firmly against hers. Taking a step back, he pulled his shirt over his head in one swift movement and dropped it onto the floor next to them.

'Are you sure you want this, Cara?' he asked, his voice guttural and low as she feverishly ran her hands over the dips and swells of his chest in dazed wonder.

'Yes.'

She smiled as he exhaled in relief and brought his mouth back down to hers, sliding his hands down to her thighs so he could pick her up and carry her over to the bed.

Then there was no more talking, just the feel of his solid body pressed hard against hers and the slide and twist of his muscles under his soft skin and—sensation—a riot of sensation that she sunk into and lost herself in. Her body had craved this for so long it was a sweet, beautiful relief to finally have what she wanted.

What she needed.

In those moments there was no past and no future; they were purely living for the moment.

And it was absolutely perfect.

CHAPTER NINE

MAX AWOKE FROM such a deep sleep it took him a while to realise that he wasn't in his own bed.

And that he wasn't alone.

Cara's warm body was pressed up against his back, her arm draped heavily over his hip and her head tucked in between his shoulder blades. He could feel her breath against his skin and hear her gentle exhalations.

Memories from the night they'd just spent together flitted through his head like a film on fast-forward, the intensity of them making his skin tingle and his blood pound through his body. It had been amazing. More than amazing. It had rocked his world.

It had felt so good holding her in his arms, feeling her respond so willingly to his demands and clearly enjoying making her own on him.

But, lying here now, he knew it had been a mistake.

It was too soon after losing his wife to be feeling like that. It felt wrong—somehow seedy and inappropriate. Greedy.

He'd had his shot at love and it wasn't right that he should get another one. Especially not so soon after losing Jemima. In the cold light of day it seemed tasteless somehow, as if he hadn't paid his dues.

He'd been in such a fog of need all day yesterday that he'd pushed all the rational arguments to the back of his head and just taken what he'd wanted, which had been totally unfair on Cara.

He wasn't ready to give himself over to a relationship again. And he knew that Cara would need more from him than he was able to give. She'd want the fairy tale, and he was no Prince Charming.

The worst thing was: he'd known that this was going to happen. From the moment he'd set eyes on her. He'd been attracted to her, even though he'd pretended to himself that he wasn't. And he'd only made things worse for himself by keeping her at arm's length. The more he'd told himself *no*, the more he'd wanted her. That was why he'd really thought it best to get rid of her quickly, before anything could happen between them. And then, once it became clear there was no hiding from the fact she was a positive force in his life, he'd pretended to himself that he wanted her to stay purely for her skills as a PA.

Idiot.

It had well and truly backfired on him.

This was precisely why he'd stopped himself from becoming friends with her at the beginning. He'd known it would guide them down a dangerous path.

His concerns hadn't stopped him from knocking on her door after she'd run away from him last night, though. Even after it had taken everything he'd had not to respond to that first kiss. But she'd looked so hurt, so devastatingly bereft that he'd found himself chasing after her to try and put it right. And, judging by her reaction when he'd been unable to hold back a second time and stop himself from kissing her, she'd been just as desperate as him for it to happen. In fact, the small, encouraging noises that had driven him wild made him think she'd wanted it for a while.

And, as his penance, he was now going to have to explain to her why it could never happen again.

Drawing away from her as gently as he could so as not to wake her, he swung his legs out of bed and sat on the edge, putting his head in his hands, trying to figure out what to do next. He wasn't going to just leave her here in the middle of rural Leicestershire with no transport, but the thought of having to sit through the whole car journey home with her after explaining why last night had been a mistake filled him with dread.

He jumped as a slender arm snaked round his middle and Cara kissed down the length of his spine, before pulling herself up to sit behind him with her legs on either side of his body, her breasts pressing into his back.

'Good morning,' she said, her voice guttural with sleep.

Fighting to keep his body from responding to her, he put his hand on the arm that was wrapped around his middle and gently prised it away.

'Are you okay?' she asked, her tone sounding worried now.

'Fine.' He stood up and grabbed his trousers, pulling them on roughly before turning back to her.

She'd tugged the sheet around her and was looking

up at him with such an expression of concern he nearly reached for her.

Steeling himself against the impulse, he shoved his hands in his pockets and looked at her with as much cool determination as he could muster.

'This was wrong, Cara. Us, doing this.'

'What?' Her eyes widened in confused surprise.

'I'm sorry. I shouldn't have let it happen. I got caught up in the moment, which was selfish of me.'

Her expression changed in an instant to one of panic. 'No.' She held out her hands beseechingly. 'Please don't be sorry about it. I wanted it to happen, too.'

He swallowed hard, tearing his eyes away from her worried gaze. 'I can't give you what you want long-term, Cara.'

Pulling the sheet tighter around her body, she frowned at him. 'You don't know what I want.'

He smiled sadly. 'Yes, I do. You want this to turn into something serious, but I don't. I'm happy with my life the way it is.'

'You're *happy*?' She looked incredulous.

He rubbed his hand over his face in irritation. 'Yes, Cara, I'm happy,' he said, but he felt the lie land heavily in his gut.

'But what we had last night—and all day yesterday—I didn't imagine it.' She shook her head as if trying to throw off any niggling doubts. 'It was so good. It felt right between us, Max. Surely you felt that, too.'

He looked at her steadily, already hating himself for what he was about to say. 'No. Sorry.' He scrubbed a hand through his hair. 'Look, I was feeling lonely and you happened to be there. I feel awful about it and I won't blame you for being angry.'

She didn't believe him; he could see it in her eyes.

'I understand why you're panicking,' she said, holding out her hands in a pleading gesture, 'because we've just changed the nature of our relationship and it's a scary thing, taking things a step further, especially after what happened to Jemima…'

'See, that's the thing, Cara. I've been through that once and I'm not prepared to put myself through something like that again.'

'But it was so random—'

'The type of illness isn't the point here. It's the idea of pouring all your love into one person, only to lose them in the blink of an eye. I can go through that again.'

'But you can't cut yourself off from the world, Max. It'll drive you insane.'

He took a pace forward and folded his arms across his chest. 'You want to know what really drives me insane—that my wife was lying there in hospital with the life draining out of her and there wasn't a thing I could do about it. Not one damn thing. I promised her I'd look after her through thick and thin. I failed, Cara.' His throat felt tight with emotion he didn't want to feel any more.

'You didn't fail.'

He rubbed a hand over his eyes, taking a deep breath to loosen off the tension in his chest. 'I'm a fixer, Cara, but I couldn't fix that.'

'There wasn't anything you could have done.'

'I could have paid her more attention.'

'I'm sure she knew how much you loved her.'

And there was the rub. He did love Jemima. Too much to have room for anyone else in his heart.

'Yes, I think she did. But that doesn't change anything between you and me. I don't want this, Cara,' he said, waggling a finger between the two of them.

She stared at him in disbelief. 'So that's it? You've made up your mind and there's nothing I can do to change it?'

'Yes.'

Tipping up her chin, she looked him dead in the eye. 'Do you still want me to work for you?' she asked, her voice breaking with emotion.

Did he? His working life had been a lot less stressful since she'd been around, but what had just happened between them would make his personal life a lot more complicated. They were between a rock and a hard place. 'Yes. But I'll understand if it's too uncomfortable for you to stay.'

'So you'd let me just walk away?'

He sighed. 'If that's what you want.'

The look she gave him chilled him to the bone. 'You know, I don't believe for a second that Jemima would have wanted you to mourn her for the rest of your life. I think she'd have wanted you to be happy. You need to stop hiding behind her death and face the world again. Like you said you were going to yesterday. What happened to that, Max? Hmm? What happened to *you*? Jemima might not be alive any more, but *you* are and you need to stop punishing yourself for that and start living again.'

'I'm not ready—'

'You know, I love you, Max,' she broke in loudly, her eyes shining with tears.

He took a sharp intake of breath as the words cut through him. No. He didn't want to hear that from her right now. She was trying to emotionally manipulate him into doing something he didn't want to do.

'How can you love me?' Anger made his voice shake. 'We barely know each other.'

'I know you, Max,' she said calmly, her voice rich with emotion.

'You might think you do because I've told you a few personal things about myself recently, but that doesn't mean you get who I am and what I want.'

'Do you know what you want? Because it seems to me you're stopping yourself from being happy on purpose. You enjoyed being with me yesterday, Max, I know it.'

'I did enjoy it, but not in the way you think. It was good to get out of the house and have some fun, but that's all it was, Cara, *fun*.'

She shook her head, her body visibly shaking now. 'I don't believe you.'

'Fine. Don't believe me. Keep living in your perfect little imaginary world where everything is jolly and works out for the best, but don't expect me to show up.'

She reacted as if his words had physically hurt her, jolting back and hugging her arms around herself. 'How can you say that to me?'

Guilt wrapped around him and squeezed hard. She was right; it was a low blow after what he'd already put her through, but he was being cruel to be kind. Sinking onto the edge of the bed, he held up a pacifying hand. 'You see, I'm messed up, Cara. It's too soon for me. I'm not ready for another serious relationship. Maybe I'll never be ready. And it's not fair to ask you to wait for me.'

Her shoulders stiffened, as if she was fighting to keep them from slumping. 'Okay. If that's the way you feel,' she clipped out.

'It is, Cara. I'm sorry.'

The look she gave him was one of such disappointed disdain he recoiled a little.

'Well, then, I guess it's time for me to leave.' She shuffled to the edge of the bed. 'I'm not going to stick around here and let you treat me like I mean nothing to you. I'm worth more than that, Max, and if you can't appreciate that, then that's your loss.' With the sheet still wrapped firmly around her, she stood up and faced him, her eyes dark with anger. 'You can give me a lift to the nearest train station and I'll make my own way back to London.' Turning away from him, she walked over to where her overnight bag sat on the floor.

'Cara, don't be ridiculous—' he started to say, his tone sounding so insincere he cringed inwardly.

Swivelling on the spot, she pointed a shaking finger at him. 'Don't you dare say I'm the one being ridiculous. I'm catching the train. Please go and get changed in your own room. I'll meet you by the car in fifteen minutes.'

'Cara—' He tried to protest, moving towards her, but it was useless. He had nothing left to say.

There was no way to make this better.

'Okay,' he said quietly.

He watched her grab her wash kit from her bag, his gut twisting with unease.

Turning back, she gave him a jerky nod and then, staring resolutely ahead, went to stride past him to the bathroom.

Acting on pure impulse, he put out a hand to stop her, wrapping his fingers around her arm to prevent her from going any further. He could feel her shaking under his grip and he rubbed her arm gently, trying to imbue how sorry he was through the power of his touch.

She put her hand over his and for a second he thought she was going to squeeze his hand with understanding, but instead she pulled his fingers away from her arm and, without giving him another look, walked away.

Cara waited until Max's car had pulled away from the train station before sinking onto the bench next to the ticket office and putting her head in her hands, finally letting the tears stream down her face.

She'd spent the whole car journey there—which had only taken about ten minutes but had felt like ten painful hours—holding her head high and fighting back the hot pressure in her throat and behind her eyes.

They hadn't uttered one word to each other since he'd started the engine and she was grateful for that, because she knew if she'd had to speak there was no way she'd be able to hold it together.

It seemed they'd come full circle, with him with-

drawing so far into himself he might as well have been
a machine and her not wanting to show him any weakness.

What a mess.

And she'd told him she loved him.

Her chest cramped hard at the memory. When the
words left her mouth, she hadn't known what sort of
reaction to expect; in fact she hadn't even known she
was going to say them until they'd rolled off her tongue,
but she was still shocked by the flare of anger she'd
seen in his eyes.

He'd thought she was trying to manipulate him, when
that had been the last thing on her mind at the time.
She'd wanted him to know he was loved and there could
be a future for them if he wanted it.

Thinking about it now, though, she realised she had
been trying to shock him into action. To reach something deep inside him that he'd been fiercely protecting
ever since Jemima had died. It wasn't surprising he'd
reacted the way he had, though. She couldn't begin to
imagine the pain of losing a spouse, but she understood
the pain of losing someone you loved in the blink of
an eye or, in this case, in the time it took to say three
small words.

Fury and frustration swirled in her gut, her empty
stomach on the edge of nausea. How could she have let
herself fall for a man who was still grieving for his wife
and had no space left in his heart for her?

Clearly she was a glutton for punishment. And, because of that, she'd now not only lost her heart, she'd
lost her home and her job, as well.

* * *

Back in London three hours later, she let herself wearily into Max's house, her nerves prickling at the thought of him being there.

Part of her wanted to see him—some mad voice in the back of her head had been whispering about him changing his mind after having time to reflect on what she'd said—but the other, sane part told her she was being naïve.

Walking into the kitchen, she saw that a note had been left in the middle of the table with her name written on it in Max's neat handwriting.

Picking it up with a trembling hand, she read the words, her stomach twisting with pain and her sight blurring with tears as she took in the news that he'd gone to Ireland a couple of days early for his meeting there, to give them a bit of space.

He wasn't interested in giving them another chance.

It was over.

Slumping into the nearest chair, she willed herself not to cry again. There was no point; she wasn't going to solve anything by sitting here feeling sorry for herself.

She had to look after herself now.

Her life had no foundations any more; it was listing at a dangerous angle and at some point in the near future it could crash to the ground if she didn't do something drastic to shore it up.

She'd *so* wanted to belong here with him, but this house wasn't her home and Max wasn't her husband.

His heart belonged to someone else.

She hated the fact she was jealous of a ghost, and not

just because Jemima had been beautiful and talented, but because Max loved her with a fierceness she could barely comprehend.

How could she ever compete with that?

The stone-cold truth was: she couldn't.

And she couldn't stay here a moment longer either.

After carefully folding her clothes into her suitcase, she phoned Sarah to ask whether she could sleep on her couch again, just until she'd moved into the flat that Amber's cousin had promised to let to her.

'Sure, you'd be welcome to stay with us again,' Sarah said, after finally coaxing out the reason for her needing a place to escape to so soon after moving into Max's house. 'But you might want to try Anna. She's going to be away in the States for a couple of weeks from tomorrow and I bet she'd love you to housesit for her.'

One phone call to their friend Anna later and she had a new place to live for the next couple of weeks. So that was her accommodation sorted. Now it was just the small matter of finding a new job.

She'd received an email last week from one of the firms that she'd sent a job application to, offering her an interview, but hadn't had time to respond to it, being so busy keeping the business afloat while Max was in Manchester. After firing off an email accepting an interview for the Tuesday of that week, she turned her thoughts to her current job.

Even though she was angry and upset with Max, there was no way she was just going to abandon the business without finding someone to take over the role she'd carved out for herself. Max might not want her around, but he was still going to need a PA. The meeting he had with a large corporation in Ireland later this week was an exciting prospect and if he managed to land their business he was going to need to hire more staff, pronto.

So this week it looked as if she was going to be both interviewer and interviewee.

The thought of it both exhausted and saddened her.

But she'd made her bed when she'd shared hers with Max, and now she was going to have to lie in it.

CHAPTER TEN

MAX HAD THOUGHT he was okay with the decision to walk away from a relationship with Cara, but his subconscious seemed to have other ideas when he woke up in a cold sweat for the third day running after dreaming that Cara was locked in the house whilst it burnt to the ground and he couldn't find any way to get her out.

Even after he'd been up for a while and looked through his emails, he still couldn't get rid of the haunting image of Cara's face contorted with terror as the flames licked around her. Despite the rational part of his brain telling him it wasn't real, he couldn't shake the feeling that he'd failed her.

Because, of course, he had, he finally accepted, as he sat down to eat his breakfast in the hotel restaurant before his meeting. She'd laid herself bare for him, both figuratively and literally, and he'd abused her trust by treating her as if she meant nothing to him.

Which wasn't the case at all.

He sighed and rubbed a hand over his tired eyes. The last thing he should be doing right now was worrying about how he'd treated Cara when he was about to walk into one of the biggest corporations in Ireland and convince them to give him their business. This was exactly what he'd feared would happen when he'd first agreed to let her work for him—that the business might suffer. Though, to be fair to Cara, this mess was of his own making.

Feeling his phone vibrate, he lifted it out of his pocket and tapped on the icon to open his text messages. It was from Cara.

With his pulse thumping hard in his throat, he read what she'd written. It simply said:

Good luck today. I'll be thinking of you.

A heavy pressure built in his chest as he read the words through for a second time.

She was thinking about him.

Those few simple words undid something in him and a wave of pure anguish crashed through his body, stealing his breath and making his vision blur. Despite how he'd treated her, she was still looking out for him.

She wanted him to know that he wasn't alone.

That was so like Cara. She was such a good person: selfless and kind, but also brave and honourable. Jemima would have loved her.

Taking a deep breath, he mentally pulled himself together. Now was not the time to lose the plot. He had some serious business to attend to and he wasn't about to let all the work that he and Cara had put into making this opportunity happen go to waste.

* * *

Fourteen hours later Max flopped onto his hotel bed, totally exhausted after spending the whole day selling himself to the prospective clients, then taking them out for a celebratory dinner to mark their partnership when they signed on the dotted line to buy his company's services.

He'd done it; he'd closed the deal—and a very profitable deal it was, too—which meant he could now comfortably grow the business and hire a team of people to work for him.

His life was moving on.

A strong urge to call Cara and let her know he'd been successful had him sitting up and reaching for his phone, but he stopped himself from tapping on her name at the last second. He couldn't call her this late at night without it *meaning* something.

Frustration rattled through him, swiftly followed by such an intense wave of despondency it took his breath away. He needed to talk to someone. Right now.

Scrolling through his contacts, he found the name he wanted and pressed *call*, his hands twitching with impatience as he listened to the long drones of the dialling tone.

'Max? Is everything okay?' said a sleepy voice on the other end of the line.

'Hi, Poppy, sorry—I forgot it'd be so late where you are,' he lied.

'No problem,' his friend replied, her voice strained as if she was struggling to sit up in bed. 'What's up? Is everything okay?'

'Yes. Fine. Everything's fine. I won a pivotal con-tract for the business today so I'm really happy,' he said, acutely aware of how flat his voice sounded despite his best efforts to sound upbeat.

Apparently it didn't fool Poppy either. 'You don't *sound* really happy, Max. Are you sure there isn't some-thing else bothering you?'

His friend was too astute for her own good. But then she'd seen him at his lowest after Jemima died and had taken many a late night call from him throughout that dark time. He hadn't called her in a while though, so it wasn't entirely surprising that she thought something was wrong now.

'Er—' He ran a hand through his hair and sighed, feeling exhaustion drag at him. 'No, I'm—' But he couldn't say it. He wasn't fine. In fact he was far from it.

A blast of rage came out of nowhere and he gripped his phone hard, fighting for control.

It was a losing battle.

'You did it on purpose, didn't you? Sent Cara to me so I'd fall in love with her,' he said angrily, blood pump-ing hard through his body, and he leapt up from the bed and started to pace the room.

His heart gave an extra hard thump as the stunned si-lence at the other end of the line penetrated through his anger, bringing home to him exactly what he'd just said.

'Are you in love with her?' Poppy asked quietly, as if not wanting to break the spell.

He slapped the wall hard, feeling a sick satisfaction at the sting of pain in the palm of his hand. 'Jemima's only been dead for a year and a half.'

'That has nothing to do with it, and it wasn't what I asked you.'

He sighed and slumped back down onto the bed, battling to deal with the disorientating mass of emotions swirling though his head. 'I don't know, Poppy,' he said finally. 'I don't know.'

'If you don't know, that probably means that you are but you're too pig-headed to admit it to yourself.'

He couldn't help but laugh. His friend knew him so well.

'Is she in love with you?' Poppy asked.

'She says she is.'

He could almost feel his friend smiling on the other end of the phone.

Damn her.

'Look, I've got to go,' he said, 'I've had a very long day and my flight back to London leaves at six o'clock in the morning,' he finished, not wanting to protract this uncomfortable conversation any longer. 'I'll call you tomorrow after I've had some sleep and got my head straight, okay?'

'Okay.' There was a pause. 'You deserve to be happy though, Max, you know that, don't you? It's what Jemima would have wanted.'

He cut the call and threw the phone onto the bed, staring sightlessly at the blank wall in front of him.

Did he deserve to be happy, after the way he'd acted? Was he worthy of a second chance?

There was only one person who could answer that question.

* * *

The house was quiet when he arrived home at eight-thirty the next morning. Eerily so.

Cara should have been up by now, having breakfast and getting ready for the day—if she was there.

His stomach sank with dread as he considered the possibility that she wasn't. That she'd taken him at his word and walked away. Not that he could blame her.

Racing up the stairs, he came to an abrupt halt in front of her open bedroom door and peered inside. It was immaculate. And empty. As if she'd never been there.

Uncomfortable heat swamped him as he made his way slowly back down to the kitchen. Perhaps she hadn't gone. Perhaps she'd had a tidying spree in her room, then gone out early to grab some breakfast or something.

But he knew that none of these guesses were right when he spotted her keys to the house and the company mobile he'd given her to use for all their communications sitting in the middle of the kitchen table.

The silence of the house seemed to press in on him, crushing his chest, and he slumped onto the nearest chair and put his head in his hands.

This was all wrong. *All* of it.

He didn't want to stay in this house any longer; it was like living in a tomb. Or a shrine. Whatever it was, it felt wrong for him to be here now. Memories of the life he'd had here with Jemima were holding him back, preventing him from moving on and finding happiness again. Deep down, he knew Jem wouldn't have wanted that for him. He certainly wouldn't have wanted her to mourn him for the rest of her life.

She'd want him to be happy.

Like he had been on Sunday night.

He was in love with Cara.

Groaning loudly into his hands, he shook his head, unable to believe what a total idiot he'd been.

Memories of Cara flashed through his mind: her generous smile and kind gestures. Her standing up to him when it mattered to her most. Telling him she loved him.

His heart swelled with emotion, sending his blood coursing through his body and making it sing in his ears.

So this was living. How he'd missed it.

A loud ring on the doorbell made him jump.

Cara.

It had to be Cara, arriving promptly at nine o'clock for work like she always did.

Please, let it be her.

Tension tightened his muscles as he paced towards the door and flung it open, ready to say what he needed to say to her now. To be honest with her. To let her know how much he loved her and wanted her in his life.

'Max Firebrace?'

Instead of Cara standing on his doorstep, there was a tall, red-haired woman in a suit giving him a broad smile.

'Yes. Who are you?' he said impatiently, not wanting to deal with anything but his need to speak to Cara right then.

She held out a hand. 'I'm Donna, your new PA.'

The air seemed to freeze around him. *'What?'*

The smile she gave him was one of tolerant fortitude. 'Cara said you might be surprised to see me because you've been in Ireland all week.'

'Cara sent you here?'

'Yes, she interviewed me yesterday and said I should start today.'

He stared at her, stunned. 'Where is Cara?'

Donna looked confused. 'Er... I don't know. I wasn't expecting her to be here. She said something about starting a new job for a firm in the City next week. We spent all of yesterday afternoon getting me up to speed with the things I need to do to fulfil the role and went through the systems you use here, so I assumed she'd already served her notice.'

So that was it then. He was too late to save the situation. She was gone.

'You'd better come in,' he muttered, frustration tugging hard at his insides.

'So will we be working here the whole time? It's a beautiful house,' Donna said brightly, looking around the hall.

'No. I'm going to rent an office soon,' he said distractedly, his voice rough with panic.

How was he going to find her? He didn't have any contact details for her friends or her personal mobile number; she'd always used the company one to call or text him. He could try Poppy, but she'd probably be out filming in the middle of the desert right now and wouldn't want to be disturbed with phone calls.

A thought suddenly occurred to him. 'Donna? Did Cara interview you here?'

'No. I went to her flat.' She frowned. 'Although, come to think of it, I don't think it was her place; she didn't know which cupboard the sugar for my drink was kept in.'

He paced towards her, startling her with a rather manic smile.

'Okay, Donna. Your first job as my PA is to give me the address where you met Cara.'

At first Cara thought that the loud banging was part of her dream, but she started awake as the noise thundered through the flat again, seeming to shake the walls. Whoever was knocking really wanted to get her attention.

Pulling her big towelling dressing gown on over her sleep shorts and vest top, she stumbled to the door, still half-asleep. Perhaps the postman had a delivery for one of the other flats and they weren't in to receive it.

But it wasn't the postman.

It was Max.

Her vision tilted as she stumbled against the door in surprise and she hung on to the handle for dear life in an attempt to stop herself from falling towards him.

'Max! How did you find me?' she croaked, her voice completely useless in the face of his shocking presence.

She'd told herself that giving them both some space to breathe was the best thing she could do. After leaving his house on Monday she'd tried to push him out of her mind in an attempt to get through the dark, lonely days without him, but always, in the back of her mind, was the hope that he'd think about what she'd said and maybe, at some point in the future, want to look her up again.

But she hadn't expected it to happen so soon.

'My new PA, Donna, gave me the address,' he said, raising an eyebrow in chastisement, though the sparkle in his eyes told her he wasn't seriously angry with her for going ahead and hiring someone to take her place without his approval.

Telling herself not to get too excited in case he was only popping round to drop off something she'd accidentally left at the house, she motioned for him to come inside and led him through to the kitchen diner, turning to lean against the counter for support.

'You did say you'd understand if I couldn't work with you any more. After what happened,' she said.

He came to a stop a few feet away from her and propped himself against the table. 'I did.'

She took a breath and tipped up her chin. 'I'm not made of stone, Max. As much as I'd like to sweep what happened on Sunday under the carpet, I can't do that. I'm sorry.'

Letting out a long sigh, he shifted against the table. 'Don't be sorry. It wasn't your fault. It was mine. I was the one who knocked on your door when you had the strength to walk away.'

She snorted gently. 'That wasn't strength; it was cowardice.'

'You're not a coward, Cara; you just have a strong sense of self-preservation. You should consider it a gift.'

She stared down at the floor, aware of the heat of her humiliation rising to her face, not wanting him to see how weak and out of control she was right now.

'So you start a new job next week?' he asked quietly.

Forcing herself to look at him again, she gave him the most assertive smile she could muster. 'Yes, at a place in the City. It's a good company and the people were very friendly when they showed me around.'

'I bet you could handle just about anything after having to work for me.' He smiled, but she couldn't return it this time. The muscles in her face wouldn't move. They seemed to be frozen in place.

Gosh, this was awkward.

'You've been good for my confidence.' She flapped a hand at him and added, 'Work-wise,' when he raised his eyebrows in dispute. 'You were great at letting me know when I'd done a good job.'

'Only because you were brave enough to point out how bad I was at it.'

She managed a smile this time, albeit a rather wonky one. 'Well, whatever. I really appreciated it.'

There was a tense silence where they both looked away, as if psyching themselves up to tackle the real issues.

'Look, I'm not here to ask you to come back and work for me again,' Max said finally, running a hand over his hair.

'Oh. Okay,' she whispered, fighting back the tears. She would not break down in front of him. She *wouldn't*.

He frowned, as if worried about the way she'd reacted, and sighed loudly. 'Argh! I'm so bad at this.' He moved towards her but stopped a couple of feet away, holding up his hands. 'I wanted to tell you that I think I've finally made peace with what happened to Jemima. Despite my best efforts to remain a reclusive, twisted misery guts, I think I'm going to be okay now.' He took another step towards her, giving her a tentative smile. 'Thanks to you.'

Forcing down the lump in her throat, she smiled back. 'That's good to hear, Max. Really good. I'm happy that you're happy. And I do understand why you don't want me to come back and work for you. It must have been hard having me hanging around your house so much.'

'I'm going to sell the house, Cara.'

She stared at him in shock, her heart racing. 'What? But—how can you stand to leave it? That beautiful house.'

'I don't care about the house. I care about us.' This time he walked right up to her, so close she could feel the heat radiating from his body, and looked her directly in the eye. 'I'm ready to live again and I want to do it with you.'

'You—?'

'Want *you*, Cara.' His voice shook with emotion and she could see now that he was trembling.

'But—? I thought you said—when did you…?' Her voice petered out as her brain shut down in shock.

He half smiled, half frowned. 'Clearly I need to explain some things.' He took her hand and led her gently over to the sofa in the living area, guiding her to sit down next to him, keeping his fingers tightly locked with hers and capturing her gaze before speaking.

'When we slept together I felt like I'd betrayed a promise to Jemima.' He swallowed hard. 'After what happened to her I thought I had no right to be happy and start again when she couldn't do that. I truly thought I'd never love someone else the way I loved her, but then I realised I didn't need to. The love I feel for you is different—just as strong, but a different flavour. Does that make sense?'

He waited for her to nod shakily before continuing. 'I don't want to replicate Jemima or the way it was with her. I want to experience it all afresh with you. I'll always love Jem because she was a big part of my life for many years, but I can compartmentalise that now as part of my past.' He squeezed her fingers hard. 'You're my future.'

'Really?' Her throat was so tense with emotion she could hardly form the word.

'Yes. I love you, Cara.'

And she knew from the look on his face that he meant every word. He'd never given up anything of an emotional nature lightly and she understood what a superhuman effort it must have taken for him to come here and say all that to her.

Reaching out a hand, she ran her fingers across his cheek, desperate to smooth away any fears he might have. 'I love you, too.'

He closed his eyes and breathed out hard in relief before opening them again, looking more at peace than she'd ever seen him before. Lifting his own hand, he slid his fingers into her hair and drew her towards him, pressing his mouth to hers and kissing her long and hard.

She felt it right down to her toes.

Drawing away for a moment, he touched his forehead to hers and whispered, 'You make me so happy.'

And then, once again, there was no more talking. Just passion and joy and excitement for their bright new future together.

EPILOGUE

One year later

THE HOUSE THEY'D chosen to buy together was just the sort of place Cara had dreamed of owning during her romantic but practical twenties. It wasn't as grand or impressive as the house in South Kensington, but it felt exactly right for the two of them. And perhaps for any future family that chose to come along.

Not that having children was on the cards *right* now. Max was focusing hard on maintaining the expansion of his Management Solutions business, which had been flying ever since the Irish company awarded him their contract, and Cara was happy in her new position as Executive Assistant to the CEO of the company she'd joined in the City. But they'd talked about the possibility of it happening in the near future and had both agreed it was something they wanted.

Life was good. And so was their relationship.

After worrying for the first few months that, despite his assurances to the contrary, Max might still be in the grip of grief and that they had some struggles ahead of them, her fears had been assuaged as their partnership flourished and grew into something so strong and authentic she could barely breathe with happiness some days.

Max's anger had faded but his fierceness remained, which she now experienced as both a protective and supportive force in her life. Being a party to his sad past had taught her to count her blessings, and she did. Every single day.

Arriving home late after enjoying a quick Friday night drink with her colleagues, she let herself into their golden-bricked Victorian town house—which they'd chosen for the views of Victoria Park and its close location to the thriving bustle and buzz of Columbia Road with its weekly flower market and kitschy independent furniture shops—and stopped dead in the doorway, staring down at the floor.

It was covered in flowers, of all colours and varieties. Frowning at them in bewilderment, she realised they were arranged into the shape of a sweeping arrow pointing towards the living room.

'Max? I'm home. What's going on? It looks like spring has exploded in our hallway!'

Tiptoeing carefully over the flowers so as not to crush too many of them, she made her way towards the living room and peered nervously through the doorway, her heart skittering at the mystery of it.

What she saw inside took her breath away.

Every surface was covered in vibrantly coloured bouquets of spring flowers, displayed in all manner of receptacles: from antique vases to the measuring jug she used to make her porridge in the mornings. Even the light fitting had a large cutting of honeysuckle spiralling down from it, its sweet fragrance permeating the air. It reminded her of their first night together after Jack's wedding. Which quickly led her to memories of all the wonderful nights that had come after it, where she'd lain in Max's arms, breathing in the scent of his skin, barely able to believe how loved and cherished she felt.

And she was loved, as Max constantly reminded her, and her support and love for him had enabled him to finally say goodbye to Jemima and the past that had kept him ensnared for so long.

She'd unlocked his heart.

She was the key, he'd told her as he carried her, giggling, over the threshold into their house six months ago.

She'd finally found her home.

Their home.

He was standing next to the rose-strewn piano in the bay, looking at her with the same expression of fierce love and desire that always made her blood rush with heat.

'Hello, beautiful, did you have a good night?' he asked, walking towards where she stood, his smile bringing a mesmerising twinkle to his eyes.

'I did, thank you.' She swept a hand around the room, unable to stop herself from blurting, 'Max, what is this?'

The reverent expression on his face made her heart leap into her throat. 'This is me asking you to marry me,' he said, dropping to one knee in front of her and taking her hand in his, smiling at her gasp of surprise.

'This time last year I thought I'd never want to be married again—that I didn't deserve to be happy—but meeting you changed all that. You saved me, Cara.' Reaching into his pocket, he withdrew a small black velvet-covered box and flipped it open to reveal a beautiful flower-shaped diamond ring.

'I love you, and I want to spend the rest of my life loving you.' His eyes were alive with passion and hope. 'So what do you say—will you marry me?'

Heart pounding and her whole body shaking with excitement, she dropped onto her knees in front of him and gazed into his face, hardly able to believe the intensity of the love she felt for him.

'Yes,' she said simply, smiling into his eyes, letting him know how much she loved him back. 'Yes. I will.'

* * * * *

THE TYCOON'S RELUCTANT CINDERELLA

THERESE BEHARRIE

This book is dedicated to my husband,
my best friend and my biggest supporter,

Grant, thank you for working so hard so that I could
follow my dream. Thank you for believing that I would
be a published author when writing was only a vague
possibility for my future. And, most of all, thank you for
loving me so well that there is no doubt in my mind that
good men and happily-ever-afters exist. I love you.

To my family and friends,

Thank you all for supporting me.
For listening to me as I went on about my dream of
writing and the plans I had to get published. To those
who allowed me to talk about plot lines and characters
even though it might have bored you, thank you.
You have all contributed to this, and I am so grateful.

To my editor,

Flo, you invested time and effort in me
even though there was no guarantee I would be worth it.
Over and above that, I have experienced so much
growth as a writer in the months we've worked together.
I can't wait to continue this journey with you.
Thank you for everything.

CHAPTER ONE

'PLEASE HOLD THE ELEVATOR!'

Callie McKenzie almost shouted the words as she ran to the closing doors. She was horribly late, despite her rushed efforts to get dressed after her shift at the hotel had ended. She wouldn't be making a very good impression on the big boss if she arrived after he did, so she was taking a chance on the elevator, ignoring her usual reservations about the small box.

Relief shot through her when she saw a hand hold the elevator doors and she hurried in, almost colliding with the person who had helped her. She had meant to say thank you immediately, but as she looked at him her mouth dried, taking her words away.

Callie thought he might be the most beautiful man she had ever seen. Dark hair sat tousled on his head, as though it had travelled through whirlwinds to get there, and set off the sea-blue-green of his eyes. He was a full head taller than her, so that she had to look up to appreciate the striking features of his face. Each angle was shaped perfectly—as though it had been sculpted, she thought, with the intention of causing every woman who looked at it to be caught in involuntary—or voluntary—attraction.

Her eyes fell to his lips as they curved into a smile and she felt her heart flutter. It was the kind of smile that transformed his entire face, giving it a sexy, casual expression that stood out against the sophistication of his perfectly tailored suit. It took her a while to realise that she was amusing him by staring, and she forced herself to snap out of it.

'Thank you,' she said, aware of the husky undertone her evaluation of him had brought to her voice.

His smile broadened. 'No problem. Which floor would you like?'

Callie almost slapped her hand against her forehead at the deep baritone of his voice. Was there *anything* about the man that wasn't sexy?

She cleared her throat. 'Ground floor, please.'

'Then it's already been selected,' he said, and pressed the button to close the elevator doors. 'So you're also going to the event downstairs, then?'

She frowned. 'Yes. How did you know?'

'Well, I'd like to think that this hotel doesn't require its guests to dress up in such formal wear to have supper.'

He gestured to her clothing, and Callie once again resisted the urge to slap herself on the head. She was wearing one of her mother's formal gowns—one of the few Callie *didn't* think was absolutely ridiculous—and nodded.

'Of course. Sorry, it's been a long day.' Callie wished she believed that was the reason for her lame responses, but she knew better. She wasn't sure why, but he threw her off balance.

'I can relate. This isn't the most ideal way to spend the evening.'

Callie was about to agree when the elevator came to an abrupt stop. The lights went out barely a second later and Callie lost her balance, knocking her head into the back wall. The world spun for a bit, and then she felt strong arms hold her and lower her to the ground.

'Are you okay?' he asked, and Callie had to take a moment to catch her breath before she answered.

She wasn't sure if she was dizzy because she was in his arms or because of the blow to her head. Or, she thought as the situation finally caught up to her, if it was her very real fear of being trapped in enclosed spaces that had affected her breathing.

'I'm fine.' Her breath hitched, but she forced it out slowly. 'I'm sure it's just a bump on the head.' *Inhale, exhale*, she reminded herself.

'Are you sure? You're breathing quite heavily.'

Her eyes had now acclimatised to the darkness, and she could see the concern etched on his face. 'I'm a little... claustrophobic.'

'Ah.' He nodded his head and stood. 'The electricity must have gone off, but I'm sure it won't take long before someone realises we're here.'

He removed his phone from his pocket and tapped against the screen. A light shone dimly between them but Callie could only see his face, disproportionately large in the poor light. She felt a strange mixture of disappointment and satisfaction that she couldn't make out his features as clearly as she had before, but she did manage to make out the scowl on his face.

'I don't have any reception, so I can't call anyone to help.'

'You could press that button over there,' she said helpfully, pointing to the red emergency button on the control panel.

Her breathing was coming a little easier—as long as she didn't think about the fact that she was trapped. She wanted to stand up, but didn't trust herself to be steady. And the last thing she wanted was to fall into the arms of her companion for a second time within a few minutes.

'Of course I can.'

He pressed the emergency button and quickly conversed with the static voice that came through the intercom. He'd been right. There had been a power outage in the entire grid, and the hotel's generator had for some reason gone off as well. They were assured that it was being sorted out, but that it might take up to thirty minutes before they would be rescued.

He sighed and sank down next to her, and Callie squeezed her eyes shut. She thought it might make his proximity—and her fear—less overwhelming. Instead, the smell of him filled her senses—a musky male scent that almost made her sigh in satisfaction. She swore she could hear her heart throbbing in her chest, but she told herself it was just because of the confines of the elevator. She opened her eyes and looked at him, and before she could become mesmerised by his looks—even in the dim light he was handsome—forced herself to speak.

'I wonder what's going on downstairs. There must be mass panic.' She couldn't quite keep the scorn from colouring her voice.

'I take it that you're not a fan of tonight's celebrations,' he said wryly.

'I wouldn't say that. I'm just…' she searched for the word '…sceptical.'

'About the event, or the reason for it?'

The innocent question brought a flurry of emotions that she wasn't ready to face. Her brother, Connor, had warned her that the hotel they both worked at hadn't been doing well for years now. Despite his efforts as regional manager, Connor was still struggling to bring the Elegance Hotel back from the mess the last manager had created. The arrival today of the CEO—their boss—held a mass of implications that she didn't want to think about.

So, instead of answering his question, she asked, 'Are you here to meet the CEO?'

'Not really, no.'

'A very cryptic answer.'

She could sense his smile.

'I like the idea of being a little mysterious.'

She laughed. 'You realise I don't know who you are, right? Everything about you is mysterious to me.'

As she said the words she turned towards him and found herself face to face with him. Her heart pounded, her breath slowed, and for the briefest moment she wanted to lean forward and kiss him.

The thought was as effective as ice down her back, and she shifted away, blaming claustrophobia for her physical reaction to a man she barely knew.

She shook her head, and was brought back to the reality of the situation. Soon she didn't have to pretend to blame her shortness of breath on her fear. She felt a hand grip her own and looked at him. She could see the concern in his eyes, and gratitude filled her when she realised that reassurance, not attraction, was the reason for his gesture.

'Your date must be worried about you,' he said, and nodded, encouraging her to concentrate on his words.

'He might be,' she agreed, 'if I had brought one.'

He laughed, and the sound was as manly as the rest of him. What *was* it about the man that enthralled all her senses?

'And yours?' Callie asked, and wondered at herself. This wasn't like her. She was flirting with him. And even though she knew that she shouldn't, she wanted to know the answer.

Their eyes locked, and once again something sizzled between them.

'I don't have a date here.'

'Your girlfriend couldn't make it tonight?'

She turned away from him as she asked the question, and leaned her head back against the elevator wall. She didn't want to succumb to the magnetism that surrounded him, but she had already failed miserably. She shouldn't be asking him about his personal life. But every time she looked at him her heart kicked in her chest and she wanted to know more. If she looked away, the walls began to close in on her.

So she chose the lesser of the two evils and turned back to him. His eyes were patient, steady, and she gave in to the temptation. 'Couldn't she?'

'There's no girlfriend.'

Was she imagining the slight tension in his voice?

'And you don't have a boyfriend, I assume?'

'You assume correctly—although I probably shouldn't be telling you that.'

'Why not?'

'Well, you're a strange man and we're stuck in an elevator together. What's going to deter you from putting the moves on me now that you know I don't have a boyfriend?'

Callie said the words before she could think about what they might provoke. But he just said, 'You don't have to worry about that. I don't "put the moves" on anyone.'

'So women just drop at your feet, then?' She couldn't take her eyes off him as she dug deeper.

'Sometimes.'

He smiled, but even in the dim light she could see something in his eyes that she couldn't decipher.

'Ah, modesty. Charming.' She said it in jest, but her heart sank. This man—this very attractive man who made her heart beat faster just by looking at her—wasn't interested in *one* woman. *Women* fell at his feet—and she wouldn't be one of them.

He laughed, and then sobered. 'Mostly I stay away from them.'

Callie felt herself soften just a little at the heartbreak she could hear ever so slightly in his voice. And just like that her judgement of him faded away. He didn't want women, or even just one woman—he wanted to be alone. Callie couldn't figure out which fact bothered her the most.

'I'm sorry. She must have been a real piece of work.'

He didn't answer her, but his face told her everything that she needed to know. She placed a hand over his and squeezed it, hoping to provide him with some comfort. But when he laid his hand over hers in return, comfort was the last thing on her mind. His hand brought heat to hers, and lit her heart so that it beat to a rhythm she couldn't fathom. He leaned his head towards hers, and suddenly heat spread through her bloodstream.

This couldn't be right, she thought desperately as she pulled her hand away. They barely knew each other. She wouldn't let herself fall into a web of attraction with a man who was as charming as a fairy-tale prince.

Before she could worry about it the elevator lurched and the lights came back on. He stood and offered a hand to her, a slight smile on his gorgeous face. Did he know the effect he had on her? Or was he simply aware that he'd helped distract her from one of her worst fears?

As Callie took his hand she had to admit that he *had* kept her thoughts off being stuck in an elevator. And she blamed that—and his good looks—on her uncharacteristic reaction.

'Thank you,' she said as the elevator doors opened. 'I hope you enjoy the rest of your evening.'

The breath of relief that was released from her lungs as she walked away was because she was out of the enclosed space, Callie assured herself, and ignored the voice in her head that scoffed at the lie.

* * *

Blake Owen stopped at the doors of the banquet hall and resisted the urge to walk away. He had never been a fan of opulence, but rarely did he have a choice in the matter. Which was fine, he supposed. In his business, events of an extravagant nature were integral to success, and the welcome for him tonight was an excellent example of that. He would be introduced to the Elegance Hotel in Cape Town in a style that would keep the hotel's name at the forefront of the media's attention while he sorted out the troublesome operation.

So he accepted his lot and walked into the room, snagging a flute of champagne from the nearest waiter's tray before taking the whole scene in.

Glamour spread from the roof to the floor and fairy lights and sparkling chandeliers twinkled like stars against the midnight-blue draping. Black-and-white-clad waiters wove through the crowd while men and women in tuxedos and evening gowns air-kissed and wafted around on clouds of self-importance.

Blake almost rolled his eyes—until he remembered the guests were there in *his* honour. The thought made him empty the entire champagne glass and exchange it for a full one from the next waiter. He noted that the power outage hadn't seemed to dampen the evening's festivities. But when he looked at the scene with the eye of a manager he could see some slightly frazzled members of staff weaving through the crowd doing damage control.

He managed to get the attention of one of them, and took the frightened young man to a less populated corner of the hall.

'What happened when the electricity went out?'

As Blake spoke the man's eyes widened and Blake thought that 'boy' might be a more appropriate description.

'It was only a few moments, sir. As you can see, everything is running smoothly again. Enjoy your evening.'

The boy made to move away, but at Blake's look he paused.

'Was there anything else, sir?'

'Yes, actually. I was wondering if you brush off the concerns of *all* your guests, or if you reserve that for just a handful of people.'

If the boy had looked nervous before, he was terrified now. 'No...no, sir. I'm sorry you feel that I did. We're just a bit busy, and I have to make sure that everything is okay before Mr Owen gets here.'

'That would be me.'

The words were said in a low voice, softly, but for their effect they might have been earth-shatteringly loud.

'Mr... Mr Owen?' the boy stammered. 'Sir, I am *so* sorry—'

'It's fine,' Blake said when he saw the boy might have a heart attack from the shock. 'You can answer my original question.' At his blank look, Blake elaborated. 'The power outage...?'

'Oh, yes. Well, it wasn't such a train smash here. The candles gave sufficient light that there wasn't much panic, and Connor—Mr McKenzie, I mean—managed to calm whatever concerns there were.'

Blake was surprised the boy had been able to string enough words together to give him such a thorough explanation.

'And that was it?'

'Yes, sir. The generator was back on in under thirty minutes, so it wasn't too long. Although I *did* hear there were people trapped in the elevator.'

Blake thought it best not to tell the boy *he* had been one

of those who had been trapped. He wasn't sure if he would be able to handle another shock.

'When was the last time the generator was checked?'

'I... I don't know, sir.'

Blake nodded and left it at that, making a mental note to check that out when he officially started on Monday. The list of what he would have to do at the hotel seemed to grow the more time he spent there, and he wasn't having it. Not any more. Somehow the Elegance in Cape Town had flown under his radar for the past few years, while he had focused on his other hotels in South Africa.

And while he focused on rebuilding his self-respect after letting himself be fooled into a relationship that should never have been.

When he had eventually started reviewing the financials he'd realised that although Connor McKenzie *had* pulled the hotel out of the mess that Landon Meyer, the previous regional manager, had made, it wasn't enough. The hotel hadn't made a profit for three years, and he couldn't let that continue.

But that wasn't tonight's problem, Blake thought as he scanned the crowd. He knew it would only take a few minutes before he would be recognised, and then he would have to start doing the rounds as guest of honour. He paused when he saw the woman he had been stuck in the elevator with a few moments ago. She was standing near a table full of champagne, and before Blake knew it he was walking towards her.

As he came closer he saw that his recollection of their time spent in the elevator didn't do justice to what he saw now. He had noticed that she was attractive when she'd walked in, but he had taken care not to stare. And with the darkness that had descended only a few moments later, he hadn't been able to look at her as he was now.

The red dress she wore clung only to her chest and then flowed regally down from her waist to the floor. Her black hair stood out strikingly against the dress, her golden skin amplifying the effect, and for reasons he couldn't quite place his finger on it disconcerted him. Her round face held an innocence he hadn't been privy to in a long time, and her green eyes persuaded him to consider pursuing her.

The thought shocked him, as there was nothing in her expression to prompt it. There was also nothing in his past that encouraged him to trust a woman again. Yet now he felt an intense desire to get to know *this* woman. One he had only just met an hour ago.

'I think that after being stuck in an elevator the least we could do is have a drink together.'

Callie heard the deep voice as she reached for a glass of champagne. Her hand stilled, and then she continued, hoping that her pause wouldn't be noticed.

'I don't know if I'm inclined to agree,' she said and took a sip of her drink. 'I never have drinks with anyone I don't know.'

'Really? But you have nothing against flirting with strangers?' He gave her an amused look, his smile widening when she blushed.

'Must have been a temporary lapse in judgement.'

'How do you date if you don't flirt?'

'I don't.' She sipped her drink.

'Which would explain the lack of a boyfriend.'

Callie aimed a level look at him. 'Yes. And it would also explain why I don't have to deal with conversations like this very often.'

'Touché.' He smiled and lifted his glass to her in a toast.

Her lips almost curved in response, but then she stopped herself. What was she *doing*? A memory flashed into her mind, of him sitting with her in the elevator, patiently talking to her to distract her from her fears. And then she remembered. She was flirting with him because there was something about him that had kept her calm when she should have had a panic attack.

Heaven help her.

'And you've told me everything I need to know about why *you're* single, then?' she asked, and immediately regretted it when his expression dimmed. 'I'm sorry, I didn't mean to upset you.'

'No,' he responded, 'it's fine.' But he changed the topic. 'Since you seem to want to know so much about me, how about you offer me the same courtesy? You can start with your name.'

She smiled. 'Callie.'

She held out her hand, proud that her voice revealed none of the strange feelings he evoked in her. He took it and shook it slowly, making the ordinary task feel like an intimate act, and she shifted as a thrill worked its way up her spine.

'Blake? I'm so glad I've found you. I was about to send out a search party.'

Callie stared dumbly at her brother as he strode towards them, his tuxedo perfectly fitted to his build and perfectly suited to his handsome features.

'Hey, Cals, I'm happy you made it without missing too much.' Connor gave her a kiss on the cheek, and angled his face so that Blake wouldn't see his questioning look. 'I see you've met the reason we're all here.'

It took a full minute before Callie could process his words. '*This* is Blake Owen?'

'Yes.' Blake intercepted Connor's reply. 'Although, to be fair, I was about to introduce myself. Connor just got here before I could.'

Blake shook Connor's hand in greeting, and Callie couldn't help but notice how much more efficient the action was now than when he had done it with her.

'How do you two know each other?'

'Connor is my brother,' Callie said, before her brother could say anything. All the feelings inside her had frozen, and she resisted the urge to shiver.

'So you're here to support him? That's great.' Blake smiled at her.

Connor laughed. 'No! Callie's a good sister, but I'm not sure she would attend an event so far out of her comfort zone for *me*.' At Blake's questioning look, Connor elaborated. 'Callie works at the hotel.'

Connor's simple words shattered the opportunity for any explanation Callie might have wanted to give. Blake's eyes iced, and this time she couldn't resist the shiver that went through her body.

'Well, we should probably get going,' Connor said when the silence extended a second too long.

'Yes,' Blake agreed, his gaze never leaving Callie's. 'You should probably start introducing me to the other *employees*—' he said the word with a contempt that Callie hadn't expected '—before I make a mistake I can't rectify.'

Callie watched helplessly as they walked away, wondering how she had already managed to alienate her CEO.

CHAPTER TWO

BLAKE WATCHED AS the crowd in the banquet hall began to thin. There must have been about three hundred people there, he thought. And, the way he felt, he was sure he had spoken to every single one of them. No, he corrected himself almost immediately. Not *everyone*. There was one person he had avoided ever since learning who she was—an employee of the hotel.

Julia, his ex, had been an employee. She had been a part of the Human Resources team in the Port Elizabeth hotel, where he spent most of his time.

He had been enamoured of her. She was beautiful, intelligent, and just a little arrogant. And she had a son who had crept into his heart the moment Blake had met him. It had been a fascinating combination—the gorgeous, sassy woman and the sweet, shy child. One that had lured him in and blinded him to the truth of what she'd wanted from him. The truth that had made him distrust his judgement and conclude that staying away from his employees would be the safest option to avoid getting hurt.

He narrowed his eyes when he saw Callie walking towards him, and cursed himself for the attraction that flashed through his body. But he refused to give in to it. He would ignore the way some strands of her hair had escaped from her hairstyle and floated down to frame her face. He wouldn't notice that she walked as if someone had rolled out a red carpet for her. He hardened himself against the effect she had on him—and then she was in front of him and her smell nearly did him in.

The floral scent was edged with seduction—a description that came from nowhere as she stood innocently in front of him, those emerald eyes clear of any sign of wrongdoing.

'What do you want?' he snapped, and surprised himself. Regardless of the way his body reacted to her, he could control it. He *would* control it.

Her eyes widened, but then set with determination. 'I wanted to set the record straight. I know you must be confused after finding out I work here.'

'That isn't the word I'd use.'

'Well, however you would describe it, I still want to tell you what happened.'

She took a breath, and Blake wondered if she realised how shakily she'd done it.

'I had no idea who you were when we were stuck in that elevator. If I had, I wouldn't have—'

'Flirted with me?'

Something in her eyes fired, and reminded him that he had flirted with her, too. But her voice was calm when she spoke.

'Yes, I suppose. It was an honest mistake. I didn't seek you out to try and soften you up, or anything crazy like that. So...' She paused, and then pushed on. 'Please don't take this out on Connor.'

Blake frowned. She was explaining to him that she'd made a mistake—and the honesty already baffled him— but she didn't seem to be doing it for herself. She was doing it for her brother, and that was...selfless.

Almost everything Julia had done had been self-serving.

But then he hadn't known that in the beginning. He'd thought that she was being unselfish, that she was being honest. And those qualities had attracted him. But it had all been pretence. So what if there didn't *seem* to be a deceitful motive behind what Callie was saying? He knew better than anyone else that she might be faking it.

But when he looked at her, into those alluring and devastatingly honest eyes, that thought just didn't sit right.

'So,' he said, sliding his hands into his pockets, 'I can take it out on *you*?'

Was he still flirting with her? No, he thought. He wanted to know what she thought he should do about the situation. Yes, that was it—just a test. How would she respond now that she knew he was her boss?

She cleared her throat. 'If need be, yes. I understand if you feel you need to take disciplinary action, although I don't believe it's necessary.'

'You don't?'

'No, sir.'

The word sounded different coming from her, and he wasn't sure that he liked the way she was defining their relationship.

'I apologise for my unprofessional behaviour, but I assure you it won't happen again.' She looked at him, and this time her eyes pleaded for herself. 'I didn't know who you were. Please give me a chance to make this right.'

Blake was big enough a man to realise when he had made a mistake, and the sincerity the woman in front of him exuded told him he had done just that, in spite of his doubts. He straightened, and saw that there was almost no one left in the room for him to meet. Relief poured through him, and finally he gave himself permission to leave.

But before he did, he said, 'Okay, Miss McKenzie. I believe you. I'll see you at work on Monday.'

* * *

By eleven o'clock on Monday morning Blake had had enough. He had got in to the office at six and had been poring over the financials since then. *Again.* But no matter how he looked at it—just as he'd feared the first time he'd reviewed them—there was no denying the fact that this hotel was in serious trouble.

How had he let it get this far? he thought, and walked to the coffee machine in the office he would be sharing with Connor. The man had set up a makeshift space for Blake, which made the place snug, but not unworkable. Right now, he was tempted to have a drink of the stronger stuff Connor kept under lock and key for special occasions—or so he claimed. But even in Blake's current state of mind he could acknowledge that drinking was not the way to approach this.

With his coffee in his hand, he walked to the window and looked out at the bustle of Cape Town on a Monday morning. The hotel overlooked parts of the business district, and he could feel the busyness of people trying to get somewhere rife in the air as he watched the relays of public transport. But he could also glimpse Table Mountain in the background, and he appreciated the simplicity of its magnitude. It somehow made him feel steadier as he thought about the state the hotel was in.

How had he let this happen?

The thought wouldn't leave his head. He had picked up that the hotel had been struggling years ago—which was why he had fired Landon and promoted Connor—but still this shouldn't have got past him. But he knew why it had. And he needed to be honest with himself before he blamed his employees when *he* was probably just as responsible for this mess.

He had been too focused on dealing with Julia to notice that the business was suffering.

His legs were restless now, as he got to the core of the problem, and he began to pace, coffee in hand, contemplating the situation. About five years ago the Elegance Hotel in Port Elizabeth had started losing staff at a high rate. When he'd noticed how low their retention numbers were, he'd arranged a meeting with HR to discuss it.

It had been at that meeting that he'd first met Julia.

She hadn't seemed to care that he was her boss, and had pushed the boundaries of what he had considered appropriate professional behaviour. But the reasons she had given him for losing staff had been right, and he'd had to acknowledge that she was an asset to their team. And as soon as he had she'd given him the smile that had drawn him in. Bright, bold, beautiful.

To this day, whenever he thought about that smile he felt a knock to his heart. Especially since those thoughts were so closely intertwined with the way it had softened when she'd looked at her son. The boy who had reminded him eerily of himself, and made him think about how Julia was giving him something Blake never had—a mother.

Until one day it had all shattered into the pieces that still haunted him.

He knew that Julia had taken his attention away from the hotels. And now this hotel was paying the price of a mistake he'd made before he'd known better. The thought conjured up Callie's face in his mind, but he forced it away, hoping to forget the way her eyes lit up her face when she smiled. He had just remembered the reason he didn't want to be attracted to her. He didn't want to be distracted either, and she had the word *distraction* written all over her beautiful face. *And*, he reminded himself again, he knew better now.

He grunted at the thought, walked back to the desk, and began to make some calls.

And ignored the face of the woman he had only met a few days ago as it drifted around in his head.

'Yes, darling, include that in my trip. I would *love* to see the mountain everyone keeps harping on about. And please include some cultural museums on my tour.' The woman sniffed, and placed a dignified hand on the very expensive pearls she wore around her neck. 'I can't only be doing *touristy* things, you know.'

'Of course, Mrs Applecombe.' Callie resisted the urge to tell the woman that visiting museums was very much a 'touristy' thing. 'I'll draw up a package for you and have it sent to your room by the end of the day. If you agree, we can arrange for the tour to be done the day after tomorrow.'

'Delightful.' Mrs Applecombe clasped her hands together. 'I just *know* Henry will love what we've discussed. Just remember, dear, that it's—'

'Supposed to be a surprise. I know.' Callie smiled, and stood. 'I'll make sure that it's everything you could hope for and more.'

After a few more lengthy reminders about the surprise anniversary gift for her husband Mrs Applecombe finally left, and Callie sighed in relief. She loved the woman's spirit, but after forty minutes of going back and forth about a tour Callie knew she could have designed in her sleep, she needed a break.

Luckily it was one o'clock, which meant she could take lunch. But instead of sneaking into the kitchen, as she did most days, she locked the door to her office and flopped down on the two-seater couch she'd crammed into the small space so that if her guests wanted to they could be slightly more comfortable.

It had been a long morning. She'd done a quick tour first thing when she'd got in, followed by meetings with three guests wanting to plan trips. Usually she would be ecstatic about it. She loved her job. And she had Connor to thank for that.

She sighed, and sank even lower on the couch. Officially she was the 'Specialised Concierge'—a title she had initially thought pretentious, but one that seemed to thrill many of the more elite guests she worked with at the hotel. Unofficially she was a glorified tour guide, whose brother had persuaded her to work at the hotel to drag her from the very dark place she had been in after their parents' deaths.

She didn't have to think back that far to acknowledge that the job had saved her from that dark place. Once she had seen her parents' coffins descend into the ground— once she had watched people say their farewells and return to their lives as usual— she had found herself slipping. And even though her brother had been close to broken himself, he had stepped up and had helped her turn her life into something she knew had been out of her grasp after the car crash that had destroyed the life she had known and the people she loved.

The thought made her miss him terribly, and she grabbed her handbag and headed to Connor's office. Maybe he felt like having lunch together, and he could calm the ache that had suddenly started in her heart.

As she walked the short distance to his office she greeted some of the guests she recognised and nodded politely at those she didn't. She smiled in sympathy when she saw her friend Kate, dealing with a clearly testy guest at the front desk, and laughed when Kate mimicked placing a gun to her head as the guest leaned down to sign something.

Connor's door was slightly ajar when she got there, and she paused before knocking when she heard voices.

'If we keep doing what we're doing, in a couple of years—three, max—the hotel will be turning a profit again, Blake.' Connor's voice sounded panicked. 'I'm just not sure *this* plan is the best option. Surely there's something else we can do? Especially after we've stepped up in the last few years.'

'Connor, no one is denying the work you've done at the hotel. You've increased turnover by fifty per cent since you took over—which is saying something when you consider the state Landon left it in. But three years is too long to have a business running in the red.' There was a pause, and then Blake continued. 'Would you rather we move on to the other option? I've told you that it would come with a lot more complications...'

'Of course I would prefer *any* other option. But you know what's best for the hotel.'

Callie felt a trickle of unease run through her when she heard her brother's voice. It wasn't panicked this time, but resigned, as though he had given up hope on something.

'All right, then.' There was a beat of silence. 'I suppose we should start preparing to lay off staff.'

The words were fatalistic, and yet it took Callie a while to process what she had heard. Once she did, her legs moved without her consent and she burst through the office door.

'No!' she said, and her voice sounded as though it came from faraway. 'I can't let you do that.'

CHAPTER THREE

'EXCUSE ME?' BLAKE LIFTED his eyebrows, and suddenly Callie wished her tongue had given her the chance to think before she spoke.

'I'm so sorry, Mr Owen… Connor…' She saw the look in her brother's eyes and hoped her own apologised for interrupting. 'I just heard—'

'A *private* business conversation between members of management. Do you make a habit of eavesdropping?'

His eyes were steel, and she could hear the implication that he thought she had more poor habits than just eavesdropping.

'No, of course not. I was on my way to ask Connor if he'd like to do lunch, and then I heard you because the door was open.' She gestured behind her, although the action was useless now, since it stood wide open after her desperate entrance. 'I didn't mean to listen, but I did, and I'm telling you that you *can't* lay off staff. Please.'

Blake's handsome face softened slightly, and she cursed herself for noticing how his dark blue suit made him look like a model from the pages of a fashion magazine. It was probably the worst time to think of that, she thought, and instead focused on making some kind of case to make him reconsider.

'There are people here who need their jobs. Who *love*

their jobs.' She could hear the plea in her voice. 'Employees here who have families who depend on them.'

'I'm aware of that, Miss McKenzie.' Blake frowned. 'I've thought every option through. This one is the best for the hotel. If we downsize now we can focus on operations and then expand again once we turn enough profit. It would actually be fairly simple.'

'For you, maybe. And for the hotel, sure. But I can assure you it would be anything but simple for the people you lay off—' She broke off, her heart pounding at the prospect. 'This is a business decision without any consideration for your employees.'

His eyes narrowed. 'I *have* considered my employees, and I resent your implication otherwise. You have no idea what any other option would require from us. This is the most efficient way to help Elegance, Cape Town, get back on its feet.'

'Are you listening to yourself?' she asked desperately. 'You've been tossing around words like "downsizing" and "efficiency" as though those are *good* things. They aren't!'

'Callie—'

Connor stepped forward and she immediately felt ashamed of her behaviour when she saw the warning in his eyes. She knew she was embarrassing him in front of their boss. She even knew that she was embarrassing *herself* in front of her boss. So, even though more words tumbled through her mind, and even though the shame she felt was more for Connor than for herself, she stopped talking.

'It's okay, Connor.' Blake eased his way into one of the chairs in front of Connor's desk. 'I understand your sister's anger. However unprofessional.'

Callie's heart hammered in her chest and she wished that she hadn't said anything. But then she thought of Kate, and Connor, and of the fact that her job meant the world to her, and she straightened her shoulders. She wouldn't feel bad for standing up for their jobs. Not when it meant that she'd at least tried to save them.

'There is another option, Callie.'

Blake spoke quietly, and she wondered if he knew the power his voice held even so.

'I've looked into other investors.'

'Why did you dismiss the idea?'

Something shifted in his eyes, as though he hadn't expected her to ask him about his reasons.

'The Elegance hotels are the product of my father's hard work, and mine, and I don't want an outside investor to undermine that. Not at this stage of the game.'

He looked at her, and what she saw in his eyes gave her hope.

'Of course I *have* considered it. Especially an international investor, since that might give Elegance the boost it needs to go international. But it would be a very complicated process, and it would require a lot of negotiation.' He turned now, and looked at Connor. 'Like I told you before, I would have to think through the terms of this thoroughly before I make any decision.'

'But you'll reconsider it?' There was no disguising the hope Callie felt.

Blake looked at her, and those blue-green eyes were stormier than she had thought possible.

'I don't want another investor. This hotel group has been in my family for decades, Miss McKenzie. It's a legacy I want to pass on to my children.' He paused. 'But if we can secure an international investor, that legacy might be even more than I thought possible. We'll talk about it.'

He gestured to Connor, and then moved to sit behind the desk Connor had had put in his office for Blake.

Callie waited, but the look on her brother's face told

her she had been dismissed. She nearly skipped out of the room, because despite his non-committal response Blake Owen *was* considering an option other than laying off staff. If Blake chose an investor it would mean that everything her brother had worked so hard for wouldn't have been for nothing.

He had toiled night and day to try and get the hotel running smoothly again, and the news of Blake's arrival had been a difficult pill to swallow—it had been a clear sign that everything Connor had done hadn't been enough. Callie knew he loved the hotel, and the last thing that he wanted was for his employees to lose their jobs. And, she thought, the last thing *she* wanted was for him to lose his job—and for her to lose hers.

So before she left she wanted to say one more thing to Blake.

'Mr Owen... Blake?'

He looked up, and she smiled.

'Thank you for reconsidering.'

Blake couldn't sleep. He had been working with Connor until just past midnight, trying to draft an investment contract that he was happy with. A contract that would require all his negotiation skills to convince an investor to accept—although he knew it was possible. He had put out feelers even before he had spoken to Connor, when he had initially thought of finding an investor, and the response had been positive. But he still wasn't convinced that this was something he wanted or if it was something he was being persuaded into by a pretty face.

He threw off his bedcovers and walked downstairs to the kitchen of his Cape Town house. He had bought the place without much thought other than that he would need somewhere to stay when he visited his father, who had retired here. Now he was incredibly grateful he had, since he didn't know how long he would be in town.

The house was a few kilometres from the hotel, and had an amazing view. He could even see the lights of the city illuminating Table Mountain at night through the glass doors that led out onto a deck on the second floor. But he wasn't thinking about that as he poured himself a glass of water and drank as though he had come out of a desert.

Since the house was temperature-controlled, he knew he wasn't feeling the heat of the January weather. No, he thought. It was because he was considering something that would complicate his life when all he'd wanted was a simple solution.

Blake had been raised in the family business. His father had opened the first Elegance Hotel four decades ago, and had invested heavily in guest relations. He had made sure that every employee knew that the Elegance Hotel's guests came first, and seen that vision manifested into action. Eventually, after two decades, his investment had paid off and he had been able to expand into other hotels.

Blake had been groomed to take over since he was old enough to understand that his father was not only building a business, but a legacy. And he hadn't been given control of the hotel until his father had been sure that he could do it.

That was why he wanted to lay off staff instead of considering an outside investor. He would be able to solve the problem that had arisen while he'd been trying to fix his relationship with Julia easily, and make the reminder of his failure disappear. It would mean that his feelings of losing control and being helpless would be gone.

A memory of himself standing at the front door, watching his mother leave, flashed through his mind, but he shook it away, not knowing where it had come from, and forced his thoughts back to the matter at hand. Laying off staff might have been the simple option, but it was also a selfish one. Especially when he thought of the hope he had seen written on Callie and Connor's faces.

He sighed as he made his decision. He would do this—but not for Callie. The slight heat that flushed through him every time he thought about her, the intensity of it every time he saw her, was a sure sign that he should stay away from her. He *wouldn't* make this big a decision based on his attraction to her or her need for him to do so. He wouldn't make that mistake again.

'Mr Owen, do you have a moment?'

Callie stood awkwardly at the door, wishing with all her might that she didn't feel quite so small in his presence. But she straightened when he looked up and gestured for her to come in.

She knew Connor had to attend one of the conferences at the hotel today, and she was using the opportunity to speak to her boss without her brother's disapproving look. And without the disapproving lecture she would no doubt receive—like the one she'd received just after midnight—which, she had been told, was when Connor and Blake had finally finished their meeting.

She knew she'd been out of line when she had spoken up, and she hadn't needed Connor to tell her that. So once again she was preparing to apologise to Blake.

She walked in and swallowed when he looked up, the striking features of his face knitted into a stern expression.

'What can I do for you, Miss McKenzie?'

'It's Callie, please.'

He nodded. 'Okay, then. What can I do for you, Callie?'

Her stomach jilted just a little at the way he said her name. She cleared her throat. 'I wanted to say sorry.'

He almost smiled. 'It's becoming a habit, then.'

She let out a laugh. 'Seems like it. I've made quite the mess since meeting you.' She stepped forward, resisted pulling at her clothes. 'But I *am* sorry. The first time I apologised it was because I'd made a mistake. This time it's because I shouldn't have barged in here and spoken out of turn.'

'I'm not upset with you because you spoke out of turn.'

Blake stood, walked around the desk and leaned against it. He was wearing a blue shirt, and the top button was loosened. She swallowed, and wondered if the temperature in the room had increased.

'I'm not your school principal.'

'Aren't you, though? In some ways?'

This time he did smile, and it did something strange to her heart.

'I won't take the bait on that one.'

He paused, and then crossed his arms. She could see the muscle ripple under his shirt, and the heat went up another notch.

'You say you're sorry for barging in here. But not that you eavesdropped?'

'No, I'm not sorry about that. If I hadn't you wouldn't have considered investors. Which you *have* been doing, right?' she asked, and knew that subtlety was not her forte.

'I have. I made a few calls this morning, and I have a few people interested.'

He walked towards her, and though the distance between them wasn't small her heart thudded.

'So the answer to your real question is yes, I am going to do this.'

'You *are*?' Relief washed over her. 'Oh, wow!' She pressed a hand to her stomach. 'That's amazing.'

'But I need your help.'

Relief turned into confusion. 'What do you mean?'

'Like I said yesterday, we need a very specific kind of investor. An international one who will be willing to invest in the hotel, but also in this city. Especially if I want him to agree to my strict terms regarding the expansion of Elegance Hotels.'

His hands were in his pockets now, and he moved until he was just close enough that she could smell his cologne. It reminded her of when they were in the elevator together— a time when she hadn't had to think of him as her boss.

She shook off the feelings the memory evoked, but when she spoke, her voice was a little husky. 'And how can I help with that?'

'You can help me sell the city. You are the "Specialised Concierge", right?'

He smiled slyly, and she realised he knew about her made-up title.

'Or, in more common terms, a tour guide,' she said.

'Exactly. So I'll need you to help me sell Cape Town to potential investors. Your knowledge of the city will be an asset to any proposal I make. I'll take care of the business side of it, of course, and once that's done we can take them on the tour you will custom-design to fit my proposal.'

'How do you know I can do it?' She felt her heart beat in a rhythm that couldn't possibly be healthy.

'Because your job depends on it.'

He smiled now, and she couldn't read the emotion that lined it.

'Callie, are you prepared to work with the boss?'

She stared helplessly at him, and despite everything inside her that nudged her to say otherwise she answered, 'Yes, I am.'

CHAPTER FOUR

'YOU'RE HERE BECAUSE you want to keep your job. You're here because you want to save Connor's job. You're here because you're saving your colleagues' jobs.'

Callie repeated the words to herself as she walked into what had previously been known as Conference Room A. Blake had turned it into an office. Not one he would share with Connor. No, that had ended the minute she had agreed to work with him. This conference-room-turned-office was hers and Blake's to share. It was one of their medium-sized conference rooms, and Callie had only been in it a few times when she'd had tours with groups of more than six. But, despite its reasonable size, Callie felt closed in. And this time she wasn't fooling herself by attributing the feeling to claustrophobia.

Her heart hammered as she saw him sitting at one end of the rectangular table, a large whiteboard behind him already half filled with illegible writing.

'Are you sure you weren't meant to be a doctor?' she asked, hoping to break the tension she felt within herself.

Blake looked up at her, his eyes sharp despite how hard she knew he had been working. The hotel had been rife with the news that Blake had been holed up in the conference room for the entire week it had taken for Callie to sort out her schedule. She'd done her tours for that week, but had cancelled everything beyond that. Blake had made it very clear that Callie's full attention would be needed for the investors, and that was what she was doing.

She tilted her head when he grabbed a cup of what Callie assumed had once been coffee from in front of him. By the look on his face, it was something significantly less desirable now.

'I'll get you some more,' she said, and placed her files and handbag a few seats away from his.

This was their first official day of working together, and Callie wasn't sure what it would be like to work with the boss. She was already distracted by being alone with him in the same room, she thought as she poured coffee into two cups that sat on the counter along one side of the conference room. The hotel staff had made sure that everything their boss could possibly need was in that room.

She'd heard them whispering amongst themselves, and had taken it upon herself to defuse their curiosity.

'We're going to try and save the hotel,' she'd told Kate, knowing her friend couldn't keep a secret for the life of her, 'and if we do things will stay the same for the foreseeable future.'

Since she'd let that little titbit go, her colleagues had done everything in their power to make sure they had the fuel to save the hotel. And maybe the world, she thought, and wrinkled her nose at the extensive display of pastries that lined the rest of the counter.

'How many people are eating this?' she wondered out loud, and set the coffee in front of Blake.

'Two today.' He sighed as he sipped from the coffee. 'It's been like that ever since I started working in here. I think they think I'm a competitive eater in my spare time.'

She laughed. 'Or a man who needs as much energy as possible so that he can work to save their jobs.' He frowned, and she elaborated. 'People were getting restless about what you being here means. I told a friend, and she told everyone else. Trust me—it's better this way. Otherwise they might have been planning to starve you instead of feed you.'

She grinned, and felt herself relax. This wasn't so bad. They were having a normal conversation. Just as she would with any of her colleagues. But then Blake smiled in return, and her heart thumped with that incredibly fast rhythm she was beginning to think was personalised for him. Like a ringtone.

She cleared her throat. 'How's everything going here?'

'Good.' He took another sip of the coffee, and settled back in his chair. 'I've created interest amongst my contacts by highlighting how beneficial it would be for them to be a part of my business, so we're looking at a few potential prospects.'

She stared at him. 'You're good.'

He grinned at her. 'Thanks. It's going to be a lot easier for both of us now that you've realised that.'

She felt her lips twitch. 'It's a good thing I have, then. Now, what do you need from *me*, Mr Owen?'

'Blake,' he said, and shrugged when she frowned. 'I feel like my father every time you call me that.'

'Fine,' she said, and forced herself to say his name without feeling anything. 'Blake, what do you need from me?'

There was a pause as the question settled between them, and it made her feel as though she'd said something inappropriate. And the way he looked at her made her feel like she wanted to give him whatever he thought he needed from her—even if it wasn't something that was strictly professional. She exhaled slowly, and hoped that the tension inside her would seep out with her breath. It did—but only because he finally responded.

'Well, we need to start working on a proposal. But, since

I'm still at the stage of securing possible investors, please start drawing up a list of places you think we can include in the tour portion of the proposal. Include your motivations for why you think we should visit them. We can take it from there.'

'Okay,' she said, and then frowned when he grabbed his coffee and hung the tie that had been carelessly thrown across his chair over his shoulder. 'Where are you going?'

'To work in Connor's office for a while. Just so we don't disturb each other while I'm busy with my calls.'

He nodded at her, and then left her wondering why he had asked her to work with him in the conference room when he wouldn't even be there.

'Welcome back,' Callie said later, as Blake entered the room.

'Thanks.' He nodded, and opted for a glass of water instead of the coffee he knew he should take a break from. Especially since his throat was nearly raw from all the talking he had been doing for the last few hours.

He had been successful—had spoken to many of the parties who had contacted him—and he could no longer justify staying away from the conference room. Not when he had insisted Callie work with him and that they should do things together.

'What do you have so far?'

Callie gave him a measured look, and immediately he felt chastised that he hadn't made small talk first. But he didn't trust himself to do that just yet. Not while he was still trying to convince himself that working with her had been a *business* decision, and had nothing to do with the way she made him feel. Especially after he had told himself that he would stay away from her.

Even now, as she sat poised behind the table, her white

shirt snug enough for him to see curves he didn't want to notice, he could feel a pull between them that had nothing to do with business.

And it scared him.

'Well, I've done exactly as you asked. I've drawn up a list of must-see locations that I think we should consider for your proposal.'

She stood and handed him the list, and he saw that her black trousers were still as neat as they had been that morning, when she'd first walked in. She looked pristine—even though, based on the papers in his hands, she had been working extensively on her planning.

'You can have a look at them and let me know what you think, but I don't think there will be a problem with any of them. I've also tentatively set up some tour ideas.'

Blake struggled to get over the way her proximity threatened to take over his senses, but he forced it to the back of his mind and listened to her explain some of the ideas she'd had. As she did, his own began to form. A business proposal that would complement what she had in mind. But he didn't know if it would work without seeing it first.

'Okay—great.' He put down his glass of water and gestured towards the chair where her jacket lay. 'Grab your things and we can go immediately.'

'What?' Her eyes widened.

'I want you to show me these must-see locations. I mean, what you have is great—theoretically—but I need you to show them to me so that I know they work in practice.'

'And you want to go right now?'

'Yes.' He walked to the door and opened it for her. 'The longer we wait, the longer we delay finalising plans. And that's not the way I work.'

Callie stood staring at him, as though at any minute he was going to say, *Just joking!* When she realised that it wasn't going to happen, she grabbed her jacket and hand-bag and walked past him through the open door.

Her scent was still as enticing as it had been that first night, and for a brief moment—not for the first time—Blake wondered if he was making a mistake. He had asked her to work with him on impulse, although he had known it was a logical, even smart way of approaching the inter-national investor angle once he'd had a chance to think about it. So why was it that he'd avoided working with her for the entire morning if he was so convinced that it was all business between them?

It didn't matter, he thought, and shook away any linger-ing doubts. He had a job to do. And that job would come first.

Callie waited as John, the parking valet, pulled up in Blake's silver sedan. This evidence of his wealth jostled her, though she knew she shouldn't be surprised. Of *course* her boss had money, she thought, and watched Blake thank John and wave him away when the valet moved to open the door for her. Instead, Blake did it himself, and she got in, her skin prickling when she brushed against him by accident.

She ignored it, instead focusing on the car. It was just as luxurious on the inside as it was on the outside—as she'd expected—with gadgets that she didn't quite think were necessary. But, then again, she drove an old second-hand car that made her arms ache every time she had to turn the wheel. Perhaps if she had thought about gadgets, she wouldn't have to worry that her car might stall every time she drove it.

Nevertheless, she was proud of the little thing. It was the first car she'd ever bought, and she'd worked incredibly hard since leaving high school and saved every last rand to buy it. Granted, she'd worked for her parents, and she knew they had been liberal in their payment.

She smiled at the memory, and caught her breath when he asked, 'What's that for?'

She hadn't realised he was paying attention to her. She should have known better. *Always be on guard*, she reminded herself.

'I was just admiring your car. And comparing it with mine. It doesn't,' she said with a smile when he gave her a questioning look.

'I bought it when I knew I was coming to Cape Town. I had no idea how long I was going to be here, and I didn't want to impose on my father and use one of his indefinitely. I'll probably sell it as soon as I know where I'm going next.'

Though her heart stuck on the information that he would be leaving, she asked, 'You didn't own a car before?'

'I did. But I sold it a while ago—when I realised I would be travelling a lot more.'

'But don't you need one for when you're at home?'

He took a right turn and glanced over to her. 'I don't have a home.'

For some reason Callie found that incredibly sad. 'I'm sorry.'

'Don't be. It's a choice.'

She wanted to ask him why, but the silence that stretched between them made it clear that he didn't want to reveal the reasons for that choice. She respected that. There were things she wouldn't want to reveal to him either.

'Blake, shouldn't *I* be driving?'

He frowned. 'Why? Can't you direct me to where we're going?'

'I can, but that won't give you the experience we'd be giving potential investors. And that's what you want, isn't it? That's why we're here?'

'I suppose so.' He signalled and pulled off to the side of the road.

They switched seats, and for a moment Callie just enjoyed the sleekness of the car. A car *she* would be driving for the day. She resisted the urge to giggle—and then the urge disappeared when she became aware of the other things sitting on the driver's side meant. The heat of his body was almost embedded into the seat. She could smell him. She traced her hands over the steering wheel, thinking how his had been there only a few moments ago.

She cleared her throat, willing the heat she felt through her body to go away. After putting on her safety belt, she pulled back into the road and aligned her thoughts. But they stuck when she realised he was looking at her.

'What?' she asked nervously. 'Am I doing something wrong?'

'No.' He smiled, and it somewhat eased the tension between them. 'I just didn't think this was how the day would turn out. You driving me around in my car.'

'Are you disappointed?' Callie turned left, a plan forming in her mind for their day. It was more of an outline, but she was sure it would suffice for something so last-minute.

'No. You're doing quite a remarkable job—especially considering I'm not a fan of being a passenger.'

'Really?' She glanced over in surprise. 'I thought you would be used to being chauffeured.'

'When the need arises, yes. But I try to keep those occasions to the minimum.'

'Because you like to be the one in control?'

He frowned, and for a minute Callie thought she had gone too far.

'Maybe, though I think it has more to do with my father. He loves his cars, and couldn't wait to share that love with me. So I like to drive him when I can so we can talk about something other than the hotel.'

Callie felt her heart ache at the revelation she didn't think Blake knew he had let slip. And, though a part of her urged her to accept the information about his relationship with his father without comment, she couldn't help but say, 'It must have made him proud that you took over his legacy. The hotels,' she elaborated when she felt his questioning glance. 'I read the article *Corporate Times* did on the two of you when he retired.'

She didn't mention that she'd read it—and many others— just a few weeks ago, when she'd heard Blake would be coming to Cape Town. When he didn't respond, she looked over and saw a puzzled expression on his face. Nerves kicked in and she felt the babbling that would come from her mouth before it even started.

'I just meant that he must be proud of you since he loved the hotel business so much. And since you're also, in some ways, his legacy, it's like his legacy running his legacy...' She shook her head at how silly that sounded. 'Anyway, that's why I said he must be proud.'

Blake didn't respond, and she wondered if she'd upset him. She should probably just have left it alone, she thought as she drove up the inclined road that led to Table Mountain. But it wasn't as if she was prying. Okay, maybe it was. But she'd only said something she thought was true. Surely he couldn't fault her for that?

'I think you might be right.'

He spoke so softly that she was grateful the radio was off or she might have missed it.

'He doesn't talk about it much, but I think maybe he is.'

Callie nodded, and was amazed at how those few words confirmed what she'd suspected earlier about his relationship with his father. She considered pressing for more information, but he asked her a question before she could.

'Where are you taking me first?'

She bit her lip to prevent her questions about his family from tumbling out. 'Table Mountain. Our number one tourist attraction, and also an incredible experience if you live here. This would be the first place I'd want to see if I hadn't been to Cape Town before.' She frowned. 'But, since you *have* been to Cape Town before, I'm sure this trip is redundant for you.'

'No. I haven't been up the mountain.'

He shrugged when she shot him an incredulous look.

'I've only been here for business or to visit my family. I don't do touristy things.'

'But…' She found herself at a loss for words. 'Don't you and your family go out together? I mean, this is the best outing for a family.'

'For certain kinds of families, yes, I suppose it is. But our family isn't one of those.'

Again, Callie felt an incredible grief at his words. They'd been driving for less than twenty minutes and already she knew that Blake didn't know if his father was proud of him or not, that their conversations mostly revolved around business, and that his family didn't do outings together.

She didn't know what was worse, she realised as she parked. Having a family—parents—and not having a great relationship with them, or having no parents but wonderful memories of them. She had always known that her parents were proud of her. And suddenly, for the first time since they'd died, she was grateful for those memories she had of her parents, no longer pushing them away.

CHAPTER FIVE

'IT'S BEAUTIFUL, ISN'T IT?'

Callie's voice was soft next to him, and he turned slightly to her, not wanting to move his eyes from the view.

'I don't think I've ever seen anything like it,' he said, knowing that the words couldn't be more true.

They stood at the top of Table Mountain, looking over the city and the harbour. If he walked to the other side, he knew he'd see the beaches and the ocean in a way he'd never experienced before. They weren't the only ones up there, but for the peace Blake felt he thought that they might as well be. He didn't think about failure or disappointment here. He felt so small, so insignificant, that thinking about his own problems seemed selfish.

Though he'd just done it, he walked back to the other side of the mountain and looked down at the ocean. There were houses scattered across the peaks of the hills above it, and he felt a tug of jealousy that the residents there were privy to such a spectacular view every day of their lives.

'I wonder if those people know how lucky they are to live there,' he said, aware that Callie was standing right next to him.

From the moment they'd stepped into the cable car to get up the mountain she'd left him to his thoughts. Thoughts that were tangled around her and her questions about his family. He hadn't wanted to talk about it, and he thought she'd realised as much when she'd remained quiet after her last question about going out as a family. But even though she was silent he had never been more aware of her presence. That peaceful, steady presence that he hadn't expected.

'Well, most of them are rich tycoons who purchase those houses and rent them out. Some are wealthy Cape Townians who invest or buy just because they can.' She paused, seemed almost hesitant to continue. 'And others are very aware of how lucky they are.'

'You know some of the others?'

'You could say so.' A ghost of a smile shadowed her lips. 'I live there.'

He struggled not to gape at her, but he couldn't resist the words. 'You *live* there?'

'Yes.'

The smile was full-blown now, and it warmed something inside him that he had thought was frozen.

'Right over there.'

She pointed, and he wondered which of the spectacular houses was hers.

'Connor said he lives in one of the main parts of town.'

'*He* does, yes. But we don't live together. He moved out of the house when he went to university. My parents were devastated, but they had me, and I had no plans for moving out. I commuted to university for my first year and then...' She trailed off and cleared her throat. 'And now I still live there.'

Her words made him want to ask so many questions. He wanted to break through whatever barrier she'd put up and find out why she hadn't continued with her story. Instead he settled for one of his many questions.

'Alone?'

She looked at him, and the pain in her eyes nearly stole his breath.

'Alone.'

Silence stretched between them while Blake tried to find words to comfort a hurt he didn't know anything about. But words failed him, and all he could do was wait helplessly.

'Come on—there's a lot more to show you,' she said, after what felt like for ever, and he followed her back to the cable car.

Somewhere in the back of his mind he was reminded that they were there for business, and as soon as the thought registered he took his phone from his pocket. He opened a memo and recorded Table Mountain as an approved place for the investors to see.

'This must be a really popular place for your tours,' he said as the cable car began its descent.

'It is.'

Was that relief he heard in her voice?

'I usually begin here or end here. Ending here usually works when the tour starts in the afternoon and we can make it up the mountain for sunset.'

'I'd love to see that.'

She smiled. 'It's definitely something to see. Maybe some day I'll take you.'

They were simple words, but Blake felt them shift something inside him. An emotion he hadn't experienced until he'd met her jolted him. *Hope.* He hadn't hoped for anything in a long time. Nor had he thought he would want to watch the sunset on top of a mountain with a woman who made him feel things he didn't want to feel.

'Where to next?' he asked when they reached the car.

'That, Mr Owen, would take all the fun out of today.'

She grinned, and he felt himself smiling back, despite what he was fighting inside.

* * *

'If Table Mountain is included in a morning tour I usually schedule it for about ten. We'd usually end there at about twelve, and then either have lunch at the top of the mountain or take a drive down to Camps Bay to have lunch.'

She nearly purred at the way the car was handling the curves of the road.

'I usually prefer driving down, because then our guests get to experience this amazing drive. And once there they can have lunch at one of the many upper-class but affordable restaurants.'

'I can't fault you on that,' Blake said, and she glanced over to see he was looking out of the window. 'This view is amazing.'

'I know.'

She smiled, and thought that her tour wasn't going badly. She hadn't shown him much yet, but she wanted to take him to the places she knew would provide opportunities to market the hotel to his investors. And she hadn't been able to resist showing him the best attraction—Table Mountain—first.

'If they like it, I tell them they can stay at the beach for the afternoon and we'll send a shuttle to fetch them when they're ready.'

'Sounds like a tourist's dream.'

'It is,' she agreed. 'Although, to be fair, it's a resident's dream as well.'

'The grateful ones.'

He looked at her and smiled, and she had to force her eyes back to the road.

'If you live here, you must drive this road every day?'

'Mostly, yes,' she said, and thanked her heart for returning to its usual pace. 'But I live further up, so I wouldn't take this part of the road. It leads to the beach,' she continued, when she realised he was probably just as much of a tourist in Cape Town as her guests were.

'Do you often go to the beach?'

She slowed down as they turned onto the road along the beachfront. 'Probably once a week. Never to swim or tan.' She smiled and drove into an underground car park. 'I usually go in the evenings for a run or a walk. It helps clear my head.'

They got out, and she suddenly realised that she hadn't told him she thought they should have lunch. Self-doubt kicked in, and she said nervously, 'Um…there isn't really much to do here unless you have your swimming trunks hidden under your suit.'

She flushed when she realised what she had said. Even more so when she thought about him in swimming gear.

'But I *can* introduce you to the management at some of the restaurants the hotel guests usually frequent during the tours. And we can grab lunch on our way to the next stop.'

She didn't wait for his response but instead led the way to the beachfront, where the line of restaurants was. The idea of sitting down and having lunch with him was still slightly terrifying to her, so she was taking the easy way out.

As she introduced Blake to the different restaurateurs she watched him slip into a professional mode that oozed charm and sophistication. He asked the right questions, said the right things, and ensured that everyone respected him. Which meant that many of them—whom Callie knew quite well—were now even more interested in the Elegance Hotel, having met its CEO. And they genuinely seemed to like him.

She grudgingly admitted that it made *her* like him a little more, too, but told herself that she was talking about her boss—not the man she'd met in the elevator.

Desperately trying to distract herself, she asked if he'd like to eat and then took him to one of stores that did take-away wraps and salads. They ordered, and stood in silence. Callie waited for him to say something—anything—about all the people they'd spoken to, but instead he sat down at one of the tables and stared out at the ocean.

She joined him, and yet the silence continued. When she couldn't take it any more she asked, 'So, do you like the beach?'

Callie knew it wasn't her best shot, but the silence had made her observant, and the more she observed, the more she responded to Blake. She felt the movement of her heart, the heat in her body, but she refused to succumb to them. She just wanted to talk, to take her mind off what being in his presence did to her.

'Who doesn't?'

His eyes didn't move from the ocean, but she could see a slight smile on his lips.

'I didn't go nearly as much as I would have liked to when I was younger. And when I took over the hotels there just wasn't time. I don't know when I was last at a beach like this.'

'You should make the time.' She offered a tentative smile when he glanced back at her. 'At both our stops so far you've seemed... I don't know...at peace with the world.' She blushed when he turned his body so that he was fac-ing her. 'I just think that if something makes you feel at peace, makes you happy, you should make the time for it.'

He didn't respond for a while, and Callie bit her lip in fear that she might have said the wrong thing. His eyes lowered to her lips then, and the heat she'd felt earlier was nothing compared to what flowed through her body at his gaze. If he had been anyone else she would have leaned forward and kissed him. But he wasn't anyone else, and she couldn't look away when he looked back into her eyes.

'What do *you* make time for, Callie McKenzie? What makes you happy or makes you feel peaceful?'

The question would have been innocent if he hadn't still been looking at her as if she was the only woman on earth.

She cleared her throat. 'Gardening. I garden.'

Blake tilted his head with a frown, and then grinned. 'I would never have guessed that.'

She smiled back at him, grateful that the tension between them had abated. 'I don't blame you. I'm terrible at it. I buy things and plant them, but mostly I pay someone to look after them.'

He laughed, and Callie couldn't believe how attracted she was to him when he looked so carefree. 'So you plant things but don't look after them? And that makes you happy?'

She nodded, remembering the first time she had done it.

'Yes, it does. It reminds me of my mother. We used to do it together—though I was just as bad then as I am now.' She stared out to the ocean, memories making her forget where she was. Who she was with. 'But my mom would just let me plant, and then she'd fix what I did wrong. When I was old enough to realise, I asked her why she let me do it.' She looked down, barely noticing how her hands played with the end of her top. 'She told me that it was because it made me happy, and that if something makes you happy you should do it.'

She looked up at him and saw compassion in his eyes, before she realised that tears had filled her own. She lifted her head, embarrassed and raw from what she'd told him, the way she'd reacted, and only looked back at him when she was sure she had her emotions under control.

He took a hand from her lap and squeezed it, but before

he could say what he clearly wanted to their order number was called.

They grabbed their lunch and without saying anything ate as they walked back to the car.

She wasn't sure what had prompted her to tell him that. Maybe it had been the moment...the setting. But the more likely answer—the one she didn't want to consider—was that maybe it was *him*. He made her feel things—things she would fight as long as she could. Feeling safe enough, secure enough to open up to someone would take a lot more than just a few hours with him.

And it wouldn't be with her boss. No, she thought as she threw away her half-eaten wrap. She couldn't open up to her boss.

Blake had wanted to say something to her from the moment she had told him about her mother. He wanted to comfort her, tell her that it was okay that she'd told him, that the fear and surprise he'd seen in her eyes when she'd realised what she'd said wasn't necessary. But instead, like the coward he was, he stayed silent and went along with the rest of the tour as though she *hadn't* just let him see such an intimate part of herself.

On their way back from the beach she drove him up to the Bo-Kaap, where colourful houses lined the streets. She told him about the rich cultural heritage of the area—how it had come to be a place of refuge for the Islamic slaves who had been freed in 1834. She pointed out the museum that had been established over a century later, and had been designed according to the typical Muslim home in the nineteenth century.

'The design is in the process of changing at the moment, but the museum will tell you quite a lot about one of the most thriving cultural communities in Cape Town.' She turned the car around and drove back down the hill. 'You should make an effort to visit it some time.'

After that she took him to the V&A Waterfront—another cultural hub of the city. It was both a mall and a dock, he discovered as they walked past a mass of shoppers to get to the actual waterfront. The large boats there were either docked for repair or in to pick up cargo, and the smaller ones either belonged to private citizens or were available for hire.

They also transported people to Robben Island, he discovered as he climbed into a boat and sat next to Callie.

Since it was the last trip of the day the boat was quite full, and he was forced to sit closer to her than he would have liked. Her perfume made him feel a need he had never felt before. Even mixed with the salty smell of the sea, its effect on him was potent. He wanted her to turn to him so that he could kiss her, just so that he could make his need for her subside.

He couldn't shake it off even when they arrived at the island where Nelson Mandela had famously spent twenty-seven years of his life. His thoughts were filled with her as the tour guide walked them through a typical day in the prison, as he told them about the ex-President of South Africa and showed them his cell.

By the time they had got back to the waterfront, it was late enough for their day to end. But he didn't want that. No, he didn't want the day to end. Because then he would have to go back to the hotel…back to being her boss.

'We should go for dinner,' he said, without fully realising it. 'It's been a long day and we've barely eaten. I think the least I can do for you after today is take you out.'

Her mouth opened and closed a few times, and his heart pounded at the prospect of her saying no. But then she answered him.

'Yeah…okay. Where do you want to go?'

'Somewhere you love.' He cleared his throat. 'I want to see more of Cape Town, but not just the side that your guests see.'

'Um…' She looked lost for a second, and then she nodded. 'Okay, I'll take you to one of my favourite places. But you can drive this time.'

He nodded and climbed into the driver's seat, following her directions until she'd finished typing the location into his GPS.

'You weren't lying when you said you haven't seen much of Cape Town, were you?'

The question was so random that he didn't take the time to think his answer through. 'No. My father and stepmother moved here when he retired, which was about eight years ago. I've probably been here twice a year since then to see them, and a few more times for the hotel. But that's the extent of my travels to Cape Town.'

'Where did you live before?'

'Port Elizabeth, for the most part. But, like I mentioned, I travelled a lot between hotels.'

'Do you miss it? Port Elizabeth?'

He thought about telling her the truth—that he didn't miss being there because it reminded him of his relationship with Julia, and how he had failed at that and let his business down. But that would only open himself up to more questions, and force him to face things he didn't want to remember.

Luckily the GPS declared that they had arrived, and he used the opportunity to deflect the question.

'What *is* this place?'

She tilted her head, as though she knew what he was doing, but answered him.

'It's called Sakari—which means "sweet" in Inuit. They

specialise in dessert and have the most delicious milk-shakes—though the food is pretty incredible, too.'

They walked inside, and Blake took a moment to process the look of the restaurant. It wasn't big, but it comfortably fitted its customers without seeming stuffy. There were even a few couches in front of a fireplace. Since it was still summer, the fire wasn't lit, but the couches were filled with people ranging through all ages. The doors were open and a slight breeze filled the room, causing the candles that had been lit for atmosphere to flutter every now and then.

It was a perfect summer's evening, he thought, in a perfect—and intimate—restaurant. He shrugged off what the thought conjured inside him and returned his attention to the hostess, who was greeting Callie with a warmth that he'd never witnessed before.

'Hi, Bianca, how are you?'

Callie spoke to the hostess as though she were her best friend.

The woman had a full head of black and blue curls that complemented her gorgeous olive skin.

'Great, thanks. Ben and I just found out we're having a girl!'

Blake only then realised the woman was pregnant as he looked at the slight bump under her apron. He figured she was probably around four months, and waited as Callie congratulated Bianca and asked if she could squeeze them in.

'Of course. Give me a second.'

Callie turned to him and her eyes were bright. 'Bianca is my father's business partner's daughter. She opened this little restaurant about eight years ago. My dad was so proud of her—almost like she was his own.'

'Was…?'

'Yes.'

Her eyes dimmed, and suddenly he put together all

the bits and pieces that she'd told him throughout the day. Her house, the almost-tears when she'd spoken about her mother, and now the past tense with her father. And just as quickly he realised he'd pressed her when he shouldn't have.

'Callie, I'm so sorry.'

CHAPTER SIX

'DON'T WORRY ABOUT IT.'

Callie cleared her throat and smiled when Bianca led them to a table in the corner. She knew the woman had probably squeezed it in herself, and she thanked her and rolled her eyes at the wink Bianca sent her after looking at Blake.

Callie busied herself with looking at the menu, and though she could feel him staring at her eventually Blake did the same. She sighed in relief, knowing that she didn't want to talk about her parents' deaths with him. She just wanted to have dinner and go home, where she would be safe from the feelings that stirred through her when she was with him.

'Their burgers are really good. And of course you should have one with a milkshake.'

She spoke because she didn't want to revert to their previous topic of conversation.

'Sounds good,' he said, and placed his menu down. And then he asked exactly what she'd tried to prevent. 'When did you lose your parents?'

She didn't want to talk about this, she thought, and shut her eyes. But when she opened them again his own were filled with compassion and sincerity. So she gave him a brief answer. 'Almost a decade ago now.'

He nodded, and was silent for a bit. 'My mom left when I was eleven. It's not the same thing, of course, but I think I may understand a little of what you feel.'

She stared at him—not because his mom had left, but because he'd shared the fact with her. It made her feel—*comforted*. That was terrible, she thought, but then he smiled at her, and she realised that comforting her had been his intention. She found herself smiling back before she averted her eyes.

How did he *do* that? And in this place that was so personal to her? She'd brought him here out of instinct, because she'd honestly had no idea what else to do. He'd put her on the spot and the only place she'd been able to think of was the one her friend owned—the one she had so often come to with her father in the year before his death.

She tried to pop in as often as possible, even just to grab one of the chocolate croissants that Sakari was known for. Maybe it was because she didn't want to lose the connection she'd had with her father. But it had taken a long time after his death for her to realise that.

'I know this isn't what you're used to.' She changed the subject to a safer topic. 'I mean, it isn't a five-star restaurant or anything, but it is highly rated.'

He laughed. 'It isn't what I'm used to—but not because I'm a snob, which you seem to be implying.'

She blushed, because maybe he was right.

'I just don't have time to find places like this. I usually eat at the hotel, or go out to dinner for business.'

'Do you enjoy it?'

'My job?'

She smiled, and wondered if he knew how cute he looked when he was confused. 'No—being so busy.'

He didn't respond immediately, and when the waiter came to take their order he still hadn't said anything. She didn't press, because somehow she knew he was formulating his answer.

'It works for me.' He shrugged. 'Keeping busy means I don't have to think about the problems in my personal life.'

She hadn't expected such a candid answer, but she took the opportunity to say, 'Your family?'

He nodded, though he didn't look at her. 'Partly, yes. And some other things.'

Callie suddenly remembered what he'd said about dating, and how he had told her without words that a woman had made him cynical about it. As much as she wanted to know, she didn't ask. She didn't want to tell him about how her parents had died, or how she'd fallen apart when they had. And clearly there were things that *he* didn't want to speak to her about either. And that was fair. Though a part of her hoped that it would change.

'Well, I hope that one day, when this mess is all over, you'll take a day to relax.'

'Relax?'

'Yes, it's this thing us normal people do—usually in the evenings or over weekends—when we try to put aside thoughts of business and enjoy the moment.'

He leaned back in his seat and grinned. 'Never heard of it.'

She laughed. 'I could show you some time. It's pretty easy.'

'I'd like that.'

He spoke softly, and suddenly the noise in the restaurant faded to the background as she held his gaze. Thoughts of the two of them spending evenings together, weekends, made her heart pound. And yearn.

He lifted a hand and laid it over hers, and suddenly the sweetness of her thoughts turned to fire. She wanted to lean over, kiss him. She wanted to know what it would be like to

feel his lips on hers, his hands on her body. His hand tightened on hers and she wondered if he knew her thoughts.
The way his eyes heated as he looked at her made her think
he did, and she leaned forward—just a bit. If this was going
to happen, then she didn't want him only to be a spectator.

And then the waiter brought their milkshakes, told them
their burgers were about ten minutes away, and the spell
was broken. Immediately Callie pulled her hand from under
his and placed it in her lap, where it couldn't do anything
ridiculous like brush his shampoo ad hair out of his face.
She drank from her chocolate milkshake, and wished she'd
ordered something that would actually help quench her suddenly parched throat.

'Do you ever bring Connor here?'

She looked up, saw the apology in his eyes—or was it
regret?—and nodded in gratitude.

'Sure. If we do supper we either do it here, or somewhere
close to the hotel. It depends on whether we're working or
just meeting up.'

They continued their conversation, steering clear of any
topics that might reveal anything personal about each other.
And, though she longed to know more, she didn't ask about
his family, or the mysterious woman in his past. She didn't
think he spoke of it very much, regardless, and she didn't
want to be the one he did it with. She ignored her thoughts
that screamed the contrary, and instead focused on eating her food.

At the end of their meal, he offered to take her home.

'No, thanks. I'll just get a taxi.'

'That's silly. It isn't that far, and it's unnecessary for
you to pay—' He stopped when he saw the look on her
face. 'What?'

'I don't want you to take me home,' she said, because

the alternative, *I'd want to invite you in if you did*, wasn't appropriate.

'Of course.' He frowned, and stuffed cash inside the bill. 'Can I at least call you that taxi?'

She smiled her gratitude at his acceptance. 'Sure.'

He waited with her for the taxi. Since Sakari was only a few kilometres from the sea she could smell it, and feel the chilly breeze it brought even in summer.

She shivered, and he glanced down at her. Without a word he took off his jacket and laid it over her shoulders. The action brought him face-to-face with her, and gently he pulled at the jacket, drawing her in so that she was pressed to his chest. She felt her breathing accelerate at the feel of his body against hers, at the look in his eyes when they rested on her face.

'What is it about you that makes me forget who I am?' he asked, his voice low and husky, and her skin turned to gooseflesh.

'I could ask you the same thing,' she responded, before she even knew what she was saying.

But their words only encouraged whatever was happening between them, she thought. Especially as they stood together, frozen in time, looking at each other. Neither of them moved—not away from each other, nor any closer— and Callie could feel the hesitation, the uncertainty that hung between them. She could also feel the want, the need, that kept them there despite the ambiguity of their feelings.

The longer she stood there, the more pressing her desire to kiss him became, and she moved forward, just a touch, so that their lips were a breath away from each other's. His eyes heated and he leaned down. Callie closed her eyes, lost in anticipation of the kiss...

The sound of a car's horn pierced the air and they jerked apart. She lost her balance, and was sure she would soon be landing on her butt, but a strong arm snaked around her waist and pulled her upright. Again she found herself in Blake's arms, almost exactly as she had been a few moments before, but the magic had passed.

She cleared her throat. 'Thanks for…um…saving me.'

'Of course.' His words were stilted. 'I assume that's your taxi?'

She turned and looked around and saw that the hoot had indeed come from a taxi. She closed her eyes in frustration and then turned back to him.

'Yeah, it is. Thanks again.' She gestured towards the restaurant and felt like an idiot. 'And…um… I hope you feel more confident about the tour for the proposal now, having seen some of the stops.'

He stuffed his hands in his pockets. 'I do. I enjoyed today. I'll see you tomorrow.'

She nodded and smiled, and then awkwardly walked to the taxi, knowing he was still watching her. She lifted her hand as the taxi pulled away, and resisted the urge to look back at him.

'Blake?' Callie pushed open the conference room door and saw him sitting at the head of the table, where she'd found him the first time.

Was that only yesterday? she wondered, and nodded a greeting when he looked up.

'Morning,' Blake said, his tone brisk, and immediately Callie's back went up. 'Grab a seat and we can start talking about the proposal.'

Callie stood for a moment and wondered if this was a joke. There was no familiarity in his tone, no semblance of the man she'd spent the day with.

The man she had nearly kissed.

When he looked up at her expectantly she walked to a seat at the table and felt her temper ignite.

'So, I've gone over your list of places—including the ones we saw yesterday.'

Oh, she thought, so he *did* remember it. 'Yes…?'

'I have some ideas on how to complement the business side of the proposal with the tour. Have a look at these and let me know what you think.'

Callie took the papers he offered her and began to look through them. But somehow she kept reading the same line over and over again.

What was wrong with him? He was treating her as he had after that welcoming event. Cold, brisk, professional. The aloof and unattainable boss. She knew she shouldn't expect more from him—or *anything* from him, for that matter—but she'd hoped that their day yesterday, the things they'd learned about one another, the attraction they'd *both* felt, would have eased things between them. She didn't want her spine to feel like steel from the tension in the room. And yet that was exactly what was happening.

She cleared her throat as she built up the nerve to address it. 'Blake, did I upset you last night?'

He barely acknowledged that she was speaking, but she pushed on.

'When I told you I didn't want you to take me home? Or when we nearly—'

'Callie, I don't need you to explain anything. I just need you to read through the document and tell me your thoughts on it.'

He continued working on his laptop and didn't see her jaw drop. Just as quickly as it had dropped, she closed it again. This wasn't the man she'd spent the day with yesterday, she realised. Now she was dealing with her boss.

The one who had made her feel as if she was dishonest and nosy when she'd first met him.

Suddenly all the regrets she'd had about not letting him take her home, about not kissing him, about not telling him more about herself faded away. All the questions she'd wanted to ask him about his mother, his father, the woman he wouldn't talk about, no longer mattered.

She should be thanking him, she thought. He was saving her, really. She didn't have to worry about developing feelings for him. She didn't have to think about opening up to him. She didn't have to open up to her boss. She could be just as brisk and aloof as he was.

'Of course,' she replied, and read through the document, making notes and ignoring the disappointment that filled her.

Blake threw his pen against the door five minutes after Callie had left for the day. It had been a week since their tour together. Seven days of complete torture, five of which she'd spent sitting across from him, answering all his questions politely, only speaking when it had to do with work.

And *he'd* done that. He'd pushed her away with his professionalism. The stupid professionalism that he'd prided himself on before Julia. No, he thought. He'd never been this bad before Julia. She'd made him into this cold person. This person who didn't open up even when he wanted to.

He closed his eyes and leaned back in his chair. That wasn't completely fair. Julia may have brought it out in him, but he'd made the decision to be cold. Just like now, when he'd decided that after the day they'd spent together—after he'd almost told her too much…after he'd almost kissed her—that Callie was too dangerous to his resolve to stay away from relationships.

So he'd ignored the fact that their day had meant something to him and dealt with her just as he dealt with any other employee. And each time he did, he could sense the animosity growing inside her.

She didn't deserve this, he thought, and loosened the tie which seemed to be strangling him. She didn't deserve to feel as if she had been the only one to want something more than professionalism.

But it had to be this way. Or else, if they started something, he might begin to need her—to want her and want things he'd forgotten about a long time ago. Julia had done a number on him, he knew, but he'd deserved it after the way he'd reacted to her. He'd been attracted to her like no one else before, and she'd had a sweet kid who'd needed a father.

He rubbed his hands over his face and thought about the first time he'd met Brent. He and Julia hadn't been dating very long—perhaps a month—when she'd brought the boy to work with her because her babysitter for the school holidays was sick that day. Brent had been sitting with Julia at the table when Blake had got to the restaurant where they'd planned to have lunch. Blake had known Julia had a son, but hadn't thought too much about it until he'd met the boy.

'I'm glad you two finally get to meet,' she'd said, her arm around her son's chair. 'Brent, this is the man that I've been telling you about.'

The boy had looked up with solemn eyes, and examined him for a long time. Then he'd asked Blake, 'Are you going to be my new daddy?'

It had shocked him, and he'd resisted the urge to laugh nervously. But then he'd looked up into Julia's eyes, seen what he'd wanted to see, and replied, 'Maybe.'

He shook his head and stood now, his body tight from sitting at the table for the entire day. And from the direction of his thoughts. Being around Callie brought up all sorts of emotions inside him, and awakened memories he'd thought he'd put to rest.

Such as the fact that he had wanted to give that boy a family like the one he'd never had.

His mother had done a number on his father as well, and since then he and his father had always focused on their joint interests instead of on family. He'd never had a normal family situation. Just as he had told Callie.

Which was exactly why being professional with her was so important. He couldn't afford to fall for her. She was everything he had tried to stay away from, and he'd already revealed things to her that he didn't even think he'd known about himself.

It was the best decision to distance himself, Blake decided. And he didn't question why it felt so wrong.

CHAPTER SEVEN

'CALLIE, BLAKE NEEDS TO see you in Conference Room A.'

Kate popped her head into Callie's office and then disappeared almost immediately. But not before Callie saw the expression on her face. She recognised that expression. It was the sympathetic one Kate usually wore when Callie told her about a horrible tour she'd been on.

Was Blake annoyed with her? She'd left him a note in the conference room to tell him that she wanted to prepare alone before their first potential investor arrived at ten. As she made her way to the conference room she faced the fact that it was certainly a possibility. He might have wanted to talk to her about the proposal and run through it one last time.

But she hadn't wanted to deal with him that morning, when her nerves had already been tightly coiled. Just being in his presence made her feel so tense that sometimes she felt sick. So this morning, before the most important tour of her life, she'd just wanted a bit of peace.

When she arrived at the room she saw Blake standing with his back facing the door.

'Blake? Kate said you wanted to see me?'

He turned to her, his face calm, though she thought she saw an eyebrow twitch. She took a step towards him and then stopped when she realised she'd mistaken calm for professional. It was the same look he'd had on his face when she'd walked in on him and Connor talking the day all this had started.

'What do you need me for?'

'Both Mr Vercelli and Mr Jung arrived this morning. Apparently Mr Jung had an urgent matter to resolve in South Africa, and so took an earlier flight to Cape Town. Instead of individual proposals, customised for two different potential investors, we're going to have to do them both today.'

Callie felt her stomach churn, and sat down on one of the conference room chairs so her legs didn't give out on her. She closed her eyes and let her mind go through the possibilities. Could they still do two different proposals? No, that wouldn't work. And nor could they make one of the men wait, do it in two shifts, since both proposals included dinner.

'Callie?'

Blake was crouched in front of her when she opened her eyes.

'Are you okay? You're pale.'

He brushed a piece of hair out of her face and her mind, which had been so busy before, blanked. And then she remembered that they had a job to do and nodded.

'I'm fine.' She stood, and he rose with her, and for a moment they were so close she could feel his body heat. 'What does this mean, though?'

'It means we need to work on a new plan that merges the two proposals.' He said it confidently, his voice back to its usual formality, as though this had always been his plan and he hadn't just shown his concern for her.

'And you aren't in the least worried that this might turn out poorly?' she asked, her own fears motivating words that she wouldn't have spoken if it didn't irk her that he had recovered from their contact much faster than she had.

'No, Callie, I'm not. This is what I do.'

He shrugged and walked around her, and she thanked the heavens when her mind started working normally again.

'And, today, this is what *we* do.'

His emphasis stiffened her spine and she realised he wanted her to step up. So she took a moment, searching through the possibilities, looking for some way to maintain the two proposals they'd worked on. She knew both tours like the back of her hand, and before she could consciously think about it she started pulling threads of commonality from each of them.

'Okay…so Mr Vercelli wants to experience the Italian side of Cape Town—family was our angle on that one.' She spoke almost without realising it, needing to hear her ideas out loud to figure out whether they made sense. 'And Mr Jung wants to experience Cape Town culture, which we know is so different from his own Chinese culture.'

She frowned, and then looked up at Blake.

'But isn't family in a place fondly called the Mother City an important part of our culture?'

Blake smiled at her, and she felt the knot in her stomach loosen.

'I'd say so, yes. I think you're on to something.'

She returned his smile. 'So we focus on the common aspect of the two proposals—family. We use tour stops and business details focused on that.'

'Yes, that should work.'

She waited for him to grab his tablet from the table to note things down. But instead he just stood leaning against the table slightly, with a satisfied look on his face.

'You'd already thought about that, hadn't you?' she asked.

'I had. But you needed to get there yourself.'

She shook her head and sat down, not sure if she was relieved that her idea was one he approved of or annoyed that he'd already thought of it and had let her panic for nothing.

'So what's the plan?' she asked in resignation, and listened as he outlined his thoughts, only objecting when she thought she had something valuable to add.

And even though she knew he was good at his job—even though his calm and commanding presence gave her some stability—she still found herself saying the words that mingled with her every thought.

'This *is* going to work, right?'

He looked at her, and something on her face prompted him to sit in the chair opposite her. He placed his hands on her arms and the heat seeped through her jacket right down to her blood.

'This is going to work. And I would know, since I've already seen you in action when you haven't had the time to plan anything.' He squeezed her arms. 'You're good at what you do spontaneously, and you still have some time to prepare now, while Connor is with them. Think about how awesome you're going to be with weeks of preparation and fifteen minutes of practice.' He smiled, and her lips curved in response. 'This is going to work.'

'Thanks,' she said as he stood, and something made her want to offer him the same comfort, even though she knew he didn't need it. 'Blake? I've seen you work. And your passion, your dedication, doesn't come close to anything I've ever seen before. I know you didn't *have* to get new investors, or do as much as you have to save our jobs when the hotel would have probably been more successful if you had downsized.' She shrugged and then continued softly, 'I'm still not sure why you agreed to this, but I'm thankful that you did. We all are.'

He nodded, with a mixture of emotions on his face that were complicated enough that she didn't try to read them.

Instead, she simply said, 'Shall we do this?'

'As you can see, this is the best place to see Cape Town from and look around. Families—tourists and residents alike—all come here to experience the best of the Mother City. This is such an integral part of the family culture of Cape Town—the culture our tourists specifically come for—and now you get to experience it for yourself.'

Blake smiled, though he was sure their two potential investors barely saw it. Not when they'd hung on to Callie's every word from the moment she'd introduced herself in the conference room that morning. She had done so confidently, as if they had always expected Mr Vercelli—who had insisted they call him by his first name, Marco—and Mr Jung to arrive at the same time.

He looked over at the two men who were admiring the view of Cape Town from its signature attraction. Mr Jung caught his eye and nodded, as though silently agreeing that this might be one of the most beautiful places in the world, his grey hair blowing in the wind. He wasn't a man of many words, but he wielded a lot of power.

Blake had his finger in pies that didn't have anything to do with the hotels, and in his previous dealings with Mr Jung he had been fair and open to suggestions. And that meant fertile ground for his expansion plans, he thought, and knew he had to do everything in his power to make sure this proposal was the best it could possibly be.

'At sunset, this experience is even more beautiful.'

Callie smiled at him, acknowledging that these were words she'd said to him once before. Except then it had just been the two of them, and Blake had felt something inside him longing, which was decidedly not the case now.

'I think that would be a…er…wonderful thing, Callie.'
Marco's Italian accent was thick, and his words were punc-
tuated by pauses every now and then, but otherwise his
English was flawless. 'I would love that.'

'And I would love to bring you up here.'

She smiled again, and Blake knew that part of the reason she was handling these businessmen so seamlessly was
because of their appreciation of that smile.

'If you invest, our hotel's connections with the staff here
would mean we wouldn't even have to wait in line.'

She smiled again, and Marco burst out laughing. She
even coaxed a smile out of Mr Jung.

'You have a firecracker here, Blake,' Marco said. 'I
might even steal her for one of my hotels in Italy!'

'You would have to get through me first,' Blake said,
and saw Callie's eyes widen. It reminded him of her expression just before they'd almost kissed that night so long
ago, when he had pulled her in closer to him…

She bit her lip and he realised that he'd been staring. And
that Marco was looking at him with amusement.

He turned his attention back to the Italian man and
smiled. 'Unless you invest, Marco, in which case we can
negotiate!'

The boisterous laughter that erupted from Marco made
him think that perhaps he hadn't lost face. But he'd nearly
lost his composure, he thought, and forced himself to focus.

Clearly the businessmen weren't the only ones captivated
by Callie's smile. Her proximity made him say things, do
things that he wouldn't otherwise. Even as she stood now,
prim and proper in a black dress and red heels, a matching
jacket lying over her arms, he wanted her with a need that
surpassed even that which he had felt for Julia.

He cleared his throat. 'Now that you've had a chance to
see it for yourself, gentlemen, you can understand how the

Elegance's proximity to Table Mountain is an asset for the hotel. We arrange for free shuttles on request, to drop and fetch our guests at the location, with the added benefit of guided tours if the guest desires it. We've also negotiated special rates for families with the Table Mountain tourism management, so all our guests will be able to enjoy this experience together.'

He assumed that the nods from both the men meant they were on board thus far. Now, he thought, to keep going for the next seven hours…

'I think we actually pulled that off,' Callie said as she watched the two businessmen being escorted back to the Elegance from their final stop at the V&A Waterfront, where they'd had dinner.

As soon as they'd been driven away she turned and grinned at Blake.

'We did,' he agreed, and shocked her by picking her up and spinning in a circle.

She laughed, but when he put her down and they stood in each other's arms she felt herself wanting him. She wanted to slide her hands around his waist and pull him close. To celebrate the success of the day. The stars gleaming down on them seemed to encourage her, seemed to tell her that it was the perfect moment to lean forward and kiss him.

But a couple of people nearby whistled at them, and broke her from her trance. She stepped back from him and smiled at their spectators. And when she turned back to Blake he was smiling at her.

'What?' she asked, wondering what the strange look on his face was.

'Nothing,' he responded, and tucked her hair behind her ear.

His hand lingered there, and again Callie found herself

wishing that he would just kiss her. Then he took his hand away and stuffed it in his pocket, as though it was being punished.

'We should go and have a celebratory drink.'

'What?' Shock seeped right through to her bones. Based on the last five minutes they'd spent together, the last thing they should be doing was spending time alone with each other.

'I think we should grab a drink to celebrate.'

He took her hand and led her through the throngs of people who were out and about, despite it being a weekday evening.

'And you can actually eat something instead of answering questions while we're at it.'

Before Callie could fully process what was happening they were walking towards the dock. She frowned, knowing that there were very few bars or restaurants on this side of the waterfront. And then she stopped dead when he led her to a boat with two men standing on either side of the steps that led to its entrance.

'What is happening, Blake?'

'We've having drinks. Come on.'

He walked towards the steps, but she didn't budge.

'Callie?'

'I don't think you understand.' Now she did take a step forward. 'This is a boat. They don't just serve drinks on private boats for people who decide that they should celebrate.'

'No, they don't,' he agreed. 'But they *do* serve drinks on boats for people who own them and decide to celebrate.'

She stared at him. 'You *own* this boat?'

'As of two weeks ago—yes. Now, will you come with me?'

Callie followed him purely on instinct. Her mind was too busy thinking about the fact that she was having drinks on a boat with her boss. And that the boat belonged to him. Two weeks ago? That had been after they'd spent the day together...

She still hadn't come to terms with it all when he pulled a seat out for her at a table in the centre of the deck. The edges of the boat were lined with tiny lanterns, which lit the boat with a softer light than the full moon offered from the sky. Champagne chilled in a bucket next to the table, and one of the men who had waited for them to get on the boat now filled their glasses with it. The other still waited at the entrance to the boat, she saw, though he didn't make any move to cast off.

'How did you do this?' She finally looked at Blake, who was wearing a very self-assured grin.

'I called a few people.'

'But when?' she whispered, afraid she would embarrass him. 'We've barely had fifteen minutes since Marco and Mr Jung left.'

'Oh, that.' He was still smiling as if he had just pulled off the world's biggest heist. 'During dinner. I knew today had been successful, and I wanted to do something on a par with what we pulled off. So I made a few calls and here we are.'

'Firstly, I'm pretty sure this *surpasses* what we pulled off. And, secondly, dinner was only about an hour ago.'

'Are you complaining?'

'No, but I feel sorry for these men. How often do they have to do this?'

'I'm not sure about their previous employers, but since they've only worked for me for two weeks this is the first time I've asked them anything. Don't worry—I've made it worth their while. Besides, this is minimal effort since we aren't going anywhere. Now...' he lifted his champagne glass '...shall we toast to what we did today?'

Callie lifted her glass and toasted, but she still couldn't

believe she was on a boat. Okay, they weren't sailing any-where, but privacy after the day they'd had was exactly what she needed. Although she wasn't sure if privacy with Blake was the smartest kind.

'Did you buy this boat after our tour together?'

'I did.'

He didn't offer anything else, and Callie thought per-haps she should be more specific.

'Did you buy this boat *because* of our tour together?'

'Not really—although our time on the boat did give me some fond memories.' He grinned and ran a hand through his hair. 'You're thinking too much about this, Callie. I wanted a boat so that I can have some peace when I need it. That's what you told me, right? To do things that make me happy.' He shrugged when she frowned at him. 'Let's just focus on tonight, okay? I wanted to do something nice for you to say thank you. And well done.'

'Well, you didn't have to. Especially not this.' She ges-tured around her, though she could see that maybe he was trying to reassure himself more than he was her. Especially after telling her that he'd bought the boat to make himself happy. 'I was just doing my job. And I wouldn't have been able to, I don't think, if it wasn't for you.'

'If you're talking about the fact that these proposals might help to save your job, and all those at the hotel—'

'Actually, no. I'm talking about what you said to me be-fore we left this morning.'

He frowned. 'That you could do it?'

'Yeah.' She laughed a little, feeling silly for telling him this. 'It made me feel like I really *could* do it. And…you know…gave me a boost of confidence.'

He didn't say anything, and she had a sudden burst of doubt. 'I'm sorry, I know that sounds corny—'

'No, it doesn't.'

She felt herself flush when he smiled at her. There was something different about this smile, she thought. It wasn't the cordial you-smiled-at-me-and-I'm-returning-the-gesture type she usually got from him. No, it was a genuine smile that made her remember the completely different Blake she'd first met in the elevator.

The memory awakened other things inside her. Like how much she enjoyed looking at him. The planes of his face, the way his hair fell across his forehead, made butterflies stumble through her stomach.

It's just the atmosphere. Which woman wouldn't have butterflies if a man took her on a boat in the moonlight?

Yeah, she thought, *keep telling yourself that.*

But before she could ponder it further the man who had poured their drinks—she realised now he might very well be a waiter—placed two platters on the table. One held a variety of cheeses and the other a variety of breads and crackers. And, she thought to herself as the waiter described them, she hadn't heard of most of them.

'So you arranged this at dinner? While we were eating?'

He grinned. 'Yes, because even from the starters I could see that you weren't eating very much.'

'Very perceptive,' she said as she spread Camembert on one of the crackers. 'Marco was incredibly interested in some of the sites we took him to. So whenever you were discussing something with Mr Jung he would lean over and ask me about them.' She chewed slowly, contemplating what he had asked her. 'I'm actually not sure if he was asking out of interest or if he was testing me.'

'Well, he definitely seemed impressed. Especially when he told me how much he'd enjoyed the novelty of today's proposal. I don't think he's ever been pitched to for business along with a tour.'

'No wonder you're doing all this. Maybe now would be a good time to ask for a raise.'

He laughed. 'I'll take that under advisement.'

'I'll have Connor put in a good word for me!'

When Blake's face sobered, Callie realised how that might have sounded.

'I was joking, Blake. Connor would never do that.'

'That's not exactly what he told me.'

She frowned, and then remembered the time when he'd told her she would have to pitch to their investors with him. He already seemed to know that her title wasn't a normal one.

'What do you mean?'

Blake drank the rest of his champagne and then asked the waiter to bring him a glass of whisky. She shook her head when he raised his eyebrows and the waiter nodded, presumably concluding that he would only need to bring one glass.

'Connor told me he gave you a job after your parents died.'

'Well,' she said, grasping for something that would make the situation sound better, 'I didn't get paid at first, so it was more of an internship than anything else.'

'He also said that you had been studying towards a degree in anthropology. A degree which, if your human resources file is accurate, you didn't complete.'

Callie opened her mouth and then closed it again. How was she supposed to respond to that? That it had been an internship was true, but she knew it didn't make sense since she hadn't studied tourism or anything related to what she was now doing. The fact that she hadn't finished her degree made an even stronger case for nepotism, she thought, and cringed when she realised that she was going to have to tell him part of what had really happened.

'Yes, that's true. But Connor was just trying to help me.' She had long since stopped eating, but the food felt like lead in her stomach. 'I... I didn't cope very well with my parents' deaths. So, yes, maybe Connor wasn't being completely professional when he got me the internship. But I've worked incredibly hard for the hotel. And I've built up a good reputation with our tours. I can show you—'

'Callie.'

Blake was looking at her strangely, and she felt her heart stuck in her throat.

'I'm not asking you to defend your job.'

'I know that,' she said, and resisted the urge to shake out her shoulders. 'I just...just thought you should know that Connor has never done anything like that again. It was a one-time thing.'

Blake didn't say anything for a while. The waiter brought his whisky and Blake thanked him. After what seemed like an eternity he drank, put his glass down and settled back into his chair.

'I was there when we hired Connor. Did you know that?'

She shook her head, wondering where he was going with this.

'My dad was still in charge then, and Connor started out as the operations manager of the Cape Town branch. During his interview I remember thinking that he was going to be a good fit for the hotel. He understood our values and seemed just as dedicated to our guests as we were. And then he worked his way up and I had the honour of seeing how much of himself he invested into the job. And the pride he took in the work he did. When I promoted him to regional manager he told me that he would make sure we got out of the mess Landon had made.'

He paused, and bit into a piece of cheese.

'Of course neither of us really knew the extent of the

damage Landon had caused. But that's beside the point. What I'm trying to tell you, Callie, is that I was always fairly sure of your brother's character. Only one thing has gone against the opinion I had of him—*your* appointment.'

Callie wished she could stand up and give her restless legs something to do. But she didn't think that would be wise, considering that she was on a boat with men who would probably think she was crazy if she did. Instead she pushed a hand through her hair, resisting the urge to pull at it.

'You know, Blake, sometimes we do things for our family that go against what we believe in.' She cautioned herself against the fury she felt behind her words, but it didn't work. 'I know *your* family wasn't like that, but in mine we did things for one another. Helped each other. Supported each other.'

She rubbed her hands over her face and almost immediately her anger fizzled out.

'I'm sorry. That was uncalled for.'

Blake's face had blanched at her words, but he nodded. 'It was.'

Callie bit her lip, and hated herself for lashing out. 'It's just that Connor saved my life with this job. No, he really did.' Tears pricked at the backs of her eyes but she forced them back. 'My parents' deaths nearly destroyed me.'

There—she'd said it. The words she'd never really said aloud to anyone else. She was afraid to look up, to see the pity she knew would be in his eyes. She didn't want that. It would remind her of how almost everyone had treated her after her parents had died. As if she was something to be pitied.

She looked up at him when she felt his hand gentle

on hers, and there was no pity in his eyes. Just compassion. And she felt the coldness that had started to chill her bones thaw.

CHAPTER EIGHT

BLAKE KNEW HE shouldn't have pushed, but he'd wanted to know. He'd needed to. Callie awakened desires in him that had been dormant since…well, since Julia. And even then, he hadn't needed to know her this badly.

Ever since Callie had told him about her parents' deaths Blake had wanted to ask her about it. He wanted to know how she'd handled it, who had been there to support her. The information he had gathered from Connor after she'd mentioned it and the little he had shared with Callie a few moments ago had only made him more curious. Especially since he knew that her specialist job wasn't something that existed in any of the other hotels.

But now, seeing her anguish right in front of him, he felt like an absolute jerk.

'I'm sorry you had go through that,' he said, wishing there was something more he could say.

She slid her hand from beneath his and laid it on her lap. 'I am, too.' She attempted to smile, but her sadness undermined its effect.

'Well, you don't need to talk about it.' He gestured to Rob, the man who had been serving them all night. 'Could you bring some tea for Miss McKenzie, please?' Rob nodded, and Blake turned his attention back to Callie. 'I figure you could use something a little more soothing than champagne.'

'Thanks.' She smiled again, and this time it wasn't quite as sad. And then she took a deep breath and said, 'Blake, I… I want to tell you what happened when my parents died, okay? But only because I need you to understand why Connor did what he did. And then can we pretend this conversation never happened?'

She looked at him with such innocent hope that he nodded, even though he knew that pretending it had never happened would probably—well, never happen.

She angled her head, and didn't meet his eyes as she spoke.

'My parents were on their way home from a weekend away. It was their anniversary, and every year they celebrated by staying at the hotel where they'd had their wedding. They'd been married twenty years.' She cleared her throat. 'A drunk driver overtook when he wasn't supposed to and crashed into them. They died instantly.'

She looked up at him.

'I was nineteen. Old enough to survive.'

But still young enough to need them, he thought, but didn't say it in case it interrupted her.

'My parents meant the world to me. We were incredibly close, and losing them…it felt like I'd lost a piece of myself.'

He reached for her hand again when he saw she was fighting back tears.

'I was incredibly depressed. I couldn't go back to university. I shut my friends out. I shut Connor out. I just felt like I was in this dark room and I was flailing around, trying to find a light.'

She paused when Rob, the waiter, returned with a pot of tea, but barely waited until he'd left before she continued.

'My friends couldn't deal with the morbid person I had

become. One by one, each of them disappeared. Until even my best friend—well, I thought she was—couldn't do it any more.'

She lifted her eyes to his, and gave him a sad smile.

'Death is one of those things that you can only truly understand when it affects you. Sure, people are there for you at the funeral, and sometimes a few weeks after. But when you realise that this is your life now—that you have to live without the family who were so integral to your existence—even those people fade away. Because how can they understand that the life you knew no longer exists when theirs is going on as normal? Connor struggled too, but he had his job. Something that gave him purpose. I think that's probably around the time he started climbing the ladder at the Elegance. But when I didn't go back to university I think an alarm went off for him and he realised how lost I was. So he pitched up at my house one morning and forced me to go to work with him.'

She smiled at the memory.

'I hated him for it, but he just told me to start shadowing the concierges. He did that every day for two months. And then one day I realised that I wasn't walking around in a coma any more. I found myself asking questions and engaging with the guests. And that's how the tours came about.'

Blake had known that it would be something like that. He hadn't been lying when he'd told Callie he knew Connor pretty well, and the man he knew would have never given his sister a job just because he could. But the truth was he didn't really care why Connor had done it. He was more interested in Callie, and in the events that had had her starting at the hotel. That now had her desperate to save it. All of a sudden, it made sense to him.

'I wondered why you wanted to save the hotel so badly.' He looked at her and wished he could do something about that wounded expression on her face. 'I knew it was because of Connor. And, of course, your job. But now I understand that the reason behind it is because they saved you. Connor and your job helped you cope with your parents' deaths.'

'Yes,' she said, surprise coating her features, 'that's exactly it.'

He drank the last of his whisky and put the glass down with a little bit of a bang. 'I'm definitely glad I listened to you, then.'

She laughed—a husky sound because of the emotion she had told her story with. 'I'm glad you listened, too. Or I might be out on the streets and not out on a boat.'

Blake grinned, and slowly began to realise that he believed what he'd said. He *was* glad he'd listened to Callie. If he hadn't he would have had to let staff go and face another example of his own poor judgement. He would have had to tell his father what had happened and face his reaction. And all the hard work he had put into building his own legacy—not merely being a part of his father's—would have been for nothing.

As he asked Rob to bring him coffee he realised that Callie's ghosts weren't the only ones that had been stirred that night.

'What's wrong?' Callie asked, holding her breath at the expression on Blake's face.

Emotions she couldn't identify flashed through his eyes, but then he shook his head and smiled at her.

'Nothing. Just thinking that it's been a tiring day.'

And it had been, she thought. Except that *wasn't* what he was thinking. Maybe he was thinking of a way to fire her. Or to fire Connor. She had just admitted that Connor had given her a job—or rather an internship—to help her through her parents' deaths. And even though Connor's intentions might have been good, that didn't matter in the real world. Professionalism mattered. Ethics.

She shouldn't have told him any of it, she thought. She had just been trying to get him to see that she had earned her job. Why did the way it had started out matter? But at the same time she had told him about the worst part of her past. She had opened up to him. Her heart accelerated at the thought. She had done exactly what Connor had encouraged her to do so often. Except she'd done it with her boss. The man who had the power to kick her out of his hotel and make sure she never worked in the hospitality industry again.

She bit her lip and searched Blake's face, hoping she would find the truth of what he was thinking somewhere. What she saw worried her even more.

'Blake…look, I'm sorry if I overstepped. I probably shouldn't have told you any of this.'

'What?' He looked up at her distractedly and whatever he saw must have alerted him to her paranoia. 'Callie, no—I am so glad you told me. I understand.'

His face softened and something made her think that perhaps he wanted to say *I understand you so much better now.*

He laid a hand over hers. 'Thank you for telling me. I know it wasn't easy for you.'

'It wasn't.' The heat from his hand slid through her entire body. 'And if you're not upset with me, that means you're thinking about something that isn't easy for *you.*'

He frowned up at her.

'Come on, Blake. We've spent almost all our time together for the last two weeks. You don't think I know when something's bothering you?'

'Look, it's honestly nothing. I was just thinking that getting investors is probably the best solution for the hotel.'

'And that upsets you?'

'No.' Rob placed coffee in front of him, and Blake waited until he was gone before continuing. 'I was just so set on saving the legacy of the hotel that I would rather have re-trenched staff whose livelihood was on the line—as you so nicely reminded me—than think about my father being disappointed in me—'

He stopped abruptly, and Callie realised he hadn't meant to say that. But because he had, things began to fall into place for her. Snippets of their conversation on the day of their tour filled her mind. His relationship with his father. His mother leaving. The legacy. As she put them together she thought she knew what was bothering him.

'There's nothing wrong with wanting to make your father proud,' she said gently.

He shook his head. 'I don't know where that came from.'

She smiled, wondering if he realised how much of a man he was being. 'You were being honest with yourself.'

He angled his head, didn't meet her eyes, and she realised he didn't enjoy being honest with himself. Which, if she knew him well enough to guess, meant that he had halted any thoughts that would continue along those lines.

'Blake, was your dad upset when your mom left?'

He looked up at her in surprise. 'Of course he was. But I don't see what that has to do with anything.'

Of course you don't.

'So they'd had a good relationship?'

'I don't know.' He shrugged. 'My dad always used to say they were partners—so, yeah, I guess so.'

'Do you know *why* she left?' Callie didn't want to ask, but she knew that the answer would help her put the final piece into place. And help Blake to do the same.

'Callie—'

'Blake, please…' she said, seeing the resistance in his eyes. 'I want to understand.'

Especially because I still feel raw from telling you about my parents.

'My father said she didn't want us any more.'

He clenched his teeth, and Callie resisted the urge to loosen the fist his hand had curled into.

'That she'd left us for someone else.'

She felt her heart break for the little boy who had heard those words. For the man who still suffered from them.

'She disappointed him?'

He drew a ragged breath. 'And me.'

'And now you don't want to disappoint him, or yourself, like she did?'

He didn't answer at first, and then he looked at her. She saw his eyes clear slightly, and resisted the urge to smile at his expression.

'I guess so.'

Now she did smile. 'Should I ask the waiter to warm up your coffee?'

'What?' He was still staring at her in bemusement.

'Your coffee.' She gestured towards it. 'It's probably cold. Actually, so is my tea.' She signalled to the man and asked him to bring them fresh beverages.

'Callie, did you just psychoanalyse me?'

'No,' she said, putting on her most innocent expression. 'I was merely pointing out why it's important to you to make your father proud.'

He stared at her for a moment, and then shook his head with a smile. 'I think you missed your calling in life. You would have had a field day with me when I got married.'

Callie felt her insides freeze. The smile she had on her lips faded and she thought time slowed.

'What did you say?'

Blake was still smiling when he answered her. 'I said you've missed your calling in life.' And then he saw her face, and his eyes widened. 'Callie—'

'You're *married*?'

'No, I'm not. I got divorced a long time ago.'

'Oh…okay,' she said shakily, and wondered why she hadn't thought about it.

He was, after all, an attractive, successful man in his thirties. It shouldn't surprise her that he had been married. Though the divorce was a surprise, she thought, and thanked the waiter—why didn't she know his name yet?—as he placed her tea in front of her.

She went through the motions of making a cup, and remembered the first time they'd met, when Blake had told her that he tried to stay away from women. She'd attributed it to a bad relationship. She'd known there was a mysterious woman. So why hadn't she considered an ex-wife until just now?

'So she was the piece of work we spoke about in that elevator?'

'I don't think we've ever spoken about that.'

'Yeah, we have.' She didn't look up at him, just kept on staring intently at the milky colour of her tea. She hadn't let it stand for long enough, she thought. 'When you said that you don't put moves on women, that you stay away from them, I told you that whoever had made you feel that way must have been a real piece of work.' She lifted her eyes to his and asked, '*Was* she?'

His face hardened. 'Callie, this isn't any of your business.'

'It isn't.' Suddenly the surprise that she'd experienced only a few moments ago morphed into anger. 'But neither was my parents' deaths yours.'

'That isn't the same thing. You told me about that because you wanted to explain why Connor hired you. And since he hired you into *my* company I had the right to know.'

She quickly realised that the reason she'd told him about her parents' deaths, about how she'd coped and how Connor had saved her—the reason he had just provided—was a lie.

'You and I both know that I wasn't telling you because I work for you,' she said in a measured voice. 'But, since we're talking about it, was what you told me about *your* parents any of my business?'

'No, it wasn't.' His tone mirrored hers, but it was lined with the coldness she was beginning to recognise he used when he spoke to her as her boss.

'And all of this—' she gestured around her '—is what you do for someone you don't want in your business?'

'I was just saying thank you to an employee for a job well done.'

She stared at him, wondering if he really believed the nonsense that was coming out of his mouth. She gave him a moment to come to his senses, to salvage the progress they'd made, but he said nothing.

'Well, in that case remind me to compare notes with Connor about employee rewards.'

She gathered her things and walked towards the man who had stood silently at the entrance of the boat since they arrived.

'Would you please help me off this boat?' she asked him, and realised that she didn't know *his* name either.

He smiled kindly at her. 'Of course, ma'am.'

Before she climbed the steep stairs up to the dock, she turned back to Blake. 'She must have done something really awful to you, Blake, for you to push away something that could have…' She faltered, but then said it anyway. 'That could have *been* something. But don't worry. The next time I see you we can pretend nothing that happened this evening actually happened. Just to ensure that we stay out of one another's business.'

He didn't move in his seat—in fact he hadn't even turned while she'd been talking to him. She shut down all the hurt flooding through her and nodded at the man who was waiting to help her.

She murmured a thank you when she reached the top, and then she was walking as fast and as far from the boat—from Blake—as she could.

CHAPTER NINE

CALLIE SIGHED AS she stared at the clock on her desk. It was almost eleven. She had been back at the hotel for almost an hour now, after taking a taxi, and she'd spent that hour clearing her office of the mess she'd made after hastily preparing for their unexpected double proposal.

She was waiting for Blake to arrive and return to his house, so that she didn't bump into him when she popped into her brother's office to give him an update. Connor had said that he'd wait for her to return, and though she knew it wasn't nice of her to make him wait even longer she didn't want to deal with Blake until she'd had a good night's rest.

Or at least that was what she was telling herself.

She sighed and paged through the file she kept on the proposals. So many things had happened that day—that evening. And the evening's events made her want to throw the file in her hand at the door. When Blake had swooped her up into his arms after they'd finished the proposal and taken her to celebrate on his boat—a *boat*—she'd almost laughed at how unbelievable it was. Now she thought that it wasn't as unbelievable as Blake's claim that he was just 'rewarding an employee' by taking her there.

After the things they had shared with one another, after the romance of the evening—and, yes, she acknowledged, to her the whole boat event *had* been heartbreak-

ingly romantic—the fact that he could claim she was just
an employee to him hurt. After she had bared her soul to
him—and she gritted her teeth at that—how could he callously say such a thing? All because he didn't want to talk
about his stupid marriage.

It hurt her more than she wanted to admit that he
wouldn't talk to her. Sure, he had told her about his parents' split, and he had been open—however reluctantly—
to her conclusion about his subsequent relationship with
his father. But then he'd completely shut down when she'd
asked him about his ex-wife, going right back to being the
stubborn boss she knew and intensely disliked. The one
she would never have considered telling about her parents'
deaths and how it had broken her.

This was the reason she didn't open up to people, she
thought as she began to gather her things. People let you
down. One day you had them around you, and you thought
that you wouldn't ever feel alone, and the next day they
were gone. It didn't matter *why* they left—those reasons
always changed—the leaving was the one thing that was
always consistent.

So she should be glad that this had happened. Blake was
saving her so much heartache by pushing her away. And
she would listen to *herself* in the future, not to Connor or
any of her colleagues, who insisted that she should open
up to people. That she should date.

It was just a waste of time, she thought, and locked her
door. Especially if the person she opened up to wasn't ready
to do so themselves.

As she made her way to the exit of the hotel she saw that
her brother's office door was slightly ajar. Guilt crept in
as she remembered that she was supposed to give him an
update, and she sighed and detoured to his office. Subcon-
sciously she was hoping that he had already gone home, and

she could send him a message when she got home with a quick summary. But he never left his door open after he'd left for the day, so she resigned herself to having to tell him how the day had gone.

It was dark when she peered into the office, with only the city's lights shining through an open window illuminating the room. When her eyes adjusted she saw the outline of a figure in Connor's chair. Her heart thudded and she rushed to his side.

'Connor, are you okay?'

Only when she knelt beside him did she realise that it was Blake, not Connor, sitting at her brother's desk.

'Oh, I'm sorry—I thought you were Connor.' She rose awkwardly to her feet and wished she hadn't let the guilt of responsibility lead her into the lion's den.

'I got that,' he said dryly, and his voice was lined with something she couldn't place her finger on. But she knew it was dangerous.

'I just wanted to fill him in on today.' She eyed the door she had shut when she'd thought something was wrong with her brother, desperately wishing she had left it open.

'I did that. He left a few minutes ago.'

'Oh, okay…' Why was her voice so shaky? 'I'll go, then.'

'No.'

She exhaled sharply. 'What do you want, Blake?'

'I want to apologise.'

'For what?'

'For being a jerk earlier.'

A part of her wanted to brush it off, to tell him that it didn't matter. But she couldn't because…*it did*. It mattered. Everything she had told herself earlier about it being for the best faded somewhere into the background of her mind as she realised this. But she didn't respond to him.

With her eyes fully adjusted, she could see that he no

longer had his tie on, and the first few buttons of his shirt were undone. She swallowed, all thought leaving her mind as she noticed that his neck was bare, ready to be kissed. She shook her head and shifted her eyes to his face. It was as gorgeous as it had been the first time she'd admired it, but the danger she had sensed from him earlier was clearly outlined there.

Somewhere at the back of her mind a voice was shouting that she should leave before she had the chance to find out what that danger meant for her. But she didn't move, not until Blake stood, and then she took a step back, bumping into Connor's bookcase. It shuddered, barely moving, but it knocked some of the breath from her.

'I… I can't do this with you, Blake.'

'Do what?'

He was a few feet away from her now. She could smell him, and the sexy scent nearly sent her to her knees. She was suddenly incredibly grateful for the bookcase behind her that held her steady.

'Whatever you have in—'

Her words were cut off as he walked slowly towards her. Her heart rate—which was never really normal around him—kicked up even higher.

'What are you doing?' she asked breathily when there was barely any space between them.

'I'm apologising,' he said, and placed his hands on either side of her.

'It's okay. It's fine.'

She didn't care that she hadn't been ready to accept his apology a few minutes ago.

'Good. But now I'm saying sorry in advance…for doing this.'

And he kissed her.

His lips were soft on hers, and she could barely breathe

from the electricity that the contact sparked. She was aware of every part of him—of his hands that were no longer braced beside her but had moved to her waist. Heat seeped through her clothing where he touched her, but it was nothing compared to the inferno of their kiss. He had deepened it, and as though she was outside of her body she heard herself moan.

Her hands slid through his hair and she loved the feel of it through her fingers. Before she knew it he'd pressed her against the bookcase, so that her body was aligned with his. She shuddered at the feel of him against her, and moaned again when he trailed kisses down her neck. She pulled at his shirt and then, with frustration, when she couldn't find his skin fumbled with his buttons. Just as she'd thought, muscles rippled across his chest when the shirt was finally opened and she greedily took them in.

And then froze when his hand slid up her thigh and settled at the base of her underwear.

'Blake…' she rasped, her breath still caught by their passion, 'Blake, we can't.'

His lips stilled at her collarbone, and she could hear that he was just as affected by what was happening between them. He lifted his head and looked at her, and something on her face had him nodding and moving back. She stayed where she was, afraid that her legs wouldn't work if she tried to move.

In the shadowed light from the window he looked amazing, his shirt undone and his abs ripped, just as she'd felt them a few moments before. She wished she could do this, she thought as she took him in. She wished that she hadn't stopped and that they could let their desires control them. But that would only get her more of the hurt she already felt when she was with him.

'I forgive you. For this,' she said breathlessly. 'But I can't do this with you.'

She straightened her dress, picked up the handbag and jacket that she had thrown across the room in her haste to get to her brother. And then she took the minute she needed to organise her thoughts.

'You may have convinced yourself that taking me out on your father's boat was an employee benefit for a job well done, but you can't claim that *this*—' she gestured between them '—is how employees and their employers behave with one another.'

'You're right, it isn't.'

She hadn't noticed that he'd fastened his buttons again. A faint wave a disappointment threaded through her.

'Callie, I meant it when I said I was sorry about earlier.' He braced himself against Connor's desk. 'You didn't deserve that.'

'No, I *did*,' she said, and ignored the surprise on his face. 'I deserved it for believing that letting someone in would do me any good.'

He looked up at her, and something had him moving towards her.

'No—stop.' She held up a hand. 'We've already let this go too far.' She sighed, wishing she could pull her hair out. Anything that would make her feel better about what she was going to say. 'Blake, your ex-wife clearly hurt you. And you'll never really let me in because of that. So, for both of our sakes, I think we should just pretend this never happened.'

'The kiss?' he asked, stuffing his hands into his pockets.

'Everything. Every single thing that's happened between us that shouldn't have happened between a boss and an employee.'

He didn't say anything, and she took that as agreement.

But as she left the office her heart ached at the thought of forgetting what they'd shared.

CHAPTER TEN

'I THINK WE should just pretend this never happened.'

Blake welcomed the cold water on his heated and fatigued body. He knew that at some point hot water would be needed to soothe his screaming muscles, but for now the cold took away the pain his two-hour gym session had yielded.

'I think we should just pretend this never happened.'

What it failed to do was wash away the memories of the previous evening. The memories of him acting completely out of character.

Completely out of control.

He'd tossed and turned the entire night, so despite the incredibly long day he'd had, and despite how tired he'd been, he hadn't been able to get a wink of sleep. Which was why he had instead, at four in the morning, made use of his home gym.

He adjusted the water when he felt the cold down to his bones, and closed his eyes as heat pounded against his body. He had probably pushed himself too far, he thought. And he knew he would pay for it the entire day. Hell, probably for the entire week. But it had kept his thoughts off the mess he had made. For a few hours, at least, he thought, when his mind yet again looped back to the single thing he couldn't stop thinking about.

'I think we should just pretend this never happened.'

He wished he could. He wished he could pretend he hadn't spent the day watching her work. He wished he hadn't noticed how well she had done—how she had taken an unimaginable scenario and turned it into what he was almost certain would be a victory for Elegance. More than anything, he wished he hadn't given in to the impulse of taking her onto his boat.

Yet that wasn't the reason why her words had haunted him from the moment she'd said them. Because, as much as he wished he could pretend everything that had happened between them *hadn't* happened, he couldn't—for one simple reason:

He didn't want to.

He turned the water off and towelled himself dry. He knew the moment Callie had started asking him about his mother that her line of questioning wouldn't be easy for him. He didn't talk about his mother to anyone—he hadn't even mentioned her to Julia—and yet he'd told Callie about her the day they'd had supper after their tour. When he had barely known her.

He had convinced himself that it had just been to comfort Callie, after he'd figured out that her parents had died—especially since she hadn't offered the information freely. But it hadn't taken him long to realise that it had also been because he'd felt comfortable with her. And, if he was honest with himself, that was part of the reason he had insisted on maintaining a professional relationship with her.

If he was comfortable enough to share his most hidden memory with her, it wouldn't take long before she lodged herself in his heart. And then she would be able to hurt him. And if his instincts weren't wrong—as they'd been before—and she'd fallen for him, he'd be able to hurt her, too.

As he began dressing for work he thought about his mother for the first time in years. She *had* disappointed him.

He had watched her pack her bags into the car, and then she'd knelt in front of him and said, 'I'm sorry, Blake. I hope one day you can understand that I couldn't do this. This life was never for me.'

She'd kissed him on the forehead and driven away, and he had watched the car fade into the distance.

He couldn't remember feeling more helpless—or more heartbroken—than at that moment when he was eleven and his mother had left. He didn't know if it mattered to him now that it had been the last time he had seen her or the last time he had known some semblance of a normal family life. But what he *did* know was that he had vowed he would never feel that way again. He didn't ever want to feel as if he didn't have control or to feel heartbroken again. Most of all, he had assured himself that if he were ever a father he would never let his child feel the way he had. He would make sure that *his* child had the family he'd never had.

Something clicked in his head and he realised that Julia had made him feel all those things—had forced him to break all those promises he had made to himself such a long time ago. And the worst thing was that now he was terrified Brent would be feeling the same way he had—helpless and disappointed.

The mess of his mother, Julia and Callie swirled through his head, and he began to think about his relationship with Julia in a way he'd never considered before. To think of why he'd reacted the way he'd reacted to her, why their relationship had broken down so completely. And though there were many layers to it—most of which seemed hazy to him at the moment—one layer suddenly became incredibly clear.

Blake closed his eyes and resisted knocking his head against the wall. And he thought one thing repeatedly— that he was a fool.

Callie got into work early that morning, not bothering with breakfast at home because she knew she could sneak into the hotel kitchen and grab some of the food that would be warm and ready for the breakfast buffet in half an hour.

After doing just that, she unlocked her office and thanked the office angels who had helped her clear her desk the previous night. Because now she could set her breakfast and her coffee on a desk that she could actually see, instead of on a pile of papers she hoped weren't important.

She sighed as she bit into a warm slice of toast, and moaned when it was accompanied by the coffee boost she so desperately needed. She hadn't slept very well, her mind muddled with thoughts, and at about three in the morning she'd forced herself to stop thinking about the events that had caused the ache in her heart and instead focused on business. She knew the proposal the previous day had gone well, but she wanted to kick it up a notch. At five a.m. she'd had a fully drafted email about what she thought would do just that. Now she just had to find the courage to hit 'send'.

She took her time eating her breakfast, and then read through the email a couple more times. When she couldn't procrastinate any longer she sent the email to Blake, and copied Connor in just in case. She hadn't spoken to him about the proposal, but he'd sent her a message congratulating her. Which she'd only read after midnight, since she had been too busy kissing her boss and dealing with the resulting anguish to switch on her phone before then.

It was barely ten minutes later when she received a response, and she held her breath as she opened it.

Come and see me.

That was it? Nothing about the perfectly outlined event she had just sent him the plan for?

She bit back her disappointment and pulled out her compact mirror to make sure she didn't have breakfast crumbs on her face. She gave herself a pep talk on her way to the conference room and told herself she was as prepared as she would ever be before seeing her boss, with whom she had so hungrily made out the night before. An image of him with an open shirt standing in the moonlight flashed through her mind, but she forced it away.

She was a professional. She could do this.

But her resolve nearly faltered when she saw him. He looked nothing like the dishevelled man she'd left in her brother's office the night before. His hair was slicked back and his suit was pressed. Worst of all, his face was expressionless when he looked up at her.

'Morning, Callie. I just got your email.'

'Yes, I know.' She forced herself to match his demeanour. She was the one who had wanted him to be like this. Except now it didn't seem to be what she wanted at all.

'So...what do you think?'

He ran a hand through his hair and just like that the neat style collapsed as a piece fell over his forehead. He didn't seem to notice, but she did, and she wanted to walk over and fix it for him. And then she could sit on his lap...and then they could continue where they'd left off last night...

She shook her head. Where had *that* come from? She had been so sure that she had made herself immune to him. She'd forced herself to replay every moment of the previous evening and repeated all those words that had hurt her so that she could strengthen her resolve. And then she had forced herself to forget the way his hands had felt on her body, the way he'd kissed like Cupid himself.

She had even dressed the part—loose white linen pants and a cream waterfall jersey that hid the curves of her body effectively. And then she had resolved never to think about him and what he did to her body, to her heart, again. She had focused on her work and come up with a pretty decent idea, even if she said so herself. Now she was just waiting for him to acknowledge it.

'It's a good idea. A really good one.' He tilted his head. 'A gala event for all our potential investors would do wonders for their interest in the hotel. Especially if they're introduced to the competition. I just don't know how you'll be able to pull it off in seven days. Maybe we should push it back?'

'Timing is important.' The words were so formal that she resisted the urge to roll her eyes at herself. 'We should hold the event when the proposals are still fresh in the investors' minds and before the negotiations start, so it can help influence their decisions. That means next Friday is our best bet.'

She sighed when he didn't respond.

'It's just an idea,' she said. 'But I think that if we do this we'll have an opportunity to show the investors the possibility of much larger events in the hotel. So far we've only done corporate events, but if we started adding birthdays, anniversaries, weddings, I think it would be a source of revenue for the hotel that will increase profits immensely.'

'Yes, I saw all that in your email. But how?' Blake stood now, and leaned against the table as he had so many times in the weeks they'd worked together. 'How are we going to pull off the best event the hotel has ever given in a week?'

She faltered. 'We *could* do it. We've racked up favours from all kinds of vendors and services, and I know a lot of them would be grateful for the opportunity to—'

'How long did it take you to organise my welcome event?'

'I didn't organise that. Connor did, mostly.'

'How long did it take Connor to organise the event?'

She bit her lip, and didn't answer him immediately.

'Callie, how long did it take for Connor to organise the event?'

'Fourteen weeks.'

He raised his eyebrows. '*Fourteen?* And you want to throw an event bigger than that in one week? In addition to working on the proposals we'll be doing for four of those seven days?'

She locked her jaw and looked at him. 'Yes.'

'I don't think—'

'Forget it—it's fine.' She turned away.

'Callie, wait,' he said, before she could leave. 'I was going to say I don't think you can do it alone. We'll have to get everyone involved. We need to call in all our favours, with every vendor and every service provider, and make this happen. Because we *can* do it. Together.'

Suddenly Callie was transported back to the previous day, when similar words had made her feel more valued than she ever had before. And she cursed him for still having the ability to make her feel that way.

'Okay, great.'

He smiled at her, though there was something behind it that she hadn't seen before. 'So let's get to it. There's a lot of work to be done.'

Her heart stopped. '*You're* going to help with this?'

He nodded. 'That's generally what's meant by "together".'

'I just thought you meant all the staff.'

'Oh, everyone will help. But you and I will be running it.' He sat down and started typing on his laptop. 'We seem to work well together.'

She stared at him, wondering who had kidnapped the surly boss she'd worked with before and replaced him with this cordial man in front of her.

'Yeah, apparently we do.'

CHAPTER ELEVEN

'ARE YOU READY to go?'

Blake stood in the doorway of her office and she nodded, scribbling a note to remind herself to check when the lights for the gala event would arrive for set-up.

'Let's do this.' She grabbed her handbag and locked up, following him to the front of the hotel. 'I think I might actually be looking forward to this.'

He laughed and nodded his thanks when John pulled the car in front of them. 'It's food—what's not to look forward to?'

How about the fact that we have to do this together?

But she smiled in response, clinging to the truce that had settled between them over the last few days. The proposals were going well, and now, since the German investor they had seen today had had to attend another meeting in the afternoon, they had some more time to work on the gala event.

Blake had arranged that they do a tasting to ensure the catering for the event was good, and she had resigned herself to the fact that she had to go. Eating together—even professionally—seemed dangerously close to a date, but Callie had agreed because she didn't want to rock the boat between her and Blake. She almost rolled her eyes at the description—why did it need to be a *boat*?—but then remembered that Blake always seemed to be watching her recently. And she didn't want to invite any questions she wasn't willing to answer.

'We never really spoke about how you chose this restaurant,' she said once they were in the car, hoping to stop her annoying train of thought.

'This is one of the rare restaurants I've actually been to in Cape Town.'

She looked at him in surprise. 'Really?'

'Yes.' He glanced over at her, but his expression was closed. 'My father has been friends with the owner since before I was born. When we did go out together, it was generally there.'

She frowned. 'Then why are we doing a tasting, if you already know how the food tastes?'

'For several reasons. One being that they've recently hired a new chef. He came with new menus, and I haven't had a chance to taste anything on them yet. Another is that I need you to make sure I've made a decent choice and not just gone with something I know because I trust that the catering will be reliable.'

It made sense, she thought, though she wished he might have said, *Oh, I see your point—we can just skip this*.

'There's a lot to be said for reliability,' she said. 'The last thing we want on Friday is to worry that the food won't be good or won't arrive when it should.'

'Which is why I hope you'll give this place the stamp of approval.'

Callie didn't answer, instead looking out of the window at the hills they passed. She didn't come to this side of Cape Town very often, she thought, as the hills become vineyards. It was a popular venue for large events—weddings, especially—and many of the vineyards offered wine-tastings. Though she had recommended it as a weekend activity for her guests, she had never considered including it on her tours since she knew they would always be battling traffic to get back to the hotel in the afternoons. And, more importantly, she didn't want to deal with tipsy guests and the potential problems they brought.

As Blake turned on to a gravel road that slowly inclined Callie looked up to the top and saw a building made mostly of glass. It was beautifully designed, with curves that spoke of specialised techniques and artistry even to an amateur eye like hers.

'Is that it?' she breathed, but didn't need an answer when Blake pulled into the car park. 'It's *amazing*.'

'It is,' he agreed. 'And the inside is even better.'

He guided her into the restaurant, where they were greeted politely, and while Blake spoke to the maître d' Callie looked around and was forced to agree with Blake about the interior design. Wooden tiles swept across the floor and chandeliers hung from the roof. The glass exterior meant that the restaurant's patrons were treated to a spectacular view of the winelands and, from their position at the top of the hill, some of the city as well.

They were led up spiralling stairs, from where Callie could appreciate the decor of the restaurant even more. It was definitely an upper-class restaurant, but the subtle touches of warmth—like the soft yellow and white table settings—made her think that the owners wanted to avoid the alienating effect more expensive restaurants often had.

When they finally stopped climbing she was out of breath, and she looked around, realising that they had climbed to the top of the building while she had been distracted by aesthetics. And then the maître d' led them through a door and she lost her breath altogether.

'Blake…' she said, but couldn't even continue as she took in the beauty of their location.

She was standing on the rooftop of the restaurant, over-looking the view she had thought so spectacular only a few moments ago. Except now she felt that description had been overzealous, since what she was looking at from here was better than the view through the glass walls.

Blake smiled at her reaction and led her to a table at the edge of the rooftop, from where she could see everything merely by turning her head to the left.

'How did you arrange this?' she asked, when they were seated and the maître d' had been replaced by a perky waitress.

'Connections,' he said, and shrugged as though sitting on the roof of a restaurant was normal. 'I take it you like it?'

'I really do.'

'So do I,' he said, and looked out to the view. There was a slight breeze that helped lessen the effect of the summer sun and rustled through Blake's hair like leaves during the autumn. 'I don't think I will ever get tired of this.'

She had been wrong, she realised. Even though getting them to the rooftop might have been easy for her boss, the experience wasn't lost on him. That loosened something inside her—something that had stuck the night she had told him to forget everything that had happened between them. The fact that something so simple, something so small, could make her heart ache for him again told her she was in trouble.

So she pulled back, forced herself to act professionally. She made the right sounds when the food was served, agreeing on some dishes, asking for variations on others. She made polite conversation with Blake about the weather, about work, about the event preparations that were coming along nicely. She had almost congratulated herself on sur-viving when the waitress brought out dessert.

'We've prepared a variety of dishes for you to taste,'

said the pretty blonde, who had been incredibly helpful throughout the tasting.

Callie wondered if she had been warned about who she would be dealing with.

'Chocolate mousse, strawberry cheesecake with berry coulis, pecan pie, and a cream cheese and carrot cake trifle.' She pointed at the individual dishes, which were lined up on a long plate. 'You can choose three of these desserts to be served at your event. Please do let me know if you have any questions.'

She smiled brightly at them and then moved to join her colleagues.

Callie frowned as she looked at the plate in front of them, and her stomach dropped when she realised that the waitress wouldn't be bringing out a second. And then she saw the spoons on the table—two of them—and mentally kicked herself for thinking that the restaurant must be encouraging romantic dessert-sharing.

'I suppose we start at each end and move in?' she said, hoping to sound logical about it.

His lips twitched. 'Yes, let's do that.'

She frowned slightly, but chose to ignore him, and instead took a bite from the chocolate mousse. She closed her eyes as it melted in her mouth. She had never tasted anything like it, she thought, and greedily dipped her spoon into the small dish for another bite.

But as she lifted it to her mouth she realised Blake was watching her, and she felt heat flush through her body when she saw the desire in his eyes.

She put the spoon down slowly and said huskily, 'I'm sorry, I suppose I'm being selfish by taking another bite.'

She cringed at her words, knowing full well it wasn't selfishness that had caused her to pause.

He didn't respond, but reached over and took the spoon

from her plate instead. 'I don't mind you being selfish,' he said, and lifted the spoon to her mouth.

She opened it on a reflex, though her eyes never left his, and felt a thrill work its way through her body. The mousse melted in her mouth, just as it had the first time, but she didn't taste it now. No, she was remembering the way *he* had tasted when they'd kissed, the way his eyes had heated just as they did now, the electricity that had sparked between them.

The sun was setting behind him, and it cast a glow over them that made everything seem a little surreal—as if they were in a romantic film and about to shoot the perfect ending. She wished it were that which made Blake look like a movie star, but she knew that Blake's looks were not an illusion. Her handsome, gorgeous boss was all too real, and with each moment she spent with him she wanted him to become a part of her reality. She wanted that heat, that electricity, his taste to be hers.

And, even though it couldn't be, for once she didn't fight showing how much she wanted it.

His eyes darkened at what he saw in hers and he placed the spoon down on her plate again and leaned over to kiss her. She felt it right down to her toes…the slow simmer of passion although his lips were only lightly pressed against hers. The taste she had longed for only a few moments earlier was sweeter than the dessert she had just eaten, and it wiped away the memory of it.

She wanted to deepen the kiss, to take more, but the sane, rational part of her brain—the part that was half frozen by his kiss—reminded her that they were in a public place and she pulled back, feeling embarrassed and needy from what she knew had only been a brief kiss.

She reached for her glass of water at almost exactly the

same time he did and she drank, grateful that the glass hid the smile that crept onto her face for one silly moment.

He cleared his throat. 'I can tell why you wanted another taste of that.'

She looked up at him in surprise, and bit her lip to stop the bubble of laughter that sat in her throat. But nothing was funny about this, she realised, and the thought banished her lingering amusement.

So she just smiled at him politely, and said, 'We should probably finish the tasting and get back to the hotel. There are a couple more things I need to do before tomorrow.'

And just like that the mood between them shifted.

'Are you done for the day?'

It was like déjà vu, Callie thought as she looked up to see Blake at her office door. It was only a few hours since she'd last seen him there, before they'd gone for the tasting. *Before they'd tasted each other.* She shook her head at the thought, resenting her mind for reminding her of the part of their afternoon that she really wished she could forget.

'Yeah, just about. Why?' She looked down at the papers in front of her, taking care not to look him in the eye.

'Great. Connor's asked me to take you home. He said something about your car breaking down yesterday?'

She was going to kill Connor. 'Yeah, it did. But he said *he* would drop me at home.'

'Something came up.'

Blake didn't seem nearly as concerned as she did about spending time alone together in a car. Even after the tension that had mounted between them on their way back to the hotel. And the awkward parting they'd shared when they'd arrived.

'It's fine. I'll call a taxi.'

Blake placed a hand on her own, which was reaching for her phone. 'Callie, I'll take you. I don't mind.'

'It's really okay, Blake. I don't want to put you out.'

'This is the second time you've said no to my offer of taking you home.'

She looked at him in surprise when his words were spoken in a terse voice.

'*Why* won't you accept my help?'

'Because you're my boss,' she said, grasping at the one thing that she could cling to. The very external thing that she held on to instead of admitting the real reasons she was pushing him away. 'It isn't appropriate.'

'Can we both stop pretending that's still a factor here?'

'Excuse me?'

'It's the card you pull out every time you want to put distance between us, Callie. We both do.'

She stared at him as he walked into her office and closed the door.

'I know I messed things up between us that night on the boat. I used our professional relationship as an excuse because I was scared. We were getting too close…and my judgement has failed me before.'

He didn't look up at her, but for some reason she could tell his expression would be tortured.

'My ex-wife was an employee. And marrying her was probably the worst decision I've made in my life.'

He lifted his eyes, and she could see that she'd been right. The look on his face tore her heart into two.

'I just don't know if I can trust my judgement any more.'

She could see that the admission had taken a lot from him. And she wished that she could take away the pain that had come with it.

Instead, she bit her lip and said softly, 'I *do* use our professional relationship as an excuse.' She played with a stray thread at the bottom of her jersey. 'To distance myself from you—yes. And because…' She sighed, and gave up on the resistance every part of her screamed out when it came to him. 'Because I don't want to have feelings for you. I don't want to open up to you and have you shut me out again.'

Or, worse, have you leave.

But she couldn't bring herself to say it.

'Do you…? Have feelings for me?'

She shouldn't have said anything, she thought immediately, and then saw the sincerity in his eyes. *Trust me,* they seemed to say, and she spoke as honestly as she could.

'I don't know, Blake. I haven't given myself the chance to entertain even the possibility.'

He nodded. 'And if I promise to…to be open with you, too. Would you entertain the possibility then?'

Her heart accelerated. 'Maybe.'

'Okay.' He held a hand out to her. 'Can I take you home?'

She laughed, and nodded. 'I guess so. I just need to put my shoes on.'

She slipped her left shoe on her foot, and was about to do the same for her right when Blake knelt in front of her.

'Let me.'

He took the shoe from her hand and fitted it onto her right foot. For one ridiculous moment Callie felt as if she was in a fairy tale. Her Prince Charming was kneeling in front of her, fitting onto her foot the shoe that would make her his princess.

But then he looked at her, and all fairy-tale notions fled from her head. There was a heat in his gaze that made her burn from the place where his hand still lay on her foot right up to the hair follicles on her head. For a moment she wondered what would happen if she pinned him against the wall and continued where they had left off a few nights ago…

She shook her head and he smiled at her. But his smile

was a wicked one, as though he knew exactly what her mind had jumped to as he'd slipped her shoe on.

He straightened and held out a hand to her. 'Shall we?'

She exhaled shakily and took his hand. 'Yes.'

CHAPTER TWELVE

BLAKE OPENED THE car door for Callie and felt his body tighten when she brushed past him to get in. He supposed he hadn't recovered from their interactions earlier today. That kiss at the restaurant... Whatever it was that had happened in her office...

He didn't know what had possessed him to put her shoe on for her, but he was glad that he had. If he hadn't he wouldn't have seen the way her eyes had sparked with a desire that matched his. She might not know if she had feelings for him, but she definitely wanted him. And that meant they were on the same page.

He watched as she typed her address into the GPS on his dashboard, and when the voice gave him his first direction he followed it. He glanced over at her, and frowned when he saw that her arms were crossed.

'Are you okay?'

'I think so.' She didn't look at him.

'What's on your mind?'

'Nothing,' she said, almost immediately, and then she sighed. 'Everything. I'm just not used to this.'

'To...us?'

She ran a hand through her hair. 'To any of it. This is all new territory for me. Worrying about work. About whatever's going on between the two of us. I don't know—I guess I just feel...*raw*.'

Blake forced himself to keep focusing on the road, even though he wanted to pull over and hold her in his arms. He wanted to comfort her, to tell her that everything was going to be okay. Instead he settled for saying the one thing he thought she might need to hear right now.

'You're not alone, Callie.'

He took a right and didn't look at her, even though he knew her eyes were on him.

'I worry about what's going on between us, too. But you don't have to worry about work, okay? Everything is going to be fine.'

He wanted to ask her if he'd made her feel worse—about her worries over them, about the things she had just told him—but he forced himself to wait. She was opening up to him again and he wanted to earn it. So he just said it again.

'You're not alone.'

The rest of their trip was quiet. Blake didn't know what she was thinking about, but her hands now lay on her lap, and he took it as a sign that maybe she didn't feel so vulnerable any more. He wanted to kick himself for making her feel that way in the first place, but there was nothing he could do about the past. When he'd realised he'd made a mistake about Callie—when he'd realised that the failure of his relationship with Julia had had very little to do with them working together—he had wanted to call her immediately and tell her that he was sorry, that he wanted to make it up to her.

But his words wouldn't have meant anything at that point, he had reasoned, and so instead he'd tried to show her through his actions. He'd made an effort not to keep up the act of being the boss she expected—the hard, cold act he had clung to in order to keep his professionalism with her. Instead he'd acted as he did with every other employee. Well, perhaps not *exactly* the same way, but he figured she'd earned some preferential treatment since her standard of work was higher than most he'd encountered.

He'd also enjoyed the way her eyes widened every time he engaged with her without the cold formality that had coloured his interactions with her before.

When his GPS announced that their destination was on the left, Blake pulled up in front of a light-coloured house with a rush of flowers planted in flower beds along the pathway.

'I'm not sure who to compliment on your garden. You for choosing the flowers, or your gardener for planting them.'

She laughed and unlocked the door. 'Both, I suppose. Thank you. I'll pass the message on to Ernesto.'

He frowned. 'Your gardener's name is *Ernesto*?'

'Yes. He's from Italy. What are the chances of finding a young, attractive male from another country to do your garden for you?'

He couldn't quite keep his face neutral when he thought about it, and she took one look at him before bursting out into laughter.

'I'm just kidding, Blake. My gardener is a lovely man in his fifties called George.'

Her eyes twinkled, and he felt himself relax. And then she gestured to the door.

'Do you want to come inside?'

He barely took a second before saying, 'Sure.'

Her house was spacious, filled with light and bright flowers from her garden. The open plan meant that the lounge, dining room and kitchen led from one room to the other, and all the furniture complemented the warm and rustic theme of her house.

'Did you do the interior of the house?' he asked, walking past a shelf that held pictures of the McKenzie family.

His eyes were drawn to a picture of Callie and Connor, standing next to a woman and a man who looked so much like them he thought that if he'd met them on the street he would have recognised them as Connor and Callie's parents. They looked so happy, he thought, and his heart broke for reasons he couldn't describe. Somehow it made him think of his own family, and the fact that Callie wouldn't ever see a picture like this anywhere in his place.

'Some of it.'

He turned when she answered him, and the compassion in her eyes tugged at his heart. How did she continue to see through him?

'But mostly I've kept it as it was when my parents were alive,' she pressed on, and took off her jersey, throwing it over one arm. 'My mom had great taste.'

'Yeah, she did.'

He was still thinking about her family when she said, 'I'm going to change. It shouldn't take too long, but feel free to make yourself comfortable.'

She walked through a doorway in the kitchen and he heard her footsteps on the floor and a door closing. He turned back to the shelf with the pictures and tried to keep his mind off the thought of her changing in the next room. But his thoughts kept shifting back to how she would be slipping off those heels that made her legs look as if they never ended. And she was probably taking off that dress that had done nothing to hide the curves that had been in his thoughts ever since he'd touched them.

He swallowed, and walked to the kitchen to pour himself a glass of water.

There was an empty glass in the sink, and he rinsed it and filled it with water from the tap. As he drank he looked up through the window that was just above the L-shaped kitchen counter. It overlooked a tidy little yard which was completely free of flowers, but had a large palm tree that shadowed a swing seat just beneath it. But the real view was of the mountain just above it.

'That's Lion's Head.'

He turned back to see Callie looking past him through the window. She had changed into a long floral skirt and a mint-green T-shirt, and had loosened her hair so that it fell in waves down her back. She looked so effortlessly beautiful that his heart stopped for a few minutes just looking at her. She walked towards him until she was next to him and then pointed to the right of the mountain he'd seen.

'Table Mountain is over there.'

But he couldn't keep his eyes off her, and her proximity overwhelmed his senses. When she looked back to him her eyes widened in that way they did whenever something she hadn't expected happened.

He put his hands on her waist, cautiously, asking permission without saying a word, and she took a step towards him so that there was barely any space between them. His arms slipped around her and his body heated at finally being able to feel hers again, and then he leaned down to her until his mouth was next to her ear.

'I'm going to kiss you now,' he whispered, and felt her shudder. He moved his head back so he could see her face, flushed and beautiful, and asked, 'Is that okay?'

'Yes.'

She had barely said the word before his lips were on hers. She had expected hunger, passion—everything that had burned with their first kiss. But there was none of that. Instead it felt as though he was trying to make up for that, to show her there was more to whatever was going on between them than just pure lust.

She thought vaguely that this might be the way their kiss on the rooftop would have felt if they'd let it continue for a while longer. And as the sweetness of their kiss swept through her she felt her heart open and be filled with it. He pulled her closer, and her heart beat at double its speed as she let her hands explore his body.

As soon as she did, the sweetness turned into need and she deepened their kiss, wanting more.

'Callie.'

Blake had ended the kiss, but he didn't let her go. She opened her eyes to see his own were closed, and he leaned his forehead against her.

'Do you want to give me a heart attack?'

She laughed breathlessly. 'I'm sorry. I didn't realise I had that in me.'

He lifted his head and smiled, and for the first time she noticed the crinkles around his eyes. She'd never really seen them before, she thought, and brushed a thumb across one of them.

'I think you have a lot in you that you don't realise,' he responded, and then took a deliberate step away from her.

As he did so she suddenly realised where she was, who she was with. Where had all this come from? Why was he was saying all the right things? About how she wasn't alone, how she shouldn't worry about the hotel, how they would deal with whatever was happening between them together. She had let her guard down enough to invite him in, and now he'd kissed her—in her own kitchen.

She turned her back to him and braced her hands on the sink as the uncertainty of the situation overwhelmed her.

'Hey,' Blake said, and moved to next to her. 'What's going on?'

'Nothing.' She turned to him and forced a smile to her face. 'Can I get you something to drink?'

'Callie, come on. I thought we agreed we were going to be open with one another.'

'Yeah, we did. So tell me where all this is coming from. How are you so calm and determined to be open with me when the last time you did this you pushed me away?'

The words had rushed from her mouth and she sighed, wishing she had some semblance of control over it. Especially when she saw the pain on his face.

'I'm sorry, Blake. I told you I was feeling a bit raw. And kissing doesn't help.' She resisted the urge to touch her lips.

He nodded. 'You're right. We should probably straighten things out before we do that again.'

Her heart accelerated even at the thought of it.

'Is that drink still up for offer?'

'Sure. Would you like some wine? I have a really good red.'

'Yeah, that's great.'

She poured the wine and joined him on the couch. It overlooked the garden when the curtains were open, and the amount of light it offered the house meant she kept them that way most of the time.

She handed him his glass and took a sip of her own wine as she snuggled into the corner of the couch. There was enough space between them that she felt safe from doing something she would likely regret if she were any closer.

'The last time I messed things up between us it was because of my ex-wife.'

He spoke suddenly, and Callie didn't know what to make of the way her stomach clenched at his mention of the woman. So she just nodded, and waited for him to continue.

'She was one of my employees at the Port Elizabeth Elegance Hotel. I met her a few years after my father retired, when I realised that the hotel in PE was losing staff at an incredibly high rate. I arranged a meeting with HR and they sent Julia.'

Callie watched as the tension on Blake's face tightened. She wanted to reach out to him, but she resisted. He needed to tell her about this without any help. But he had stopped talking.

She waited, then finally she asked, 'What was it that made you fall for her?'

He looked at her, and she saw a mixture of emotions in his eyes. Emotions that almost mirrored her own. She didn't really want to hear about what it was that had attracted Blake to this woman. But she needed to if they were going to make any progress together.

Then he exhaled sharply. 'I don't exactly know, to be honest with you. I guess it was because she had all the ingredients of the perfect woman. She was smart and beautiful, and I was attracted to her. But I didn't want to date her because—well...' he smiled wryly '...I was her boss.'

He continued now without any help, and she thought it was almost a compulsion for him to tell her.

'But professionalism didn't really mean as much to me back then, so after about six months of resisting I asked her out. And it felt good. But what drew me in was Brent—her son.'

Blake didn't look at Callie but he paused, as though letting her process what he was telling her. She already had so many questions, but she refused to speak. Especially when she didn't think she would have the voice to do so.

After a few more moments he continued. 'She had always been honest with me about him. She'd told me that his father hadn't been in the picture from the beginning and that she'd been raising him by herself. And the way she told me that...'

He leaned forward now, bracing his elbows on his knees, and Callie realised he had long ago placed his wine, untouched, on the coffee table in front of them,

'That was, I think, what made me fall in love with her. She had this softness about her when she spoke about Brent that seemed so out of place in this woman who was all sass all the time.'

Callie didn't realise she was holding her breath until he looked at her, and the torment she saw in his eyes made her untangle her legs from under her and move closer to him. They sat there for a while in silence, and Callie thought about what he'd said. She remembered the way his eyes had dimmed when she'd spoken to him of his mother on the boat, what felt like a lifetime ago. It was quite simple for her to come to a conclusion then.

'She was a good mother. So different to what you'd had.' She hadn't realised she'd spoken out loud until he took a shaky breath.

'Yeah, I think that was it. And when I met Brent I fell in love with him, too. He reminded me a lot of myself.' He frowned, as though unsure of where that had come from. 'In hindsight, I suppose I fell for Brent more than I did for Julia, but they were intertwined. And then one day I found her crying in my office. She told me that she didn't think she was a good enough mother to Brent, that she wasn't giving him stability because he didn't have a father. And just like that she had me.'

He pushed off from the couch so fast that Callie felt her heart stop.

'I thought she was being honest with me. That she was being unselfish, thinking of her son first. Maybe she was. But the way she did it...' He shook his head.

She'd shown her son all the things Blake hadn't had

growing up, Callie thought, and wished she could have been there for him then.

'I fell for it. I comforted her, told her she was an amazing mother, and started making plans to propose. I'd only known her for a year then, had been dating her for six months, and I *married* her.'

He looked at her, and she thought she saw embarrassment in his eyes.

'I married a woman I barely knew because she pulled at my heartstrings. My father insisted that we sign a prenuptial agreement, and we did—though she made some noise about that. The right noise, too. About how we didn't need a prenup when we were going to last. We were a family, and we were going to make it work. And for a year we did.'

He joined her on the couch again, and Callie took his hand, wanting to provide as much comfort as she could.

'Callie, I didn't think I would *ever* be as happy as I was being a husband and a father. We were a family. *I* had a family.' He rubbed a hand across his face. 'But I was in a bubble, and I only noticed the way Julia had changed when it began to affect Brent. She had become snarky and mean. Only to me, luckily, but she was doing it in front of Brent, and I could tell that he hated it. When I challenged her on it she told me it was none of my business because Brent wasn't even my son.'

He looked at her, and then lowered his eyes.

'I tried to save the relationship—I really did. I even went so far as to look into adopting Brent. I hired an investigator to find Brent's father so that I could ask him to relinquish his parental rights to me. I was going to surprise Julia with it. But then one night she told me it wasn't working, and that what was happening between us was hurting Brent. That was the last thing I wanted, so I agreed to a divorce. I had just wanted to give Brent a home, a family.'

'I'm so sorry, Blake.' Callie spoke because she had to. She couldn't take the pain in his voice any longer.

He looked at her now, smiled sadly. 'Thanks, but I was in that relationship for the wrong reasons. For my own reasons. Julia had her reasons, too, so we were both wrong—though I do think she thought she was doing the right thing for Brent. She wanted to make sure that he never lacked for money.'

'Wait—what?'

Blake shot her a confused look. And then he nodded. 'Oh, yeah, I didn't mention that. When we spoke about the divorce she told me she had only married me so that she could live the life she knew she and her son deserved. And then she realised that she was hurting him instead, and she didn't want that.' He shook his head. 'That was pretty much the end of it.'

'Did she get anything in the divorce?' Callie didn't want to ask, but it was one of the pieces of the puzzle she needed to understand him better.

'No, the prenup prevented that. And Brent didn't either, since the contract stated he needed to be legally mine before I was required to pay anything.'

'Do you still see him?'

'No, I don't. Julia resigned shortly after we divorced and moved to back to Namibia, where she's from.'

'Blake...' Callie shifted over and put an arm around him. 'I'm sorry.'

He lifted his own arm, put it around her, and sat back so that she could lay her head on his chest. They sat like that for a while, and Callie wished she had words to say that would take the pain away. Suddenly everything made sense to her. His resistance to dating an employee. His pushing her away when she got too close. He was broken inside, and he didn't want anyone to know.

'I've created a trust fund for him.' Blake spoke softly. 'When he's twenty-five—old enough to decide what to do with his own money—he'll get something from me. It may not mean much to him—'

'But you needed to do it.' She leaned back and watched him nod, before putting her head on his chest again. 'You're a good man, Blake Owen.'

CHAPTER THIRTEEN

CALLIE LOOKED AT HERSELF in the mirror and tried to be critical. She was wearing a blue floral dress with a white jersey and matching heels, and her hair was tied into a loose
bun. She had to lead a meeting about the gala event that
day, and she wanted to look her best. She placed a hand on
her nervous stomach and forced herself to admit that she
wanted to look her best for Blake, too.

He hadn't stayed for very long after they'd spoken last
night. Callie knew that telling her about his past had made
him feel uncomfortable, so she hadn't pushed him. Instead
she'd brushed a kiss on his cheek and waved him away, all
the while worrying about what it meant for *them*. She could
no longer deny that there was something between them,
but even the thought of it terrified her. Especially as they
hadn't defined it yet, and she didn't even know how long
Blake would be staying in Cape Town.

Or if he would be staying at all.

She shook her head and told herself that there was no
point in worrying about it now, when everything was still
so new and fresh. She would just have to wait and see how it
played out. She sighed, and wished that was enough for her.

She grabbed her handbag when she heard a car hoot outside and locked up quickly, not wanting Connor to wait.
Her car would probably be ready after the weekend, her

mechanic had told her, and he had also cautioned her that it didn't have much life left in it. This she knew—though part of her wanted to keep it, even if she left it in the garage, just because it reminded her of the days when she had been part of a family.

'Hey, Cals. How are you?' Connor asked as she climbed into the car and kissed him on the cheek.

'Fine—no thanks to you. What were you thinking, throwing me to the wolves yesterday?' Callie wasn't sure why she'd said that, but somehow she felt it was what he would expect her to say if she hadn't shared anything personal with their boss.

'Sorry about that.'

He grimaced and she thought her gut instinct had been right.

'Urgent matter at home.'

She looked at him in alarm. 'Is everything all right?'

'Not really.' Connor focused hard on the road ahead of him and didn't even look her way.

'Connor,' she said, in the stern voice she only used with him, 'what's going on?'

After a few more moments of silence he said tersely, 'Elizabeth is pregnant.'

Her jaw dropped before she consciously realised. 'Oh, Connor...'

'She only found out a few days ago. Told me yesterday.' He shrugged, though the movement was heavy with tension. 'I guess I'm going to be a dad.'

Callie wished she had the right words for him, but she didn't. Connor had been dating Elizabeth for less than six months. And, while she was a perfectly lovely girl, she knew Connor didn't want to start a family this way. Family was a responsibility that deserved attention, and she and Connor had lived by that because that was the way *they* had been raised.

Her heart cracked for him, but she knew that all she could do was offer her support. 'How do you feel about this?'

'I'm not sure. I think I'm still a little numb from the shock. It wasn't planned.'

She laughed a little. 'Yeah, I got *that* part.'

He gave her a wry smile, and then sobered. 'But… I *want* it, Cals. I want to keep the baby. And so does she. You know how much family means to me. And after Mom and Dad died I thought I'd lost that. Do you know what I mean?'

'Yes, I do.'

'Now I get to have my own…and I don't think that's a *bad* thing.'

'Of course it isn't!' She felt excitement bubble inside her at the prospect of seeing her brother as a father. And ignored the voice in her head that threatened to temper it. 'I think you're going to be an amazing father. I mean, an amazing brother, not so much—but definitely an amazing father!'

He laughed, and she could tell some of the tension had gone from him. Feeling an urge to make even more of it go away, she placed a hand over his and said, 'I think Mom and Dad would be so proud of you. There's no doubt in my mind that you're going to give your child what they gave us—a good, solid, wonderful family.'

He smiled at her, and they drove the rest of the way to the hotel in silence.

She'd meant every word she had said to him. She could picture Connor running around with a little boy or girl in the backyard, could see herself spending holidays with him and his family. So why did she feel so strange? Perhaps it was because she wished her parents could have been there to see their grandchildren? Yes, she knew there was some truth in that. But something niggled inside her, and she knew that wasn't quite all of it.

No, she thought suddenly, it was because now she wondered where *she* would fit into Connor's new life.

Something inside her broke, though she couldn't explain why. But before she could examine it they'd arrived at the hotel.

'Thank you.'

'Of course. Cals?' Connor looked over at her. 'Are you okay?'

She forced her doubts and her fears away, and smiled over at him. 'Yeah.' She got out of the car and hugged him when he joined her. 'It's going to be okay, Connor. I promise.'

She repeated the words to herself as she walked to her office, and then tried to force the situation out of her mind altogether so that she could focus on preparing for the meeting in less than an hour.

But her mind kept wandering, until finally she sighed and went to get herself a cup of coffee. Before she got to the kitchen she saw a flurry of activity around it, like bees weaving in and out of a beehive, and did a neat three-sixty turn and instead headed for the conference room.

Her heart beat a little faster as she knocked at the door, and it accelerated one hundredfold when she heard the muffled, 'Come in.'

'Hey,' she said as she walked in.

'Hi.' Blake smiled at her, and stood up at the end of the table. 'What are you doing here? I thought you were going to prepare for the meeting in your own office.'

'I was, but then I couldn't really focus and I needed coffee. And, since nowadays coffee in the kitchen comes with the dozens of questions my colleagues seem to have every time they see me, I thought I might persuade you to share.'

'No persuasion needed.' He grinned and walked to the counter to grab a mug. 'Can I pour you some?'

She nodded, and wordlessly took in how attractive he looked. She would never tire of it, she thought. Admiring him in a suit was definitely on the list of things that she most enjoyed doing.

'Black, one sugar, right?'

She shook herself, and blushed when she saw the amused look on his face. 'Yes, please.'

She walked to one of the conference room chairs and sat heavily, needing a moment to process everything. She was all over the place, she thought, and forced herself to be *present*. To be in the moment. She had so many important things to do. Her job depended on the tours she still had to do this week, and so did her brother's. And while she *was* struggling with processing her brother's announcement, she still wanted to support him. One of the biggest ways she could do that was to fight for the hotel he loved…and the job that he needed if he was going to be a father.

Then there was Blake, and all her feelings for him that were knotted in a ball at the base of her stomach. She took a deep breath in, and exhaled slowly.

'Hey, is everything okay?'

Blake handed her the coffee and sat on the chair next to hers.

'Thanks,' she said, and then answered him. 'Everything is fine. Just the usual concerns.' She smiled, but she could feel that it was off.

'About the event?'

She nodded, because she didn't know what else to do.

'Look, I know this isn't your thing. I remember the night we met Connor mentioned it was out of your comfort zone,' he elaborated when she looked up in surprise. 'Which makes me respect your suggestion for doing it all the more. But you don't have to worry. After the meeting today we'll know exactly where we stand with the planning, and we can take it from there.'

She stared blankly at the cup of coffee in her hands, and blew at the steam in an attempt to cool it down. She had heard him, but her thoughts had almost immediately drifted away to Connor's situation. What would it mean for *their* relationship? She knew his child would come first, of course, but would that mean that she would lose him, too?

'Callie?'

'Mmm?' She looked up at Blake and realised he was waiting for a response when she saw the questioning look on his face.

'Yes, I know it's going to be fine.' She laid a hand on his cheek, finding the warmth there comforting, and then stood. 'I need to prepare. Thanks for the coffee.'

'Are you sure you're okay?'

'I'm fine.' She brushed a kiss on his lips. 'I'll see you at the meeting.'

She walked out the door, her mind already wandering back to Connor.

Blake leaned against his car and resisted the urge to pace.

Callie had been so unlike herself today that he had wanted to corner her as soon as he could to demand that she give him something other than her generic 'I'm fine.' He hated to think that it was about him, but after what he had shared with her the previous evening, the thought kept strolling through his head, making him restless.

He knew he hadn't stayed very long after he'd told her about Julia, but he'd thought it was best for them to spend some time apart to process what had just happened. Because something had shifted between them, and he'd wanted to give her space—and, yes, give himself space too—to come to terms with it.

He hadn't worried that he'd done the wrong thing until he'd seen her in the conference room. She'd been pale, and her usual vibrant demeanour had seemed almost brittle. She had looked...*fragile*.

Again he despised the thought that it might have been because of him. But the more he'd seen of her that day, the more he'd thought that it might be. She had still been professional—she had handled the meeting with a grace and leadership that had had him thinking about her future at Elegance—but underneath it he'd been able to see that something was wrong.

So he had gone rogue and told Connor that Callie would be working late that night, that he shouldn't worry about getting her home because Blake would drop her. Connor had dubiously accepted, but had thankfully been distracted enough not to verify it with Callie. He knew the man had been under a lot of strain lately, and there were rings under his eyes that looked like thunderclouds. But it would be over soon enough, and none of his employees would have to worry about their future any more.

He looked at his watch and wondered if Callie had got his message that *he* would be taking her home. He was just about to call when he heard the click of heels coming towards him. He looked up and was blown away by her beauty all over again. He had been right that first night they'd met, he thought, about her walking as though on a red carpet. She was so graceful, so elegant, that it made him square his shoulders and take his hands out his pockets.

She looked up at him and smiled—an utterly exhausted smile, but a smile nevertheless—and tightened her grip on the handbag under her arm.

'Are you making up for lost time with these lifts?' she asked easily, and something in Blake's heart released.

'Maybe. Or maybe I just like seeing if I can trick your brother into forgetting how protective he is of you.'

Her smile dimmed, and then she said, 'We should probably get going.'

Blake frowned, wondering what he had said wrong, but he opened the car door and waited as she got in. Then he decided to drive to his house instead.

She didn't say a word to him—not even when he drove in completely the opposite direction to her house. She only looked up when the gates to his house opened.

'Where are we?'

'My place. I figured I could make you some dinner.'

She looked at him in surprise. 'You *cook*?'

'Yes, I do. And I'll try not to be offended by the incredulity in your eyes.' He smiled at her. 'Do you have anything against steak?'

CHAPTER FOURTEEN

CALLIE TRIED TO KEEP a neutral expression on her face as she looked up at the place where Blake lived.

The house was a combination of brick and glass, with brown frames outlining the doors and windows. A deck on the upper level of the house overlooked a vast estate, including a small pond that Callie could see from where she was standing outside his car. She walked forward, caught a glimpse of the city lights, and imagined that standing on his deck would be quite an experience.

When Blake had unlocked the large oak door he stepped aside for her to walk past and her neutral expression gave way to a jaw-drop.

Brick walls, wooden furniture and sparks of green were scattered across the living room in a design that screamed warmth. A fireplace was the focal point of the room—and rightly so, she thought as she took in its impressive design, and then walked through the room to a passage that opened onto the kitchen and dining room.

The kitchen space was huge, and had the same homely yet modern design as the living room. Granite counters were highlighted by pops of colour and a window looked out onto a garden that made her salivate. The dining room was more elegant—wooden floors and a black dining room set that was decked out with cutlery and crockery that looked incredibly expensive.

'This is not what I expected from you.'

'Did you think I lived in a cold black and white room?' He smirked as he said it, but his eyes grew serious when she nodded.

'Something like that. This is a lot more...*inviting* than I expected.'

He looked around, as though seeing it for the first time. 'It is, isn't it? Though it's wasted on me. I've barely spent any time here, and the decor was pretty much left to the interior designer I hired.'

'Perhaps they decorated according to what they thought the house needed instead of thinking about its owner.'

He narrowed his eyes. 'I'm not sure if you just complimented me or insulted me.'

She laughed, and felt a bit of the tension of the day leave her. 'I was only agreeing with you that this house needs to be somewhere people are invited to.' She ran a hand over the kitchen counter. 'It deserves a family.'

The words felt fatalistic as she said them, and although she knew why it felt that way for her, she wasn't sure what the expression on Blake's face meant.

Then it cleared and he smiled. 'Well, you haven't seen the second floor, where I spend most of my time. It's a lot colder than this.'

He winked and she laughed.

'Now, shall we have some supper?'

She nodded, and settled back on a bar stool at the kitchen counter. Though she wanted to offer her help, there was something about watching him go through the motions of making a meal that helped soothe the turmoil inside her. She also wanted to speak, to tell him of all that was going through her head, but she couldn't bring herself to interrupt what seemed surprisingly easy for him. So she just sat and watched him—watched as he spiced the meat, seared it in a pan, and popped it into the oven.

He took out two wine glasses, poured a liberal amount of wine into each, and handed a glass to her.

'Now, will you tell me what's happening in that head of yours?'

'What do you mean?' she asked, but she didn't look him in the eye.

'Callie, come on. You and I both know you've been distracted today. We promised each other we would be open.'

She looked up at him when he paused, and felt alarm go through her as he clenched his teeth.

'If this is because of Julia, then—'

'What?' she exclaimed, and then she placed her wine down and walked around the counter until she was in front of him. She brushed the piece of hair he should really have cut out of his face and kept her hand on his cheek for a moment. 'No, Blake. This isn't about Julia—or you.'

He took her hands and squeezed. 'Then what's wrong?'

She bit her lip and then she said, very softly, 'Connor is going to be a father.'

Blake felt his eyebrows lift, and then carefully rearranged his features. 'And that's a *bad* thing?'

'No, I don't think so.'

She walked back around the counter, and Blake thought it might be symbolic, somehow, her placing an obstacle between them.

'I mean, it isn't the *best* thing that could happen to him right now, what with our jobs being on the line and him only knowing his girlfriend for six months...'

This time Blake didn't try to hide his surprise, and Callie grinned at him.

'That's not like the man you thought you knew so well, is it?'

'No, it isn't.' He looked up at her, and saw something in her eyes that prompted him to ask, 'Or is it?'

'I'm beginning to think it is.'

She lifted her wine glass slowly, not meeting his eye. And when she did, he saw a flash of pain that quickly settled into something he couldn't quite identify.

'I mean, not the getting-a-girl-pregnant thing. But the baby…' She trailed off. 'I think it helped Connor cope with my parents' deaths when he had to help *me*.'

'What do you mean?'

She looked at him, then sighed. 'Should we be making a salad, or something else to go with the steak?'

He didn't respond, recognising her ploy, but walked to the fridge and started removing vegetables. He was glad he had made a visit to the shop the day before—he'd wanted steak and his conscience had guilted him into buying the ingredients for a salad. He'd have to do it more often if Callie visited regularly.

And then he stopped, remembering her earlier words about his house needing family, and something nudged at him. But he forced it away and handed her cherry tomatoes and an avocado to cut. Before he knew it—and, he thought, before she was ready—they were done.

'Nothing left to distract you now,' he said, and laid a hand on her cheek. 'Tell me.'

She sighed again, walked back around the counter and sat down. Then she spoke without looking at him. 'I just mean that family has always *meant* something to Connor. To both of us, really, but to him most of all. And when our parents died they left a void that we both felt.' She paused. 'I thought that we'd filled it for one another. But I think this baby is going to do it for him.'

Blake watched her as she spoke. Her shoulders were tight, and he realised that she was embarrassed by what she was saying. Suddenly it clicked.

'And you're going to be left alone?'

She didn't look up at him, but he thought he saw a tear roll down her cheek.

'Yeah, that's it. Except that admitting it makes me sound selfish.'

Before she had finished speaking Blake pulled her into his arms. He wanted to comfort her—needed to, perhaps—because he was feeling less and less comfortable with what she was saying and he wasn't sure why. So he focused on her, and said what he thought she needed to hear.

'Callie, I know that Connor helped you get through your parents' deaths. And you have every right to be grateful to him for that. But he isn't the reason you got through it.' He leaned back so he could look into her eyes. '*You* are.'

She blinked, and two more tears escaped from her eyes. 'Connor *did* help me get through my parents' deaths.' She said it slowly, deliberately, as though trying to convince him of the fact.

'I know he did. But just because he helped you, it doesn't mean he's the *reason* you made it through.'

He repeated it, stopping only to check how his words were affecting her.

'Callie, when you told me about how you dealt with everything you said that *you* were the one who became interested in your job. *You* chose to start interacting with the guests. *You* were the one who took the initiative to start tours. Connor could never have forced you to do it, even if he'd waited outside your house every single day for a year.'

He stopped, trying to gauge whether she was taking it in.

'I know Connor is important to you, and that the two

of you have been through a lot together, but that doesn't mean you can't do it alone. Besides, you won't be alone.'

She looked up at him now, and the hope in her eyes knocked him in the gut.

'I mean, I don't think Connor won't be there for you any more just because he's having a baby.' He said the words quickly, for reasons he didn't want to examine. Not when they were so entwined with feelings he couldn't explain. The hope in her eyes was quickly dimmed, and although he knew he had spoken in response to that hope its extinguishment disappointed him.

'Yeah, maybe you're right,' she said, and was quiet as she waited for him to dish up.

And even though the meal was one of his favourites to make on the rare occasions he was at home, he didn't taste it. His thoughts were too busy with why he had tried to back out of the support he wanted to offer her.

'I think I forgot that Connor's baby will be my family, too.'

Callie spoke softly, and dragged him from his thoughts. Her expression was pensive, but when she met his eyes there was a sparkle there that had been missing the entire day.

'I've been thinking selfishly all day.'

'Your reaction was completely normal. You weren't being selfish.'

'Maybe normal, but definitely selfish.'

She smiled at him, and his lips curved in response. 'Maybe just a little.'

She laughed lightly, cut another piece from her steak, and then looked at him. 'You're the first person who's ever made me feel like it's okay to be alone. Or that I might have helped *myself* get out of my depression. Thank you.'

Her words were so sincere that they ripped at his heart,

and immediately he felt like a fraud. He didn't deserve her gratitude when he couldn't even tell her that he would be there for her. When her simple comments about family had frozen him up.

'You're welcome.'

They ate the rest of their meal in silence, each lost in thought, and when they were done she ran the water for washing the dishes. He sat back, watching her as she pulled plates into the soapy water, rinsed them, and then placed them on the dish rack. Slowly, almost without realising it, he began to picture her there after a long day at work.

He could almost see the rain outside the window above where she was washing up, could hear the fire roaring in the living room. He even saw himself walking to her and offering a hand, drawing her close to him as he touched her stomach, where she was carrying their child...

'You know, I think before today I hadn't thought about family outside of my parents and brother. But it's nice to think that we could expand.'

He was ripped out of his fantasy, felt his heart racing faster than he'd thought possible. 'Yeah?'

'Yeah.' She turned to him and her expression softened. 'Wasn't your time with Brent good?'

His heart still pounded as he answered her. 'Yes, it was.'

'I thought so.' She nodded, and started washing again. 'Connor's going to be an amazing father. And being an aunt won't be so bad.'

It was almost as though she was thinking out loud.

'I'll get to practise for when I have my own kids one day. *Ha!* I hadn't even thought about having my own family until now.'

'Do you *want* to have a family?' he asked, before he could stop himself. He didn't think he would have been able to stop himself even if he'd had the chance. Not when he still saw that picture of her pregnant in their house—no, *his* house—vividly in his mind.

She turned around and wiped her hands with a dry cloth. 'Yeah—yeah, I think I do.' She tilted her head and said, 'It's our legacy, I guess.' She smiled at him. 'Building on the foundation of family that our parents gave us.'

The words hit him right in the stomach, and finally he realised what it was that was bothering him. *Family.* The word that described his biggest disappointments. And now, he thought in panic, his biggest fear.

'Callie, do you mind if I take you home?' he asked, and ignored the voice in his head that called him a coward. 'It's getting late and I still have a couple of things to do before our next proposal tomorrow.'

'Um…okay—sure,' she said, and his heart clenched when he saw her bewildered expression.

He helped her with the dishes in silence as he tried to work through the thoughts in his head. He wanted it. Family. With Callie. Never before had he felt a need more intense. Never before had he seen something this clearly. But he'd lost things before. Things that hadn't meant nearly as much to him. And those things had nearly broken him.

Like Brent, he thought as they made their way to the car. He'd loved that boy more than he'd thought he could, and his heart was still raw from not being near him. And like his parents, who had both, in their own way, left him. He fought the memories of those heartbreaks every day, still carried the scars of them with him.

More so than he had realised, he thought, remembering his conversation with Callie on the boat when she had pointed it out to him.

If somehow this didn't work out between them—if, for some reason, Callie left him—he knew he wouldn't be able to go on as though nothing had happened. No, he would be a broken man. And she would carry the pieces of him with her, so that he would never be able to put himself together again.

And even if she didn't leave he would risk disappointing her. He knew nothing about family. Nothing about the foundation she spoke of—her *legacy*. He didn't have much to contribute to that. His mother had left him and his father was more business partner than parent.

It didn't matter that he wanted to be a part of her life, he thought sadly, and it didn't matter that he wanted to have a family with her. What mattered was that he would fail her—just as he had Brent. And he knew that it would kill him if he failed her. And more importantly, he realised, it would devastate him to hurt her like that.

'Hey, what's going on?' she said softly, taking one of his hands.

Blake turned to her and realised that he had pulled up in front of her driveway. He wondered when that had happened.

'Nothing,' he answered, feeling his heart hurting from the lie, but knowing it was for the best.

The only way to avoid disappointing, failing or hurting her—*and* himself—was to put some distance between them. And, though it killed him, that meant not talking to her about the way he felt. Not when he still needed to figure out what to do about it.

'Really?' she scoffed. 'So we've been sitting here for ten minutes for you to think about *nothing*?'

He resisted the urge to tell her what was wrong, and forced himself to think about the look on Brent's face the last time Blake had seen him. The memory of the mixture of emotions in the little boy's eyes—especially the heartbreak—helped him steel his heart.

He *never* wanted to see that expression on Callie's face.

'It's just been a long day, that's all.'

She looked at him for a while, and then moved her hands to her lap. 'So, is this "being open" you reminded me of earlier something that only *I* have to follow?'

Though his heart tightened at the emotion in her voice, he ignored it. He was doing the only thing that would protect both of them. 'Look, there really isn't anything going on. I've just had a long day, and I still need to get things done. I was thinking about that.' He tried to smile, but knew he was failing miserably at it.

'Fine. If that's what you're going with.'

She picked up her bag and got out of the car, but the tiny moment of relief Blake felt was shattered when she slammed the door shut.

'Callie.'

He got out quickly, not knowing what he could say—not when he wanted space to think about everything—yet he needed her to be okay with him.

'Please.'

She stopped on the first step of the path up to her house and then turned to him. He knew the hurt in her eyes was a picture that would stay with him through the night.

'Look, if you need time to work through whatever's going on, that's fine. But don't lie to me about it.'

He walked towards her, but stuffed the hands that itched to take hers into his pockets.

'Okay.' He paused, then exhaled slowly. 'I need time.'

She nodded. 'Okay.' She kissed his cheek and walked to her house, shutting the door after a slight wave.

And for a long time afterwards Blake stood outside her house, thinking about the choice he needed to make and why he needed to make it.

CHAPTER FIFTEEN

IT WAS FINALLY FRIDAY, the day was gorgeous, and the final arrangements for the gala event were going well.

It was being held on the Elegance's rooftop—an idea Callie had had after she and Blake had gone for the tasting. It had taken some planning—and a lot of convincing—to change the venue so soon before the event, but as she looked around she was glad she'd managed it.

Pillars stood at each corner of the rooftop, with mini-lanterns draped between them. A stage had been set up at one end, adorned with light. The band they'd hired were setting up there, and any speeches during the evening would be made from it. Tables had been set around the centre of the roof, with white flower centrepieces and napkins on black tablecloths, leaving space for a dance floor. The food would be plated, there was a bar up and ready, and the bustle of the staff doing the final touches should have given Callie a sense of accomplishment.

Except that as she stood there, looking at everything, she wasn't feeling anything except dread.

All she'd been able to think about for the last few days was the way Blake had decided to take her home after the dinner they'd had at his house. The way he'd lied to her about what was bothering him. And although she told herself to be patient, although she reassured herself that he would tell her when he was ready, every time she saw him the feeling of dread deepened.

Because somehow she knew he was slipping away from her.

She'd tried to brush it off at first as paranoia. He wasn't acting differently around her—at least not on the surface. But her heart knew that there were no more lingering looks, no more affectionate touches. Those had been replaced with smiles that had no depth and words that didn't say what he meant. She'd hidden the hurt, hidden the concern, and waited in vain for him to tell her what was wrong.

And the wait was breaking her.

'It's amazing.'

She turned to see Blake surveying the area. He offered her a smile, and again she was struck by how different it was.

'Yeah, I can't believe we actually pulled it off.' She looked around again, and then returned his smile tentatively. 'I think it's going to be a success.'

He nodded, and she saw something flash across his eyes.

And then he said, 'Shouldn't you be busy with your hair? We only have four more hours until the event. You're cutting it close.'

She tilted her head, trying to figure out his mood. 'No, I have my things downstairs. I'll get ready once I'm sure everything is done up here.'

He stuffed his hands into his pockets. 'I was joking, Callie.'

'Were you?' She shrugged, ignoring the pain in her heart. 'I can't seem to tell with you lately.'

'Look,' he said, and then took a deep breath.

He stood in silence for a moment—his hands still in his pockets, his face tense—and Callie felt her nails cutting into her hands as she clenched her fists, waiting for him.

'Did you say you have your things downstairs?'

'What?'

'You don't have an afternoon of pampering planned after this week?'

'No, Blake, I don't.' She brushed off the irritability that threatened. 'I didn't have time to make the appointments this week nor do I want to spend a ridiculous amount of money on a new dress—'

'You don't have a dress to wear tonight?' he interrupted her.

'Of course I do,' she said defensively. 'It's just not new. It's one of my mom's. But what does that have to do with anything?'

Callie was ashamed of the desperation that coated her tone.

He looked at her for a few moments, and then pulled out his phone, his fingers speeding over the screen. A 'ping' sounded almost immediately, and he nodded and put it back into his pocket. Then he looked at her, and something in his eyes softened her heart.

'Would you come with me?'

His voice was hesitant, as though he wasn't quite sure of what she was going to say. That, combined with the look in his eyes, made her insides crumble, and she took the hand he offered. Even though everything inside her wanted to say no, wanted to ask him why he was allowing this uncertainty to eat at them, she let him lead her down the stairs.

And felt hopeless when the thought that she would follow him anywhere flitted through her mind.

They didn't speak when they reached the parking garage, and she waited for him as he moved to open the car door for her. But his hand stilled on the handle and he stepped back.

'What's wrong?' she asked—and then she saw the look in his eyes and felt herself tremble.

She was standing just behind the front door of the car, and when he took a step towards her instinct had her moving back against it. Her heart thudded as his hands slid around her waist and he pulled her closer, until she was moulded to his body. She looked up at him, breathless, and her knees nearly gave way at the need, the desperation in his eyes.

She closed her own eyes when he moved his head—closed them against the onslaught of emotions that flooded through her at the look on his face—and thought that their kiss would be filled with hunger, with the passion that need brought.

But instead it was so tender that she nearly wept. She slid her hands through his hair and shivers went down her spine when he deepened their kiss, taking more. She felt herself being swept away with it, but her heart cracked, just a little, as she thought that he must be trying to memorise the way she tasted, the way she felt.

Her heart demanded the same, and she slowly opened the buttons of his shirt and slid her hands up and down his chest, over his abs and back up again. She shook when the muscles beneath her hands trembled.

And then he moved back, breathing heavily, with his forehead against hers. She realised that she was breathing heavily too, and she stepped away from him, laying a hand on her racing heart. Finally, time and place caught up with her and she looked around, half expecting to see a colleague looking at them with shock. But the parking garage was empty, and for some strange reason she felt disappointment.

'I'm sorry,' he said, and she saw that he had buttoned his shirt up.

'Why are you apologising?' she asked, and braced herself for his answer.

But he simply said that someone might have seen them,

and she nodded, not trusting herself to speak when she realised *why* she felt disappointed that no one had.

Because now there was no proof that everything that had happened between her and Blake hadn't only been in her head.

He opened the car door for her, and when he'd got in he pulled out of the parking garage and started driving towards the business centre of Cape Town.

'Where are you taking me?' she asked, when she thought she had her thoughts—and her body—back under control.

'To a friend. You'll see when we get there,' he said quietly, and again Callie wondered what was going on with him. With them.

She had never felt this unsure in her life. Even when her parents had died she had had certainty. She'd known they were gone, and the only thing she'd been unsure of then had been herself. Now she was wondering if she'd made up their relationship—could she even call it that?—in her head. The feelings, the sharing... Had that just been wishful thinking? Was she just a fling to him? Someone to pass the time with?

No, she thought. That couldn't be it. Not when they'd shared things that she knew had been new for both of them. Besides, he'd never tried anything besides kissing with her. And, yes, the kissing had been hot and delicious, but he'd had the opportunity to press for more. Like the evening they'd been at his house... But instead he'd just dropped her off at home. That didn't seem like a man who wanted a fling.

But why hadn't he defined what they were? an inner voice asked her. He'd never told her that she was his girlfriend. A mistake, she realised, and suddenly she was immensely tired of the back and forth of her thoughts. She was going to ask him, once and for all. She would demand to know what they were to one another, and why he had pushed her away that night. She would demand the truth from him.

Satisfied with her resolution, she opened her mouth to speak—but the words stuck when he pulled up in front of two large bronze gates. Blake pressed the buzzer and told the crackly voice who he was, and the gates opened.

Callie held her breath as they drove up the path and she saw the large white house in front of them. Blake pulled into one of the designated parking bays and they walked to the front door, barely having enough time to press the button before the door opened and a woman stepped out and pulled Blake into her arms.

Callie might have felt threatened if the woman had done it in a remotely flirtatious way. But her hug was almost maternal, and Callie felt interest prickle when the woman drew back and said, 'Let me take a look at you.' She scanned Blake from his head to his toes and back up again, and then she smiled, and Callie thought it made her look years younger. 'Blake, you're an adult. I can't believe it.'

He laughed. 'Yes, Caroline, I have been now for quite some time.'

'Which I would have known, had you visited me at any point during that time.' She gave him a stern look, and then waved a hand. 'But that's water under the bridge now that you're here.'

She turned and Callie felt her back stiffen as she was sized up.

'And who are *you*, darling?'

'This is Callie. She's…a friend of mine.' He paused, as though thinking about what he had called her, and then continued. 'She needs a new dress for an event at the hotel tonight.'

'Oh, why didn't you just say so? Come on, let's go in.'

She walked past the two of them down the passage, and entered a room right at the end. Callie and Blake followed, and she whispered, 'Who *is* this woman?'

'She's an old family friend. My mother's, actually, though she didn't want us to hold that against her when my mother left. Her name is Caroline Bellinger.'

Callie stopped in her tracks. 'You *know* Caroline Bellinger?'

'Yes. Why?'

'*Why?*' She looked at him incredulously. 'Caroline Bellinger is Cape Town's top designer. She's designed dresses for local celebrities for almost all of our glamourous events. She isn't just someone's "family friend".'

'Do you plan on joining me, or are you going to stand in the passage whispering about me all day?' Caroline called from the room.

Blake grinned. A genuine one this time, she noted.

'She's astute, isn't she? Come on, let's find you a dress for tonight.'

From that moment Callie felt as though she had been selected for a makeover show. Caroline examined her even more critically than she had when they'd met, and Callie had to resist the cringe that came over her when Caroline announced that she had a body 'like a movie star'. She could tell Blake was enjoying the show, but Caroline shooed him out before she pulled out any dresses.

'You can follow Darren, Blake. He'll take you to the restaurant where we make all the men wait while we do this.'

The man who appeared when his name was called nodded at Blake, and Blake gave Callie a reassuring nod before leaving. She held her breath when she realised that Caroline was now looking at her, and she felt the weight of the woman's stare.

'So, you and Blake are...*friends*?'

Caroline didn't believe it for a second, Callie thought, but answered, 'Yes, I think so.'

'I didn't need an answer, dear. I just wanted to see your face after my question.'

Caroline didn't elaborate on what she'd seen there, and walked past Callie to a rack of dresses on the other side of the room.

'I met another friend of Blake's a while ago. Except it was at their wedding.'

Callie quickly realised what Caroline was implying, and it had her shaking her head. 'No, no. This isn't anything like him and Julia.'

Caroline raised her eyebrows. 'No, it can't be if he's told you about her.'

She returned to Callie with four dresses, each of which looked as though they were fit for royalty.

'He didn't bring her here, you know.'

'Excuse me?'

Caroline handed her a midnight-blue dress that Callie worried might not cover nearly as much of her body as she would have liked before answering.

'I always thought I would be the one to make Blake's bride's wedding dress. Though he didn't even ask me.' She looked at Callie again, and this time the gaze felt distinctly more piercing. 'And yet here you are. For a dress for an event at the hotel.' She paused again, and then simply said, 'You can get changed over there.'

She pointed to a dressing screen and Callie followed, not sure what else she was supposed to do. Or whether she was supposed to speak at all. The woman had given her so many innuendoes that Callie wasn't sure she was able to process them all.

She dressed as quickly as she could, and almost sighed when she felt the silk on her skin. It was luxurious, she thought, grateful for the distraction of something as simple as a dress. Except that this dress was anything *but* simple. She thought she could easily become used to such luxury... until she walked out and Caroline shook her head.

'Oh, *no*, that's dreadful.'

Callie felt her face blanch, but Caroline waved a hand.

'No, darling, it's not you—it's the combination of you and that dress. Try this one instead. I think it'll do wonders for that rich skin tone of yours. And it won't hide your curves either.'

She winked, and Callie took the dress wordlessly.

She knew that artists could be eccentric—but, honestly, she hadn't ever experienced it first-hand before. It was strange that this woman was a part of Blake's life. Her conservative boss—she'd settled on using that term, since she wasn't sure *what* to call him personally—didn't strike her as someone who would be familiar with a person so—well, *unique*. Especially when Caroline seemed to see things Callie didn't think most people would want her to see—especially not someone as private as Blake.

She looked down at the dress, noting how much tighter it was than the previous one, and resisted pulling at the neckline that lay just a touch too low for her liking. When she walked out in the emerald dress Caroline clasped her hands together in what Callie could only imagine was delight.

'This is *it*. This is the *one*.'

Callie doubted the dress required that much enthusiasm, and was still thinking about it when Caroline asked her what size shoe she wore. She responded automatically, even though she wanted to tell the woman that she had some shoes she could wear with the dress. But then Caroline brought out the most gorgeous silver pair Callie had ever seen and she kept her mouth shut.

'Gorgeous—though there's something missing...' She

looked at Callie for a few more moments, and then went to fetch something from a glass cabinet.

Callie didn't realise what it was until Caroline presented her with a diamond necklace.

'Oh, Caroline, I couldn't—'

'You can, and you will.' She fastened the necklace around Callie's neck herself, and then led her to the mirror.

Callie was almost afraid to look, but she caught her reflection before she had a chance to close her eyes and nearly gasped. She looked… *Wow*, she thought. Maybe the dress *had* required that much enthusiasm. She almost didn't recognise herself.

Caroline had been right about the colour, and the gown fitted her perfectly. The necklace sparkled up at her, matching the shoes that she could see beneath the slit that ran up her left leg. She had never seen herself like this before. Not even on the night of Blake's welcome event had she looked this elegant.

She remained silent when Caroline stood behind her and twisted her hair into some kind of chignon.

'You should wear your hair like this. And just a touch of make-up. We don't want to hide any of your natural beauty.'

Callie nodded wordlessly, not trusting herself to speak. What could she possibly say to this woman who had made her look like a princess?

'It's okay, dear. You don't have to thank me. That look on your face is more than enough.' Caroline smiled at her, and for the first time since they'd met Callie could see what it was about the woman that Blake cared about.

She returned Caroline's smile and walked back behind the screen, undressing slowly so that she didn't do any damage to the dress. When she was done, she handed it over to Caroline along with the shoes and the necklace.

'Caroline, I don't think I can take these from you.' She

gestured to the accessories she knew must have cost a fortune.

'You can't have the dress if you don't.'

'What?'

Caroline put the dress in a clothing bag and said again, 'You can't wear this dress if you don't take the accessories.'

'Why…why not?'

'Because you need the whole package for Blake to get that feeling *you* had when you looked in the mirror.' Caroline smiled kindly when Callie lifted her eyebrows. 'You don't think I saw the surprise on your face when you looked at yourself? I think it would give Blake a good kick in the behind to see you like that. And, from what I know about that man, he could use it.'

Again, Callie didn't respond.

'I'm *so* glad he brought you here.'

Suddenly Callie found herself in Caroline's arms.

Hesitantly, she put her arms around the woman, and she felt an odd sense of comfort when she said, 'Be patient with him. He'll get there eventually.'

She drew back, and Caroline smiled again, and for a moment Callie wondered what 'there' meant. She realised too late that she'd asked Caroline out loud, and waited with bated breath for the answer.

'You'll know soon enough, dear,' she said, before calling Blake, and Callie knew her chance to probe was gone.

'Are you sorted?' Blake asked when he walked in.

'Yes, she is.' Caroline patted his cheek. 'No need for thanks. You can just send the things back after the event.'

'Of course. We can sort out payment at a later point.'

Callie immediately wanted to offer payment too—even though heaven only knew how she would be able to afford it—but Caroline had narrowed her eyes.

'Blake, you say something that offensive to me again,

and I swear I will tell the world that you stole this dress from me.'

He laughed, and then sobered. 'I appreciate it, Caroline.'

'Anything for you.' For the first time, Caroline looked completely serious. 'I'm just so happy to see you, Blake. You look good.'

As they drove away Callie didn't say anything. Caroline's cryptic words kept swirling around in her head, rousing the thoughts she had refused to have for such a long time. Rousing feelings she had ignored even when they had demanded attention. Because she couldn't give in to them. Not when she didn't know where she stood with Blake.

One moment she felt as if she didn't know this man she'd spent so much time with, the next he was kissing her as if he was a dying man and she was his last breath. And then he'd arranged this trip to a fairy godmother.

How could she love a man like that? she thought, and then went very still when she realised it.

The very simple truth that made his strange behaviour so difficult to swallow.

She looked away, out of the window, although she didn't see any of the buildings they passed. She just needed to look away from him. She didn't want him to know that she loved him. That she—Callie McKenzie, who hadn't thought she would ever open herself up enough to fall in love—was in love with her boss.

She squeezed her eyes closed, letting herself process the novelty of her thoughts.

Except that they weren't new, she thought. They had been there since—well, she didn't even know. But then Caroline had nudged her and cracked the armour she'd protected the thoughts in. She was in love with an incredible man. A man who cared about his company, about people, about *her*. A man who made her feel she wasn't alone. A man who had helped her work through feelings from the most difficult part of her past.

If she'd had to pick him from a list on paper, Callie would have put money on herself picking Blake, and a part of her took joy from that. But that joy was quickly dimmed by the fact that the man she had fallen in love with wasn't the man who was sitting next to her. And it terrified her—wholly and completely—to consider the reasons why that was the case.

She was so deep in thought that she didn't even notice that they'd stopped until Blake put a hand on her thigh.

'Callie?'

'Yeah?'

'We're here.'

She looked around in surprise. 'This isn't the hotel.'

'No, it isn't. This is the salon my stepmother goes to. I made an appointment for you, and a car will come and get you in a few hours.'

'Blake, this really isn't necessary…'

'A car will come and get you and bring you back in time for the event,' he repeated, and then he continued, 'There will probably be someone inside to help you with all the make-up stuff, too.'

'Blake—'

'No, don't say it. Don't tell me that you don't want this. Because this isn't about you. This is *for* you. You deserve this. After all you've done…' He lifted a hand to her face and she thought that it was as if he *needed* her to believe him. 'You deserve a few hours of relaxation. When people do things for *you*. Let me do this for you, okay?'

She wished she could just accept his words at face value. Her heart was full of him, of his compassion, of his gesture for her. But something told her that he'd said them out of obligation. Out of a need for her to accept this from him. And how could she resist such a plea?

'Okay.'

He leaned over and kissed her cheek. 'I'll see you in a little bit. Go and have fun.'

CHAPTER SIXTEEN

BLAKE WAS SURE he would burn a trail in the carpet if he didn't stop pacing.

But he felt unsettled and couldn't stop. Not when some of his employees passed him, smiling politely to hide their curiosity, or even when guests did, aiming puzzled looks at him as he walked back and forth in front of one of the rooms. He wasn't sure if it was adrenaline for what was to come during the evening that fuelled his legs, or anticipation at seeing Callie when she finally emerged from the room she was using to get ready in.

He hadn't seen her when she'd got back, so he didn't know what she had thought about the limo he had sent to pick her up. It might have been overkill, but he wanted her to feel like a princess tonight. He wanted her to know that the effort she had put into the hotel hadn't been for nothing. He wanted her to know that what they'd shared together *meant* something to him. Especially when he wouldn't be able to tell her himself…

He paused. He didn't want to think about those plans. He didn't want to think about the way he had put distance between them, about Callie's face every time he'd done so. He didn't want to think about leaving her when it was all too painful. When he was doing it because he couldn't bear to lose her, to disappoint her. He just wanted to spend one night with her without worrying about what it would do to them when he left. Or, worse, what it would do to her if he stayed and couldn't give her what she wanted.

But he wasn't running, he assured himself. He was just saving them both from the potential hurt.

But all thoughts froze in his head when she opened the door and hesitantly took two steps towards him.

The neckline of her gown lay lazily over her chest, hugging her curves and accelerating his heart. Especially when he saw a diamond necklace sparkling just above her breasts, as though it wanted to distract him and draw his attention to them at the same time. The rest of the dress was just as flattering, clinging to her curves and revealing legs that Blake now realised he had vastly under-appreciated. She wore silver shoes that wrapped around her legs from just below her knee, and never before had he found a pair of shoes more attractive.

Finally, when his body had settled, he rested his eyes on her face. Her hair was like silk, tied into some kind of intricate knot at the base of her skull. And her face was glowing, slightly red at his appraisal, and absolutely gorgeous.

'Hi...' she said huskily, and Blake had to check himself before he could speak.

'Hi. You look amazing.'

She smiled hesitantly, closed the door behind her, and Blake had the pleasure of seeing how much skin the back of the dress revealed. He wasn't sure which side of it he appreciated more, he thought, and smiled when she turned back to him. Just one night, he promised himself—and his conscience—and offered his arm.

'Thank you,' she said as she straightened the tiny train of the dress behind her.

When they got to the elevator he looked at her in question.

'It would probably be best if we took the elevator today,' she said, without moving.

He squeezed her hand. 'Don't worry, the electricity won't go off tonight. And if it does I've made sure the generator is working, so we won't get stuck.'

'Famous last words…' she breathed, and then straightened her shoulders and walked into the small box.

He smiled at her bravado, and selected the button for the rooftop. He knew she held her breath as they steadily moved up, and when the doors pinged open she let out a huge sigh of relief.

'You ready?' she asked, and turned to him, the tension of a few moments ago only slightly abated.

He refused to think about what the remainder of that tension meant.

'I think so.'

'Then let's do this.'

'Dance with me.'

Callie turned to Blake and had her refusal ready when she saw he had the same look on his face as that afternoon when he'd kissed her.

But he didn't wait for an answer. Instead he took her glass and placed it with his own on the closest waiter's tray. Then he led her to the dance floor and pulled her in close. Every nerve in her body was awakened and prickled with awareness at the feel of him against her. His hand pressed against her naked lower back and sent shivers down her spine, and when she looked up at him her breath caught.

He looked at her with longing, with a sadness she hadn't expected. But she didn't want to think about it. She didn't want to think about all that had plagued them over the last few days. No, tonight she wanted to stand in the middle of the dance floor on the rooftop, under the moonlight, and sway to the music with the man she loved.

'Callie?'

She lifted her head and the illusion of a few moments ago was gone. And it had taken any thoughts she had about love with it.

'What is it?'

He looked at her, his eyes filled with an emotion she knew only too well.

'We need to talk.'

She clenched her jaw as a voice in her head told her that she wasn't being paranoid. She stiffened in his arms and looked at him, trying to read him even though it pained her to do so. And what she saw gave her the answer to all the questions she'd had.

'You're leaving.'

His arms tightened around her, and she had to stop herself from pulling away from him.

'Callie—'

'Don't.' She didn't look at him, and was grateful when the song ended. 'Just *don't.*'

She wanted to hate him for it—for doing this to her after making her feel like a princess. After making her fall in love with him. But she forced all feelings aside and worked the room, pretending everything was normal.

She clapped along with everybody else when Blake walked up onto the stage to thank everyone for coming, and laughed jovially when he told them he looked forward to taking their money the following week. But when the formalities were done she couldn't take it any more. She slipped away to Connor, and asked him if he could wrap things up for her.

'Yeah, sure. Things shouldn't go on too long anyway.' He looked at her, and then frowned. 'Are you okay?'

'I'm fine.' She brushed a kiss over his cheek. 'Thanks. I've spoken to all the investors, so I know they're happy with the event. You just need to facilitate the clean-up afterwards. I'll see you soon, okay?'

She didn't wait for his response, though she could tell that his gaze was on her as she walked away from the event. She didn't look back as she took the stairs in her evening gown, too distressed to take a chance on the elevator. They had pulled it off, she thought, and immediately felt grief at the use of 'they' for her and Blake. There would be no more of that, she knew.

She laid a hand on the railing of the staircase, bracing herself for support, and took a moment—just one—to close her eyes and soothe her aching heart. But she knew that soothing wouldn't be possible—not when her pain could only be compared to what she'd felt after her parents had died. But still she stood, rubbing a hand over her chest, as though doing that would make a difference somehow.

The look on Blake's face flashed through her eyes—the look that had told her all she needed to know about the awkwardness between them over the last few days—and another wave of grief rushed through her.

But instead of giving herself another moment, she hurried back to the room she had got ready in to change and get her things. Before she changed she looked in the mirror for one last time, wondering who the woman who looked back at her was. That woman looked so glamorous she might be royalty—nothing like the broken woman Callie knew really stood there. The one who was using every last bit of her strength to keep standing, not to fall into a heap on the floor and cry until she couldn't think about him any more.

Until she couldn't feel the pain that sliced through her at every memory of him.

She carefully took off the necklace and the shoes, placing them back into their boxes, and peeled the dress from her skin. When she was done she laid the dress bag over her arm and took the boxes in one hand, her own things in the other. She struggled out through the door and smiled her thanks when Tom, one of the bellboys, offered to help her.

She'd just handed over her things and asked him to call her a taxi when she heard Blake's voice.

'Callie—wait. Callie!' he said, more loudly when she didn't stop. 'I've been looking for you all over. We need to talk.'

She gestured for Tom to go ahead, and stiffened her spine when she saw Blake walking towards her even as the pain crushed through her chest.

'I'm on my way home. I was going to put this in your office with a note for Caroline. Actually, I think I'll do that now.'

She walked past him to his office, silently thanking Kate for getting her a room on the ground floor, so that she didn't have to get into an elevator again. She opened the door and laid the things gently over the desk Connor had put up for Blake, and turned when she heard the door slam.

'Let me explain,' he said, tension in every part of his body.

'Explain what?'

'Why I'm leaving.'

'So you *are* leaving.' She nodded as her heart broke, but coated it with anger. 'I thought you were just going to let me assume something was wrong, like you've been doing for the last few days.'

'I'm sorry. But—'

'I don't want to hear it, Blake.'

'Callie, I think the least you can do is let me explain myself.'

His tone was testy now, and she felt anger clutch at her.

'*Why*, Blake? Why should I let you explain yourself? You've been pushing me away for days. You've lied to me. And now you're leaving. So give me one reason why I shouldn't walk out of here right now and forget about whatever we had?'

'Because we care about each other. At least I care about you.' His hands were on his hips; his face was fierce. 'I care enough that I'm leaving because it's what's best for you.'

'What's *best* for me?' she repeated, almost shocked at his audacity. 'You've decided what's best for me based on what?'

'Based on the fact that I know you,' he said angrily. 'You need someone who can be a father to your children. I can't do that.'

Pieces began to fall into place somewhere at the back of her head, but she didn't take the time to see it. 'Of course you can't. Not when you're so stuck in your own world that you don't really care about how I feel.'

'Excuse me?'

Although she heard the warning in his voice, she couldn't stop now. 'I can't actually believe that I thought you might tell me what was going on in your head. I made excuses for you. I went against my gut.'

Tears pricked at her eyes, and for once she didn't care.

'That night you took me home from your house—the night you lied to me—I told myself that you needed time, and that I needed to be patient. But I waited and waited and waited. And all I got was distance, a day of pampering— because you needed to distract me from the fact that you were leaving, right? And from a decision made for my best interests. All because of what?'

She wiped at the tears that came when she realised that he had been saying goodbye to her from the day he'd dropped her at home. Today had just been the finale.

'Because you couldn't have a conversation with me about having a family?'

The shame she saw in his eyes confirmed her words.

'You have no idea what it's like to care about someone and realise that you can't give them what they want,' he said.

'*You* have no idea what it feels like to have someone you love decide they don't want to *give* you what you want,' she snapped back at him, and then stopped when the words fell between them like the blade on a guillotine.

'You *love* me?'

'I'll get over it—don't worry.'

It felt like a weakness, now—a mistake. Loving him. One she would rather have kept to herself. But she hadn't, and now she had to keep herself from falling for that expression on his face. It made her want to beg him to stay, to face his fears, to let himself love her.

To let her love be enough for him—for them.

But then she saw the sadness behind his surprise at her declaration—the sadness that told her he wouldn't let go of whatever was keeping them apart—and she felt devastation rip through her. With tears still threatening, she walked to the door, and then she paused, the fire inside her burning just enough for her to turn back to him.

'You could've missed it, because I made the mistake of saying I love you, so I'm going to say it again. You think that you're leaving because you can't give me what I want. But what I want is exactly what *you* want—a family. So don't use me as an excuse, Blake. The real problem here is *you*.'

'Callie… I'm trying. I mean, I've tried it before, and I failed miserably at being a father.' He said the words through clenched teeth. 'I'd rather walk away than have you witness me failing at it again.'

She choked back the sob that threatened, and felt completely helpless as she said, 'Well, then, luckily for both of us I'm used to the people I love leaving me.'

And with those words she walked out through the door, slamming it shut on him and on their relationship.

And breaking whatever had been left of her heart.

CHAPTER SEVENTEEN

BLAKE STOOD LOOKING OUT of the window of the office he shared with Connor, and felt the weight of his decision heavy on his shoulders. The weight that had settled there the moment Callie had shut the door to the office—to them— what felt like years ago.

He rubbed a hand over his face, tried to get his thoughts in order. The first day of negotiations had gone well—he thought he already knew who would be giving him a call, even though they still had four more days to go. It would take a few days after that to draw up the contracts, and then that would be the end of the personal responsibility he felt after letting the Elegance Hotel, Cape Town, slip through the cracks because of Julia.

He wouldn't be needed in Cape Town after that. He could run operations for the hotels from anywhere in the country. From anywhere in the *world*. Logically, he knew that. Which was why he couldn't figure out why every part of him wanted to stay in Cape Town.

Except that was a lie. He knew exactly why he wanted to stay. The part he couldn't figure out was how he could even consider it. He'd broken things off with Callie—whatever they'd had was now completely and utterly broken. His heart seemed to be, too—so much so that he couldn't remember the reasons he had given her, had convinced himself of, for why they couldn't be together. The reasons that had seemed so clear before.

'You should be at home, celebrating the deal that will be coming in soon.'

Blake turned to see Connor behind him, his hands in his pockets.

He nodded, failing to muster the energy required for a smile. 'I'm not in the mood.'

'I can see that. Seems you and Callie may have taken a drink from the same fountain. She's as miserable as you are.'

Blake hated it that there was a part of him that took comfort in that. 'She is?'

'Yes.' Connor waited a beat, and then said, 'In case you didn't pick it up, the fountain was a metaphor. The reality is that you two have been in a relationship that has now broken up. Correct?'

Blake stared at Connor, wondering why on earth his heart was thumping as though he had been caught making out with a girl by her parents, like some teenager. 'How did you find out?'

Connor let out a bark of laughter and Blake wondered if he had spoken with the guilt he felt.

'Blake, *you* may be able to hide your feelings quite well, but my sister can't.'

He smiled at that. 'Yes, so I've realised. She told you?'

'She didn't have to. I could see it from the way she looked at you.'

Connor studied Blake for some time, and Blake had to resist the urge to shuffle his feet. He was becoming increasingly aware of the fact that he was being sized up by his employee. No, he corrected himself. By the brother of the woman he cared about.

'Blake, do you know how long it took for me to get Callie to consider dating?' Connor shook his head. 'It was like talking to a rock. She would let me speak for however long my words of encouragement for that day required, and then she'd smile and tell me she wasn't interested. So, as much as I'd like to avoid getting involved in my boss's affairs, the fact that Callie opened up to you tells me that she cares about you. What happened?'

Blake felt another blow to his heart at Connor's words, and wondered why the reminder that Callie had been willing to let him in hurt so much.

'It doesn't matter. We can't be together.' He shrugged, as though to show that he had come to terms with it.

'Well, clearly it *does* matter—to both of you—because of exactly that.' He stopped, gave Blake a moment to contradict him, but when it didn't happen, he nodded. 'That's what I thought. Was it you or her?'

'What do you mean?'

'I mean did you end it or did she?'

Blake thought about it. 'I'm not actually sure. I suppose it was me—though she was the one who actually walked out.'

Connor stared at him, and then shook his head. 'Of course she would fall for you. You're *safe.*'

'Excuse me?'

'You're safe,' he repeated. 'You're not here permanently and you're her boss. She wouldn't have to worry about falling for you because you would never feel the same way about her.'

'That's not—'

'In fact she probably never told you how she really felt. She may not be able to hide her feelings, but verbalising them is completely different. So if you weren't looking, and she didn't say anything, you'd never know and she'd be able to tell herself that she tried and then move on.'

'Stop.'

The single word was said so sharply it might have sliced through metal.

'You have no idea what you're talking about. She put *everything* on the line for me.' Blake ran a hand through his hair. 'She told me exactly how she feels, and she was perfect. *I'm* the problem.'

Finally, after repeating the words had Callie told him the last time they'd spoken, something cleared inside his head. He *was* the problem. He had pushed her away because he'd thought that was best for them—for her.

He turned to Connor, saw the look on his face, and realised he'd been baited.

'How did you do it?' he asked Connor, who was watching him with serious eyes. 'How did you get over your parents' deaths? In your relationship?' He saw the surprise on Connor's face and realised there was no point in pretending he didn't know. 'Callie told me you're expecting. Congratulations.'

'Thanks.' Connor paused, as though trying to gather his thoughts, and then he said, 'I'm sure you know that losing our parents broke both of us.' He rubbed at the back of his neck. 'When I found out Elizabeth was pregnant it scared me. I don't know how to be a father, and I was terrified of caring about her, about our baby, and then losing them. And then I realised that going through life being scared wasn't living. I thought about coming home to Elizabeth, to our child, and I realised my parents would have *wanted* that for me. They wanted me to live, to be happy.'

Blake thought about how he'd imagined the same thing, and how it had thrown him into a panic. 'And that was it?'

'Pretty much.' Connor shoved his hand back into his pocket. 'I'm still scared of losing them. I still don't know how I'll be a father. But the thought of not being with them, of *not* being a father, scares me more.'

Something shifted for Blake as he realised he felt the same way. The misery he felt now because he had lost her—the irony of that gave him a headache—was testament to that. But he still couldn't shake off that one thing…

'You had a father to learn from.'

'We all do. Even if they aren't perfect,' Connor continued when Blake opened his mouth to interrupt. 'We learn from them. We learn what to do and, sometimes more importantly, we learn what *not* to do. And we should have a partner to help us through it.' He smiled slightly. 'It's not so scary when you realise you're not alone. Unless, of course, you choose to be.'

He stopped, and then nodded at Blake.

'I think I'll head home now. And by the way…' Blake looked at Connor. 'I don't care if you're my boss. If you hurt her again I'll kick your butt.'

Blake smiled wanly in response, and then sat down heavily at his desk. Connor had a point. With Brent, Blake had tried to be there as much as possible, and he'd thought he had succeeded until the divorce. It was still a sore point for him, the fact that he couldn't be there for Brent now. One he had used when he'd decided he couldn't give Callie the family she needed.

She would be an amazing mother, he thought. She was caring—passionately so. And she would sacrifice her own happiness before letting anything happen to the people she cared about. He could only imagine what she'd do for her child, for her family. She would never leave them—not for one moment…

She would *never* leave, Blake realised. If Callie had any choice in the matter she wouldn't leave the people she loved. But *he* had left. He'd left her, failed her, disappointed her, lost her. All the things he'd wanted to protect her—

and himself—from had happened, because he'd chosen to leave the woman he loved.

The realisation hit him like a bomb, and he leaned forward, bracing his arms on his knees. He loved her. And he had hurt her. So much so that the woman he knew in his heart would never leave the person she loved—*him*— had left. Because he had left her first. He'd done the very thing she'd been afraid of. He'd shown her that opening up to him had been a mistake.

Convincing her to take him back would mean she'd have to trust that he wouldn't leave again. And how could he do so when he'd already left?

The weight on his shoulders nearly crushed him.

Callie's heart broke over and over again each time she thought about it—which felt like every second of every day.

She had taken the week off work, which no one had questioned, despite the fact that she hadn't taken any time off since she'd started—because she couldn't bear to see Blake every day. Not when there was a hole in her chest where her heart was supposed to be.

She knew the pieces lay somewhere, broken in her chest, and would no doubt remind her of their brokenness when she saw him. She would forget, just for a second, about the fact that he had left her and she would run into his arms, feel his warmth, smell the comforting musk of his cologne.

And then she would break when she realised that would never happen again.

She shrugged her shoulders and forced herself to breathe as she walked into the hotel on Friday. Kate had called, telling her that a young honeymooning couple had begged her to arrange a tour for them, and since Kate had no idea what to do she'd called Callie. Her favourite tours were those she organised for honeymooners—they were always so happy to be with one another it was infectious—so she'd reluctantly agreed to come in.

Even though she didn't want to see the man who'd broken her heart. The man who, according to her brother, was a negotiation tsar.

Of course she was happy that the negotiations were going well. But somehow it just didn't seem important any more. So she would just focus on what she'd come to do.

Kate had told her the couple wanted to see Table Mountain at sunset. That would be in an hour, giving her enough time to introduce herself and travel there with her guests. And to remember that the last time she had been up there had been with Blake.

She stopped when he materialised in front of her. And blinked just to make sure she wasn't imagining things. That she wasn't dreaming of him again.

'Callie.'

'Blake.'

She nodded, and hated it that her body heated at the memory of his. Even worse, that her heart still longed for him.

'I've missed you around here.'

'I've…er…' She cleared her throat. 'I've been on leave.'

'I know.' He put his hands in his pockets. 'I was hoping we could talk.'

'Yes, well…let's pretend you've left already, when there won't be any more talking between us,' she said, and then tried to walk past him.

But she stopped—as did her heart—when he placed a hand on her arm.

'Callie, please. I have to tell you something.'

She looked up at him, and though her heart urged her to agree her mind warned her not to. And for once she chose to listen.

'I think it would be best if we didn't speak any more.'

Their eyes locked for a moment, and then he let go of her arm.

'Okay.'

She nodded and walked away with an aching heart and the sinking feeling that this might be the last time she spoke to her boss.

To the man she loved.

CHAPTER EIGHTEEN

'AND IF YOU look over there you'll see Camps Bay Beach and the Atlantic Ocean. Beautiful, isn't it?'

Callie pointed out the area for her guests, and watched the sun cast its orange glow over the city, grateful that Cape Town was showcasing its romance for the couple. She smiled and walked to the other side of the mountain, giving them privacy. And giving herself time to think, to grieve for the man she would have loved to share the experience of sunset on the mountain with.

'I don't think I've ever seen anything quite as beautiful in my life.'

Callie heard the words and for a brief moment wondered if she had conjured him up again. But when she turned around Blake was standing in front of her, looking directly at her.

She squared her shoulders. 'What are you doing here?'

'I came to talk. I thought that you would have no choice on a mountain.' He smiled slightly.

She bit her lip, feeling the heat of tears threaten. Why couldn't he just leave her be?

'How did you know I was here?'

'Kate. Connor. A number of other people who gladly offered me the information when they realised we were together.'

'You told them that?'

He took a step closer. 'I did. I wanted them to know how serious I am about the talk we're going to have.'

Her heart ached with longing, with heartbreak. The combination left her a little breathless.

'I have guests here, Blake' She gestured to the couple. 'I don't think I'll have much time to talk.'

'That's okay. They're with me.'

It took Callie a moment to process that. 'What do you mean, they're with you?' She repeated the words slowly, hoping it would help her make sense of it.

'I mean I asked some friends of mine to request a tour. I knew you wouldn't come if it wasn't for your guests, so I called in a favour.'

His eyes were so serious, so hopeful, that her indignation faltered. And her heart wondered what was so important that he'd had to pull strings to see her. She turned to the couple, who waved gaily at her, and felt the ends of her mouth twitch. And then she noticed that the mountain had cleared in the moments she'd spent with Blake, and that her pretend guests were also moving in the direction of the cable car.

'Blake, I think the last cable car of the day is leaving.' She said the words even as her mind told her that it wasn't supposed to happen for at least another hour.

'No, there's one more. For us.'

She looked at him in surprise. 'How did you…?' But she trailed off when she saw the determination and the slight desperation in his eyes. 'You did all this for a moment alone with me?'

He nodded and took her hand. Tingles went up her arm as he led her to the end of the mountain where it overlooked the ocean. They stood there like that for a while, and then he spoke.

'I've been trying to find the words to tell you how sorry I am since the moment I realised how wrong I was.' His hand tightened on hers, and then he stuffed it in a pocket. 'I did things so poorly. I made decisions for you, for us, without talking to you. I let my fears become more important than my need for you.'

He turned to her and she resisted the urge to comfort him.

'And I *do* need you—more than I've needed anything else in the world.'

Her lips trembled and she took a deep breath, trying to figure out what to say. But he continued before she had a chance to respond.

'I have been so miserable since you walked out through the door of that office. I justified my actions, and cursed them, and I went back and forth doing that for a long time. And then I spoke to Connor, and I knew I was wrong.'

'You *what*?'

Blake gave her a nervous smile. 'He caught me moping in the office and offered me some advice.' Then he grew serious. 'My whole life I've tried to avoid disappointing the people I care about. I thought that by being in control I could do that. And then you came along, and I've never felt less in control in my life.'

He exhaled, looked out to the ocean.

'I was falling for you even when I was trying not to. Then we got to know one another, and I knew the falling would never stop. Not with you.'

He looked back at her and she felt her breath catch.

'It scared me, Callie. I've *never* felt the way I feel about you. And I began to think about how I'd lost my mother, how much it would break me if you left. I thought about Brent, about disappointing him, and how it would hurt if I did that to you. How I had failed in my marriage, with my family, and how I wouldn't survive if I failed *you*. If I failed to give you the family you deserved.'

He reached a hand up and touched her cheek, and without even realising it Callie leaned into it. 'I thought the only way to prevent that was to leave. I couldn't break you, disappoint you or fail you if I left. But by doing that I did *all* those things, and I'm so, *so* sorry.'

His voice broke and Callie took a step forward, wanting to comfort him.

'I know, Blake. I know that you thought you were doing the right thing.' She looked up at him, drew a ragged breath. 'I was scared, too. I realised I was in love with you but I had no commitment from you besides the things we'd shared. I convinced myself that it was enough. I convinced myself that loving you would be okay even if I lost you. *Because* I loved you.'

She couldn't stop the tears now, even if she wanted to.

'And then I *did* lose you, and it hurt more than I could imagine because you *chose* to leave me.'

'I'm sorry.'

He pulled her into his arms, and the pieces of her heart stirred.

'For everything. I can't imagine ever hurting you like that again.' He drew back. 'I'm not going to leave, Callie. I will *never* leave you.'

'Why should I believe you?' She whispered the words that whirled around in her mind, keeping her from accepting what he was saying.

'Because this week has been the worst of my life.' He gently brushed a piece of hair from her face. 'And it's made me realise that I want to give you the family you want. I want to create a legacy with you.' He tipped her chin up so that she could look at him. 'Believe me, because I'm telling you I won't leave you. Trust me.'

'Why?'

'Because I love you, Callie. And if you still love me let me prove to you for the rest of my life that I will stay with you. That I will fight for you. For *us*.'

And with those words—the words she'd dreamed about hearing from him—her broken heart healed and filled.

'I still love you.'

He smiled tenderly at her. 'I hoped you would.'

'So much that it scares me.'

She looked at him, and the agreement in his eyes comforted her.

'I am, too. So let's be scared together.'

He got down on one knee and Callie's heart pounded and melted at the same time. Suddenly she became aware that the sun had set and that their only source of light now came from candles and lanterns, all over the top of the mountain. And then she saw the ring—a large diamond sparkling brightly up at her surrounded by what seemed like a thousand smaller ones—and she realised Blake was offering her the biggest assurance he could that he was staying.

'Will you marry me, Callie McKenzie?'

'You want to *marry* me?'

'I really, really do.'

She laughed, and nodded, and was swept up into his arms before she had a chance to wipe the tears from her cheeks. Her hand shook as he slid the ring on her finger, and then he kissed her, and any remnants of fear she'd had disappeared. The kiss was filled with all the longing they'd felt for one another since they'd been apart, with the joy of their future together, with the heat of their passion. And when they finally drew apart they were both breathing heavily.

'We're engaged,' she said when she'd recovered, and she looked at the ring on her finger.

'We are.' He smiled and drew her back against him. 'I'm

thinking we should get married at the hotel. A rooftop sunset wedding could be pretty amazing.'

'I think that would be perfect.' And then she realised she hadn't even asked him about the deal. 'Did we get an investor?'

'We did. Marco signed the papers a few hours ago. He's going to be a silent investor. Although he *did* say he will still actively try to poach you.' He waited as she laughed, and then said, 'I have so many plans for the hotels. I can't wait to do it all with you.'

'So I'm going to help with the Owen legacy, huh?' She smiled and drew his hands tighter around her waist as they looked down at Cape Town at night.

'Yeah. Which means it's probably only fair that I help you with *your* legacy.' He looked down at her with a glint of amusement in his eyes. 'Family, right? I think the best way for me to show my commitment to you is if we start on that as soon as possible.'

Her laughter rang out on the top of Table Mountain, and for the first time since her parents had died Callie finally felt whole.

EPILOGUE

'ARE YOU READY for that?'

Blake gestured towards the chubby toddler who was steadily making his way over the grass in their backyard to his father, knocking down every toy they'd put out for him. He gave a happy gurgle when Connor picked him up and spun him around, and Callie smiled when she saw the absolute love in her brother's eyes as he did so.

'I keep thinking about a little girl with your eyes, or a boy with your hair. And every time I do I fall in love with the little person in my imagination.' Callie snuggled closer to her husband—she would never tire of the thrill that went through her when she thought that Blake was her *husband*—and kicked at the ground so that the swing seat they were sitting on would move.

She couldn't quite believe they were already celebrating her nephew's first birthday. Tyler was such a little ball of happiness, with his father's steady presence and his mother's zest for life, that it made her excited to see what combination her own child would be.

She resisted the urge to rub her stomach and imagined how happy her parents would have been if they'd been there. They would have loved enjoying their grandson in their home—the home that she and Blake now shared and had gladly offered to host Tyler's birthday at—and feeling the comfort of family. Connor and Elizabeth hadn't wanted a big party for their son when he wouldn't remember it, so instead they'd just organised a day when the McKenzies and the Owens—she *and* her brother had married within a few months of each other—could spend time together.

Callie couldn't think of a more perfect way to celebrate. Or to share her very exciting news.

'What if they have *your* eyes or hair?' Blake said, distracting her from her thoughts.

He pulled her in and she felt the warmth right down to her toes, before it quickly turned into a sizzle the moment he began to run his fingers up and down her bare arm.

'I suppose we'll have to accept them as they are. It won't be *their* fault after all.' She gave a dramatic sigh, and smiled when Blake laughed.

She loved seeing him like this—relaxed, happy, content. He had become a part of their family so smoothly she sometimes felt that he had always been a part of it. And she wondered where the man who had feared family so much had disappeared to.

'Look how beautiful it is,' Blake said, and gestured to the mountain and the ocean they could see from the swing seat. She smiled when she saw the peace settle over him, the way it always did when he looked out onto that view.

'Are *you* ready for it?' she asked quietly, not wanting to be overheard by her brother and sister-in-law.

'What?' He followed her eyes with his as she looked at her nephew, and then settled them back on her. 'I was ready the moment I met you. And then again when you told me you'd marry me. I believe I was willing to start right at that moment.'

She laughed. 'You were. But there were a few things we needed to sort out first.'

He rolled his eyes—a clear indication of a man who had

heard the words before. 'Yes, I know. We had to set up our operations for the hotels from Cape Town, and then we had to support Connor and Elizabeth during their wedding and Tyler's birth, and then we had our own wedding.'

'Exactly. Points to you for remembering.' She grinned at the amusement in his eyes, and then felt it soften to a smile. 'But all that's done now.'

'Yes—thankfully. So I don't have to be reminded about it all the time.'

She felt her lips twitch. 'No, Blake, all that's done now.'

'I heard you the first time.' Blake frowned at her, and then sat up a little straighter. 'You mean we can start trying for a family?'

'I mean that it's happened without us really trying.' She whispered the words, unsure, even though she knew that this was what they both wanted. 'I think my body knew about our timeline, too.'

He took a moment to process her words, and then whispered back, 'Do you think you're pregnant?'

'I *know* I am. The doctor called yesterday.'

She had barely finished saying the words before Blake pulled her into his arms, needing the contact with her more than he'd thought possible. His heart was exploding, and it was a long time before he let Callie go.

'Hey, none of that in front of my kid.'

Blake heard Connor's amusement and smiled, unable even to pretend that he was upset. 'Well, I think expressions of love are important. Maybe we should start making notes of all the things we've learnt from Connor about what to do and what not to do before *our* baby gets here, honey.'

Connor's eyes widened. 'You're *pregnant*?'

Blake laughed, and thought he had never felt this good in his life. 'No, not me personally—but Callie is.'

The announcement was met with laughter and congratulations, and even though he accepted the hugs of his family, even though he toasted his unborn child, he couldn't take his eyes off Callie. She was radiant, he thought, and saw her blushing every time she caught him looking at her.

It made him love her even more.

When Connor and Elizabeth had left, Callie and Blake moved back to the swing seat in the backyard. It would be a special place to him for ever, he thought. This house where he had finally found a home, where he had finally found himself be a part of a family. This yard where he had celebrated his godson's first birthday. And now this swing seat, where he had found out he was going to be a father.

'How have you made every dream of mine come true?' he asked, his heart filled with the love that overwhelmed him every time he looked at her.

She gave him that soft smile of hers and moved closer to him. 'We've made each other's dreams come true.' She laid a hand on his cheek. 'You're going to make the best father, Blake Owen.'

'Our child will have the best parents in the world.'

And then he kissed her, and knew without a doubt that he had finally found his home.

* * * * *

A BRIDE FOR THE
BROODING BOSS

BELLA BUCANNON

To my special husband, whose extra help enabled me to conquer the challenge of a deadline.

To Brett for expert advice, once he and other friends had stopped laughing at the idea of technically inept Bella's heroine being a computer problem investigator.

To the Paddocks Writing Group
for support and encouragement,
and to Flo for her advice and belief in me.

My grateful thanks to you all.

CHAPTER ONE

Lauren Taylor alighted from the taxi, smiling in surprise. A multi-storey glass and cement edifice had replaced the six-storey building with a bank at ground level she remembered from years ago.

Anticipation simmered through her veins. A rush job. Urgent—which usually meant challenging.

Her initial reaction to her employer's Monday morning call had been to refuse. She had managed to squeeze in a much-needed week off and had planned on some 'me' time—seeing movies, reading in the park, aimless walking... The promise of an additional week on completion of the assignment, plus a bonus, had won her over. A few days of Adelaide in March wouldn't be too hard to take.

The flight delay at Sydney airport the next afternoon meant it was three o'clock by the time she'd booked into her hotel and caught a taxi to the address. A quick phone call to a brusque Matthew Dalton raised some apprehension but he *was* the one with the critical dilemma.

Dalton Corporation's reception area on the eighteenth floor suited the building. A patterned, tiled floor drew the eyes to a curved redwood desk and up to the company name, elaborately carved in black on a gold background. Sadly the lack of human presence, along with the almost complete silence, detracted from the impact. The three doors in her sight were all shut.

Scrolling for the contact number she'd used earlier, she stopped at the sound of a crash from behind the second door along. Followed by a loud expletive in a woman's voice.

Lauren knocked and opened the door.

A blonde woman stood leaning across a desk, her hands shifting through a pile of papers, a harassed face turned towards Lauren. A document tray and its previous contents lay scattered on the floor.

'You want Mr Dalton.' Uttered as a hopeful statement. 'Sorry about this. I'm usually more organised. Last door on the left. Knock and wait. Good luck.'

Her words heightened Lauren's unease as she obeyed, instinctively smoothing down her hair before tapping on the door. The light flutter in her pulse at the raspy 'Come in' startled her. As did the unexpected allure in the deep guttural tone.

Without looking up, the man with a mobile held to his left ear gestured for her to enter and take the seat in front of his desk. Matthew Dalton was definitely under pressure. No jacket or tie, shirt unbuttoned at the top, and obviously raked through, thick chestnut-brown hair. He continued to write on a printed page in front of him, occasionally speaking in one- or two-word comments.

Lauren sat, frowning at the oblique angle of his huge desk to the wall-to-wall, floor-to-ceiling windows with an incredible view of the Adelaide Hills. Made of dark wood, it held only a desktop computer, keyboard, printer, land phone and stacked document trays. The only personal item was a plain blue coffee mug.

The man who'd requested her urgent presence swung to his right, flicking through pages spread on the desk extension. His easy fit in the high-back leather chair with wide arms suggested made to measure. And he needed a haircut.

She continued her scan, fascinated by the opulent differences from the usual offices where she was welcomed by lesser employees. From the soft leather lounge chairs by the windows to the built-in bar and extravagant coffee machine, this one had been designed to emphasise the power and success of the occupier.

The down light directly above his head picked up the red

tints in his hair, and the embossed gold on his elegant black pen. She shrugged—exclusive taste didn't always equate with business acumen. If it did she might not be here.

Reception had been bare and unmanned, the blonde woman agitated. How bad *was* the company's situation?

Normally tuning out sounds was an ingrained accomplishment. Today, nothing she tried quite prevented the gravelly timbre skittling across her skin, causing an unaccustomed warmth low in her abdomen. She steadied her breathing, mentally counting the seconds as they passed.

Then the man she believed to be a complete stranger flicked a glance her way. Instantly, with a chilling sensation gripping her heart, she was thrown back ten years to *that* night.

The dinner dance after a charity Australian Rules football game organised by interstate universities and held here in Adelaide. Limited professional players were allowed and her parents insisted the whole family come over in support when her elder brother agreed to represent Victoria.

The noisy function seemed full of dressed-to-kill young women draped over garrulous muscular males, many of whom twitched and pulled at the collars of their suits. Though only two or three years separated her from most of them, at sixteen it was a chasm of maturity and poise. Unfamiliar with the football scene and jargon, she blushed and stammered when any of them spoke to her.

Escaping from the hot, crowed room, she found a secluded spot outside, at the end of the long balcony. Hidden by tall potted plants, she gazed over the river wishing she were in her hotel room, or home in Melbourne. Or anywhere bar here.

'Hiding, huh? Don't like dancing?'

The owner of the throaty voice—too much enthusiastic

cheering?—was tall. Close. Much too close. The city lights
behind him put his face in shadow.

She stepped back. The self-absorbed young men whose
interests were limited to exercise, diet, sport, and the
women these pursuits attracted held no appeal for her.
Men like her brothers' friends who teasingly came on to
her then laughed off her protests. Never serious or threatening, merely feeding their already inflated egos. Shy and
uncomfortable in crowds, with a tendency to blush, she
was fair game.

'I saw you slip out.' She detected a faint trace of beer on
his breath as he spoke. When he took a step nearer, causing her to stiffen, a fresh ocean aroma overrode the alcohol. Not drunk, perhaps a little tipsy.

'We won, you should be celebrating. You do barrack for
South Australia?' Doubt crept into the last few words, the
resonance telling her he'd be more mature, maybe by two
or three years, than she was. So why seek her out when
there were so many girls his age inside?

'Y… Yes.' How could one word be so hard to say? How
come her throat dried up, and her pulse raced? And why
did she lie when she didn't care about the game at all?

He leant forward. 'I did kick two goals even if I missed
out on a medal. Surely I deserve a small prize.'

He *was* like all the others. Her disappointment sharpened her reply.

'I'm sure you won't be disappointed inside.'

'But an elusive prize is much more rewarding, don't
you think?'

Before she could take in air to answer, he gently covered her lips with his.

And she hadn't been able to take that breath. Hadn't been
able to move. Hadn't been able to think of anything except
the smooth movement of his mouth on hers.

The urge to return the kiss—have *him* deepen the kiss—

had shaken her. Terrified her. The quick kisses from the boys she knew were just being friendly had been gentle, nice. Never emotionally shattering.

Why did she sigh? Why were her lips complying, pressing against his, striving to be in sync? Until the tip of his tongue flicked out seeking entry and she panicked.

Frantically pulling away, she fled past him to the safety of the packed ballroom and a seat behind her parents and other adults in a remote corner. As she drank ice-cold water to wet her dry throat, she realised all she could recall was a glimpse of stunning midnight-blue eyes as his head had jerked back into the light.

The same midnight-blue eyes that had fleetingly met hers a moment ago.

Why was she so certain? She just knew.

Would he recognise *her*? He'd had a drink or two and it had been dark. She finally had a reason to be thankful for her mother's instructions to the hairdresser. Darker colouring with extensions woven into a fancy hairdo on top, plus salon make-up, had altered her appearance dramatically.

She'd been a naive teenager who'd panicked and run from an innocent kiss. He'd been an experienced young man who'd have known scores of willing women since.

Gratitude that she hadn't seen his face flowed through her veins as she studied the man to whom she'd attributed so many different features over the years in her daydreams. If, along with those memorable eyes, she'd imagined high cheekbones, a square firm jaw and full lips, she doubted she'd have slept at all. Even his lashes were thicker and darker than she'd pictured.

She dipped her head whenever he looked at her, wasn't ready for eye-to-eye contact. Forced steady breathing quelled her inner trembling.

Matt Dalton's mind ought to be totally focused on the

information he was receiving. Instead his eyes kept straying to the brunette sitting rigid on her seat, politely ignoring him. The one who'd caused a tightening in his gut when he'd glanced up at her.

In an instant he'd noted the sweet curve of her cheek framed by shoulder-length light brown hair. If she hadn't dropped her gaze, he'd also know the colour of her eyes.

Shoot! He asked the caller to repeat the last two figures. Blocking her out, he carefully wrote them down. After ending the call, he clipped all the pages together, and dropped them into a tray.

He could now concentrate on this woman, and her technical rather than physical attributes. Her employer's high fees would be worth it if she found out what the heck had happened in the company's computer system.

'Ms Lauren Taylor?' He pulled a new document forward.

She turned, and guarded brown eyes met his.

He immediately wished they hadn't as a sharp pang of desire snapped through him and was instantly controlled. Women, regardless of shape, colouring or looks, were off his agenda for the foreseeable future. Probably longer. Betrayal made a man wary.

'Yes.' Hesitant with an undertone he didn't understand.

He'd requested her services on a recommendation, without any consideration of appearance or demeanour, which for him were unimportant. The female colleagues he'd associated with overseas were well groomed, very smart, and always willing to offer their opinions. His equal on every corporate level.

Lauren Taylor was neatly dressed in a crisp white blouse under a light grey trouser suit, and wore little make-up. With her reputation, she ought to project confidence, yet he sensed apprehension. Was it a natural consequence of her temporary assignments or the confidentiality clause creating a desire to keep a distance from company employees?

No, this ran deeper, was more personal. He cleared his thoughts, telling himself his sole interest was in her technical skills, conveniently discounting his two reactions towards her.

'I'm Matt Dalton. I contacted your employer because I'm told you're one of the best computer problem investigators. My friend's description. Was he exaggerating?'

A soft blush coloured her cheeks, and her eyes softened at the compliment. They were actually more hazel than brown with a hint of gold flecks, and framed by thick brown lashes. He growled internally at himself for again straying from his pressing predicament.

'I don't... I rarely fail.' She made a slight twitch of her shoulders as if fortifying her self-assurance.

He gave a short huff. 'Please don't let this be one of the times you do. How much information were you sent?'

'The email mentioned unexplained anomalies a regular audit failed to clarify.'

'Two, one internal, one external. The detectable errors were fixed but no one could explain the glitches or whatever they are, and I need answers fast.' Before his father's condition became public and the roof caved in.

'May I see the reports?' Again timidity, which didn't fit the profile he'd received, though to give her credit she didn't look away.

'In the top drawer of the desk you'll be using along with a summary of our expectations, file titles et cetera. I assume you can remember passwords.'

She frowned, making him realise how condescending he sounded. Was he coming over as too harsh, overbearing? Her impression of him wouldn't be good either.

'Staff turnover has been high in the last two years, sometimes sudden with no changeover training. Recently I found out passwords had been written down and kept in unlocked drawers.'

She waited, and he had the feeling he was being blamed for some personal misdemeanour. He decided he'd divulged as much as she needed to know to start. Anything else necessary, she'd learn as the assessment progressed.

'Most of the errors were from incorrectly entered data, exacerbated on occasion by amateur attempts to fix them. Apparently not too hard to find and correct if you know what you're doing.'

'But surely the accountant…?' Her hands fluttered then her fingers linked and fell back into her lap. 'Why weren't they picked up at the time?'

Damn, she was smart. And nervous.

'The long-term accountant left, and was replaced by a bookkeeper then another. Neither were very competent.'

Her eyes widened in surprise. For a second there was a faint elusive niggling deep in the recesses of his mind. As her lips parted he forestalled her words.

'I'd like you to analyse from July 2014 up to the present date. Everything your employer requested is in the adjacent office. How soon can you start?'

Too abrupt again but it was imperative he find out what had been going on. The sooner the better. Four weeks ago, at his original inspection of his father's company accounts, would have been best.

'If I can see the set-up now then I can begin early tomorrow morning. Being a short week because of Easter doesn't allow much time.

'Are two days enough?'

'Doubtful if I'm a last resort. I have a family commitment in Melbourne for the weekend then I'll come back.' She made it sound like an obligation rather than a pleasant reunion.

'That's acceptable.' He flicked his hands then put them on the edge of the desk to push to his feet.

'Human error and deliberate action are different. Is it the latter I'm searching for?'

He sank back into his chair. She was *too* smart.

Lauren had been in critical corporate situations before and recognised desperation, even when well hidden. This man was heading for breakdown. His taut muscles, firm set lips and weary dark eyes all pointed to extreme stress.

And her question had irritated him so he definitely suspected fraud, probably by someone he'd trusted. She certainly wasn't going to push it now. Not when she'd behaved like the skittish child she'd thought she'd conquered years ago.

'I won't make guarantees I might not be able to keep. I can only promise to do my best. Having the straightforward errors already adjusted helps.'

He relaxed a little, and his lips curved at the corners, almost but not quite forming a smile.

'Thank you.'

He rose to an impressive height, letting his chair roll away, indicating a door to her left.

'Through here.'

Lauren picked up her shoulder bag and followed, wishing she were one of those women who were comfortable in killer heels all day. And an inch or two taller. Having to tilt her head gave him the advantage. When he suddenly stopped and turned, her throat tightened at the vague familiarity of his cologne. Not the same one, surely? Yet she recognised it, had never forgotten it. And this close, the lines around his mouth and eyes were much more discernible.

'I apologise. I should have offered you a coffee. Do you—?'

'No. No, thank you.' The sooner she was out of his presence, the better. Then she could breathe and regroup. 'You're obviously busy.'

His relief at such a minor point enforced her opinion of the strain he was under.

'Like you wouldn't believe. Any answers you find will be extremely welcome.'

He opened the door and ushered her in, the light touch of his fingers on her back shooting tingles up and down her spine, spreading heat as they went. Unwarranted yet strangely exciting.

The décor in the much smaller room matched his office, and included two identical armchairs by the window. But the position of the desk was wrong, standing out from the wall facing the door they'd entered. She walked round to check the two desktops and a keyboard, all wired up ready to go. He followed, stopping within touching distance.

'Your employer asked for the duplication. Easier for comparisons, huh?'

'Much. What's the password?'

He told her. While she activated the computer, he removed a blue folder from the drawer, and placed it on the desk.

'Anything else you require?'

'I'll need a copy of the report for highlighting and a writing pad for notes.'

'Help yourself to anything in the cupboard. The copier is in Joanne's office off reception.'

'The blonde lady?'

'Yes, currently we don't have a receptionist. If you have any questions regarding your task ask me. If it's office related Joanne or any one of the other five employees can help.'

He walked out, not giving her a chance to say thank you, leaving his heady sea-spray aroma behind. Did he treat everyone in the same offhand manner?

Lauren felt like pounding the desk. She'd handled ruder employers who'd been under less pressure with poise and conviction. I'm-the-boss males with autocratic, archaic, even on occasion sexist, views were certainly not an endangered species. It didn't wash with her. They were in a predicament and she was the solution so she made it clear: no respect and she walked.

The personal aspect here had shaken her composure, giving the impression she doubted her abilities. She'd show him. Tomorrow she'd be the perfect detached computer specialist.

She selected stationery from the cupboard, skim-read the printed files, then spent ten minutes perusing the computer data prior to closing down. The few pertinent notes she'd written would save time in the morning.

Carrying the audit reports, she tried the door leading to the corridor. Finding it locked, she went into Matt Dalton's office. He was standing, sorting papers on his desk. His gaze was less than friendly to someone he'd hired to solve his problems.

'I'll copy these then I'll be leaving. What time is the office open in the morning?' Polite and stilted, following his lead. The fizz in her stomach could and *would* be controlled.

'I'm here from seven. Do you need transport?'

'I'll sort that out.'

'Good.' He returned to his papers.

She swung away, heat flooding her from head to feet at his dismissive action. All her fantasies came crashing down. Spoilt, rich, I-can-take-what-I-want teenager had become arrogant, treat-hired-staff-with-disdain boss. Was that why people had left without notice? She'd never wished bad karma on anyone, but she was coming close today!

Long deep breaths as she went out helped to settle her stomach and stop the trembling of her hands.

Before re-entering Mr Dalton's office, printouts in hand, she reinforced her prime rule of contract work. Never,

never, ever get involved. Someone always ended up heart-broken.

Swearing the oath was easy. Sticking to it when confronted with those hypnotic blue eyes that invited her to confess her innermost secrets was tougher than she'd expected. Especially when his lips curled into a half-smile as he said goodbye.

She stabbed at the ground-floor button, angry that she'd smiled back, dismayed that even his small polite gesture had weakened her resolve. The thrill of the chase ought to be in his computer files, not in dreaming of— She wouldn't dream of anything. Especially not midnight-blue eyes, firm jaws or light touches that sent emotions into a frenzy.

CHAPTER TWO

MATT STARED AT the open doorway, perplexed by his reactions to a woman so unlike the outgoing, assured females he usually favoured. He raked his fingers through his hair. They were strangers, so why the censure in her alluring eyes when they'd met? It irked. It shouldn't have affected his attitude but he knew he'd been less than welcoming.

His finding her delicate perfume enchanting was also disconcerting. And she'd stiffened when he'd touched her. Had she felt the zing too? Please not. He had enough complications to deal with already.

Would it make her job easier if she knew the whole story? Loath to reveal family secrets to outsiders, he'd tell her only if it became relevant to her succeeding. Despite his friend's glowing report, he'd been less than impressed.

Dalton Corporation was in trouble. His only choice was to trust her on the corporate level. He had little reason to trust her, or any other woman, personally. Especially as her manner said she'd judged him for some transgression made by someone else.

Had she suffered the same indignity as he had? The soul-crushing realisation that you'd been used and played for a fool. The embarrassment of how close you'd come to committing to someone unworthy, incapable of fidelity or honesty.

The dark-haired image that flared took him by surprise. Any affection he'd felt for Christine had died when she'd proved faithless. He hadn't seen her since he'd walked out of her apartment for the last time after telling her the relationship was over, and why. He'd rarely thought of her either.

They'd both spent nights in each other's homes but he'd held back from inviting her to live with him. Looking back that should have been a red flag that he had misgivings. Thankfully he'd told no one of his plans to propose to her.

Admitting he'd been stupid for assuming mutual friends and lifestyle expectations would be a good basis for a modern marriage hadn't been easy. He wasn't sure he'd ever consider that life-changing step again.

God, he hated being here handling this mess. He'd hated even more being in London where people gave him sympathetic looks and wondered what had happened.

Letting out a heartfelt oath, he banished both women from his mind. There were emails to read and respond to, and he'd promised his mother he'd be there for dinner. He grabbed his coffee mug, feeling the urgent necessity for another caffeine boost.

Nearly two hours later he pulled into the kerb outside his parents' house, switching off the engine to give himself time to prepare for the evening ahead. He regretted the loss of unwavering respect for his parents, wished he'd never found out his father had been having affairs. He'd lost a small part of himself when he'd come home that evening nine years ago, and had never been able to obliterate what he overheard from his mind.

'I suppose this one's as gullible as the rest and believes she has a future with you. How many more, Marcus?'

'Man wasn't meant to be monogamous. If you want a divorce, be prepared to lower your standard of living.'

'Why should I suffer for your indiscretions? I'm giving up nothing.'

Somehow his mother's acceptance of his father's infidelities made her complicit. In disbelief he'd fled to his room, changed into a tracksuit and taken off, pounding the footpath trying to drive what he'd heard from his mind. His hero had fallen. He'd returned to a silent, dark house where, for him, nothing would ever be the same.

He scowled, thumping the wheel with an open hand. He'd always been confident, sure of himself and his judgement of cheating and affairs. Now he felt remorse as his father had turned into a stranger who'd made drastic mistakes in the last eighteen months, sending Dalton Corporation on a downhill path.

Pride dictated he fix those glitches and return the company to profit status, along with preserving its good name. Only then could he consider his own future, and for that he'd need a clear head. The only people he'd give consideration to would be family and his partners in London.

He started the engine, and drove through the elaborate gates, grimacing as he entered the luxurious house. This was his father's dream, a symbol of wealth and prestige, bought during Matt's absence abroad. He hadn't told his mother their financial status was in jeopardy. If Lauren Taylor was as good as her reputation, and he'd inherited any of his father's entrepreneurial skills, he might never have to.

Adelaide had a different vibe from the city Lauren remembered. Not that she'd seen much of the metropolitan area when she'd lived here, or much of anywhere besides ovals and training grounds. Beaches in summer, of course— swimming and running on the sand were part of the family's fitness regimen.

As she'd strolled past modern or renovated buildings a window display advertising Barossa Valley wine triggered a light-bulb moment. The Valley, the Fleurieu Peninsula and the Adelaide Hills, plus many other tourist areas, were all within easy driving distance, and she'd been promised a two-week vacation as soon as the assignment ended. All she'd need were a map, a plan and a hire car.

She picked up Chinese takeaway, and spent the evening poring over brochures and making notes. In full view from her window a group of young athletes were training in the parklands over the road. On the side-lines some adults watched and encouraged. Others sat on the grass with younger children, playing games or reading with them.

Her eyes were drawn to a man sitting with a boy on his lap, their heads bent as small fingers traced words or pictures in a book. Her chest tightened and she crossed her arms in a self-hug. Why didn't she have any memories of those occasions? Why had she never asked either parent to read to her or share a favourite television show with her? She'd always been too afraid of rejection.

Why had *they* never noticed her quietly waiting for some of the attention claimed by her boisterous brothers? If it had been intentional maybe it wouldn't hurt so much. Being overlooked cut deeper than deliberately being ignored. And she'd never been able to summon up the courage to intentionally draw attention to herself.

The boy looked up, talking with animation to his father. Eyes locked, they were in a world of their own.

It conjured up the image of Matt Dalton holding her gaze captive as they'd talked. Even thinking of those weary blue eyes spiked her pulse, and memories of that long-ago kiss resurfaced. Her balcony secret she'd never revealed to anyone. Never intended to.

Lauren chose a different route to work in the morning. She felt more herself, determined to show her new boss she was the professional his friend had recommended.

Last night no matter how many positions she'd tried or how often she'd thumped the pillows, sleep had eluded her. Reruns of her two encounters with Matt Dalton had kept her awake until she'd given in, got up, and researched the company. Something she normally avoided to keep distance and objectivity.

There'd been no reference to him, only a Marcus Dalton who'd become successful by investing in small businesses, and persuading others to participate too. The website hadn't been updated since November last year, indicating there'd been difficulties around that time.

No, wait. She'd been asked to assess twenty-one months. So the anomalies had been discovered only recently but long-term deception was suspected.

The sleep she'd eventually managed had been deep and dreamless, surprising since her last thoughts and first on awakening had been of full grim lips and jaded midnight-blue eyes.

The door adjacent to Mr Dalton's was still locked. From the piles of folders on his desk and extension, he'd arrived very early. He appeared even wearier, the shadows under his eyes even darker.

Lauren tried to ignore the quick tug low in her abdomen, and the quickening of her pulse.

'Good morning, Mr Dalton. Would it be possible to have the outer door unlocked so I won't disturb you going in and out?'

Or be disturbed by my immature reaction to you.

Intense blue eyes scanned her face, reigniting the warm glow from yesterday.

'Good morning, Ms Taylor. I'm not easily disturbed.'

Of course you're not. You're a cause not a recipient. Ignite a girl's senses with a soul-shattering kiss then forget her. Though to be fair she'd been the one to run.

'My watch alarm is set for an hourly reminder to relieve my eyes, stretch and drink water. To ease my back, I sometimes walk around or up and down a few flights of stairs.'

'Not a problem.' He glanced at the bottle in her hand. 'Keep anything you like in the fridge under the coffee machine or there's a larger one in the staffroom.'

Without looking, he flicked a hand towards a door in

the wall behind him. 'There's an ensuite bathroom here or, if you prefer, washrooms on the far side of Reception.'

Why the flash of anguish in his eyes? Why was she super alert, her skin tingling during this mundane conversation?

'Thank you.' She turned towards the bench, away from his probing gaze, popped her drink bottle and morning snack into the fridge, then went to her desk. Keeping her eyes averted didn't prevent his masculine aroma teasing her nostrils as she passed him.

She settled at her new station and, while the system booted up, filled in the personnel document he'd left for her. Once everything was laid in her preferred setting, she stood by the window to stare at the distant hills for a slow count of fifteen.

Now she was ready to start.

For two hours, apart from a short break for her eyes, she focused on the screens in front of her. But like a radio subliminally intruding into your dreams, some part of her was acutely aware of each time the man next door spoke on the phone or accessed the filing cabinets in this room.

The feeling in the pit of her stomach now was different, familiar, one she found comfortable, the exhilaration of the chase. The minor errors matched those in the audits. The one anomaly she found was puzzling enough for her to recheck from the beginning, puzzling enough to tease her brain. A challenge worthy of the fee her boss charged Dalton Corporation.

She headed for the ensuite to freshen up ready for coffee, cheese crackers and relief time. There was one door on her left, another along the corridor to her right.

She regretted choosing the latter the moment she saw the iron-smooth black and silver patterned quilt covering a king-sized bed. For a nanosecond she pictured rumpled sheets half covering a bare-chested Matt, his features composed in tranquil sleep. She blinked and pivoted round. Not an image she wanted in her head when she locked eyes with this cheerless, work-driven man.

On her return to the office, his posture enforced her last description. His chin rested on his hands, his elbows on the desk, his attention fully absorbed by the text on his screen.

Stealing the opportunity to observe him unnoticed, she stopped. A perception of unleashed power bunched in his shoulders, a dogged single-mindedness showed in his concentration. The untrimmed ends of his thick hair brushed the collar of his shirt, out of character to her perception of a smart, city businessman.

His mug had been pushed to the edge of his desk, presumably empty. She picked it up, startling him.

'Would you like a refill?'

He nodded. 'Thanks. Flat white from the machine, one sugar. How's it going?'

'Progressing. Do you want details?'

His eyes narrowed.

She pre-empted his next remark. 'People who hire me have varying knowledge of technology and require different levels of explanation.' *Many don't like to betray their ignorance in the field.* 'My daily report will be comprehensive.'

'Do whatever's necessary to get results. I'll read the report.' Again an undertone of irritation further roughened his voice, a darkening glint of angst flashed in his eyes.

Matt made a note in red at the top of the paper in front of him, and regretted being repeatedly terse with her. He closed his eyes, clasped his neck, and arched his back. He felt bone tired from sitting, reading, and trying to make sense of his father's recent actions.

He wished he could shake the guilt for not being around, for not noticing the subtle changes on his trips home for family occasions. Maybe if he'd spent more one-on-one time with Marcus he would have. Instead he'd apportioned blame without considering it was their lives, their marriage.

For nine years he'd kept physical and emotional distance from two of the most important people in his life.

He heard the soft clunk of a mug on wood. By the time he straightened and looked, a steaming coffee sat within reach, and Lauren was disappearing into her room. She'd discarded the light jacket she'd worn on arrival. Tired as he was, the male in him appreciated her slender figure, her trim waist. The pertness of her bottom in the grey trousers.

Inappropriate. Unprofessional.

As he drank the strong brew the sound of a quirky ringtone spun his head. The friendliness of Lauren's greeting to someone called Pete rankled for no reason. Her musical laughter ignited a heat wave along his bloodstream.

He strode to the ensuite to splash water on his face and cool down.

'Hey, it's nearly twelve o'clock.'

Lauren started, jerking round to see her temporary boss standing in the doorway, the remoteness in his eyes raising goosebumps on her skin. She blinked and checked her watch.

'Two minutes to go. Are you keeping tabs on my schedule?' Some clients did.

'Not specifically.' He moved further into the room, closer to her desk. To her.

Her pulse had no right to rev up. Her lungs had no right to expand, seeking his masculine aroma.

'Your work's high intensity.' His neutral tone brought her to earth.

'I've learnt how to manage it. Results take patience and time.'

He gave a masculine grunt followed by a wry grin. 'The latter's not something we have plenty of. Take a lunch break. I need you fully alert.'

Eight floors by foot before taking the elevator to the

ground helped keep her fit. She smiled and walked out into the light drizzle. Adelaide was like a new city waiting to be explored. Chomping on a fresh salad roll, she strolled along, musing on that dour man, wondering what, or who, had caused the current situation. And why Marcus Dalton was no longer in charge.

Matt was clearly related. He bore a strong resemblance to the photograph on the website she'd accessed. Even with the ravages of the trauma he was under, he was incredibly handsome with an innate irresistible charisma. Was he married? In a relationship?

She chastised herself, chanting silently, *Never let anyone get to you on assignments*. Stupid and unprofessional, it could only lead to complications and tears. However, she had never been in this situation before…she'd never been kissed by one of her clients.

'There's definitely a recurrent anomaly. Finding when it started may tell me how and what,' Lauren informed Matt as she gave him her report prior to going home.

She was leaning towards it being deliberate because of the number of identical anomalies. No reason to mention she had no idea how it had been achieved.

He nodded and dropped the report in a tray. 'How's the hotel? I asked Joanne to book somewhere not too far out.'

'Oh.' Was he trying to be sociable? Make amends for his abruptness? 'Very nice, and my room overlooks the parklands.'

'Not too noisy on that corner?'

She couldn't suppress her grin. 'I live in Sydney, remember. You tune it out or drown it with music.'

His gaze held hers for an eon, or longer. The darkening in the midnight-blue coincided with heat tendrils coiling through her from a fiery core low in her abdomen. Her eyes refused to break contact, her mouth refused to say goodbye. Her muscles refused to obey the command to turn her away.

It was Matt who broke the spell, flinching away and shaking his head. His chest heaved as his lungs fought for air. He clenched his fists to curb the impulse to—no, he wouldn't even think it.

'Did you bus or taxi?' He didn't particularly care but was desperate to keep the conversation normal. To ignore those golden specks making her eyes shine like the gemstones in his mother's extensive jewellery collection. His voice sounded as if he'd sprinted the last metres of a marathon.

'I walked. It's not that far.'

His eyebrows shot up. 'Walked?' To and from a bus stop or taxi rank was the furthest most women he knew went on foot, apart from in shopping centres.

She shrugged. 'Beats paying gym fees and clears my head.'

'I guess. Just take care, okay.' He had no reason to worry, yet he did.

'Always. Good afternoon, Mr Dalton.'

'I'll see you tomorrow, Ms Taylor.'

As soon as she'd gone he slumped in his chair, stunned by his reaction to her smile, quick and genuine, lighting up her face. His pulse had hiked up, his chest tightened. And his body had responded quicker and stronger than ever before.

His fingers gripped the armrests as he fought for control. This shouldn't, couldn't be happening. Women, *all* women were out of bounds at the moment. Even for no-strings, no-repercussions sex. She was here on a temporary basis. She was an employee, albeit once removed.

He groaned. She was temptation.

He forced his mind to conjure up visions of the life he'd left behind in London, crowded buses and packed Tubes, nightclubs, cafés and old pubs. Teeming, exciting. Energising. Attractive, fashionably dressed women in abundance. Great job, great friends. And one woman he'd thought he'd truly known.

It had been a near perfect world prior to his trust going down the gurgler and his existence being uprooted into chaos. Now he had little social life, even less free time, and collapsed wearily into a deep dreamless sleep every night. And woke early each morning to the same hectic scenario.

CHAPTER THREE

MATT WAS PACING the floor, talking on the phone when Lauren arrived Thursday morning, hoping for a repeat of yesterday when she'd been left pretty much alone all day. He'd been absent when she'd finished so she'd left her report on his desk.

On the way to her room she returned the preoccupied nod he gave her, grinning to herself at the double take he gave her suitcase and overnight bag. She'd booked out of the hotel, confirmed she'd be returning on Monday and been promised the same room.

She did her routine and began work, fully expecting an apologetic call some time from her eldest brother, who'd been delegated to pick her up on arrival in Melbourne. She'd long ago accepted she was way down on her family's priority list.

Her priority was to complete her designated task. Her expertise told her a human hand was involved. If—*when, Lauren, think positive*—she solved what and how, fronting Matt Dalton was going to be daunting. The few occasions she'd had to implicate someone in a position of trust had always left her feeling queasy, as if she were somehow to blame.

In two days she'd become used to the sound of him in the background like a soft radio music channel where the modulations and nuances were subtle, never intrusive. Every so often the complete silence told her he'd left the office. Occasionally someone came in. Few stayed more than a couple of minutes.

There was no sign of him when she went to the fridge, though an unrolled diagram lay spread out on his desk. She resisted the impulse to take a peek, and consumed her snack while enjoying the view from her window.

Matt's return was preceded by his voice as he walked along the corridor not long after she resumed work. She glimpsed him as he strode past her doorway to the window, ramrod-straight, hand clenched. Not a happy man.

His temper wouldn't improve when her report showed all she'd written down so far today was a slowly growing number of random dates.

'Dad!'

His startled tone broke Lauren's concentration.

'Sorry, mate, I'll call you back. *Dad*, what are you doing here?'

He came into her view and stopped. By craning her neck, she could see him clasping a greying man to his chest.

'You came alone?' There was genuine concern in his tone.

'Haven't been in for weeks so I thought I'd come and find out what's happening.' Apart from the slower pace of the words, the voice's similarity to Matt's was defining.

'Everything's going smoothly. Come and sit down. We'll talk over coffee.'

Blocking his father's view of her, he guided him towards the seating, then continued talking as he passed her door on the way to make the drinks. Without breaking step he made a quick gesture across his throat when their eyes met.

'There's a new espresso flavour you've never tried, rich and aromatic.'

He wanted her to shut down and not let his father know what she was doing. What if Marcus came in here? Asked who she was? As far as she knew, it was still his company. And it was his son's fault she couldn't escape through the locked door.

The papers and folder were slipped into the drawer, a fresh page on the pad partially covered by random notes for show. Acutely conscious of the mingled sounds of the coffee machine and Matt's muted voice making a call, she reached for the mouse.

Matt slid his mobile into his pocket, and picked up the two small cups. What the hell had prompted his father's arrival? If his mother was aware he'd come into the city, she'd be worried sick. Had Ms Taylor understood his silent message? Could things get any worse?

'Here, Dad, try this. Tell me if you like it.' He sank into the other armchair, torn between the desire to hug his ailing father, and the recurring craving to demand why he'd cheated on his wife. So many times.

He'd never understood why so many people he knew treated cheating casually, as part of modern life. To him it was abhorrent. Why claim to love someone and then seek another partner? Why stay with someone who had no respect for your affection?

He had never declared the emotion, deeming that would be hypocritical, but had always insisted on fidelity. He'd found out the hard way that for some people promises meant nothing.

It churned Matt's stomach that his father considered affairs a normal part of life, his due entitlement as a charismatic male. The man he'd revered in his youth and aspired to become had seen no reason why they should affect his marriage.

He was torn between the deep love of a son for his father and distaste for his casual attitude to being faithful. And behind him, hidden by the wall in Matt's eye line, was the room where he brought the women. His coffee turned sour in his mouth.

Marcus sipped his drink cautiously, savouring the taste.

'Mmm…good, real coffee. I'll take a pod home and ask Rosalind to buy some.'

'Take a box.' Matt cleared his throat, hesitant to ask the

vital question. *Please don't let the answer be he drove.*
'How did you get here, Dad?'

'Caught a cab at the shopping centre near home.' He
glared at the desk, set not too far away. 'You've twisted
my desk.' It was an accusation.

'Don't worry, it suits *me* that way. We can always put it
back.' He'd never place it in the former position that had
given the user a direct eye line to the person working at
the desk next door.

'Hmph. Now I need the bathroom.'

Marcus put his cup on the table, and went to the ensuite.
Matt let out a long huff of breath, and took another drink of
the hot, stimulating liquid. A glance at his watch told him
his cousin should be here in a few minutes.

Swearing softly when his desk phone rang, he strode
over to answer. He missed his father's return as he searched
his in-tray for the letter the caller had sent.

Lauren stopped typing as Marcus came into her office.
The eyes were a similar colour, the facial features bore a
strong resemblance, but he lacked the firm line of his son's
jaw, his innate sense of character.

'You're new. What happened to Miss...?' He tapped his
palm on his forehead. 'Um, long dark hair, big blue eyes.'

'I believe she left. Can I help you?'

His gaze intensified, then he came round to stand beside
her, and stared at the screen.

'She was a good typist. Fast and accurate.'

'Dad.'

Matt stood in the doorway, the same forbidding expression he'd worn at her interview directed at her. She lifted
her chin, determined not to be part of whatever games this
family was playing.

The older man spoke first. 'There's too many changes,
Matthew. My girl was good. She left. People kept leav-

ing.' Slow with pauses at inappropriate times. 'Who hired this one?'

He tapped her on the shoulder as he spoke, and she involuntarily flinched, knew from the frown on Matt's face he'd seen. He came over, and wrapped his arm across his father's shoulders.

'Let's leave Ms Taylor to her work, Dad. Come and finish your coffee?'

Although Matt barely glanced at her screen, he gave her a reassuring nod as he led his father out. He'd seen the bogus letter she'd started typing up.

'It'll be cold.'

She heard the outer door open, and saw Matt's body sag in relief.

'Here's Alan, Dad. He and I will drive you home and Mum will brew you another when we arrive.'

They moved out of her sight and she heard muffled exchanges then Matt's clearer words.

'Give me a minute. Grab that box of pods from the bench.'

He came into her room, his grateful expression telling her she'd pleased him, creating fissions of pleasure skittling from cell to cell.

'Quick thinking, Ms Taylor, thank you. I'll be gone for an hour or so. Joanne has a key to lock my office if you go out.'

He paused, swallowed as if there was more he wanted to say but couldn't find the words, then disappeared leaving her with a bundle of questions she'd never be game to ask.

The man she'd just met hadn't looked all that old but his behaviour and actions were certainly not those of a fast-thinking entrepreneur who'd built a thriving business.

She deleted the text as soon as she heard the door close, and brought up the files she'd been scanning. The events replayed in her mind as she sat, hands lightly resting on the keyboard.

Matt had been protective yet somehow detached from his father, desperate to get him out of here. He'd called this Alan to come and help, not wanting to escort him alone.

From Marcus' remark she deduced Matt had taken over his office. A woman had worked in here so he'd been elsewhere, probably the empty room by reception. Had Marcus kept such tight control Matt had no idea what was happening in the accounts and records?

That would explain his underlying antipathy and hostile manner but why towards her? She was his solution, his last resort. She was used to being warmly welcomed and treated with respect.

Matt was an enigma, his words and tone not always matching his body language and often conflicting with the message in those stunning blue eyes. He resented whatever it was that sparked between them, and must have a reason she couldn't fathom.

At all costs she had to find and fix his problems and get away without him finding out they had a past.

Matt quietly placed his keys into his desk drawer, wondering what he was going to say to Lauren.

My father has Alzheimer's. He's losing his memory. He's lost most of his good staff in the last year, and he's possibly screwed up the company.

His condition had escalated in the last month and Matt's mother was finding it harder to cope. Some very tough decisions would have to be made in the near future.

Matt would never blame Marcus for anything that could be attributed to that hellish affliction. But it was his father's screwing around that had sent him to the other side of the world. If he'd been here, possibly working with him, he'd have noticed the deterioration in time to prevent this debacle.

He would have. His fingers bunched. He squeezed his eyes shut and gritted his teeth. *He would have.*

Only the family, their doctor and a few select friends knew. Matt believed his chances of success hinged on keeping it a secret, and Lauren's employer had emphasised her discretion and trustworthiness. He was about to test it to the max.

She stopped working as he came to her doorway, her face inscrutable, her eyes wary. His stomach clenched.

'We'd better talk. Please come in here.'

Once they were seated by the window he paused to think, weighing up how much to tell her.

'There aren't the words to thank you enough for your understanding today. The man you saw isn't the same person who started this company. He has Alzheimer's.'

She leant forward. 'I suspected something like that. I'm sorry. It must be so hard on your family.' Empathy rang true in her voice and showed in her expression.

'Unfortunately, he kept his illness a secret from everyone, including my mother. We have no idea how long he faked his way until the progression sped up and his errors in the business became obvious. I'd have come home sooner if I'd known.'

'You weren't here?' She recoiled, eyes big and bright, fingers splayed.

She didn't know? There'd been no reason to tell her but he'd assumed she'd guessed. He nodded. 'I've been living in England for seven years.'

'Oh. Did you ever work here with your father?'

'In my late teens. My interests are in different fields of business.'

A pink blush spread up her neck and cheeks.

'Is something wrong?' He tensed, flexed his shoulders, and his hand lifted in concern.

Lauren cursed her lifelong affliction. What *could* possibly be wrong?

Only that the instant he mentioned his teens she remembered the balcony. Only that the sight of his mouth forming the words had her lips recalling the gentle touch of his.

'No, and I promise never to divulge any personal or company information to anyone.' Her hands clasped in her lap, she could barely take in that he'd shared this most personal secret with her. Now she understood.

His unplanned return from abroad to take control of a company in financial trouble explained the tension, the curtness. The urgency. She couldn't begin to imagine the daunting task he'd had thrust upon him.

'I'd appreciate it.'

'You're welcome. That's why you wanted my scanning hidden from him and called a friend for help.'

'He has good and bad days. Normally he becomes agitated whenever anything to do with the company is mentioned yet today he gave the taxi driver the correct address for the office. There was no hesitation in finding his way here or to the ensuite.'

'And he remembered the girl who worked here, though not her name.'

'He would.' The bitterness in his voice shook her and she jerked back, receiving a half-smile in apology as he continued.

'I was told her departure a few months ago was acrimonious to say the least. There were others who left because of his behaviour too, but replacements have to wait until you succeed and we sort everything out.'

She'd go and new staff would come. There'd be another woman at her desk, chosen by him...what was she thinking? This was not a valid reason to be depressed. Did he prefer blondes or brunettes?

Must. Stop. Thinking like this.

She snapped herself out of it and went to stand. 'On that note, I'd better get back to my task.'

He stood, and held out his hand to help her. The warmth from his touch spread up her arm, radiating to every part of her. She doubted even ice-cold water would cool her down. She prayed he couldn't detect her tremor and didn't demur as he kept hold.

'I am truly grateful, Lauren. I owe you big time and I never forget a debt.'

The message in his smouldering dark blue eyes painted a graphic picture of the form his gratitude might take, scrambling every coherent thought in her brain. Her throat dried, butterflies stirred in her stomach and it felt as if fluttering wings were brushing against every cell on her skin.

His grip tightened. Her lips parted. He leant closer.

The phone on his desk shattered the moment, and he glowered at it as he moved back, and reluctantly released her. She caught the arm of the chair to avoid collapsing into it.

His rasping, 'We'll talk again later,' proved she wasn't the only one affected.

As he picked up the handset he added, 'Alan's my cousin, family.'

The instant he answered the call he was in corporate mode. That irked because she needed time to compose herself, cool her skin, but he clearly didn't. When she returned from the ensuite, he was leaning on his desk, phone to his ear, watching for her. His engaging smile and quick but thorough appraisal from her face to her feet and back threatened to undo her freshen up. Not so calm and composed after all, just better at covering it up.

* * *

Lauren closed down early, allowing time for the ride to the airport, loath to suspend her search for four days. She had an inkling of an idea she'd heard somewhere but couldn't remember where or when. There'd be plenty of time to dwell on it in Melbourne.

Collecting her luggage, she took her report to Matt, whose stunned face and glance at his watch proved he'd forgotten her early departure.

'That late already? Have you ordered a taxi?'

'I'll be fine. I've noticed they always seem to be driving past.'

He grinned. 'Unless you need one. I'll finish this page and drive you.'

'There's no—'

'Humour me.'

Lauren's knowledge of cars was limited—there wasn't a necessity to own one in Sydney—but she recognised the Holden emblem on the grill. Matt's quiet assurance as he eased into the traffic didn't surprise her.

'Did you drive in Europe?'

'Yes, rarely in London, a lot through the country. Nowhere is too far if you can put up with dense traffic and miles of freeways. So different from Australia. Driving in Paris was a unique experience. Have you travelled?'

'A week in Bali with friends two years ago. We're planning a trip for this year if we can decide on a destination.'

She was aware of him glancing at her, but she kept her focus on the road where his should be.

'You mentioned family in Melbourne. Do you visit often?'

'Three or four times a year. This is my niece's first Easter.'

Matt willed her to look his way. She didn't. The ten-to-fifteen-minute drive in heavy traffic was hardly conducive to a meaningful discussion. That would have to wait until she returned.

'Why did you move to Sydney?' Why did he want to know? Why the long silent pause as she considered his question?

'Why did you go to London?'

Because I couldn't stand the sight of my parents feigning a happy marriage when it was a complete sham.

Because even moving into a rented house with friends in another suburb hadn't given him sufficient distance.

'Rite of passage to fly the nest and try to climb the corporate ladder without favour from associates of my father.'

'And you succeeded. It'll all be waiting for you when you've got Dalton Corporation back on track. Your family must be glad to have you home even under sad circumstances. I'm sure they've missed you.'

Matt picked up on the nuance in her voice, but didn't respond as he flicked on his indicator and turned into the airport road. So she had an issue with family as well. She'd rather not go.

He pulled into a clear space at the drop-off zone and switched off the engine. Before he had a chance to walk round and assist her, Lauren had unlatched her seat belt and jumped out.

He wiped his hand across his jaw, fighting the urge to reassure her, feeling he'd left so much unsaid today. He'd make time when she came back. She *was* coming back, and that pleased him.

She let him lift her luggage from the boot, and seemed reluctant to say goodbye.

'Thank you for the lift, Mr Dalton. I'll see you on Tuesday.'

'My pleasure. Enjoy your long weekend.'

I don't understand why, but I'll miss you.

CHAPTER FOUR

DRIVING BACK, MATT felt like laughing out loud at the incongruity of the situation. They could have spent time together during the four-day break, working alone, sharing lunches, maybe even dinner. Learning more about each other. Instead they'd be in different states paying lip service to family traditions.

With a complete turnaround, he wondered what the hell he was thinking. This was insane. Lauren Taylor was a temporary employee. Not his type at all. Yet he'd been so close to kissing her today in the office. The action and location were both bad ideas. So why did he wish that call hadn't come at that moment?

And how the hell had she managed to avoid answering his question?

Lauren closed her novel, and stared at the landscape rushing by then disappearing as the plane gained height. How could she concentrate on spine-thrilling action when her mind was in turmoil because of a man? She had male friends, a few of them treasured and platonic with whom she felt completely comfortable and totally at ease.

There were none who made her forget to breathe, who created fire in her core and sent her pulse into an erratic drumbeat. The thought of the magic those now skilful lips might evoke had her quivering with anticipation, earning her an anxious mutter from the older woman in the adjacent seat.

She gave her a reassuring smile, and turned back to the window. The fantasies she'd concocted for the last ten years had been childish daydreams based on teenage romance. The two relationships she'd drifted into had been more from affable proximity than passion. That they'd remained friends to this day proved how little anyone's heart had been involved.

No way would any woman accept friendship after an affair with Matt Dalton. His touch created electrical fissions on her skin, turned her veins into a racecourse and curled her toes. If they ever made it to the bedroom… She gulped in air, imagining the tanned, hot muscles he hid under expensive executive shirts.

'Are you sure you're okay?'

Her head swung round to meet a concerned gaze.

'Yes, thank you. I'm fine.'

Opening her book, she pretended to read, flipped pages and didn't take in a solitary word.

Late on Saturday night Lauren curled into the pillows in the guest bedroom, wondering what Matt was doing. She almost wished she'd gone with her parents and the grandchildren to visit friends. Her brothers were having the inevitable barbecue in the back garden.

She'd spent a great day with friends from university, who had insisted on driving her home, dropping her off at the corner because of all the cars parked in the street. Deciding to try to be more sociable, she'd attempted to join in with her brothers' party.

She'd lasted ten minutes among the raucous crowd, with whom she had little in common, then she'd finished her sausage sandwich, drained the soft drink can and said goodnight. A chorus of, 'Night, little sister!' had followed her into the house, most of it slurred.

She'd gone slowly up the stairs, reappraising her attitude to her upbringing. Had she been the one to pull away, uneasy with the openness of the rest of her family? Had she taken their leave-her-in-peace approach for indifference?

Not understanding why she'd begun to analyse her relationships, she'd shaken it away. She had a good life, a great job and supportive friends. Maybe she'd talk it through with them when she went home.

Putting on headphones and turning her music up loud, she'd logged into her computer and accessed her favourite game, which necessitated super concentration, blocking everything else out.

Now it was quiet except for an occasional passing vehicle. Was Matt asleep? Did he live alone or with his parents? Did he have siblings? There were so many questions that might never be answered.

Matt laughed out loud as he stood chest-high in his parents' pool on Sunday afternoon, pretending to fight off his nephews. He picked up Drew, the youngest, and tossed him, squirming and shrieking, about a metre away. Alex immediately latched onto his upper arm.

'Me next, Uncle Matt. Me next.'

He obliged, knowing this game could last until they were exhausted. He was surprised they had so much energy after the active Easter egg hunt around the garden this morning. One after the other, they kept coming at him and he revelled in their joy of the simple pleasure. They rejuvenated him whenever he was with them.

These were the times he regretted never marrying, and having children of his own. He took a splash of water in the face, shook his head, and laughed again. Hell, he wasn't even thirty, he had plenty of time.

He grabbed them both, one in each arm. Knowing what was coming, they giggled and clung to his neck. 'Deep breath.' Taking one himself, he dropped to the bottom of the pool, bending his legs to give him leverage. Pushing up, he surged from the water in a great spray, their happy squeals deafening him.

'Again. Again.

'Time out.'

His sister, Lena, was walking across the lawn carrying a tray of drinks and snacks. He let the boys go and they immediately swam for the ladder. Hoisting himself up onto the side, he took the beer she offered. She sat beside him, letting her feet dangle into the water, and studied him as he drank.

'What?' He looked at her and grinned. 'Am I in trouble?'

She shook her head as her eyes roamed over his face, and rested a caring hand on his arm. 'There's something different about you, Matt. I can't quite work out what.'

'I'm bone-tired, grabbing fast food most days and need a haircut.'

And I am inexplicably missing a woman I have only known for three days.

'Nothing's changed there since I last saw you. Bigger problems at work? No, that you'd handle in your usual indomitable manner.'

She tilted her head and arched her eyebrows, a ploy that usually produced a confession. They were as close as siblings could get but Lauren was new and he hadn't quite worked out how and why she affected him. And what he was going to do about it.

'Every trip you made home I hoped you'd have found peace from whatever drove you to go so far away. It never happened though you hid it well, and I know you only came now because Dad needed you.'

He didn't reply because he couldn't explain. He shrugged, put his arm around her and drew her close.

'I missed you, Mark and the boys more than I can say, Lena. You're the biggest plus on the side of me staying for good.'

Her face lit up at his remark he was considering relocating back to Adelaide. He meant it, wanted to be here for all his nephews' milestones. Skype was no substitute for personal hugs.

She kissed his cheek. 'You'll tell me when you're ready. In the meantime, add an extra plus sign.'

He frowned then grinned even wider and bear-hugged her. 'That's great. When?'

'November. You're the first to know.'

'Whatever happens I'll be here.' It was a promise he intended to keep.

When the boys went inside with their mother, he slid back into the water, working off restless energy with strong freestyle laps. His strokes and turns were automatic, leaving his mind to wonder what Lauren was doing and who she was with. And why the hell it was beginning to matter to him.

'Hang on, Lauren. The door's locked.'

Lauren turned her head towards the sound. It was ten past seven on Tuesday morning. Where was Matt? He'd said nothing about being absent today.

Joanne appeared, carrying a small bunch of keys, and they walked along the corridor.

'Mr Dalton's at a site meeting in the northern suburbs, called me last night. If he's not back by morning break, I'll join you for coffee.' She pushed the door open and left.

Being alone in the office didn't daunt Lauren, who'd always preferred having no surrounding noise or motion. Today her body was all keyed up as if waiting for some fundamental essential that was missing.

She had no interruptions until ten-thirty when Joanne walked in carrying a plate of home-baked jam slices.

'Family favourite. Let's sit by the window. Tea or coffee?'

'Tea, thanks.'

Lauren never indulged in gossip at work. She couldn't define why she felt tempted now, unless it was because Matt Dalton had invaded her peace of mind, and aroused her curiosity. The more she learnt about him, the easier it might be to resist him. If she couldn't she knew who'd end up heartbroken.

'How long have you worked for the Daltons?'

'Over six years. Since my youngest started secondary school. Of course, that was in a smaller office near the parklands. I like having familiar faces around. How do you cope, travelling and working with new people all the time?'

'I prefer it. I'm not much of a people person, never quite got the hang of casual socialising.'

'Mr Dalton senior was a natural and had no problems persuading people to invest with him. He was good with computers, installing quite a few new programs himself, and very easy to work for until a few years ago. We lost good long-term staff because he became secretive and less approachable.'

'And now Matt's in charge.'

Of everything. Thankfully he was unaware that included her emotions, unaware of how intriguing she found him.

'He came back from Europe when his father's heart trouble was diagnosed. Put a great career on hold, I understand, and not very happy to be here. I'm not sure whether it's the business, the problems or having to leave London, maybe all of them. He'll be heading back once his father's in full health again.'

Lauren let her babble on, regretting she'd instigated the topic. Matt had led her to believe he trusted Joanne yet he'd given the staff a fabricated story and let them believe his father would be coming back.

Did he really think any of them were involved in the computer anomalies? If not, it was cruel of him to give them false hope. Why did he keep giving out mixed messages? Or was she misinterpreting them?

Oh, why wasn't he older, content with a doting wife, and heading for a paunch from all her home cooking?

* * *

Lauren's mobile rang as she wrote notes on the last hour's work. Convincing Matt of her beliefs wasn't going to be an easy task.

'Ms Taylor, I need a favour.'

No preamble. No 'how are things going?' And the rasping tone was rougher. Why did she sympathise with his stress when he obviously intended to unload some of it onto her?

'Yes, Mr Dalton.'

'This is taking longer than I anticipated. If a Duncan Ford arrives at the office while I'm out, can you entertain him until I arrive?'

'Me?'

Meet and socialise with an unknown corporate executive?

Dealing with them when they needed her skills and the conversation centred on their technical problems was a world away from casual chit-chat. Knowing she was capable gave her confidence.

'You. Will it be a problem? Joanne's compiling figures for our meeting later.' He sounded irritated at her reluctance.

'That's not what I do. The few businessmen I've met have only been interested in how quickly I can fix their problems. A comment about the weather is as personal as we'd get.'

'It won't be for long. I'll be there in an hour or so, depending on traffic.'

She heard another voice in the background, followed by his muttered reply.

'Please, Ms Taylor. He's just a man.'

Yeah, like you're *just a man.*

His coaxing tone teased goose bumps to rise on her skin, and the butterflies in her stomach to take flight. She'd do it for him, and he knew it. She could hardly tell him fear of messing it up for him contributed to her reticence.

'Give him coffee. Ask him about the weekend football or his grandkids. Pretend he's an android.'

She pictured him grinning as he said that, and sighed.

'Okay, I'll try.'

After an abrupt 'thanks' he hung up, leaving her with a sinking stomach and a strong craving for chocolate, *her* standby for stress. Grabbing her bag, she raced for the lift and the café in the next building, mentally plotting dire consequences for all the too-good-looking, excessively privileged, overly confident males who'd ever tried to manipulate her. Including her three brothers.

'Mr Ford has arrived, Lauren. I'll bring him along.' Joanne phoned to give her warning.

Shoot. Only ten minutes since Matt called to say he was finally on his way. She swallowed a mouthful of water, pulled her shoulders back and prayed she didn't look as apprehensive as she felt. On her way through his office she added an extra plea he had a clear traffic run.

Mr Ford was average height, slightly overweight, and wore an apologetic smile. So much for Matt's word picture. He also held a small boy by the hand.

'Ms Taylor? Thank you for offering to look after us until Matt gets here.'

Offering? Us? Someone tall and desperate had bent the truth a tad.

'You're welcome. Come on in.' She indicated towards the armchairs. 'Please take a seat. Would—?'

Squealing with excitement, the child had broken free and was running to the window.

'Look, Granddad. Look how high we are. Look at the tiny cars way down there.'

Granddad smiled at Lauren and shrugged. 'The world's a wondrous place at that age.'

He walked over and hunkered down, his arm around the boy's shoulders, and let the child point out the amazing things he could see.

Pain clamped round Lauren's heart and she couldn't bear to watch them. She clasped her hands together over her stomach and stared at the floor. She'd never shared a special moment like this with either of her parents. They'd been happy to supply her with books, computers and assorted accessories, hoping they would keep her occupied. Never seemed to have time to spend exclusively with her.

There'd never been other relatives either. Her father's family lived in Canada, her mother had left home in her teens, and contact was limited on both sides. No wonder she felt inept in any new social situation.

'I believe you were about to offer coffee, Ms Taylor.'

She looked up to meet a quizzical gaze. Knew she was being appraised and managed a shaky smile. Matt had requested her to hostess and he was paying her wage, so a hostess she'd try to be.

'Of course. We have water or soft drinks if the child is thirsty.'

And then what do I talk to you about?

Take out the economy, sport, politics and local events, none of which she was up with, and she was left with the weather.

Matt Dalton, I hate you for putting me in this position.

He'd hired her to sit and scan his computer files, not make small talk, which she'd never ever been able to comprehend.

'Flat white for me and lemonade for Ken, thank you. I came in to take care of him while my wife and daughter saw a specialist, took a punt that Matt might be free. Ken has a game pad, and I have a magazine to read so we won't be a bother.'

He reached for the satchel he'd placed on the floor and opened it.

It's no trouble,' she lied.

His expression said he didn't believe her, and knew exactly how she was feeling. He'd be a formidable opponent in a boardroom. She turned away, heart hurting, stomach churning. Still the same tongue-tied girl she'd always been. Always would be.

Mr Ford was settled into a chair and Ken sitting cross-legged on the floor when she brought the drinks over. The boy was frowning as she put his on the low table.

'Thank you. Granddad, the frog won't jump.'

Without hesitation she dropped down alongside him.

'Show me.'

He studied her with narrowed eyes, assessing if she could be trusted with his new favourite toy. He gingerly handed it over, shuffled closer and didn't take his eyes off the screen as she read the game rules and started tapping.

Matt couldn't remember breaking a mirror or running over a black cat but he sure as hell was raking in bad luck. At least there'd been some positives in his inspection of a new recommended site today.

Duncan Ford was a man reputed to be fair and honest in business, a trustworthy partner and an admirable opponent. A man he'd met on a number of occasions over the years, usually with his father. Lately through a business acquaintance and his own initiative.

If Lauren had managed to keep him happy, he'd have a chance to pitch his proposition in the near future. If he secured a deal with Duncan Ford on the development of a vacant factory, it would go a long way to solving the company's present dilemma. Unfortunately ifs weren't solid happenings.

He strode towards his office, his heart sinking. No sound, no voices. Until, as he reached the open door, he heard a triumphant 'yes' in a child's tone.

The man he'd hoped to impress was sitting in one of the armchairs reading a magazine. Lauren and a young boy were kneeling by the coffee table, heads bent over a bright yellow pad.

'Matt.' Duncan stood, and came forward to shake hands. After putting the cardboard tube containing site plans on his desk and his satchel on the floor, Matt willingly complied.

'I apologise for not being here, Duncan.'

'Hey, it was an off chance. Lauren's been the perfect hostess.'

Matt flashed a grateful smile in her direction. He'd thank her properly later. The daggers she sent back warned him he'd have to grovel, big time. To his surprise he found the prospect stimulating rather than daunting.

'I got a call late yesterday to say this particular site goes on the market next month. I couldn't refuse the chance to inspect it.'

'We'll schedule a meeting when you've finalised your proposal. My coming into town was unexpected and I should be hearing from my daughter any minute. Once she and young Ken are on their way home, I'd like you and Lauren to join my wife and me for lunch.'

'Me?'

Matt's head swung at the panic in Lauren's voice. Exactly the same as earlier, yet, whatever her fears, she'd obviously impressed Duncan, which didn't surprise him. She certainly fascinated him.

'My treat for keeping Ken amused.'

'Thank you but no. I have work to do and I've brought my lunch.'

Her agitation was clear in her voice, and, though she managed to keep her features calm, Matt saw the plea in her wide-open eyes. And that intangible niggle flicked in his memory, and was gone just as fast.

The gentleman in him leaned towards letting her off the hook. The desperate male striving to secure a solid future for the company and its employees won.

'It'll keep 'til tomorrow, Ms Taylor. Never refuse a chance to eat out in Adelaide.'

If she was about to protest, Ken forestalled her, patting her arm and holding up his pad.

'Your turn, Lauren.'

She knelt to attend to the child. The chagrined look she gave Matt ought to have annoyed him, as she'd be wined and dined in style. Instead he was already planning ways to help her relax with the Fords.

CHAPTER FIVE

CLAIR FORD AND her daughter were Lauren's idea of true corporate wives, dressed in the latest fashion and groomed to perfection. If their greetings and appreciation hadn't been so sincere and friendly, she might have cut and run.

With young mother and son safely on their way home, the remaining four walked to the Fords' chosen restaurant. They led the way, allowing for private discussion.

'I owe you big time for today.' Matt's voice was low and subdued, proving the tension he was under.

'I'll keep tally, Mr Dalton. This counts too. What do I have in common with Mr Ford and his wife? The nearest I come to their world is walking past executive offices.'

'Under the current circumstances, Lauren, I think you should call me Matt.'

Lauren. Matt.

This made it personal, more familiar.

She'd liked the way he'd remembered the pronunciation of her name from her first phone call. She wasn't so sure about the butterfly flutter in her belly as he said it or the pleasurable shivers over her skin every time he guided her past oncoming pedestrians.

'I don't understand. You meet and deal with new people all the time. Why the reluctance?'

How could he understand how she felt? He oozed confidence and charm, would have no qualms on walking into a room full of notable people he'd never met. He'd been brought up to meet and greet strangers with ease.

'I can't do small talk. My family are all outgoing, garrulous, and at ease with anyone. I was shy. I'd freeze up and hide in my room. I...'

Duncan turned to check where they were as he and Clair turned off towards a waterside restaurant. The warm glow to her belly from Matt's gentle squeeze at her waist eased her misgivings. The tingles from his hot breath as he bent to her ear generated entirely different reservations.

'She's a down-to-earth mother and grandmother who enjoys serving on charity committees. He's into football and car racing. Trust me, Lauren, I'll be right beside you.'

They were escorted to a round table by the window. Matt held her chair, leaning over to whisper, 'Just be yourself, Lauren. I like you as you are.'

His fingers gently brushed a strand of hair from her shoulder, making her quiver, making her heart expand 'til her chest felt full and tight. So much for her internal lectures on the return flight to Adelaide, reinforcing how vital it was to keep distance between them.

Clair insisted on sitting next to her rather than opposite. 'The men will talk shop,' she said without rancour, smiling as she accepted a menu. 'Always say they won't. Always do. Nature of the beast.'

At the moment the two of them were discussing wine with one waiter while another poured iced water into their glasses. Lauren drank some, and felt cooler, more in control.

'What do you fancy, Lauren? The veal scaloppini is always delicious, and the perfect size to leave room for dessert.' Clair put down her menu, her decision made.

After ordering the same, Lauren almost refused wine until she caught Matt watching her, and decided why not? It was a light refreshing Sauvignon Blanc and one glass might give her courage. It would also fortify her for later if she told him the most likely outcome.

'Duncan's a stickler for supporting local wineries and we're rarely disappointed,' Clair said, leaning closer. 'Ken really enjoyed himself today, told me you taught him how to win games faster.'

'He's very bright, picked up what I showed him easily.'

'Maybe I ought to get him to teach me. I'm hopeless. My

worst fault is somehow sending files into folders they're not supposed to be in. Then I can't find them. I've also seized everything up a few times.'

'Have you taken any courses?' Chatting came naturally when someone took a genuine interest in you. Knowing they were all grateful to her, albeit for different reasons, helped too.

'A couple. I read the notes, and try to remember. Drives Duncan crazy. He says I rush too much. How do you do it all day?'

'Different people, different skills. Put me in a kitchen with any more than four or five ingredients, and I'm in trouble. Or rather, whoever wants to eat is.'

Their meals arrived, and the conversation became general until Clair suddenly announced, 'I'm thinking of asking Lauren to give me a lesson or two on my computer.'

Lauren saw a delighted smile replace the initial surprise on Matt's face. Duncan's exaggerated groan and loving expression towards his wife filled her with a longing she couldn't explain.

'I'm sure she's dealt with more incompetent people than me, Duncan Ford.' Clair's put-on piqued expression caused laughter round the table. Three pairs of eyes turned to Lauren for a reply.

'I'm sure I have. The trickiest ones are usually when they've tried to rectify the error but can't remember what they did. Or when they deny knowing.'

She shared a story of an ongoing promotion feud where two women had been sabotaging the other's computer, costing both of them their jobs. With encouragement she continued.

'A friend was asked to retrieve permanently deleted emails from the client's wife's laptop. He'd found romantic messages between her and another man, lost his temper and deleted them. Became angrier when he realised he now had nothing to confront her with.'

'Teach him to be destructive even *with* provocation. Did he get them back?' Clair asked.

'My friend refused to get involved so I have no idea.'

'Duncan, remember when…'

Clair's voice faded and Duncan's took over but Lauren barely heard his words. As she'd told the story, she'd become aware of Matt tensing beside her, hadn't dared look that way. She forced herself to focus on their host.

They were all laughing at the anecdote of his son-in-law wrongly directing an email about a surprise party when she glanced sideways. Matt was looking at her, a speculative expression on his face.

The world around them blurred until she could see only him. Her heart blipped then began to race. Warmth spread up her throat and cheeks. He arched his neck and his eyes darkened to almost black. She didn't dare guess at the thoughts behind them as he reached for his glass.

In fact Matt was wondering what the heck had happened. The quiet woman, who was so guarded with him, was captivating their hosts. There was only a hint of the hesitancy he'd perceived in the office. She listened to Clair with a genuine smile on her lips, and gave the same consideration to Duncan as he spoke.

So why the barrier with him? Instinct told him Lauren had a history with someone, painful enough to make her wary of men, or a particular breed of men. He was torn between letting it alone or finding out more and proving to her he couldn't be categorised.

It would be treading dangerous ground trying to discover the woman behind the technical façade. But, oh, it would feel good to see her smile focused on him, feel those sweet lips yield under his, trail a path of kisses down her slender neck as he held her in his arms.

'Have you finished, sir?'

He flinched as the waiter's arm appeared at his side.

*Finished? Unless he lost his mind, he had no intention
of starting.*

'Oh. Um... Yes, thank you. The steak was perfect.'

He met Clair's knowing look across the table, and knew
by the heat his cheeks were flushed. She was as astute as
her husband; he'd bet she wasn't easily fooled. He had to try.

'Great restaurant. I'll keep it in mind for entertaining.'

Thankfully the wine waiter distracted her as he topped
up her glass. Matt noted Lauren declined.

As they left the restaurant Clair caught his arm.

'I like her, Matt. She's very natural, down to earth. Pity
she'll be returning to Sydney.'

'It's her home.'

'Adelaide used to be.'

He didn't answer. He hadn't known.

Duncan hailed a cab, telling Matt they'd drop him and
Lauren at the office on their way. As they said goodbye
Clair tapped Matt's arm through the window.

'We'll see you Saturday night. I do so love dressing up
for corporate dos.'

'I'll be wearing my best tuxedo.'

He took Lauren's arm to guide her into the building, and
sensed her guard was back up. Which made his burgeon-
ing idea even more incongruous.

Lauren strove to keep her emotions under control in the
lift, fought to keep her fingers from fisting. She didn't have
proof yet, only assumptions. Saying anything would detract
from the positives of the day.

Matt unlocked his office door, moved aside to let her
enter then suddenly stiffened and caught her arm.

'You're trembling. Why?'

She looked into concerned blue eyes, and was swamped
by the desire to caress the shadows away from underneath,
to ease his burden. To say it was all okay.

'It's been an eventful day. I'd better get back to work.'

'Hmm, and I have to check in with Joanne and the others.' He let go, shrugged off his jacket, and hung it on his chair. Halfway back to the door, he swivelled round and gave her an ironic smile.

'I know I haven't been the easiest of people to work with or approach since taking charge. You're a courageous lady, Lauren Taylor, and I will find a way to repay you for stepping in for me.'

His unexpected compliment threw her. Her first opinion of him eroded a little more as new aspects of his enforced position emerged.

Opening up to her on Thursday wouldn't have been easy. He'd been forced by circumstances to take her into a confidence he'd rather have kept private. Something he only shared with those close to the family.

She went to her desk, determined to crack this puzzler and alleviate the pressure he was under. Her life in Sydney was on hold, her friends were there. When she returned everything would revert to normal. Except her vague fantasy was now a handsome, magnificently built real live male whose aroma, and every look, every touch weakened her knees and sent her pulse skyrocketing.

Her professionalism partially blocked him out at the office, and she managed to focus when dealing with hotel staff and other people. During those hours he was like an undercurrent in her head, surging to full force as soon as she was alone. With his muscled torso—clearly defined under his shirt—his trim waist and flat stomach, his image flicked through her mind like pages of a fireman calendar.

She'd succeed and then she'd have to leave him behind.

Matt returned to his office an hour later. Talking plans and strategies hadn't kept his thoughts from straying to Lauren. The way her chin lifted when she became defensive. The way her hair swung across her shoulders when she turned her head. Her soft hazel eyes betraying every emotion.

They'd crossed a threshold today, and he wasn't sure where it might lead. Surely they could become friends and stay platonic? Yeah, tell that to whatever part of his body was revving up his pulse and stimulating his libido. Initiating a closer relationship while she worked for him was fraught with danger.

She leant forward over her desk as if being closer would make something happen, her eyes riveted to the screen. Delightfully intense. She hadn't noticed his arrival, and started when she did, falling back with her hand covering her heart.

'Sorry, I didn't mean to disturb you.'

She'd gone a delicate pink again, a shade fast becoming a favourite of his. Leaning on the door jamb, he wondered how far it spread, immediately banishing the enticing image.

'I've got a call to make then we'll talk.'

Why? Lauren blinked, stretched, and changed her mind about going for a cold drink. She did a few leg raises, wriggled her fingers, and resumed work.

She tried to ignore the steady drone of his husky voice, interspersed with laughter and long pauses. The gentle tone she'd never heard him use before implied it had to be a woman he cared for. Her stomach knotted and her fingers curled. If she'd dared, she'd have closed the communicating door so she wouldn't have to hear.

His call ended, and she sighed with relief, entered a date for checking, and scrolled down peering at the screen. Neck tingles alerted her as he walked in and sat on the edge of her desk.

Letting her hands fall into her lap, she looked up. Her throat dried, and she wished she'd gone for that drink. Her chest tightened under the intensity of his gaze. It was as if he were searching for her innermost secrets.

'Do you have plans for Saturday night?'

'What?' She jolted upright, gripping the armrests for support. Stared, mouth open, too shocked to think.

His sudden wide smile confused her more, sending her body temperature soaring. Heart-stoppingly handsome before, even with the ravages of fatigue, he was elevated to drop-dead gorgeous.

'It's a simple question. Are you free on Saturday night?'

'I may not be here by then.' Breathless and throaty, not sounding like herself at all.

'No.' Sharp. Irascible. 'No.' Gentler, more controlled. 'Even if you find the cause of the anomalies, there'll be tidying up to do.'

'Why are you asking?'

What could he possibly want from her?

His light chuckle skimmed across her skin.

'I'd like you to be my partner at a corporate dinner.'

'Dinner? Why me?' Her common sense brain patterns seemed to have deserted her.

He leaned forward, and what little breath she managed to inhale was pure ocean breeze.

'A thank you for having my back today. Duncan and Clair like you, and we'll be at their table.'

'Surely there's someone else you could take.'

'After seven years away and working up to eighty hours a week? Anyone I knew is long spoken for. My sister only consented to accompany me out of pity.'

His sister. She flopped. She'd been jealous of his sister. *No! Not jealous.*

'Well?' His eyes were like laser beams searching for the answer he wanted.

'Won't she be disappointed?'

'Ah, that's where my negotiating skills came in. I've offered to babysit my two nephews, and shout her and her husband dinner at the restaurant of her choice. She'll have a romantic evening for two instead of set menu, speeches and dancing with her brother.'

Dancing. In his arms.

Too close. Too dangerous. You're already in too deep. Say no, thank you.

The phone on his desk rang. He muttered a low hoarse sound, and appeared reluctant to move.

'Will you come with me, Lauren?'

'Yes.'

Wrong. Idiot. Wrong.

He stroked a feather-touch path down her cheek, immobilising her senses, then smiled again, sending them all haywire.

'Thank you. I promise you won't regret accepting. Do you want to take an early leave? You've had an eventful day.'

'I'm fine. I'll keep going, and you need to reply to that call.'

Fine didn't come near to describing how she felt. Adrenaline coursed through her veins, her lungs were having trouble pumping air and her heart was pounding. And she couldn't tell if it was joy or fear driving them.

Matt had avidly watched the ever-changing emotions in her eyes. Confusion, surprise, shock when he mentioned his sister, and then pleasure as she blurted out her answer. It was as if she were afraid her brain would rebel and refuse his request if she dithered any longer.

He'd gripped the desk to prevent his arms reaching for her, the urge to hold her stronger than he'd ever felt. And then what? He had no idea; with her he was in uncharted waters.

He was, however, determined that before he let her go he'd persuade her to reveal her inner torments, and help her overcome them. He knew with an innate certainty the inner woman was as beautiful as her outward appearance.

* * *

Lauren arrived early the next morning even though she'd taken extra time on her hair and make-up. She'd fallen asleep thinking of ball gowns—she'd have to buy one, plus matching accessories—romantic music and dancing with a stunning male in tailor-made formal wear.

It had been dark when she'd woken, her mind buzzing with an idea generated by her discussion over the phone with Pete in Sydney. Eagerness to try it had warred with the desire to look extra good for Matt, so she'd skipped breakfast and bought a sandwich on the way.

The disappointment at his absence was countered with optimism that she'd be able to give him the answers he'd requested. Her fingers hesitated over the keyboard. If she was correct, today might be her last day in this room, so close to him. Even when he was elsewhere in the building, she felt his presence, and his unique aroma lingered in the air.

She'd spend the rest of her working life breathing in expectantly and being disenchanted. Not even the same brand would suit because it wouldn't have his essence.

She booted up. She'd promised to do her best for him, and would, even if it meant she lost out.

Matt arrived mid-morning, eager to see her. He was perplexed by her reticence on the phone when he'd called to say he'd been delayed. If she was having second thoughts about Saturday, he'd have to talk her round.

In his hurry to see her he left his jacket in the car. Not caring, he barrelled through his office to her door where her grave expression pulled him up short. Even as the truth hit home his subliminal mind noted she wore extra make-up. Subtle and captivating.

'You've solved it.' It was what he wanted, had hired her for. So why the heaviness in his chest, and the sudden nausea attack?

She nodded and he swung away to fetch his chair, wheeling it over to her desk. His gut told him it wasn't good and he braced for the worst. Her delicate fragrance taunted him with every intake of air.

Her blue screen was blank except for a familiar symbol.

'And this is…?' He already knew—wanted confirmation yet dreaded receiving it.

Lauren hesitated, hating that what she was about to reveal would hurt him, She had no choice, pressed enter, and a box with a request for a password appeared.

'It's deliberate and there are limited people who had access. Joanne said—'

'You've discussed this with her?' His body surged forward. Anger flashed in his eyes, giving them more animation than she'd seen since they met.

'No! We shared a coffee break yesterday, and she said they'd lost good employees. You referred to the staff turnover last Thursday.'

'I did. I apologise.' It was terser than he'd been lately, with no relenting of his indignant stance.

'It wasn't gossip. Joanne admires your father very much. I got the impression his health had worried her for ages. She said how well he and the staff got on, what a great boss he was, and that he'd installed a number of the programs himself.'

'I didn't know. I wasn't here.' He ground one fist into the other palm.

'It has to be my father.'

CHAPTER SIX

HIS WORLD HAD imploded at the sight of the icon. This was confirmation of the suspicion that had grown as he'd checked the records, hoping his father's worsening dementia had been responsible for the unaccountable swings. Saying the words out loud enforced the actuality.

He moved closer and typed in the heading on the plaque in his father's home study, his fingers surprisingly steady in contrast to the agitation in his gut. Two screen changes and he had the answers he needed. And a whole new bunch of complications.

Elbow on the desk, hand clenching his jaw and mouth, he gaped at the folder titles, anger building at the subterfuge of the man he'd admired. What the hell had he been planning?

'Would you like me to leave while you examine the files?'

He didn't turn, couldn't face her. Needing air and time to come to terms with the harsh reality in front of him, he pushed away from the desk, shot to his feet and swung away from her.

'No. Close it down.'

He strode out of both offices, his mind churning with distasteful words: fraud, embezzlement, jail. Ignoring the lift, he went to the stairwell and headed down. There was no more doubt, no more hope of technical glitches, or outside scamming.

If he reported what they'd found his father would be investigated. If he didn't...not an option. He'd fight like hell to save the company and his new enterprise with Duncan but the appropriate authorities had to be informed. Whatever the cost to his own personal reputation, everything had to be open and above board.

He wasn't sure how many floors he pounded down and

up again. As his head and his options became clearer, he realised he'd left Lauren in the lurch. She'd succeeded in the task he'd given her, and he'd growled and walked out. Had she left? Would she equate him with his father?

His angst eased a little when he found her sitting by the window in her office writing in a small notebook. She raised her head and he gazed into sweet hazel eyes, full of compassion and offered with complete sincerity. A haven from the tempest.

Lauren sat stunned after he'd barked out the order to shut down and stormed out. He hadn't even glanced at her, just bolted.

After closing down and writing out instructions to access the files, she went for a drink of water, pondering her future, which might be closer than she'd expected. She'd done the job, found what the anomalies hid. Not knowing what the folders contained, she assumed they'd need to be audited, and that wasn't her expertise.

Did this change his invitation for Saturday night? Would she be starting her exploration of rural South Australia earlier than anticipated? She was no longer required so why didn't she feel the usual elation of success? The bubble of enthusiasm for the next assignment?

She took a notebook from her bag and tried to makes notes and failed. Her mind was on the distraught man who was trying to come to terms with his father's deceit. This was a major blow for him. He deserved privacy to come to terms with tangible proof of his father's duplicity and the fallout effects to his family.

His entrance was as abrupt as his departure. He paused for a second in the doorway then walked slowly towards her, midnight-blue eyes dark and unsure of his reception. Her skin tingled, and her heart somersaulted. She trembled as she met his gaze, stood and dropped the book and pen onto the chair.

He took her hands and squeezed them, his Adam's apple convulsing, and his mouth opening and shutting without sound. Slowly, gently he caressed up her arms to hold her shoulders, and inched closer. He stroked her cheek, caught a strand of her hair and twined it round his finger. When she placed a hand on his chest, he shuddered.

If Lauren's heart swelled an atom larger, it would burst from her body. Heat spiralled from deep in her belly, drying her throat, searing her from within. He evoked feelings she'd never have believed herself capable of, made her aware of a physical wanting she'd only read of in books. He coloured her dreams in brilliant shades and sunshine.

His eyes were searching for her soul and she couldn't look away. Mesmerised by their power, she leant forward in a mirror image to his movement. Stilled when he straightened up, a guttural sound coming from deep in his throat. His hands dropped to his sides, leaving her cold where his fingers had been.

'I... This... *Hell.*' Forceful. Passionate. 'I'd planned for a special lunch with you so we could talk.'

He rubbed the back of his neck and his face contorted as he stared at the computer.

'I have to deal with this now and find out what he's done.'

She understood the battle he was fighting—his family's good name was in jeopardy—but it hurt. She felt as if she'd been dismissed. Gathering up her pen and book, she moved to the desk for her bag and took a sheet of paper from the top drawer.

'These are the access instructions.' She put it on the desk top, Had to get out before she broke down and cried.

'Lauren?' The anguish in his voice tore at her heart.

She turned and saw a different battle in his eyes, one that clogged her throat and tripped her heartbeat.

'Thank you. I may not seem grateful at the moment but I do appreciate all you've done.' He gestured at the computer. 'If possible we'll have lunch tomorrow or Friday.'

'I'd like that.' Much, much more than like.

'There can't be much you don't know or haven't guessed so you must know the ramifications could send us under.'

The potency had gone from his voice, giving him an endearing vulnerability, making her care for him even more. With his strong will, it would only be a temporary effect of the devastating blow.

'If there's anything I can do.' She moved forward until she inhaled his cologne. She was so going to miss the fragrance. The walks she always enjoyed along windswept beaches, especially prior to an impending storm, were going to be a mixture of pleasure and pain for ever.

His rueful smile made her long to wrap her arms around him for comfort.

'I'm sure there will be at some stage. There's nothing now so take a few hours off.'

When she left he was talking on his mobile, an open file on her screen in front of him.

The size of the hidden program astounded Matt. There were accumulated folders and files dating back six years, money transferred in, none out. He studied names and figures, made calls to his accountant, lawyer and Alan. No amount of trying could curb the resentment at his father's deception beginning long before the onset of his dementia.

Cheating was unjustified, in any form. Marcus, acquaintances, even friends deemed nothing wrong with bending rules or breaking promises. A few months ago he'd let himself be fooled by a scheming woman, and had been on the verge of pledging his life and honour to her. She'd claimed to love him, a blatant lie.

Now he was more cynical, and had no faith in romantic declarations. He'd make that clear before entering into any relationship. No emotions, no lies, and nobody got hurt.

Which meant no involvement with Lauren. She was a for-ever kind of girl who'd weave romantic dreams around kisses and…hell, again he'd come so close to kissing her today.

It might be for the best that she'd be leaving soon. It wouldn't be until he was sure there was nothing else hidden, and not until he'd treated her to a night she'd always remember.

He clicked the mouse, and rechecked the folder list. He'd need hard-drive copies of everything plus paper copies of the folder list, maybe others. Lauren's help would be invaluable as he dealt with any authorities who'd have an interest in any aspect of the clandestine accounts.

Bracing himself, he accessed another file, and resumed his onerous task.

Lauren rarely shopped for social events. Her new 'uniforms' of trouser suits and blouses were purchased in the January and June sales. Outside work she wore casual clothes, unless on special occasions. What she did have was in Sydney but nothing in her wardrobe came close to being suitable for a corporate dinner.

She fluctuated between longing to go and fearing she'd embarrass him as she wandered from shop to shop, sifting through racks of dresses and tops. Standing in the change rooms of an international brand store, she almost gave up.

Why this alien urge to buy something bold and extravagant? *So* not her, sleek and clinging, showing off every curve and a seemingly long expanse of leg? Like the low-cut sapphire-blue on the wide-eyed image staring at her from the mirror.

'Do you require any assistance?' the salesgirl called through the door.

No. Though, if she were ever to wear anything like this out in public, a huge hike in self-confidence would definitely help.

'I'm fine, thanks.'

She found what she was searching for in a small off-the-mall boutique. A dress that fitted perfectly and boosted her self-esteem, one she hoped would make Matt proud to escort her. Shoes and a matching clutch bag were bought in a nearby shop, and by mentioning Joanne's name she managed to book an appointment for Saturday at her recommended hairdresser.

Stepping towards the kerb to hail a taxi, she remembered he'd spoken of lunch, a special lunch for two. She dropped her arm and headed back into the mall.

The driver who took her and her parcels to the hotel waited and drove her to the office. She'd rather be there helping him than on her own in her impersonal rented room.

Lauren watched the file names speed through as they were copied to the second hard drive, so many more than she'd expected. Surely this would have a huge effect on the company. Had any of it been declared to the tax office?

She'd be long gone before anything official happened. Matt might remember her as part of his father's downfall, not much more.

He'd been making and taking calls since she'd returned to the office, a pleasant background to her thoughts. She was going to miss his gravel tone when she left. Rougher under stress; she doubted it would ever be smooth. Not even in moments of passion. Which she so should not be thinking about. Ever.

He was absent when she'd finished so she made herself a cup of tea. The man who walked in as she deposited the used tea bag in the bin was tall, handsome and had to be related. His resemblance to Matt was striking, and his instant smile in a familiar face reminded her of Matt's when he'd invited her to the corporate dinner.

Hi, is Matt here?'

'Right behind you, mate.'

She watched enviously as the two men hugged and slapped shoulders, indicating a very strong bond.

'I've made a couple of calls, thought I'd come round to talk. It's quieter here than my office. Then I'll shout dinner. Shall we make it for three?'

Whoever he was, he spoke to Matt but looked at her, with unashamed interest in eyes that were a much lighter blue than Matt's.

Matt noticed the direction of his gaze, his brow furrowed and his eyes narrowed. For the first time since they'd been in high school, he was loath to introduce his charming cousin to a girl. They walked over to her.

'Lauren Taylor, our computer expert from Sydney. Lauren, my cousin Alan Dalton.'

Her quick glance at him told him she'd heard the edge to his voice that surprised him as well.

'Hello, Lauren.' Alan held out his hand, and she accepted it.

'He said he'd hired an expert from Sydney, didn't say *she* was young and beautiful.'

Matt tensed, his breath lodged in his throat. She'd never acknowledged the few times he'd touched her, though he'd sensed her reactions. He'd barely been able to hide heat rushes from contact with her.

She certainly didn't seem to mind Alan holding on longer than protocol required while he continued his smooth talk. Bile surged in his stomach. He knew how persuasive his cousin could be and felt an indefinable impulse to move between them, break them apart.

Thankfully Lauren appeared to be impervious to his charms, deftly stepping away as she freed her hand. In fact she wore a similar guarded expression to the one he'd first encountered on the day she'd walked into his office. So perhaps it was all eligible men she had a problem with... not just him.

'Thank you. I have plans for tonight.'

Matt knew she didn't and her words inexplicably pleased him.

'Maybe the three of us could have lunch another day.' Not if Matt could prevent it. Alan was a persistent devil.

'I'll be leaving soon so probably not. Matt, the hard drives are in your top drawer. Excuse me.' She took her drink and went to her office.

'Wait here, Alan.' Matt followed her to the chairs by the window, and dropped onto the vacant one. Her sombre hazel eyes caught at his heart.

'You've finished the copying?'

'Yes, is there anything else you want me to do?'

A hundred things flashed through his mind, none of which he could voice out loud. All of which he'd be happy to participate in with her, however inappropriate. A complete reversal of his earlier decision.

'I have no idea until I've seen the accountant and solicitor. I do know I don't want you to leave yet.'

She smiled, her eyes lit up and he fervently wished his cousin were back in his own office two city blocks away.

'It's heading for five. Go home, and if you want time off tomorrow to shop for the dinner that's fine.'

'About that...'

His finger covered her mouth, preventing her from changing her promise and creating a zing along his arm.

'Alan's waiting. We'll discuss details tomorrow. The

function's black tie so it's long dresses, or pants and glittery tops. The women usually scrub up good too.'

'Idiot.' Her stuttered laughter raised the hairs on his nape, made his fingers itch to reach out and pull her from her chair onto his lap. He liked that his teasing had rekindled the sparkle in her eyes.

Feeling happier, he stood up, inhaled her enchanting perfume and fought the impulse to stroke her hair.

'I'd better get back to Alan and pick his brains.'

She looked puzzled.

'He studied both law and commerce at university. They make a useful combination and I need all the good advice I can get.'

Alan was perched on his desk checking his mobile when Matt walked in.

'Too busy to make the coffee, huh?' He set the machine for two cappuccinos as his cousin came over to join him.

'I've never been able to work that machine. Too elaborate for me.' Alan leant on the bench, picked up a teaspoon, and twirled it through his fingers.

'How long will Lauren be in town?'

'As long as I need her, and I'd rather she wasn't distracted.'

'You've got to admit she's cute.'

'She's also quiet and dedicated to her job. Not your type at all, cuz.'

The spoon stilled in Matt's peripheral vision. He looked up to find a wide grin and knowing eyes.

'Getting territorial, are we, Matt?' The smile faded as Alan's gaze intensified. 'You *are*!'

'She's here to work—an employee. I have no idea if she's free. I'm strictly solo for a long time. Take your pick of reasons.'

He heard the curtness in his tone, regretted being terse with the one person he trusted unconditionally. The only person he'd confided in when he broke off his relationship. The one secret between them was his father's infidelity and he hadn't been able to admit to his father failings, or his mother's acceptance of them, to anyone.

'Alan, I'm sorry. You've been my rock throughout this mess. Put it down to fatigue and frustration.' And, he admitted to himself, maybe jealousy.

'No problem. I'd have buckled weeks ago.'

They were seated by the window when Lauren came through and said goodbye. Alan replied in kind.

Matt held her gaze for an instant, wishing they were alone. 'Enjoy the rest of the afternoon. I'll see you tomorrow.'

'Definitely territorial,' Alan stated after she'd gone. 'Don't give me the guff you spouted earlier. I know you, Matt Dalton. What's the problem?'

'Trust.'

'Hers or yours? I thought you were over the woman in London.'

'There was really nothing to get over. I was angry as hell that she'd cheated on me but my pride took more damage than my heart. So how do you tell if it won't happen again?'

'I reckon Lauren's worth taking a chance on.'

Matt silently agreed.

Thursday morning was muggy with depressing grey clouds and intermittent showers. It was a perfect day for Lauren's mood as she kept close to the city buildings, avoiding raindrops and dodging umbrellas. Which she'd always hated, even the one she'd received on her last birthday. Transparent and shaped like a dome, it made her feel like one of those stuffed birds you saw in old houses and museums.

She'd been rehearsing how to approach Matt since she'd woken, hadn't found an easy way or the appropriate words. Every hasty decision she'd ever made had brought remorse.

Though doubtful, proximity might lead to him remembering their meeting on the balcony. Their lives were different. They were different.

She shook out her light raincoat in the building's entrance and folded it over her arm. Sensible, coherent excuses ran through her head as she entered his office, and scrambled in her brain with one look at his striking features, his toned chest muscles moulded to his light blue shirt, and one long leg crossed over at the ankle as he leant against the bench.

'I've changed my mind.' She blurted it out without a greeting, not allowing him to charm her with his gravelly voice or expressive eyes. Not giving him the chance to captivate her with his smile.

CHAPTER SEVEN

HE TURNED HIS head towards her and his body stiffened. His jaw tightened, eyebrows arched and eyes widened, darkened. His lips curled as he did a slow, oh-so-slow scan from her flustered face to her feet. When he finally looked her in the eyes he wore a wide grin and his raspy voice dropped an octave.

'Is this for my benefit?'

'What? Oh.' So focused on her speech, which she'd stuffed up anyway, she'd forgotten she was wearing the new green dress. At the time of purchase she'd hoped the scooped neckline, fitted waist then flared skirt to just above her knees would impress him. Seemed as if she'd succeeded big time.

'You look too exquisite to be spoiling for a fight, Lauren Taylor. I like the dress. Colour suits you.'

'I thought it…you're trying to confuse me.'

He didn't need to try. A look, a smile, a touch and her brain addled.

'I truly don't think I should be your partner at the dinner.'

The mug in his hand clanked as it hit the bench. In two strides he stood in front of her, a determined gleam in his eye. Close. As close as he'd been on the balcony. If he leant forward…

Blushing at her thoughts, she stepped back, out of range. Maybe not. He had long arms. The long, muscular arms she'd last night dreamt of encircling her as they danced to a Viennese waltz.

His lips firmed as her cheeks warmed.

'Okay. We are going to talk this out now and then forget it.'

With surprising tenderness he took her arm and guided her to the chairs, settling her into one then placing her bag and raincoat on the floor. He sat opposite and didn't say a word until she looked up at him.

'I confirmed you'll be my date when I called in to see my sister last night.'

There was an implacable edge in his tone. His eyes, now alert and locked with hers, were corporate mode. She tamped down her longing to surrender and mustered logical arguments.

'You can phone her. I should never have agreed. I'll get tongue-tied and embarrass you.'

'No, I won't. You're beautiful, intelligent, and the Fords want you there. In fact it was Clair who subtly put the idea into my head.'

He thought she was beautiful? Clair had really liked her? Her heartbeat kicked up.

'It's a woman's privilege to renege, of course, but then you'll be the one who has to break the news to my sister and nephews.'

She lifted her chin and glared at him. He was teasing. The gleam in his eyes was back, more compelling than before, and his lips seemed tantalisingly fuller. It was a complete change from her interview meeting. Did he really believe she'd relent on that flimsy statement?

'Why? You can stay with them another night so their parents can go out.'

'No problem there. The camping trip they decided to have seeing they now had no commitments for the weekend might be. The boys were writing a packing list when I left and I'm not going to be the one to disappoint them.'

'Oh.' Her bubble burst. She broke eye contact, fighting not to hug her stomach to quell its churning as she squeezed her legs together to hide their trembling. She gulped when he leaned towards her, fingers linked between his knees.

'You meet and deal with new people every day, Lauren.

Your boss receives glowing reports about your interaction with others. How is this different?'

Because it's not work, not technical. Not transient. She realised she'd linked *her* fingers and was grinding her palms against each other. Stopping the action, she drew in a deep breath.

'Those are usually people who want my help. I fix the glitches and leave. And, yes, there are a few regular clients, and our rapport has built up over a number of visits. Not the same and mostly workers on my level.'

Matt held back the chuckle that threatened to erupt. She sounded so earnest, so desperate to have him believe she'd be a hindrance. So scared of putting herself in an unfamiliar environment.

'Lauren, it's just a roomful of couples wanting to have a good night out and raise money for charity. There'll be set tables for dinner, then people tend to mix once the dancing starts.'

'That's another thing, the dancing. I'm not sure I can in company like that.'

'Ah. Which worries you, traditional or modern? In the first I promise you won't be pressured to join in. And my experience with modern is there are no rules, and the men with the least coordination seem to have the most fun. Especially after a few good wines.'

Her brow cleared, her stiff posture loosened. He was making headway. She knew about his father's condition and financial deception. If either leaked out saving the company could become almost impossible. And he needed her to understand the evening wouldn't be a prelude to a personal relationship.

'You're smart. You must know Dalton Corporation is in trouble. As things stand, your findings could tip us either way. I've been upfront with Duncan Ford and promised he'll be kept informed of all proceedings. Thankfully he has faith in me.'

He reached out and unclasped her hands, covering them with his.

'Please, Lauren. If it will make it easier to accept, treat the evening as an extension of your assignment.'

The gold specks in her darkening eyes were becoming more pronounced. They brightened and softened with her unconcealed changing emotions. He willed her to agree, his own responses heightened by the softness of her skin under his fingers, and the gentle blush on her cheeks. His pulse quickened, and every muscle felt taut as he willed her to agree.

She raised her chin, and her lips curled into a sweet smile.

'You'll come.' If she still wavered, he'd go down on his knees. And pray no one came in while he was there.

'Only so your sister can have her romantic evening.'

If punching the air wouldn't have seemed patronising he'd have done it. He didn't care about her motive, which he suspected she'd grasped at rather than admit she wanted to come.

'Thank you, Lauren. I promise to give you a night you'll never forget.'

She pulled her hands free and leaned away from him as if needing space and distance.

'So what would you like me to do today?'

'I know it's not your field but Joanne says the day-to-day data is behind. I've got meetings this morning and later this afternoon, which should give me some idea of what repercussions I might be facing. Midday's free so I've booked our table for one o'clock'

Shame flooded Lauren. He was fighting for the future of the company and its employees and she'd dumped her insecurities on him. He'd even allowed time to take her for lunch.

'I'm sorry, Matt. I've been selfish, worrying about myself when you've got much bigger problems.'

He stood and held out his hand, his eyes sending a message that weakened every resolve she'd made, and every muscle in her body. Her legs threatened to buckle as she accepted his assistance to stand.

'I'll forgive you almost anything as long as you keep saying my name, Lauren.'

That would be breaking down another barrier between them, and she wasn't sure how many were left. She smiled and stepped away.

'I'd better go and find Joanne.' Her head had demanded poise and self-control. Her voice had proved breathless and aroused.

Wind had blown the dark rain clouds away, bringing in their place white fluffy banks that drifted slowly across the now bright blue sky. The sun had dispelled the morning chill and raincoats could be left behind. The taxi dropped them off at the gates to the botanical gardens and they walked to the restaurant inside.

There were so many shades of green, so many different plants and flowers, all fresh and glistening from the showers. Ducks waddled over the lawns and birds swooped from tree to tree, their different calls mingling in the air. For Lauren it had become a magical spring day. Made doubly so by the sight of the shimmering white pavilion at the edge of a pond.

'This is where we are eating?' She drew them to a stop to drink in the image, and fumbled in her bag for her mobile to take a photo, though she knew she'd never forget.

'Here, let me.' Matt took it from her. 'Turn around.'

She faced him, the building behind her, the breeze teasing her hair and her heart twisting while she smiled on his command. Twice for her camera then, to her surprise, twice more for his.

The interior was as pristine. White linen covered the

tables and chairs, even extended to the serviettes. Silver cutlery, crystal glasses and a delicate floral centrepiece completed an impressive décor.

They were seated by one of the open arches overlooking the waterfall and pond featuring a reed-covered island and a family of colourful ducks. Matt declined wine, opting to share the water she'd asked for. As the waiter left with their orders she gazed round full circle in awe.

'It's so incredible. I can't believe I never came here in all the years I lived in Adelaide. I have a vague recollection of the zoo so that must have been when I was young.'

'You never came to the city on weekends or in the holidays with friends?' As if that made her unique but not in a good way. 'How old were you when you moved?'

'No and thirteen. My family life revolved around my brothers' sporting events. And before you judge, it wasn't so bad.'

Why was she defending what she'd always decried? Unless she was beginning to understand her own personality's part in it all? She sipped water from the delicate glass and smiled. If she had visited the gardens, it would have been in a plastic bottle on the benches outside.

Matt stretched across the table, stroking her hand with his long fingers.

'Believe me, Lauren, I never make judgements on anyone's family. The reason you're here is proof you can never tell what happens behind closed doors.'

Nausea gripped his stomach as he recalled the moment she'd shown him evidence of his father's duplicity. The secret deals and bank accounts, even the location of a large amount of cash. Preparation for what, a new life with another woman? A suspicion he'd keep to himself as long as he lived.

He gazed into hazel eyes, and found warmth and understanding. Something tight around his heart shifted and softened unexpectedly.

'How do you explain nearly five years of lies and deceit, Lauren? What the hell was he planning?'

'Will he even remember?'

'I have no idea how much is real or how much he's been faking, and I'm praying I can keep the truth from my mother. She's defended his behaviour all my life, and I can't bear to disillusion her.'

He found the simple act of caressing her small, delicate hand comforting. The kitchen could take all the time they wanted; he was in no hurry.

'Does she have to know anything?'

'If there are legal proceedings against him or I fail to revive the business, yes. In either case I won't be able to protect her from the consequences. I've accepted my father is guilty and I'll handle whatever happens as it occurs.'

He noticed the waiter approaching with their meals, grudgingly removing his hand.

'No more work talk. This was intended as a get-to-know-you meal before the dinner.'

Get to know you? Lauren already responded to him in ways she hadn't believed were real, much less that she'd be capable of. He could turn her inside out without any visible effort. He was going to haunt her for ever.

She picked up her knife and fork, and made the mistake of looking into his contemplative midnight-blue eyes. It was as if he were seeking a path out of the quandary he'd been coerced into handling, and she might be his beacon.

He ran his finger over his mouth—oh, heck, the mouth that had covered hers so gently, so masterfully. So long ago.

'So, do you follow the footy at all?'

About to begin eating, she almost bit her tongue. Had he remembered?

'Only as a talking point with clients. Sport's never interested me.'

'What does?' He bit into his bread roll, showing neat white teeth.

'Why the sudden interest?' She heard the words, hadn't meant to say them out loud.

'Indulge me. Saturday night I'll be your escort. It would help if we knew something about each other.'

But we are strangers and I have to keep it that way so I can relegate you to 'memories never to be intentionally accessed'. Ever.

He started on his meal, chewing slowly, and studying her as if committing her to *his memory*. Agreeing to go to this dinner was so one of her worst decisions ever. Though it could turn out to be one of the best.

'Does it work both ways?' Again she voiced her thoughts. She didn't wanted to know, hoped he'd refuse.

'I'm an avid Adelaide Crows supporter, and watched every match on the Internet while I was overseas. I played competitive squash—now I fit in games or workouts with Alan whenever I can, and run. My movie taste is for high adventure, fast action. And there's not much I won't eat.'

Wow, more detail to flesh out her fantasies and spice up her dreams of an unsuitable, never ever for her, completely unattainable man. She instinctively squirmed in her seat and pushed into the back.

'Your turn.' He wasn't going to let her off.

'I rarely watch sport, enjoy any well-made science fiction, and Australian historical movies or series and walk whenever possible. I use a gym on a casual basis. I enjoy spicy food, not too hot, and eat limited takeaway when I'm home.

'And you like your job?'

'I love the challenge of a mystery and the adrenaline rush when I succeed. Unfortunately most jobs are mundane, the result of human error and complications when they try to undo without really knowing what they did.'

She heard her own dissatisfaction. Maybe it was time for a change.

'Is there anything else you'd like to do?'

'I'm not sure. It's a new concept.' She frowned at him then smiled. 'Talking to you might not be good for my career. Where did you live in London? I heard houses and units are super expensive.'

'Correct. I got lucky. I own a one-bedroom suburban flat within walking distance of the Tube. Actually, the bank has a major share, but my name is on the deed. And I could buy a new three-bedroom house in Adelaide for less. It's rented out to a colleague while I'm away, which looks like it's going to be much longer than I anticipated.'

He pushed his empty plate aside.

'New topic: favourite ways to relax.'

Matt didn't mention Saturday night arrangements during their meal or on the way back, and kept the taxi waiting while he came in to pick up the folder he needed for his meeting with the solicitor.

He turned to go, made a move towards her and the air stilled between them. The flash in his eyes triggered a surge in her pulse. She waited, holding her breath. His eyes narrowed, his lips parted then his Adam's apple bounced as he struggled for words. The sound he made was guttural, masculine. She felt its effect skittle down her spine.

'Don't go until I get back, okay?'

She could only nod as his finger brushed her lips and he walked out through the door.

Joanne hadn't been kidding about the backlog but by normal finishing time Lauren had made good progress. She tidied up, then went to the nearby shop and bought a magazine and a packet of chocolate biscuits.

She was curled in a chair by his window, filling in a cross-word when he appeared and dropped the folder on his desk.

'Stay right there. Another drink?' He indicated the mug by her side.

'No, thank you.' She closed the book and watched him. She'd expected dejection with the prospect of prosecution for Dalton Corporation, his father or both hanging over him. Couldn't see it in his face or movement.

He sat and stretched out his long legs, taking a deep swallow before putting his mug down.

'That tastes good. Thanks for waiting for me.'

His attitude puzzled her. Blasé as opposed to taut as a wound spring as he'd been most of the time she'd been here. As if he read her mind, he arched his back, linked his hands behind his head and smiled.

Where had the dour, weary-eyed man from ten days ago gone? Only the dark shadows under his eyes and the deep lines around his mouth and eyes proved the strain he'd endured.

'Not the same guy you first met, huh? Your finding that screen has taken away the uncertainty, the unknown factor hanging over every decision I made. Now I have true facts and figures to deal with. We'll be audited and investigated but if we're honest we'll survive.'

'So your meetings went well.'

'I've told the truth, and produced all the records and Dad's medical assessment. Now I can concentrate on the new project while the experts work it all out. My priorities are to keep the company going, even if I change its direction, and to protect my mother from any fallout from Dad's actions.'

He drained his coffee, and stood, pulling her to her feet. Close but not quite into his arms.

'You've already exceeded expectations and completed

your original assignment. Now I'm asking you to stay here a little longer in case I need you. Please, Lauren?'

How could she refuse when his fingers clasped hers, his voice dropped low with emotion and the pleading in his eyes wrenched at her heart.

The urge to step closer, reach out and trace his strong jaw line, to feel the slight rasp of his almost undetectable stubble, consumed her. Her pulse fluttered, her legs trembled, and swallowing had no effect on her dry throat.

'As long as you think I can be useful.'

'Thank you.'

A buzzer sounded from the reception area, newly installed for visitors. 'Anyone here?'

'That's for me.' He led her to the door and called out, 'Be right with you,' before giving her a quirky smile.

'No peace, as they say. You go home and I'll see you in the morning.'

He didn't. He called as she walked to work telling her he probably wouldn't be in the office at all. How could such a short sentence turn her day cloudy?

'I wanted to talk to you about tomorrow night. Pre-dinner drinks start at six-thirty so I'll pick you up at your hotel around then. It's only a short drive.'

That meant thirty-four hours until she saw him again. She hid her disappointment with a cheerful voice.

'I'll be ready. Call me when you're nearly there and I'll come down to the lobby.'

'I'm looking forward to it.'

In a crazy way with mixed feelings, so was she.

'I'll see you then, Mr Dalton.'

'The name's Matt, remember?'

Matt. Imprinted on her brain, hero of her dreams. Of course, she'd never forget.

CHAPTER EIGHT

MATT WASN'T A teenager on his first date so why did his heart race, his chest feel tight? Why were his palms sweating? Escorting a colleague to a corporate dinner hardly qualified as a date anyway.

Quit fooling yourself, Matt Dalton. She's not a colleague. She's a beautiful woman you are attracted to. And it bugs you that she's so wary of men like you.

He'd called her as the taxi was pulling into the hotel driveway, wanting to be there when she walked out of the lift. The look on her face as she'd agreed to stay on Thursday was imprinted in his brain.

It had been a mixture of fear and hopeful expectancy. If it wasn't complete delight when he brought her home tonight, he'd deem himself a failure. His aims were to see her smile, hear her laugh. And to develop his bond with the Fords.

Cold and objective maybe, but he'd learned that love and happy-ever-afters were more advertising hype than reality. Tonight he'd forget business, relax and enjoy himself. Lauren would go home with happy memories rather than those of nights spent alone in a hotel room.

The lift came down twice while he paced the foyer. She'd said five minutes, four had passed so…

His jaw dropped, his heart pounded. He looked into big anxious hazel eyes and the resolution to keep the relationship casual and platonic shot into Netherland.

She was exquisite, captivating. Every red-blooded man's dream. From her gleaming newly styled, honey-brown hair framing her lovely face, to her red-painted toes peeping out of strappy gold shoes. Her sunshine-yellow dress, which fell loosely to her ankles from under her enticing breasts, shimmered as she walked towards him. A double gold chain around her neck enhanced her smooth peach skin. And she had to be wearing higher heels because she barely had to tilt her head to meet his gobsmacked gaze.

He took both hands in his and held them out, felt *her* speeding pulse under his thumb, and had to clear his choked throat before he could speak.

'Stunning. Lauren Taylor, you are enchanting.'

Her eyes misted. Her glossed lips—oh, he so wanted to kiss them right now—parted.

'I am?' She was genuinely surprised by his compliment. Didn't her room have mirrors?

The lift beside them pinged and opened. As soon as the occupants left, he ushered her in, facing her towards the mirrored wall, and standing behind her.

'Look at yourself, Lauren. You are gorgeous. I'll be the envy of every male in the room.'

His first aim was achieved as she smiled at their reflections. A soft glow appeared in her eyes and grew until they sparkled, and all apprehension disappeared. His arms ached to wrap around her, and if they didn't leave this instant he most definitely would claim a kiss.

After they'd buckled in their driver handed him the corsage he'd left on the front seat.

'I chose this one without knowing what colours you'd be wearing. It seemed…well, you.'

'It's beautiful, perfect.'

He echoed her words in his head, not referring to the flower.

When she reached out to touch the delicately shaded orchid with its deep purple centre, he caught her hand and slipped it onto her wrist. Resisting the whim to press his lips to her pulse, he compensated by linking their fingers and keeping hold. He gave her the same advice he'd given himself.

'Relax and enjoy the evening. It's one of the biggest events of the year, all profits benefitting children's charities.'

He felt her fingers twitch against his, saw the colour in her cheeks fade. But her eyes were clear and steady when they met his.

'Big crowds are less daunting than smaller ones. They're easier to hide in.'

A puzzling remark that intrigued him. Why wouldn't she want to be seen?

'No hiding tonight. Not that you could looking the way you do. Duncan arranged our tickets, and the other two couples at our table are friends of theirs so you'll be in good company. I'll stay as close as I can and make sure you're never alone.

Which was going to be a pleasant task, not difficult at all.

Matt being close might well be her biggest problem, Lauren thought, floating on air from his compliments. He wore formal wear with an innate ease. Had he been so elegant when he'd kissed her years ago? She could only remember those devastating startled blue eyes.

As the taxi joined the line-up waiting to discharge their passengers, she craned her neck to watch them heading for the entrance. These were the elite, the rich and influential, and the corporate climbers—a mingling horde of people eager to see and be seen by their peers. Unlike her, they'd be at ease with each other or skilled at hiding any nerves.

'Lauren?' She turned her head to find Matt regarding her with a pained expression.

'I'll need that hand to eat dinner.'

With a gasp she realised how tightly she was gripping his fingers, and let go.

'I'm so sorry. Does it hurt?' Mortification stung her cheeks.

He gave a low chuckle and wriggled his fingers. 'My friends will say any damage can only improve my guitar playing.'

The car inched forward, stopped and a uniformed man opened Matt's door. She sidled across as he alighted and offered her the hand she'd squeezed. She felt his strength as she allowed him to help her, felt hot tingles race along her veins as he drew her closer for protection in the throng.

The foyer was a kaleidoscope of colours, bold and lurid, pastel and muted, interspersed with the stark black of tuxedos. The overhead lights glistened off the dazzling displays of precious gems adorning necks, wrists, and fingers, hanging from ears and even woven into elaborate hairdos.

Being part of the excitement was worth the initial sick feeling in her stomach, the harsh dryness of her throat. Matt pressed her to his side in his efforts to manoeuvre them to the designated meeting point with the Fords, and the adrenaline rush was intoxicating.

Even he seemed surprised by the number of people who greeted him and held them up. So many inquired if his parents were attending. Others asked when he'd arrived in Adelaide, how long he was staying, and when they could catch up.

They declined drinks until they'd joined their hosts, Matt selecting a white wine and Lauren a soft drink. Duncan introduced them to a middle-aged couple then, when the men began to discuss today's games, Clair drew the two women aside and grinned at Lauren.

'And at these occasions they talk sport.' She turned to the other woman. 'Lauren's a computer expert and I'm—'

'A danger to any active program,' the woman cut in playfully.

They laughed and Lauren noticed Matt's short nod of approval in her direction. She'd also felt the reluctance with which he'd released her hand. Or was she reading too much into his protective mode?

The doors to the dining area opened and they were asked to locate their seats. As she began to follow Clair, Matt appeared beside her, drawing her close.

'This is incredible,' she whispered, admiring the ornate decorations on the uncountable number of tables.

The dimmed lights gave everything a magical feel, coloured spotlights played across the room, randomly picking out guests for a second or two then moving on. Classical music was supplied by a string quartet on stage, and along the backdrop hung brightly coloured banners bearing the names of sponsors and the charities that would benefit.

Matt guided her to her seat at a table near the front and sat alongside. Duncan and Clair were on her left. She swung her head, determined to memorise every detail, and shared a menu with Matt as bread rolls and wine were being served.

'Main course is served alternately, chicken or steak. If you'd prefer what I'm given, we can swap. The other courses are set.'

'Thank you. I'm not keen on steak unless it's well done.'

'Good evening everyone.' A deep voice boomed through the sound system urging latecomers to take their seats so the caterers could begin serving entrees. The welcoming thank-you speech was short and amusing, and the quiet music during the meal allowed over-the-table conversation.

Matt and Duncan made sure Lauren was included and she felt at ease enough to join in. Not often and not unless she was sure of the subject but it felt good. Except when Duncan asked if she had siblings. Giving a quick glance to check Matt wasn't listening, she admitted to three brothers, found herself telling him they were all professionals, two footballers and one cricketer. He seemed impressed, wanted more detail. To her their jobs were no different from hers, his, or any other person's.

As the waiters cleared the dinner plates, people began to move around the room, stopping in small groups to talk or wander out into the foyer. Band gear was set up on the stage and the group began to play a slow ballad.

There was a trickle of couples at first then more and more until the floor was crowded. No room for any more, she thought with relief.

'Dance with me, Lauren.' Matt's eyes gleamed, his breath tickled her ear, and his hand on her bare shoulder evoked a quivering in her stomach that had nothing to do with nerves.

'You promised no pressure.'

'True. If you refuse I won't push. But I'll be disappointed, and regret not having even one dance with you.'

Oh, so smooth. No wonder he'd won the Fords over and, according to Joanne, been very successful in England. She'd regret it too; the difference was she'd always remember.

She stood, and accepted the hand he offered. 'Do you always win?'

'The important battles, yes.' The victorious sparkle in midnight-blue eyes proved he believed this counted with those.

He led her onto the dance floor, and slipped his arm around her waist, enclosing her hand in his over his heart. Her legs trembled and her head clamoured for her to cut and run. Her heart leant into him, taking her body along.

Matt had planned his move. The packed floor gave him the excuse to hold her nearer, move slower. Her body aligned with his perfectly, she followed his steps with ease, and her perfume—or her—stirred feelings he'd been denying all week.

Somehow in the last two days the anger he'd carried for

weeks had begun to dissipate. Tonight the pain of betrayal had been replaced by an unfamiliar emotion. It took him a few minutes to recognise the alien feeling as contentment, and a little longer to realise that his thumb was caressing her fingers.

The music stopped, and as other couples split to applaud the band they stayed together, his eyes on her face as she looked towards the stage. She was happier and more relaxed than he'd ever seen her. Suddenly however long she'd be here was too short.

'Lauren.'

Bright hazel eyes met his, her lips parted, and only the first few notes of a classic seventies heartbreaker stopped him from kissing her there and then. The couple behind nudged her and he automatically pressed her closer for protection. Her head nestled on his shoulder, his cheek brushed her hair. And he wanted the music to last for ever.

It didn't of course. The singer announced desserts and coffee were being served, and the band was taking a break. He escorted her back to the table, pleased she seemed as reluctant as he was.

'Duncan's gone walkabout,' Clair said, moving along next to Lauren, beckoning her female companion to join them. 'Are you planning to network too, Matt?'

He ought to, it was the sensible thing to do, the best action for the company. Their desserts arrived, and he grinned and took his seat.

'And miss double chocolate gateau with strawberries and cream. Maybe after.'

'Have Duncan's too, if you like. I'm watching his weight,' Clair offered.

'You want double delight, Lauren?' he teased and was rewarded with a rosy blush.

'I'm not sure I can handle what's in front of me,' she countered without breaking eye contact and his heart leapt into his mouth. Heat flared in the pit of his stomach, and his fingers itched to reach for her and…

'Coffee for anyone?' A waiter held up cups and saucers on the other side of the table.

Yeah, black and strong for me to drown in. And is that a tiny smirk on her face?

If they were alone he'd be kissing it off in an instant.

'I'll take one, thanks.' Duncan loomed up behind Matt and sat down. 'After that, and the dessert I'm going to be scalded for eating all weekend, I want you to meet a trusted friend of mine, Matt. If we decide to proceed with the bigger project an extra investor might be welcome.'

Matt glanced at Lauren.

'You go. I'll be fine.'

She was. Too much so. Catching up with business acquaintances and meeting new contacts should have been a pleasure but his mind was on Lauren, and how long he'd been away. He'd left her talking to Clair and her friend. When he returned she was in deep conversation with a blond-headed man who, in his opinion, was leaning too close.

His gut hardened, his jaw clenched and he strode over to where the two of them sat alone.

'Sorry I've been so long, Lauren.' Not much regret in his tone.

They turned, and the man rose to his feet, extending his hand.

'Matt Dalton, isn't it? I'm sure I played high-school footy against you a few times. I'm John Collins, a friend of Lauren's brother. Haven't seen her for five or six years so this was a pleasant surprise.'

Matt's irritation abated and he accepted the greeting.

'Your face is familiar though I can't remember the name. Too many over the years.'

'Yeah, I know.' John glanced at his watch. 'I'd better go

find my wife and say our goodbyes. My mother-in-law's babysitting. Great catching up with you both.'

'Where is everyone?' Matt asked as soon as he'd gone, shaking off his discomfort. An old friend of the brother's. Married and bending close, as *he* was now, because of the constant hum of voices combined with the now louder and upbeat music.

'Out there having fun.' Lauren laughed and pointed at the dance floor.

It was hard to tell who was partnering who as arms were waving, bodies writhing and legs kicking, stomping and twisting. Clair was easily spotted in her bright red dress, grinning and waving as she recognised friends. Duncan, now coatless, followed no rhythm but his enjoyment was clear.

'Let's join them.'

She demurred.

'Look at them, Lauren. No rules. No cares.' He seized her wrists, lifting her to her feet. 'Come on.'

She'd shrunk. He looked down at her stockinged feet. Felt the grin spread across his face.

She grinned back. 'My new shoes started to pinch. Besides, I can hardly dance like that in those heels.'

'Not without spiking someone, probably me. Hang on while I ditch my coat.'

This was the best and the worst idea he'd had all night. The way Lauren's body synchronised with the rhythm created havoc in his. Her dress outlined shimmering hips as she swayed. Her lustrous hair brushed her shoulders as she swung her head and her skin glowed under the spotlights. Even watching her delicate energetic feet with their red tips gave him a warm glow.

Completely in the moment she'd let go of whatever cares she had, given herself to the magic of the music, and was in a world of her own. A world he wanted to be part of for as long as possible. He tasted bile in his mouth at the thought of her leaving, swallowed it down. Emotion-inspired happy-ever-afters were a myth.

'Last dance, ladies and gentlemen. Slow or fast?'

Couples were already coming together, calling out 'slow' and drowning the requests for fast. A few left the floor. Lauren's eyes shone as he stepped closer. She didn't resist at his pressing her head to his shoulder. She was smaller without her heels, making him feel more macho, more protective. He caressed her back, drawing her tightly against him, and swore he heard a contented sigh.

Lauren sighed again as the taxi eased into traffic. This was an enchanted evening. A night to cherish always, for so many reasons. The man responsible for those unforgettable memories shifted across the seat, put his arm around her, and nestled her into his side.

'Glad you came, Lauren?'

His voice was low, gruff, his breath tickled her ear. She turned, put her hand on his chest, and wished she could snuggle into him and fall asleep. Any dreams she had tonight would surely be pleasurable.

'Mmm, it was wonderful. I didn't want it to end.'

'It hasn't yet.'

Her fingers curled, her heart chilled and she stopped breathing. He didn't think, wouldn't expect... No. That wasn't the man she...could she possibly learn the true man within less than two weeks, four days of which were spent apart?

'We have the drive home and I'll ask the cab to wait while I escort you to your room.'

'There's no need.' Her words came out in a rush of air.

'My pleasure. Would you like to hear the compliments Duncan paid you?'

'He and Clair are nice, so easy to talk to though she

made a few enigmatic remarks during the evening, and asked twice how long I'd be here. Said she'd like to meet for lunch before I go. Oh.'

She gasped as he suddenly squeezed her as if annoyed at her remark.

'Don't think about leaving yet. Don't think about anything but tonight. Did I mention you were the most beautiful woman in the room?'

She smiled up at him. He was smooth and charming, handsome as hell and his midnight-blue eyes glowed with an intensity she'd never seen. Ever. From anyone.

'Once or a dozen times. Thank you for everything.'

He tapped the folder under her clutch bag on the seat. 'And you have the photos.'

'They're mine?'

'All yours.'

So he didn't want any reminders. She'd behaved as he'd asked, been a helpful social partner, and he was simply grateful. But in the end she was just the skilled technician hired to fix his system. A chill settled over her. The gloss faded. The evening was tainted.

A few moments ago she'd been elated, not wanting the evening to end. With two simple words, he'd burst her blissful bubble. She felt tired, numb... She wished she were alone, yet contrarily didn't want to leave the warm haven of his arms.

CHAPTER NINE

HE PUT DISTANCE between them in the lift as if sensing her withdrawal. She kept her eyes downcast, and hung onto the photos like a lifeline. They and the exotic orchid on her wrist were mementoes she'd treasure for ever.

She should be grateful. She would be, when common sense rid her of the dull ache. Not now. Maybe once they'd shared polite platitudes, and she was alone.

Her key card. She'd better have it out ready and limit any awkward time. The doors opened and he guided her towards her room, turned her to face him, gripping her elbows, his features composed, his eyes dark as ebony.

They held her captive, mesmerised her. Seconds. Minutes. She was drifting, vaguely aware of him freeing her arms.

'Sleep peacefully, Lauren.' Rough as if forced over jagged stones.

Then, like déjà vu, his lips were on hers, moving smoothly yet more masterful, more mature. Like ten years ago their only physical contact. And like ten years ago she instinctively responded, wanting his kiss to last for ever.

Breaking away, eyes now narrowed and puzzled, he stepped back, and gave a slow short shake of his head.

'Goodnight, Lauren.' He sounded bewildered before walking away.

Had he remembered? Realised who she was? Her hand shook as she blindly tried to swipe her card without taking her eyes off his rigid departing back. She froze as he turned, strode back and yanked her into his arms, taking her mouth with a fierce male grunt. Causing her to drop everything and cling to him.

This wasn't the exploratory tenderness of the teenage boy, or the polite goodnight of a moment ago. This was raw, masculine need, a hunger that swept her up and demolished any inhibitions. He caressed her back in wide strokes, urging her closer, searing her skin wherever they touched.

A yearning to arch into his warmth overwhelmed her. She couldn't breathe, didn't care. Her legs shook, her body quivered, fire flared in her core. And her lips parted willingly as he deepened the kiss.

She tasted wine and rich coffee, a hint of chocolate and—

His head flung back, his chest heaved. His stunned eyes raked her face, and his lips parted without sound. He backed away, arms wide. He hit the wall opposite and swallowed, dark eyes roaming her face as if he'd never seen it before.

With his gaze locked with hers, he came slowly forward and lightly traced shaking fingers down her cheek, settling under her chin.

'Wow.' Incredulous. Deep and husky. He seemed to struggle for breath. 'I… I'll see you Monday.'

By the time she'd blinked he'd gone, heading for the stairs.

Lauren fought for composure, unable to move. What had she done to provoke such a reaction? Where had *her* response come from?

The lift's ping brought her back to the present. She scooped up her belongings and a moment later was secure behind her closed door. Dumping the stuff on the desk, she flung herself onto the bed, reliving every second since they'd exited the lift.

She studied the photo of the two of them, searching for something to explain his behaviour and sudden flight. There was no clue in his open expression or his smile. Nothing to indicate he had anything but enjoying the function on his mind.

So it had to be her. What deficiency did she have in her personality that discouraged more familiar contact? Did she give out negative vibes? She had close friends, some from back at school and uni in Melbourne.

Their common interests had been the original base but their friendships now went much deeper. She knew she could always depend on their support in any situation. It was her family who seemed to find excuses not to be with her. Or was it she who put up barriers, subliminally deterring closer intimacy for fear of being rejected?

She set the photo against the lamp on the bedside table, placed her corsage in front of it, and prepared for bed. They were clearly visible in the light from the street lamps. She fell asleep with her fingers on her lips.

Matt fisted one hand into the palm of the other as the taxi drove him home. He could smell her perfume on his shoulder, see her shocked expression when he'd pulled away and left. He still savoured the taste of her on his lips.

He'd meant that first kiss to be gentle, an affectionate ending to a memorable night. Her initial response hadn't surprised him. Its effect on him had been astonishing. His libido had gone into overdrive and that damn niggle had drummed in his head. Breaking free had been instinctive.

But he hadn't been able to walk away. The invitation he'd seen in her hazel eyes had driven him back and he'd let his pent-up desire run free. He'd moulded her body to his, caressing her back, and exploring the curves he'd delighted in all evening. He'd invaded her mouth, savouring her sweetness, craving more.

Her soft moan had slammed him back to reality. To the shame of his actions. He'd never lost control before. Getting the hell out of there had seemed the only option; now it branded him a coward.

Going back to apologise while he still ached for more intimate contact would exacerbate the pain he'd caused.

Phoning would be even more cowardly. He hadn't felt so much like a louse since…

Since the night he kissed a girl hiding in the dark on a balcony. The niggling cleared like a light-bulb moment in his head. An irresistible allure. A barely heard sigh. Soft lips under his.

The kiss he'd never forgotten, had relived so often in his dreams, and that had been so entrenched in his memory that his body had known her the instant their lips had met tonight. He'd never had a face to picture, only a curled mass of dark hair, and a recollection of a slender body in a blue dress. And throughout the ten years since, no lips had ever felt as soft or tasted as sweet.

He'd searched the ballroom for her, and spent the rest of the evening repeatedly scanning the crowd without success. Deep inside he'd never given up hope of finding her.

Now he understood the guarded look and apprehension the day he'd interviewed her. She'd recognised him, must have remembered their meeting as well.

Tomorrow he'd begin to make amends for tonight's ending. Monday morning was going to be very interesting.

Matt's jacket hanging on the back of his chair was the only indication he was in the building. Lauren wasn't sure if she was upset or relieved.

Tucked into her purse was the florist's card that had accompanied the arrangement of orchids delivered to her hotel room yesterday morning. Another memento, personally inscribed, *Forgive me, Matt.*

For the kiss or for running?

She'd imagined a number of scenarios for when they met again, none of which eased her apprehension. She couldn't shake the re-emerged doubts. Their lives, their interests, their personalities, all were polarised. If it weren't for the undeniable attraction, they'd have nothing in common. She sighed and gazed out of her window lost in a daydream of music, lights and feeling cherished as they'd danced.

'Why were you hiding?'

She jumped, spun round to find him standing halfway across the room. Her heart stuttered. She covered it with her hand, and fought to steady her erratic breathing. How come he looked so cool and calm? So unruffled?

'I wasn't.' She cursed her wobbly voice. 'I'm just doing my normal preparation.'

Three rapid paces brought him an arm's length from her side, leaning on the glass nonchalantly. The firm set of his jaw belied his calm demeanour, giving her composure a tiny boost. He gestured in the general direction of the river.

'On the balcony, a good cricketer's throw away from where we had lunch with the Fords.'

He knew—had to see the blush heating her neck and face, the embarrassment in her eyes. Her teeth as they bit on her lip, something she hadn't done since she was a child.

As she struggled for breath and an answer, his lips—lips that had filled her waking hours since he'd strode away—curled into an apologetic smile.

'I have no idea why I followed you. I saw a mass of dark curls and a hint of blue dress going through the door alone and wondered why. Couldn't find you at first.'

He inched a little closer.

'You running away shook me. I swear I looked for you to apologise, and I've always regretted frightening you but never the kiss, never the sweet taste of your lips.'

'I hated being there,' she blurted out without thinking. 'Hated the way I was forced to be part of a world I had no interest in. Places like the balcony were sanctuaries. I didn't belong inside with those people.'

Fleetingly stunned by her outburst, he recovered to run his fingers in a light path down her cheek and under her jaw, sending fissions of delight skimming across her skin.

If he let go, her legs would give way and she'd end up a trembling mess on the floor.

'And I invaded your peace. Did you know who I was before the interview or recognise me then?'

She felt her skin heat again and dropped her gaze, only to have him tilt her head until she looked him in the eyes. His eyebrows quirked.

'Lauren?'

'There were lights behind you that night. I didn't see your face but as I pushed away your eyes became visible. They're very distinctive.'

His low chuckle zinged through her. Laughter shone in his eyes and they crinkled at the corners.

'My eyes, huh. We'll have to talk more but not *here*.'

He grated the last word and then his tone softened.

'The next few days are going to be gruelling. I'll be juggling appointments regarding Dad's actions with meetings, on and off site, about new projects. They'll all take time away from where I want to be.'

His affectionate expression said he meant her. The gap between them diminished. His movement or hers?

'Come to dinner with me tomorrow night.'

There was an edge to his voice that she didn't understand. Her first inclination was to refuse but then she'd always wonder.

He claimed he'd tried to find her. If she agreed—and her heart and logic warred about the sensibility of that—she'd have personal time to learn more about him, be able to return to Sydney with no what-ifs. His persuasive voice, his hypnotic gaze, and his touch on her skin were an irresistible combination.

She meant to nod, swayed forward instead. As if in answer to her silent plea, he bent his head. Suddenly jerked away.

'Not here.'

Growled in anger. Why?

His fingertips tracked lightly across her neck, triggering a goose-bumps rush from cell to cell, from her scalp to the soles of her feet. Awareness flared in his eyes, his chest heaved, and suddenly there was a wide space between them.

'I have to make a couple of calls, and talk to Joanne before I leave.'

'What am I supposed to do after I've finished the data entries?'

He spread his arms, fingers splayed.

'Whatever Joanna needs help with. I know it may be below your expertise but...'

He struggled for words. 'I don't want a stranger coming in when we transfer those accounts into the mainstream. I want you.'

The inflection in the last three words was personal, nothing to do with accounts or computers. Leaving wasn't an option.

'I'll stay.' Data entry. Filing. Basic office work. Tasks that would allow her mind to wander to midnight-blue eyes and smiles that lit up her day.

'You're an angel. I'll be here for half an hour then out for the morning. My mobile will be off most of the time so leave a message if you want me.'

His hand lifted towards her. Dropped. He walked out, picking up his jacket on the way.

If she wanted him?

Her body hummed with a need more disturbing than anything she'd ever felt. So much stronger than the mild desire she'd felt during her two previous relationships. She now recognised them as more mind melding and merely physical rather than zealous ardour.

There'd be no 'let's be friends' when the passion died for Matt. He'd walk away and she...she'd survive. Somehow.

* * *

Matt strode to the boardroom, praying it would be empty. He was pleased he'd been able to persuade Lauren to stay. Having her at his home for dinner was risky, considering the way they both responded to the proximity of the other. But how else were they going to talk without interruptions? How else could he find out why she hadn't trusted him before she knew him?

He'd almost kissed her again this morning. Never, ever going to happen here. He would never follow in his father's footsteps. Would never use that bedroom, no matter how late he worked or how tired he became.

Footsteps sounded in the corridor. He refocused on the project he and the team were working on, the one he was determined would revitalise the company.

Everything hung on a precipice. His father could be facing fraud charges. He and, in his doing, Dalton Corporation had probably committed tax evasion. Duncan Ford might decide to suspend their talks of investing until Matt could prove he and the company were clean.

He should be broken, anxious of the future. Instead, now he knew the truth he found the challenges stimulating. If it all collapsed around him, he'd start again. Staying down wasn't an option.

Lauren collected information needed from Joanne's office and settled at her desk. She tingled from his touch, her stomach had barely settled, and her brain was in the clouds.

Logging in took two attempts at the password. When she went to write the date on her notepad, she'd left her pen in the drawer. Unless she pulled herself together, today would be a shambles.

Get it together, Lauren.

A fingertip tap on each of her work tools, a muscle-loosening back-stretch, followed by her slow-count-to-fifteen habit, and she moved the cursor.

Engaged in more simplistic tasks, she found her mind had a tendency to wander, always to Matt and his effect on her. After an hour, she took a break, ran up and down eight flights of stairs and refocused. Apart from taking messages from occasional phone calls, she was undisturbed.

At midday she joined Joanne and three of the male staff for lunch for the first time, making an effort to contribute to the weekend football match discussion. She didn't comment when one of the men raved about her youngest brother, who'd kicked four goals including one as the siren sounded.

'Mr Dalton seems happy with the progress we've made on this new venture, Joanne. It's completely different from anything we did for his father, quite stimulating. Do you think the changes will be permanent?'

Lauren lowered the mug she'd been raising to her lips. She noticed Joanne's hesitation at the man's question. How much did she know of the true situation?

'I know he's doing all he can to sort everything out and he'll be tied up with meetings most of the week, nothing else.' She rose and went to stack her utensils into the dishwasher. 'Break's over. Do you have enough to do, Lauren?'

'Yes, I'll find you if I need more.'

Every employee she'd met addressed him as Mr Dalton. Although he used their first names, he kept distance between himself and his staff except for her. Because he intended to return to London?

Was there someone special there? Someone prepared to wait for him? Someone he'd taken to Paris?

A no-strings arrangement by two mature people. How did they do that? She couldn't imagine becoming involved with anyone who also dated other women.

Reinforcing that in her head didn't stop her stomach from fluttering at his call sign on her mobile.

'How's it going, Lauren?'

'Fine. Joanne says she can keep me occupied today and part tomorrow, after that I may be on cleaning duty.'

He laughed as she'd hoped he would, deep and raspy, making her ear tingle.

'Anything to keep you here. I won't get to the office until late today, or tomorrow morning. I'll call you when I can.'

'Is it bad?'

'I'm dealing with reticent legal and financial professionals. They hardly commit to black or white coffee but at least it's not all doom and gloom. Hang on.'

She heard his name and him replying, 'Thank you.'

'I'm being summoned back to the world of ifs, maybes, and it all depends. I'll see you tomorrow, Lauren.'

'Tomorrow.'

She sat as still as stone, staring at her mobile. He'd called her Lauren twice; she hadn't said his name at all. He used hers every time he spoke to her. At the function she'd made a deliberate attempt to say 'Matt' in the presence of others. In front of work colleagues it was 'Mr Dalton', to conform with them. Alone with him she omitted to call him anything.

He was smart, quick to notice nuances and actions. He'd have to know she deliberately avoided the intimacy of first names.

CHAPTER TEN

MATT DIDN'T WANT to be sitting in his parents' dining room that night pretending nothing had changed. His head ached from all the legal jargon, the implications of what might or might not happen, and from reading some of the complex forms and documents he'd been given. And the processes had only just started.

It had taken supreme effort to keep focused and not picture Lauren alone in her office or Joanne's. Or ponder on dinner tomorrow. No disruptions, no phone calls with both mobiles on silent. Quiet time for conversation.

It's more than talk you want.

'Matthew?'

'Sorry, Mum. Miles away. It's been a long day.'

'This is all taking a toll on you. I wish I'd acted sooner, but Marcus kept assuring me he was just tired and overworking.'

'It's okay, Mum. I've got good help and everything's coming together.'

Though there's a fair chance it might implode in my face.

'His mood swings are more frequent, and persuasion doesn't work as well as it did. Today he became angry when I suggested he shouldn't go for a walk alone.'

His jaw tightened, and he glared at his father, nonchalantly eating his meal. He softened his features as he asked, 'When's his next appointment with the doctor? I'll make sure I'm available and then we'll have a family meeting.'

'I want to keep him at home as long as possible. Please, Matthew.'

He reached across to cover her hand with his.

'For as long as possible, Mum. We can arrange for day help and, if necessary, I'll move in.'

His gut churned at the thought of living here again, in

the house where his naive adulation of his father had been shattered, and his admiration for his mother diminished in a single stroke. Where he'd discovered human weakness could overrule honour, and betrayal could be overlooked if it meant the continuation of a preferred lifestyle.

His honour dictated he had no choice. His heart demanded he call into his sister's on the way home to spend time with a truly happy couple. And to kiss his nephews as they slept.

Crouched behind the desk in Reception, Lauren almost missed Matt's arrival at five past two the following day. Checking the stationery, she sprang upright at the faint hint of sea-spray aroma.

'Matt.' Instinctive. Spontaneous.

As natural as the smile he gave her. He looked frazzled and energised at the same time, jacket slung over his shoulder and sleeves rolled up to reveal muscular arms covered with fine dark hair. One glance at finger-ruffled hair and blue crinkled eyes, and her senses sprang to attention.

'Hi, how's it going? Come and tell me over coffee. With normal everyday words.'

'Joanne's run out of work to give me.' She straightened the desk phone as she glanced up, and met narrowed eyes and a scowl.

By the time she come round to his side, they'd gone. He patted his satchel as they walked to his office. 'And I'll be occupied for days. How's your legalese?'

'My what?'

'Legal mumbo jumbo. Guaranteed to cause headaches or a craving for alcohol.'

She laughed. 'Sorry, all I know is the few foreign phrases I learnt from friends at uni. Unless it's cyber-speak.'

'Might just as well be for me. So what time are you finishing?'

'Ten minutes and I'm all done.' She swallowed, glad he wasn't looking at her. Thankful he couldn't see her disappointment.

His brow creased again as he held the door open for her, not moving aside, ensuring she brushed against him as she passed. He dumped his satchel on his chair, draped his coat over the back, and scraped his fingers into his hair. When he spoke she swore there was a catch in his voice, growing more pronounced towards the end.

'You're not going home?'

She shook her head. 'I promised I'd stay.'

'You're one of the few people aware of the full situation and I trust you. We'll find something for you to do.'

He trusted her. Her heart soared and dipped, raced for a moment then blipped. She couldn't deny she had continuing issues with where he'd come from, the class he associated with.

'You don't have to. I decided last week to spend my promised fortnight vacation being a tourist in South Australia.'

His face cleared and he caught her hands in his, skittled her breathing with his beaming smile.

'Two weeks, huh? That's good. Can you fit any work I need done between trips?'

'If I'm needed.'

'You are—very much.' His intense appraisal was unnerving, as if commanding she hide nothing from him. His undisguised admiration made her insides glow, yet roused a prickling unease on her nape.

'Is there a special dress code for tonight?'

'Neat casual. Whatever you feel comfortable in.'

Your arms.

Thankfully thought and for once not voiced. She cursed her seesawing responses.

'I'll call when I leave here and pick you up.'

'I'll be ready.'

* * *

She was sitting on a bench near the revolving doors two minutes after he phoned. It gave her a clear view of the curved driveway and the road beyond the garden bed. Her fingers tapped on her right thigh and she clasped them with her left hand.

It was just another dinner in a public place, nothing to make her nervous. Unless you counted the confident, charismatic male striding, head high, on the opposite side of the road. At twenty-six, she really ought to be able to control these sudden spikes in her pulse and these inexcusable urges to run to meet him.

She went to the kerb, keeping track of him between passing vehicles. He stopped when he noticed her, his smile easily visible at this distance, and beckoned her to come across. Took her arm as she reached his side.

'Hi, has anyone ever told you that you are remarkably punctual?'

'For a woman?' She tilted her head, and raised her eyebrows. Relished the pleasurable quiver in her stomach as he laughed.

'For a human. The car's not far.'

He didn't speak during the short walk, obviously preoccupied. Lauren was all too aware of his guiding touch on her arm. Warm and protective.

The lights flashed to unlock his car but he didn't open the door. He leant on it instead, placing his hands on her waist. He looked at the grass under their feet and exhaled.

'When I said dinner, I meant takeaway or home delivery to the unit I'm renting. You and me. No phones, no demands from anyone. No distractions. I should have been explicit. If you'd prefer, there's a local hotel with good food and friendly atmosphere.'

His preference matched hers. No noisy chatter or waiters hovering to serve, clear dishes or top up glasses.

'Do I get to choose what we pick up?'

She hadn't realised how tense he was until his shoulders dropped.

'Food, wine and anything else you want.' He moved aside, allowing her to get into the car. 'You amaze me almost every day, Lauren Taylor.'

Lauren was the one surprised as she entered the modern single-storey town house not far from the city. He'd driven into the garage, led her through the door into a laundry and then along a hallway into one of the most sparsely furnished rooms she'd ever seen.

There was a long soft leather lounge, a coffee table and a television on a wooden cupboard. No rugs, no cushions. No books, ornaments or pictures.

She appreciated he was renting, and had been working long hours under extreme pressure, but...

Matt's eyes followed her astonished gaze, and for the first time he saw his home as it was. He'd bought the barest necessities, hadn't been planning on long term or entertaining.

He shrugged and gave a rueful grin.

'Not exactly home beautiful, but I don't spend a lot of time here.'

'Are the other rooms the same?'

Leaving the Thai food and bottle of white wine on the table, he held out his hand.

'Guided tour included with the meal. Any constructive opinions welcome.'

She didn't say a word as he pushed open doors to reveal a desk and office chair in one room, suitcases and boxes in another, the bathroom, and finally the main bedroom.

It contained bedside drawers and a rumpled king-sized bed, which dominated the space but he never slept well in anything smaller. Since moving in he'd crashed every night into deep, unbroken sleep, including a few times in the lounge. Except for the last two nights, and his restlessness was evident from the unmade bed.

His senses were on super alert, tuned for her slightest reaction. He heard the faint intake of breath, saw her shoulders twitch and the convulsive movement in her throat.

Berating himself for his insensitivity, he drew her away, and pulled the door shut behind them, praying she didn't think he had an ulterior motive bringing her here. He couldn't ignore the picture that had flashed into his head as he'd looked from his bed to Lauren, or its effect on his body.

'I signed the lease in the morning, made the saleswoman's day in the afternoon, and moved in two days later,' he said, hoping to distract her as he took her to the kitchen area.

'No dining setting?'

'Not yet. The only person who visits is Alan, and we eat while we watch TV, usually the footy.'

She winced and he remembered her outburst yesterday morning. She hadn't exaggerated her dislike of sport. Tonight he was determined to find out why.

'We'd better eat before the food goes cold. Plates are in the corner cupboard. I'll bring the glasses and cutlery.'

Clicking on the TV, he scrolled to the relaxing music channel, keeping the volume low. He sat, giving her space, and opened the Riesling, poured a glass and slid it in front of her.

'Thank you. I'm guessing you like leftovers, from the amount of food you bought.'

'It'll taste as good tomorrow.' He lifted his glass in salute. 'To you, Lauren. You have my eternal gratitude for everything you achieved.'

She tapped her glass to his. 'Even with all the angst it's going to cause you?'

'Hard facts can be dealt with. The uncertainty is what

fuels suspicion and creates tension. I'll be guided by the professionals and handle any repercussions.'

Lauren savoured the tang of the sweet and sour pork, and the mellow taste of the wine, but found the depth of the settee uncomfortable. It was built for taller people or for curling up on. A few thick cushions would solve the problem.

She put her plate on the table, slid onto the floor, and folded her legs.

'Can we pull this closer so I can lean against the sofa? I don't have your long limbs.'

He complied immediately. 'I'm not rating too well, am I? I'm all set up for myself, didn't expect to have visitors very often if at all.'

Then why that huge bed, looking as if there'd been plenty of action there last night? Did he have similar expectations tonight?

She choked on a piece of pineapple, took a soothing drink of wine, letting it glide down her throat. He'd said only Alan visited and she had no reason to dispute his word.

'Are you all right?'

No, but admitting it might start a conversation she wasn't ready for, probably never would be.

'I'm fine. This is delicious.'

'Hmm.' He relaxed, elbow on the leather arm, his legs stretched out with one ankle over the other. Looking as hassle-free as a newborn baby.

Unlike her. Sitting down here might be easier on her spine but now he was only in her peripheral vision and other senses heightened. She became aware of muted sounds as he shifted or flexed muscle against the leather, and his ocean aroma teased her nostrils, overriding the piquant sauces of their meal. Occasionally his foot twitched.

The companionable silence stretched, the music soothed. She picked up her glass and sipped, letting her mind drift to a gentle touch, a guiding hand. A bewitching dance she'd never forget.

She turned her head, and caught him watching her, his lips curled, his dark eyes gleaming with unconcealed desire. He blinked and it vanished. Or had it been a reflection of her own?

'Full?'

She could only nod, her throat too clogged to form words. He wanted to talk; she'd prefer to delay it any way possible. If he wanted her history, dared she ask for his? Wouldn't it be better to have only memories of *their* time together untainted by his past?

The dishwasher was stacked, the food containers stored in the refrigerator. Lauren curled up in the corner of the settee cradling the remnants of her drink.

'Top up?' Matt waved the bottle in front of her.

Why not? She'd make it last 'til the end of the evening.

He half-filled hers, gave himself more then took the remainder to the fridge. Settling at the far end, he twisted towards her, one ankle balanced on the other knee. His arm lay along the back of the lounge, forming a perfect angle with his body for someone to snuggle into.

She stifled the sigh that threatened as she remembered the firm warmth of him, and the way her head rested cosily on his shoulder during the slow dances. A quick self-rebuke, a sip of wine and she met his gaze with a bravado her internal fortitude didn't match.

'So you didn't inherit the sporting gene like your brothers?' A coaxing tone, probably developed with his nephews, with an edge that said he wouldn't give up until he'd learned all he wanted to know.

'I was uncoordinated, couldn't catch, throw or jump and had no interest in being coached to improve. Lately I've been wondering if I was the one who withdrew from my family rather than it being them who ignored my interests.'

'Maybe lack of compromise on both sides.'

'I believed I didn't count so I stopped attending anything sporty and made a life on my own.'

He scooted along the cushions, stopping inches from her knees. His fingers caressed her neck and tangled into her hair.

'You count, Lauren, in every way that matters.'

'I know that now, just not sure how much with them.'

She suddenly hit him, flat-handed over his heart, making him jerk away.

'Admit it, Matt Dalton, you were one of those guys like my brothers, who assumed being athletic made you better than those who weren't. And more deserving of attention from girls.'

Matt's fingers stilled, his stomach clenched. She'd nailed him. Major benefits of being in the school's A-grade had been the accolades, the admiration of lesser-gifted pupils. The chicks he could take his pick from.

Hell, that sounded egotistical.

'And I'll bet you barely noticed anyone who wasn't beautiful, confident and out there.' Her jaw lifted and one finger tapped on his chest. Her hazel eyes flashed with challenge.

'Ah, but I did.' He grinned at her defiance. 'I was nineteen, surrounded by adoring girls yet I followed a shy, unknown escapee into the dark and kissed her. She ran and I ended up going home alone because I couldn't find her again.'

'You didn't?'

She doubted his word. Understandable maybe but it irked. He prided himself on his honesty. Taking her drink, he plonked it on the table heedless of the splashing droplets. He bent forward, splaying his hand on the lounge arm, enclosing her and forcing her to lean away.

'You don't believe me? How can I persuade you it's true?'

'You can't.' Proud and playfully stated.

She had no idea how provocative she looked arched over the armrest, enticing full lips parted and bold eyes sparking.

Or did she? The tapping stopped. Pity, he'd liked it from her. She sucked in a deep breath, her head tilted and wariness drove defiance from bright hazel.

Ashamed of his brash behaviour, he shifted but kept within reach. Picking up the glasses and holding hers out, he noticed the motion of the wine. *From his trembling.* He drained the remainder of his, shaken by his reaction.

'Forgive me. I said tonight was for talking. I won't make that promise for the future though. There's something between us, Lauren, something too strong to ignore.'

'It'll pass. There'll be other women in your life.'

'You're the only one now. It's you I want.'

Her head swung from side to side in slow motion as if that would change his statement. He halted the movement by cupping her chin.

'I don't lie, Lauren. And I can wait until you're ready to admit it too. In the meantime, we could call Alan, who'll confirm my story. I shared a cab with him and his date.'

She flicked him a half-smile. 'No phones tonight, remember.'

Almost an admission she believed him. He feigned an affronted air.

'You questioned my word. I deem that an emergency.'

Her instant laughter hit a spot deep inside, denting the armour he'd placed around his heart. Scaring the hell out of him. He'd sworn never to be vulnerable again.

'So why Sydney?' Out of the blue to give him recovery time.

'I was offered a challenging position interstate from Melbourne.'

'A long way from your family.'

'I didn't disown them. I keep in touch, visit reasonably regularly, and always see them when they come to Sydney for a sporting fixture.' She spoke defensively as if she'd heard censure in his voice.

'Which you don't attend.'

'No. They seem to have accepted I'm different. I'm hoping they give this new consideration to their grandchildren.'

'My eldest nephew loves anything involving kicking or hitting a ball, the younger one can take or leave it. We're trying to keep it all fun for as long as possible.'

'There's only the two?'

'Alex and Drew.' He recalled Lena's expression when she'd told him she was pregnant, felt the same rush of affection he'd had then. 'Lena and Mark would love a little girl as well.'

'I wish them success. What did you do in London?'

CHAPTER ELEVEN

STUPIDLY BECAME INVOLVED with a scheming adulteress. Confused physical idolisation with love and almost got sucked into a nightmare.

'I'm a partner in a consultancy firm. We tailor business strategies, give advice and bring investors and companies together. Unlike my father, we don't invest in them though I do have my own portfolio. And I'm very good at what I do.'

She looked away, tightened the hold on her glass, and seemed to shrink in front of his eyes. He thought through his statement, trying to pinpoint what might have upset her.

It hit him like a hammer to his gut, almost overridden by the elation that flooded him. The present tense, still committed. Planning to return.

His heart flipped and his pulse raced. Had she already thought about making love with him and now believed she'd end up hurt if they became involved? It didn't have to be that way if they were completely open and honest. If they didn't let emotion rule their heads, they'd have no regrets when it was over.

He fought the urge to reach for her, draw her into his arms, and tell her that was how it would be. She wasn't ready for such a declaration yet.

'I haven't changed my status as a partner because of the uncertainty. The best scenario would be to get everything legal at Dalton Corporation, and any due taxes paid. I'll get the new project running then I can decide on my future.'

Her sceptical gaze met his. Somehow he had to convince her he was telling the truth, that his main objective was to make the company strong and viable. He hadn't allowed himself to think beyond that.

'Legal proceedings allowing, I'll try to use the same procedure we have in London with Dad's clients, making them independent. The project with Duncan is different, a change of direction for me, but it will stabilise Dalton Corporation.'

Her body had inched forward as if drawn by a magnet. Now the only movement was the slow rise and fall of her chest. Her eyes didn't waver from his.

'It sounds long term.' Husky with a hint of hope. Dared he wish too?

'Anyone's guess. There are too many factors involved.'

Lauren's anticipation deflated. She stared at the glass in her hand, wondering when she'd drunk the remaining wine. From the moment they'd met tonight her emotions had taken her on a loop-the-loop ride, twisting her in knots, ending with a crash landing.

The agenda he'd described would take time and effort. He'd shrugged it off as no big deal, easily done. Then Europe and his partnership would beckon and he'd go with no looking back. And while he might caress and cajole, he'd never pressure her against her will.

She just wished she could decide what she wanted most.

'Your glass is empty.'

His fingers brushed hers as he took it and she trembled. Something fiery flared in his eyes.

'Would you like a hot drink?'

'No, thank you.' She snuck a glance at her watch as he turned away, torn between wanting to stay and having space to fortify her defences against his charm.

'Hinting it's time to go home?' The laughter in his husky voice teased, and she dipped her head to hide the inevitable blush.

He shuffled closer, avoiding contact, the glasses clinking in his hand, and waited silently for her to raise her head. And the funfair ride took off again at his tender expression. Her stomach flipped, her heartbeat pounded and, she wasn't exactly sure but…had her toes curled? Without even a touch.

'Your choice, Lauren. I'll call a taxi if you want to.'

'Taxi?' Sending her home alone. Shortest funfair ride ever.

'I haven't long finished the second wine. We'll take a taxi now or have coffee and wait a little longer. I don't take chances when I drive.'

A cosy trip in the back seat or more disclosures here?

'Make mine weak white. Do you need help?'

He only had big mugs so hers wasn't full. It was rich and sweet, complementing the meal. She sipped and enjoyed, noticed he took fewer, bigger swallows.

'Sydney's an expensive city to live in too. Do you live alone or share?'

His polite words were belied by the set of his shoulders, the slight tilt of his head and the heat in his midnight-blue eyes. There'd been no necessity to say he wanted her. Every look, every touch proved he did.

Did she give out the same signals? Her curiosity about him was all consuming yet he'd managed to avoid revealing much personal information.

'Three friends and I put in a bid for one floor of an un-built apartment block. One of them is in banking and arranged the mortgages. We got a special price and an input into the layouts and décor.'

'And?'

And what? The other half of his question. He was fishing about her private life.

'I live alone. The other three have partners so it's rare there's not someone around. What about you?'

He ran his hand up her arm creating electrical zings on her skin. All over her skin. He faced her full on, his shoulder pressing into the leather back of the lounge, his arm flat along the top. His fingertips played with her hair.

'Occasionally I have guests.' His face darkened for a second as if remembering an unpleasant experience. 'Not for a while.'

Matt brushed away the past, trying to concentrate on the now. She lived alone, she was single. There was no one who'd have cause to feel offended if he kissed her again.

A companionable silence settled. He gazed into his empty mug, multiple questions racing through his mind, each one too personal to ask unless he intended to make a move tonight. Common sense said it was too soon, they knew little about each other, needed time to build trust. However, would he ever fully trust a woman again?

His libido said he knew all he needed. He wanted her and he'd bet whatever part of the London flat he owned that she wanted him too.

A movement in the corner of his vision broke his reverie in time to see Lauren try to smother a yawn behind her hand. Guess it wasn't going to be tonight.

'You're tired. What do you have planned for tomorrow?

'I'm picking up a hire car and heading to the Barossa Valley for a couple of days. No schedule, just drive and stop whenever something takes my fancy. I'll book into a local hotel each night.'

Two nights.

Plus almost three days without seeing her.

He straightened, tried to swallow past the lump in his throat, tried to ignore the tight band constricting his lungs.

'You'll be back in Adelaide on Friday?' He had to know. Didn't understand why.

'Will you need me then?'

He choked back his instinctive reply.

'I'll keep in touch. Now I'd better get you home.'

He took her hand, led her to the laundry and reached for the door knob to the garage. His brain urged caution.

Every muscle tensed with craving. Every cell in his body clamoured, 'Ask her to stay.'

Lauren wasn't his ex, she was as wary as he was. He saw his knuckles whiten and he let go, slamming his hand onto the wall beside her head.

Her eyes widened, her lips parted and her breasts lifted as she sucked in air. He drew her into his arms, his forehead resting on hers. He heard her bag hit the floor and felt one arm encircle his waist. The other hit his chest between them.

It felt good, so good. But not enough. He ached for something unattainable, something that didn't exist. He'd have to settle for whatever she was prepared to give. For being close and building up memories that wouldn't turn sour in acrimony.

She leant into him, and had to be aware of his harsh breathing, how hard his heart was thumping. How aroused he was.

He bent his head. She lifted hers to meet him. He kissed her gently, using every ounce of restraint he could muster, shuddered as her fingertips pushed up his chest to trace a fiery path over his already heated skin. Her unique aroma stirred him with every breath.

He teased her lips into opening, and tasted sweet coffee, mellow wine and Lauren. Encouraged by her muted sighs, he strengthened his hold, stroking and caressing, binding her to him. Only when his lungs screamed for air did he break the kiss, trailing his lips across her neck.

Her eyes moved under closed lids. Her trembling vibrated through him, or were his tremors affecting her? He willed her to look at him and his heart slammed into his ribcage when she did. Gold specks glittering, her hazel eyes smouldered with desire. She wanted him. Primal macho pride surged through him.

But before he allowed himself to accept what her eyes

were offering, that same pride decreed he be totally honest, even if it meant she didn't stay. He pressed her head to his shoulder, not wanting to see her expression change, fighting for a softer way to tell her.

There wasn't one. He watched his breath stir her hair as he forced out the words.

'One thing life's taught me is there's no rose-covered cottage with two dogs and a cat and a happy-ever-after waiting for you to find it. Flowers don't last and having a one true love is as rare as a priceless diamond.'

She made a strangled gasp into his shirt. He cupped her chin, raising her head until their eyes met, and felt a strong urge to take it all back just to see the pain vanish. He couldn't. He wouldn't deceive her.

'I want you, Lauren. I want to make love to you so badly it's driving me crazy. But I won't lie. I don't believe in soulmates and endless romance, I've seen too much anguish caused when others have. However, I do believe in and expect complete fidelity.'

Lauren's heart twisted. Someone *had* hurt him, broken him, making him doubt every other woman he met. She fought for composure. If she gave in to desire, she'd be the one counting the cost.

Her heart didn't care, deeming every moment spent with him worth any pain. There was no yesterday, no tomorrow, only now. There was only Matt Dalton, his skin hot under her hand, his body trembling in sync with hers and his heartbeat pounding against her breast.

She inhaled, drew in ocean spray and aroused male. Wanted, ached for more. All-consuming heat coils spiralled from her core. Her fingers itched to unbutton his shirt and caress the muscles it defined.

'Matt?' A dry whisper, pathetically weak for the powerful emotions controlling her.

Passionate blue eyes darkened, his nostrils flared, his

lips parted. Something akin to euphoria swept through her. He was no longer the aloof, self-contained executive of fourteen days ago. This was primal man. And tonight she would be his.

'Lauren. I…' Rough. Grating. Emotional.

She touched one finger to his mouth. 'No promises. No tomorrow. Only us tonight.'

With a triumphant growl, he scooped her up, claiming a conqueror's kiss as he strode towards his room. To that massive bed with its rumpled sheets and pillows sure to smell of ocean waves.

The sudden shudder from head to feet took Matt by surprise. His body resonated with the aftermath of the most intense, satisfying sex of his life. As if they'd been transported to a new dimension where only they existed. Lauren had been his, totally, utterly his from the moment he'd lain beside her, kissing and caressing her, moulding her body to his form.

Tightening his arms around her, he held on, riding out the incredible feeling, wishing he could see her beautiful face and her lovely expressive eyes. There was only the faintest light seeping round the edges of the window blinds, only enough to see shadowy outlines.

She was stroking his chest, threatening to reignite the fire that had consumed them both. His willingness to be engulfed by the flame warred with the suspicion that she didn't realise the fervent effect her gentle action evoked.

He placed his hand over hers, sought and found her lips. Keeping the kiss soft and light, he tried to let her know how he felt, elated yet humble, primal yet emotionally moved.

Her soft sigh motivated action.

'Don't go away.' He went to the ensuite, turned on the light, then left the door ajar, allowing subdued light to spill into the room. Bunching up the pillows, he slid into bed and nestled her tight against his side, her head on his shoulder. Her breath blew across his chest, tickling his skin in the nicest sensation imaginable. Her hand lay over his rapid-beating heart.

He'd never initiated after-sex talks, curtailed them as quickly as possible if his partner did. This new desire to learn all he could about Lauren was unnerving and compulsive, so not him. Confidences led to familiarity, which equated with vulnerability. And that he'd determined never to risk.

He stroked her hair for a moment, pressed a kiss on her forehead.

'Why are you so wary of guys like me? Maybe not me so much any more, but it's there. With Alan too.'

Lauren didn't answer. Her body stiffened, she stared at his chest, and her fingers curled. Idiot, he'd pushed too soon. If he could see her face…hell, he knew what he'd see. Fear. Reluctance.

He'd had no choice but to tell her about his father, had given her no reason to believe she could confide in him.

'There was a woman in London I'd known and dated for quite a while. I liked her a lot, though after I wondered if she'd shown her true self to me at all. We shared mutual interests and friends, got on well and I believed we could have a mutually advantageous marriage. It's surprising how many people settle for that. Love wasn't a factor at all.'

He had no idea why he'd confessed his humiliating experience unless it was to show her she could trust him, that she was different from other women he'd known. His calm, rational approach to the relationship with Christine was worlds away from the mind-blowing emotions Lauren aroused simply by being in the same room.

She stirred as if preparing to pull away. He held on, needing contact, and rushed the end of his embarrassing story.

'Luckily for me I discovered she was also involved with a married man before I proposed. I ended the relationship immediately.'

She raised her head and he was stunned by the honest sympathy in her eyes, not a hint of disapproval for his cold approach to a lifetime commitment. He kissed her, holding back the passion that flared. Having her confide in him was paramount even if he wasn't sure why at the moment.

'We've all done things we regret or had them done to us. I have no right to judge anyone, Lauren. Will you tell me? Whose actions did you brand me, Alan and umpteen other guys with?'

Her eyes clouded a second before she dropped her gaze to his throat. She quivered, and sucked in a long breath. Feeling like a louse, he was about to tell her it didn't matter.

Lauren blurted the first words out in a breathy rush then steadied as Matt soothed her back with rhythmic caresses.

'Just after Christmas, the same year you and I…you know… There were often weekend barbecues in our place, crowded, noisy, lots of drinking. My brothers' friends got a kick out of teasing me, and calling me little sister to make me blush and get tongue-tied. To them it was harmless fun. I hated it.'

The almost forgotten feeling of helplessness crashed back, clogging her throat, rendering her speechless. Followed just as suddenly by an empowering sensation. She was no longer a victim. She'd grown and moved on. Hadn't she talked to them at Easter without any childish awkwardness?

'I can see now it was thoughtless but never ill intentioned. If I'd been closer to any of my family I'd have been able to tell them how I felt. Instead I used to spend most of my free time with friends. That night the house was quiet inside when I was dropped off. I didn't see my brother's best friend leaning on the dining room door jamb until he lurched out and grabbed me in a bear hug.'

Matt pushed up against the bedhead, taking her with him. 'Lauren, if you—'

'He mumbled, "You're pretty, *li'l sister*," and kissed me. He stank of beer and sweat and to me it was gross. I remember kicking his shins, breaking free and looking over the top of the stair rail with revulsion. He was slumped against the wall, finishing off his can of beer.'

'And you lumped our kiss on the balcony with that?' His incredibility was tinged with anger.

'No! You were…' In her eagerness to appease him she almost divulged how special his kiss had been, how she'd created fantasies of him over the years.

'Matt, I'm sorry, truly sorry. I let one drunken incident influence my judgement of certain types of good-looking men. From his attitude on the few occasions we've met since, I'm convinced he doesn't remember it at all.'

'Lauren Taylor.'

She recognised the corporate tone from their earliest meetings and squeezed her eyes shut as if that would prevent the coming declaration. He tilted her chin up, coaxing her to look into determined midnight-blue eyes.

'You are very special and I intend to banish every skerrick of that image from your memory. In the best, most personal way possible. And I promise you won't want to run from me.'

His kiss was sweet and tender, and, for her, much too short. Humour glistened in his eyes as he raised his head.

'So you think I'm good-looking? Tell me more.'

CHAPTER TWELVE

THERE WERE FEW vehicles on the roads as Matt drove home after leaving Lauren at her hotel room in the early hours of the morning. Gently nudging her through her door and not following tested his resolve. Pulling it shut to enable him to walk away from her sweet smile, flushed cheeks and slumberous hazel eyes was the hardest action he'd ever taken.

He could still feel her soft lips responding to his in the longest, sweetest goodnight kiss he'd ever had. No holding back. No expectations.

He'd asked her to stay all night but understood her need for distance after their shared confessions and lengthy conversation after. It had been soul-searing for them both. They'd have distance all right, three days, two nights and who knew how many kilometres.

He parked in his garage, switched off the engine and clicked the remote to wind down the roller door. Didn't move. Didn't want to go into that empty unit where her tantalising perfume lingered and her presence was now indelibly implanted into the atmosphere.

Reclining the seat and pushing it back, he lay staring at the roof. New, clean, unmarked, like everything else he owned in Australia. Limbo land. Between the old and the unknown.

He closed his eyes—body weary, mind wide awake. His impulsive kiss so long ago had caused repercussions he'd never have believed, and distress for Lauren. He'd allowed his perception of his parents' relationship to affect his attitude. Love might not be blind but maybe it blurred faults in those you cared for.

Lena and Mark, Duncan and Clair. There were other happy couples he knew too. Did his mother's love override the pain of his father's affairs?

He yawned, ought to go in, get a few hours' sleep to cope with the long day ahead. He'd miss her in his bed— probably lie awake remembering the passion they'd shared. Had those harsh, ecstatic groans of release mingling with her joyful cries come from him? His lips curled, his body shifted as he remembered her kittenish mews. He slept.

Lauren woke early, a faint ray of daylight competing with the street lamps to dispel the night. She quivered as memories teased her from sleep, and grew stronger, more vibrant. More intimate.

She blushed as she recalled how forward she'd been, so unlike the compliant participant in her other relationships. Matt had gently encouraged her, kissed her until she was molten lava in his arms then taken her to the stars and beyond.

It was because of those new and tumultuous sensations, followed by the sharing of their innermost secrets, that she'd asked him to take her back to the hotel. Part of her had longed to stay, to sleep cradled to his body and make love in the morning as the sun rose. The other half had felt vulnerable, shocked by her ardent responses, and needing solitude to decipher why now? Why him?

A similar duel had her torn between knowing how much she'd miss him and feeling an inexplicable inclination to re-erect the defence shield round her heart. She had three days to…who was she kidding? Her surrender had been complete.

Thirteen hours later she pushed her dinner plate to the far corner of the table and opened the green patterned spiral notebook she'd bought in the quirky gift shop a few hours ago. Along with presents for friends' future birthdays.

She'd never been one for writing copious holiday descriptions, relying on photos, brief notes and her memory.

She'd kept Matt's image at bay as she drove, forcing her mind into work mode where nothing was allowed to intrude on the task at hand. New vehicle, new roads, though there were fewer freeways than in New South Wales.

As she wrote and sipped delicious rose tea she noticed the small ceramic vases on the dining-room tables, each one unique and holding two fresh flowers and a sprig of greenery. *Her* vase with orchids was swathed in bubble wrap and secured behind the passenger seat of the car.

Laying her new special green pen down, she cradled her cup, recalling his tenderness and sensitivity, and the way his passion, matching hers, had overridden both. No one had ever made her feel so feminine, so aroused. She relived the evening from the initial eye contact across the road to his reluctant expression as he'd closed her hotel-room door.

Lost in reminiscence, she jumped when her mobile rang, rummaged for her phone with unsteady fingers.

'Matt.'

'Hi, having a good day?'

His now oh-so-familiar raspy voice triggered a rush of heat through her veins. She leant her elbow on the table, and pressed her mobile tighter to her ear as if the action would bring them together.

'Yes, I turned off at any interesting sign, and stopped at almost every town I went through. The autumn colours are incredible. I took lots of photos and bought a few presents.' She was babbling, couldn't seem to slow down.

'Did you miss me?' Deeper, hopeful tone.

'If I say yes, you'll claim an advantage. How did your meetings go?

'Chicken. I missed *you*. Only had one. Where are you now?'

She clutched her stomach to quell the fluttering his confession created, steadied her breathing, and fought for her normal placid tone when she replied.

'Nuriootpa for the night. Tomorrow, who knows?'

'You will be back on Friday?' The teasing note disappeared. He sounded serious, surprisingly uncertain.

'That's the plan. Is there a problem?'

'Not from my end. You'll be getting a call from Clair in the next hour or so. We've been invited to their home in the Hills for the weekend.'

'We?'

'As in you and me, Lauren. Duncan wants to discuss the company's current position, and the business proposal I pitched to him a couple of weeks ago in a relaxed atmosphere. They want you to come with me.'

'Why? I'm not part of your deal at all.'

'They like you.'

Not exactly the answer she wanted to hear.

'Lauren, *I* want you to come. You know them, said you liked them. If it's our relationship worrying you, I promise nothing will happen between us unless you want it to.'

Of course she wanted it to; the location was irrelevant. Last night had been the most wonderful experience of her life. The dilemma was the when and where.

'A whole weekend in someone's home is a giant leap from having dinner with them.' With added pressure if they believed she and Matt were involved.

He made an exasperated noise in his throat.

'I wish I could see you, reassure you. Will you please consider it? Talk it out with Clair?'

She shared the same desire to be with him but she was also aware of how much he was counting on making a deal with Duncan Ford. Would it make a difference if she could see his expression? Moot point so far apart.

'Okay. I'll decide when I talk to Clair.'

'Let me know. Now tell me where you went and what you did.'

* * *

Matt almost rolled off the lounge as he lunged for his mobile an hour or so later, failing to stifle a harsh groan as his elbow hit the side of the coffee table, and his mug fell off.

'Lauren.'

'What was that?'

Simultaneous voices, then silence.

'Matt, are you there?' He liked, more than liked, the concern in her tone.

'I knocked my elbow on the table. You can kiss it better on Friday.' He sat on the sofa's edge, ramrod straight, stomach taut.

'Try pawpaw ointment, it works quicker.'

'Not as much fun. Clair phoned?' He held his breath.

'The two of you are very persuasive. She reminded me I offered to have a look at her computer some time, so I could hardly refuse. And she promised it'll be a weekend to remember.'

His commitment as well. He rose to his feet, adrenaline surging, his free hand fisting and pumping the air. Couldn't, didn't want to stop the grin from forming but managed to keep his voice steady.

'It will be. Are you tired?'

'A little. I'm in the motel room ready for bed.'

A vivid image from his bedroom filled his head, he barely managed to stifle the zealous groan.

'Too sleepy to talk? You're a long way away, and I don't want to say goodnight.'

'What about?'

'You and your family. Why you took the job in Sydney.'

He waited as she pondered his question, a habit he'd learnt to expect, professionally and personally.

'What I went through might have been because I was so different, too shy and inhibited to join in boisterous games. My parents and brothers were all extroverts, loved any kind of physical sport and had no problems interacting with strangers.'

A decidedly male growl resonated in Lauren's ear.

'They didn't allow for you being quiet and gentle, didn't make time to understand who you were?'

She sensed Matt's anger, found his defending their lack of sensitivity towards her exhilarating.

'I'm beginning to see how I contributed to the problems. I wasn't interested so I didn't make any effort. I never complained or told them how I felt except to refuse to attend any more sporting events once I turned thirteen. To them I seemed happy to bury myself in books and homework. At least I always got good grades at school.'

Another growl so she quickly added, 'If I hadn't I might not be working with computers. Might not be here.'

'Eighty odd kilometres away. Much too far.'

She snuggled into the pillow, striving to keep grounded. He made her feel warm and light-headed even along a phone line. With each word, her pulse had quickened, electric tingles danced over her skin, and the overwhelming desire to touch him, feel his strength surrounding her was almost frightening. He could make her feel strong, empowered. He could also hurt her more than anyone else in the world.

Lauren returned the hire car early Friday afternoon, and was given a sealed package Matt had left for her containing a key to his unit. Finding a round dining setting in the appropriate place and three large bright blue cushions on the settee left her speechless.

She texted him to say she'd arrived, found a tea towel in a kitchen drawer, and set it on the new table. It was the perfect place for the orchid arrangement he'd sent her. They were as fresh as when she'd received them, having suffered no ill effects from their journey to the Barossa.

A cup of tea, an open packet of chocolate biscuits, and

she was ready to sort out her belongings in the lounge room. The items she chose for the Hills visit were packed into the new suitcase she'd purchased, everything else was wrapped and stored in her original one ready for the trip home.

Home. Her own apartment. Her sanctuary. It was never going to feel quite the same. The memories she'd be taking with her would change the way she viewed her life, her work. Her future. She chomped into another biscuit and vowed, no matter what, there'd be no regrets. Her friends would be there for her though she'd never be able to tell them the full truth. Matt would be her special *good* secret, hers alone.

She heard his car pull into the garage, his footsteps in the passage, his delighted raspy tone. 'You're here.' She saw his captivating smile, was swept into his embrace, and held as if she was fragile and precious. She slid her arms around his waist, revelling in his strength and the satisfying sense of security.

His lips feather-brushed her forehead. She cuddled up, wanting this serenity to last, and he seemed in no hurry to end it either. Quiet harmony. An idyllic memory to cherish.

'You kept the orchids?'

She arched her neck to meet questioning eyebrows and curved lips. 'Of course. They're beautiful, Matt.'

His eyes shone as he gathered her in. 'So are you, Lauren. Beautiful and intoxicating.'

His kiss was light, gentle, spreading a warm glow from head to toes. Her lips instinctively moved with his. Her heart soared, and she wanted to freeze-frame this precious moment for ever.

With evident reluctance he eased away.

'If I don't let you go now, we'll arrive in the dark. I know which I'd prefer…'

'But the Fords are expecting us for dinner. I'm packed and ready.'

'Give me ten minutes to shower and change.' He dipped his head for a brief hard kiss and walked out of the room.

When they left Lauren kept silent at first allowing Matt to concentrate on the driving through peak traffic. She stared out of the window, trying to identify the suburbs and buildings, surprised by the number of new houses and renovations on main roads.

Once they hit the freeway to the hills, he turned on the radio, keeping it muted in the background.

'Any listening preference, Lauren?'

'Whatever you usually have on is fine.'

'Which would mainly be news and sport. Not for you. How are you on county and western?'

He had to be teasing. One look at his profile said he wasn't.

'As long as it's ballads and not yippee-ki-yay stuff.'

'Whatever pleases you.' He glanced over and her mouth dried up at the fire in his eyes. She quivered inside at the thought of the two nights and two days ahead.

'I've been meaning to ask you for days, kept forgetting because you have a habit of distracting my mind and scrambling my brain. What's the name of your perfume?'

She couldn't answer, her own brain turning to mush at his compliment. He was claiming to be as affected as she was when they were together. Did he have the same heat rushes, the tingles? The heart flips?

She'd been wearing the same brand for years, had one of the fragrances in her suitcase. So why couldn't she remember either name?

'It's from a small rural company who produce different aromas from Australian native flowers. I keep three and wear whichever suits my mood at the time.'

'It's been the same one every day since you arrived. Are the others as enticing?'

'I've no idea. Why do you always wear the same sea-spray cologne?'

'The truth?'

'Yes.' *Please don't let it be because it was a gift from a girlfriend.*

'I forgot to pack mine for when I changed after a game and borrowed Alan's. Apart from when I've been given others, it's the one I use.'

'You wore it that night.'

'For the first time.' He flicked her an incredulous look. 'You remembered how I smelt?'

'You did get pretty close, Matt.'

'Yeah, and then I lost you.'

They drove in silence for a while, both lost in thoughts of their meeting on the balcony, Matt's focus on the road and Lauren's out of the window.

Because of the long hot summer, the vegetation wasn't as green as she'd hoped. Sneak views of houses between the trees, horses and sheep grazing, and colourful native plants drew her avid attention. Seeing a herd of alpacas in a small fenced area of a paddock thrilled her.

After exiting the freeway, they followed the signs through the small typical hills town and onto a winding, tree-lined road. High overhanging branches covered with autumn leaves of brilliant orange and brown shaded them from the setting sun. The verges were covered with more, tempting walkers to romp through them.

'This is so peaceful. So Australiana. When we lived in the suburbs I used to dream of moving to a hills town. Any one of them.' She shrugged. 'Didn't happen of course.'

Matt pulled over, switched off the engine and unbuckled his seat belt. He stretched his arm and unclipped hers, unfazed by the sudden apprehension in her eyes. Twisting to face her and taking her hands in his, he yearned for the glowing satisfaction he'd seen after they'd made love.

'You had a few unfulfilled childhood wishes, didn't you?'

She shrugged. 'Doesn't everyone?'

'No.' He ignored his ambition to work as a partner with his father. 'Most of mine came true. I played Aussie Rules for the school, graduated from uni and travelled overseas. Considering my lack of vocal ability, becoming an international singing sensation was never going to happen.'

His heart swelled at the sight of her hesitant smile. Give him time and he'd make her radiant and happy.

'I dreamt of being a dancer for a year or so.' She gave a self-conscious laugh. 'Of course, in my imagination I had no fear of appearing on stage in front of hundreds of people. The one time I was selected to read a poem I'd written at parents' night, I took one look at all those faces, froze and bolted.'

'So you wrote?'

'I have a stack of notebooks full of poems and short stories, only ever shown to my best friend. Childish and not very good but fun. I haven't written anything for years except reports or emails.'

Her fingers gripped his. His pulse accelerated. The temperature in the car rose rapidly.

'I've been reflecting on my life lately and I'm beginning to realise my family and I just didn't gel. Maybe they weren't as much insensitive as bemused by the alien in their midst. And there were no other relatives around who might have made a difference.'

'Will you discuss it with them when you see them?'

'No.' Short and sharp. 'There's no way it wouldn't sound accusing and the past can't be changed.'

He silently agreed with fervour.

'I'm an adult with a good career and great friends. It'll achieve nothing, and only cause pain.'

A car drove past, the driver beeping in customary rural

friendship. Matt checked the time, then cradled her face in his hands.

'Most assuredly an adult, Lauren Taylor. Beautiful and desirable.'

He intended the kiss to be gentle, reassuring, but almost lost control when she returned it with enthusiasm. Her hands slid up his chest to tease his neck, heating his blood to near boiling. Her body pressed to his fuelled the urge to have her alone somewhere quiet and private.

He broke away, expelling the air from his lungs, gasping in more as he feasted on her blushed cheeks and brilliant eyes. His hand shook as he redid his seat belt and started the engine.

As he struggled to find his voice again he mulled over her confessions of the last few days. He needed to know everything if he was to help her completely overcome her insecurities before she left.

Before she left. The very idea depressed him. Having her near lifted his spirits.

'In five hundred metres turn right.'

The GPS interrupted his thinking and he slowed down.

CHAPTER THIRTEEN

LAUREN'S LIPS TINGLED from his kiss, and her heartbeat loped along in an erratic rhythm. She wanted to be alone with Matt, wasn't ready for a whole weekend with comparative strangers who'd probably invited her for his sake. Her first sight of the property increased her reservations.

Well-maintained tall hedges formed the property's boundaries with ornate stone columns and high elaborate gates protecting the entrance. She could see neatly trimmed red- and green-leafed plants skirtinged the winding gravel driveway, and a variety of trees and shrubs hid the house from view.

Matt pressed a button on a matching bollard, answered a disembodied voice and the gates swung open. They passed through, and for Lauren it was like entering another world, where money was no object and the traditions of genera- tions would be strictly upheld. She had no logical reason for the feeling yet it was strong and overwhelming, negat- ing all the assurances Matt and Clair had given her.

She gripped her hands in her lap, drops of sweat slid down her back and her stomach churned. Having lunch in public, with eating and waiter service taking up time, hadn't been as bad as she'd expected. The dinner function had been so noisy, so crowded and bustling, interaction had been kept to a minimum.

She'd been coerced into a weekend with Matt and the Fords, dining with them three times a day, sitting with them in the evening. She'd be alone with Clair while the men discussed business. What did she have in common with a rich, influential woman whose life revolved around her husband, family and society friends?

She… Oh, they'd stopped as the car rounded a curve. Wide expanses of lawn had been laid as a fire break on the sides she could see. Ahead stood the house, a beautiful sprawling example of a colonial family homestead with a shady wide veranda on all four sides. It was painted in muted shades of green and brown, including the shutters, to blend with the surroundings. A peaceful harmonious haven. A millionaire's paradise.

She was vaguely aware of the lack of engine noise, then Matt's hand covering hers, raising the hairs on her skin, triggering warmth deep inside. Somehow it intensified the trembling she tried to hide.

She looked into sympathetic blue eyes and wished she'd been more honest and refused the invitation. So much hung on the impression he made this weekend, and she'd be a liability he'd regret.

'I'm sorry, Matt. I made a mistake. This is a mistake. The dinner was one thing—this is way bigger. You and Duncan talk business, sport, topical news. You were brought up in the same social environment, probably went to the same private school. I'll never fit in with your elite circles.'

A guttural rumble came from his throat and he placed two fingers on her lips. She swatted them away.

'Clair is a caring, generous person with all the social skills. I'm a computer geek with hardly any. We'll run out of conversation in minutes.'

His features hardened, sending an icy chill shooting across her skin as if she'd entered a supermarket freezer. She pressed into the seat, wishing she could disappear into it.

'Those statements are beneath the person I believe you are, Lauren. They met you and thought you were a charming, intelligent, and gracious young woman. Duncan's exact words when he asked me to thank you for your kindness to Ken. And, believe me, Clair would never have invited you just to make equal numbers.'

He stroked her hair, clasped her nape and gently drew

her upright. His gaze intensified as he studied her face. What was he searching for? And why? His smile obliterated her logic and created chaotic fantasies.

'They'd like you to have a relaxing weekend in one of the most beautiful places in South Australia, the same as I do. I'm sure Clair knows we're attracted to each other but there's no way she'll say or do anything to make you feel uncomfortable.'

Shame made her blush and she bit her lip. She gave him a remorseful smile, and flattened out her hands with linked fingers in supplication.

'I guess deep inside I know that's true. Sometimes the insecure child overrides the logical technician. Being with you plays havoc with my rationality.'

Too late she heard what she'd admitted, knew from his smug grin he'd understood, and wouldn't hesitate to use it to coerce and cajole her.

'You've just paid me one of the nicest compliments I've ever had. If I wasn't parked in view from the house, and constrained by my seat belt, I'd put it to the test.'

He covered her lips, teasing and coaxing yet with an underlying restraint. She returned the kiss, safe in the knowledge it could go no further. For now. She wound her arm around his neck to hold him closer then let it slide slowly away when he lifted his head. Embraced the surge of power at the emotion in his voice when he whispered in her ear.

'And don't think for a second I won't remember every word and every touch next time we're alone.'

Bringing her breathing under control as they drove up to the house, she silently echoed his words. Except *she'd* remember them as long as she lived.

Clair was waiting on the front steps and came out to meet them, leaning into Lauren's window.

'Glad you made it. We've opened one of the garage doors

for you round the back. I'll meet you there.' She didn't comment on the five-minute time gap from gate to front door.

They parked and Matt was unloading the boot when she joined them, giving Lauren a warm hug and a kiss on the cheek. So different from the casual greetings from her family. Did her reticence cause the awkwardness between them?

'Do you need a hand with the luggage?'

'She's brought less than any woman I've ever travelled with,' Matt chipped in as he received the same greeting. 'And that includes the carton of wine from the Barossa.'

'Oh, how thoughtful. Let me take your suitcase.'

She led the way to the steps, wheeling Matt's case, accompanied by Lauren with hers and an overnight bag. Matt locked the car and followed carrying the wine, his satchel and parka.

'I've put you in the guest wing, three bedrooms all with an ensuite, a sitting room and small kitchen. Completely self-contained if needed.'

As they stepped onto the veranda two black and white dogs raised themselves from their snug positions in the corner and came over to sniff and be introduced. The larger one, a mixture of collie and a few unknowns, nuzzled at Lauren's hands and she dropped her bags and stroked him. The other sat by Clair and studied the two newcomers.

'Cyber's an addict for attention. He'll stalk you the whole time you're here if we let him. Cyan is pure collie, and quieter. Both are very protective and great guard dogs. Go settle, you two.'

Turning to the right, she walked a few steps and opened a door to reveal a wide corridor with a high ceiling. Entering first, she placed the suitcase by the wall.

Lauren's eyes widened at the incredible décor, presumably historically accurate with the appearance of being freshly painted in shades of blue. She'd always enjoyed colonial movies, now she felt she was on the set of one. The carved wooden mirror on the wall with a narrow matching table fascinated her. She moved closer. Clair came to stand behind her.

'We inherited these and a lot more furniture with the house. Tomorrow I'll take you on a tour if you like.'

'I'll look forward to it.'

'You'll find we've mixed and matched different time periods. If we like it, we fit it in. Use any rooms you want and join us in the main lounge when you're ready. Shall I take the wine?'

'It's heavy so I'll bring it. We won't keep you waiting.' Matt had already put it on the floor.

'I just need a quick freshen up,' Lauren said.

'Take all the time you want, then come through here.' Clair left through a door midway along the hall.

'Well, Lauren, would you like to choose where you sleep?'

At odds with its rough timbre, his voice glided as smooth as silk over her skin and the only answer in her head was, *With you.*

The first room was a cosy corner lounge with windows on two sides. Matt opened the next door to reveal a king-sized bed with a padded green headboard and quilt. The light green wall complemented white woodwork and built-in wardrobes.

Shuttered windows overlooked the veranda, and the Queen Anne dressing table and stool between two closed doors matched the bedside drawers. One door led into a very modern ensuite, the other to an almost identical bedroom with a floral theme.

Lauren gazed from one to the other then to Matt's inscrutable expression. His taut jaw and the slight curl of his fingers showed the depth of his tension.

She bent her head to hide a smile. If she said separate

rooms, he'd accept her decision without censure though she'd bet he'd use his charm and every seduction technique he could think of to change her mind.

Her stomach quivered and she trembled as she imagined a few of them. In an instant, he was holding her arms, sombre eyes scanning her face.

'Whatever feels right for you, Lauren. This is for happy memories, no regrets.'

She reached up to caress his cheek, and felt his tremor through her fingers. Felt a surge of elation at the power her touch had on him. She tilted her head, and curled her lips in what she hoped was a beguiling smile.

'I've never been a flowery décor girl, and I can't imagine *you* sleeping under a floral quilt.'

His smile lit up her world, his bear hug squeezed her ribcage, and his deep, passionate kiss had her craving to be in the bed behind them right now.

Lauren expected dinner to be in a formal room. Instead the round dining setting overlooked a native garden scattered with inconspicuous bollard lights, illuminating colourful flowers and leafage of all shades of green. Picture perfect scenery.

Duncan opened a red wine she'd purchased in the Barossa Valley and one of his own chilled whites.

'Lauren, which would you like? We are firm advocates for indulging in your own preference.'

She chose white, the others elected to try the red. They toasted good friends and she was complimented on her choice, making her relax and laugh.

'I can hardly claim responsibility. Matt recommended two of the wineries and I merely asked the people in those, and a third near Angaston, for a selection of their bestsellers. It's a gift from both of us.'

'Very much appreciated. Shall we take our seats?'

Clair went to fetch the starters, declining Lauren's offer to assist.

'They're all ready to be served. You can help clear and bring in the other courses.'

Any apprehension Matt had felt regarding this visit faded away as conversation flowed. Lauren was curious about the plant varieties in the garden, admitting she'd had a successful vegetable plot in Melbourne and missed the straight-from-the-ground taste. When laughingly challenged by Clair to name the home-grown on the table, she amazed them all by being correct.

'I thought I'd get you on the peas from the market. We'll pick some fruit for you to take home on Sunday.'

The conversation ranged from orchards to the history of the house and the restorations the Fords had undertaken over a number of years. Matt admired the gentle banter between them, the friendly teasing solidly based on an enduring love and evident companionship.

He'd been convinced he'd never feel such a bonding, yet lately that belief had become blurred. Was it possible he might be wrong?

His eyes met Lauren's as she stood to help with the dinner plates, and her smile tripped his heart. His mind flashed to the night ahead with the enchanting woman who'd agreed to share it with him.

Pavlova, coffee and liqueurs rounded off a delightful meal, his senses heightened by the promise of a perfect ending to the day.

All Lauren's senses were acute, tuned like a maestro's violin, as they approached the door that would shut them off from the rest of the house. Matt's fingers were laced with hers. She could hear the long breaths he took. His aroma surrounded her, tempting her lungs to breathe deeper.

Tonight there'd be no drive back to her hotel. She'd nestle into his warmth and fall asleep. And wake in his arms to be kissed and loved some more as the sun's rays lit up the room.

No expectations. No recriminations. She'd accept what he freely gave and not regret what he was not able to give. Every moment spent with Matt inched her further along the path of surrendering her heart. There was no going back and in front she could see no happy ending.

As soon as the door closed behind them, he twisted her round, and stepped closer, trapping her against the wall. He stroked her cheek with his knuckles, and she could feel his heart pounding under her palm. His free hand slid around her neck and he bent his head to claim her lips.

The fire that had smouldered since he'd arrived home roared into flame, and she returned his kiss with an ardour that shook her to her core. He quivered then his arms enfolded her, tightening until there was no space between them.

Time stood still, stretched endlessly to infinity. Too short an eon later, he raised his head to take a shuddering breath. Her own came in gasps, and she let her forehead rest on his chest.

'Wow.' Placing one hand on the wall above her head, he blew air out and inhaled new in. Stared at her for a long time as if trying to see inside her head, trying to puzzle something out.

'I've missed you, Lauren. Ached for you for three long days and two endless nights and I can't wait any longer.'

He lifted her into his arms, carried her into the bedroom, and laid her on the bed. Without relinquishing hold, he settled beside her, rolling onto his side to lean over her. His fingertips skimmed across her shoulders and arms then over her hips, making her squirm with anticipation. His lips kissed a path from the pulse by her ear to the corner of her mouth, driving her crazy with need.

'Matt?' She hardly recognised the breathless, needy plea as coming from her. Her hand pressed on the back of his neck, dragging his head down to hers, and her fingernails scraped his skin.

'You're mine.' His voice was harsh, deep with passion. Macho. Triumphant.

'Yours.' Hers was breathless. Elated. Proud.

For as long as he needed and wanted her.

Lauren leant on the veranda rail waiting while Matt showered so they could join their hosts for breakfast. The universe was different, sharper, brighter. *She* was different.

She huffed and watched her breath evaporate in the cool air. She'd been changing since Matt had glanced up at her with his mesmerising midnight-blue eyes. A little every time they were together, stronger from the kisses outside her hotel room and a giant leap when they first made love.

Last night the metamorphosis had become complete. There'd been no sign of the shy, vulnerable caterpillar. She'd given herself to him completely, no hesitation, no restraint. And been shown a realm of soaring passions and sensations far beyond her imagination.

She'd fallen into contented sleep wrapped in his arms, his lips on her forehead, her hand on his thundering heart.

She felt a nudge at her side, and hunkered down to pat Cyan, almost fell over as Cyber also claimed attention.

'Save some for me.' Matt stood in the doorway, hair damp, eyes gleaming.

He could have all of her for as long as he wanted.

Breakfast was served on the balcony facing the large vegetable patch. Lauren loved the crispness in the air, and the light breeze stirring the foliage, making the garden appear to be alive. She could imagine sitting here all day and into the evening enjoying the changes of light and sound.

'This is all so idealistic. I can't imagine a more soothing place. Working in the city must be so much more tolerable if you know you have a haven to go home to.'

'And work's better now I can do a lot electronically,' Duncan chipped in. 'You can keep your high-rise views. Nothing beats what we have here.'

'Do you get out of the city much, Lauren?' Clair asked as she buttered her toast.

'Occasionally. We drive up to the Blue Mountains or along the coast to go hiking. Beach walking is fun any season and easily accessible in Sydney.'

'And who's we?'

Lauren noted she gave no apologies for being inquisitive, didn't need to. It was part of her caring nature.

'A group of friends I've met since moving there. We now live in the same apartment block so we're like family.'

As she spoke she looked across the table at Matt's thoughtful expression, remembered earlier conversations and wondered if he'd come to the same sudden realisation. She had a second family, of her own ilk, and who she gelled with comfortably.

He quirked an eyebrow and his lips curled, causing fluttering in her belly and heat waves in her veins. She lifted her glass, drank the remainder of her freshly squeezed orange juice, and tried for a nonchalant demeanour.

CHAPTER FOURTEEN

MATT STRUGGLED FOR the same effect. His body still buzzed from the exhilaration of waking from deep satisfying sleep with Lauren curled into him, warm and irresistible. He had no idea what he'd eaten, drunk or said since they'd joined Duncan and Clair for the meal.

She was radiant. Her skin glowed and her expressive hazel eyes shone as brightly as any stars in a country sky. He'd heard and understood what she'd said. She had friends and support. She'd be all right when she went home.

Home. His half-empty barren unit. She'd taken three days of her leave. Allowing for the day or two he'd need her at work, she'd only be here for two more weeks. Forget the hotel. He'd ask her to stay with him.

The prospect of spending long evenings with her was intoxicating. The image of her sharing breakfast and dinner across the new table he'd bought because of her upped his pulse to uncountable. And as for the nights…

'Matt?'

He crashed to earth with a thud. Clair's eyes twinkled as she held up the coffee jug.

'More coffee?'

'Um… Please.' He pushed his cup and saucer over to her, hoping his face wasn't as red as it felt. She'd caught him out again.

'As you two will be in Duncan's study for most of the morning, Lauren and I will walk the dogs then I'll show her over the house,' Clair said, topping up her husband's drink.

'Just don't let her get you in the small room off the lounge, Lauren,' Duncan quipped. 'That's where her troublesome computer lurks and you'll be trapped in there until dinner.'

'Brute.' Clair gave him a playful flick of her hand and they smiled blissfully at each other.

The painful gut wrench took Matt by surprise. Their affection was obvious after nearly thirty-five years of marriage. Duncan had mentioned their anniversary was in June and he intended to make it an extra special occasion.

He'd assumed it would be for show like his parents' celebrations. Not any more. Like Lena and Mark, the interaction between them proved their feelings ran deep and true.

The dogs bounded down the back steps as soon as Lauren and Clair came out of the door, raced halfway across the lawn then stopped to ensure they were following.

'They're better than any exercise programme I've ever tried,' Clair remarked. As the two women caught up with them, they shot off again.

'Walking anywhere around here would never seem like training to me. This trip has got me rethinking my priorities and future,' Lauren replied.

'The trip or the man?'

Lauren wasn't sure how to answer as they went through a gate and onto a bushland path.

'It's complicated.'

'It needn't be, Lauren. The way you look at one another, whenever you touch, the attraction's obvious but there's also constraint. My children tell me not to interfere…'

'Advice is always welcome.' Lauren would gladly accept guidance. 'It's whether it can be acted upon that counts.'

'Don't give up on him, Lauren. Matt's mother and I belong to the same organisations, and she's hinted at Marcus's medical problems. Apart from that and the company situation, I sense Matt has personal demons to conquer.'

'You may be right.'

He's certainly determined to have me exorcise mine.

'He also has a reputation for tough, ethical dealing. If he

didn't Duncan wouldn't be considering a partnership. Let him find his own way and be there when he does.'

As things stood she'd be on the east coast fixing glitches, living on memories and dreaming of midnight-blue eyes.

'Cyber. Cyan.' The dogs had darted to the left at a fork, and obediently returned to Clair's side.

'There's a magnificent view this way. Luckily the koalas don't seem at all perturbed by our noisy pets so keep an eye out for them in the gum trees.'

'I envy you all this beauty and peace. Matt told me the property was quite run-down when you moved in.'

'I inherited the estate from two wonderful stubborn-as-mules grandparents who refused help and died within weeks of each other. Life wasn't easy, especially in those early years, but it's always worth fighting for what you love.'

But what if the one you are fighting for doesn't want to be won?

The talks with Duncan couldn't have gone better; now all Matt wanted to do was find Lauren, and see her smile. Had she had a good morning? Was she happy she'd come?

He found her in the kitchen helping Clair prepare a salad lunch, and restrained the desire to kiss her in company. Until her face brightened at the sight of him and the invitation in her bright eyes was too hard to resist. He slipped his arm around her waist and softly covered her enticing lips with his.

She laid her hand on his arm, and welcomed the kiss, recreating the heat sensations from last night. His pulse tripled and his heart pounded. All overridden by an unfamiliar longing to hold on for ever and cherish.

Shaken by this new emotion, he broke the kiss, fighting for control. He wanted to find solitude to assess what was happening, and perversely ached to scoop her up and carry her to a quiet place and be with her.

'How'd the walk go?' Reality slammed home at Duncan's remark from the doorway.

Matt set Lauren free, nearly pulled her back in at the sight of her sweetly bemused expression.

'The air was fresh and crisp at the south lookout and the hills were shrouded in mist—very bracing,' Clair replied. 'You two can carry the salad bowls and meat plates. Lauren and I will bring the rest.'

The dogs padded round the veranda to join them, squatting close in anticipation of being fed as well.

'We also had a session on my computer,' Clair announced with pride as they helped themselves to food.

'And?'

Duncan wasn't merely playing lip service to his wife. Matt heard the genuine interest in his tone, saw it in his eyes. She was his number one priority as he was hers. So different from his parents. A cold fist crushed his heart, and his chest tightened.

'I'm not so bad after all. Lauren gave me a beautifully covered notebook and bright green pen and I wrote down everything step by step as she told or showed me.'

Lauren's knee bumped against his and stayed. A simple nod of her head plus a look that said 'you were right' sent heat surging throughout his body. He echoed her action then concentrated on Clair.

'No one's ever explained the things I have trouble with in simple English I can understand. Lauren did, and I have her email address and phone number so I can contact her any time I need help.'

Matt couldn't prevent the swell of pride even though all he'd done was persuade Lauren to come. With a start, he realised it was pride in her, something he had no justification for. She was her own person. An enchanting, self-sufficient woman.

'So I'm going to take her into Hahndorf this afternoon. What do you have planned?'

The men exchanged glances.

'Another couple of hours and we'll break for the day. You'll find us on the side veranda with a bottle of wine and a selection of cheese and crackers.' Duncan grinned at Matt. 'They'll have to come get us to carry all the shopping from the car.'

Clearing the table was accomplished in a few minutes with everyone helping then Matt went with Lauren to fetch her coat and shoulder bag. And to kiss her, longer and deeper than he'd be able to do in front of their hosts.

It left them both hot and gasping for air. And bedtime was a lifetime away.

'Glad you decided to come, Lauren?' He watched her face for any sign of regret.

'Got coerced you mean. Yes, I'm very glad.' Her eyes darkened, highlighting the gold flecks. His body responded to the thought she might be remembering last night.

'Clair says she'll take me round the house tomorrow.'

He'd been in umpteen old renovated homes. A few days ago he'd have politely declined joining them. Today the chance of seeing what the Fords had achieved through Lauren's eyes was appealing.

'Tell her I'd like to be included.'

His wanting to join them delighted Lauren. When the offer of two weeks' leave had been made it had sounded like ample time for a break. Now, with three days taken, it was a pitiful amount to store memories to last a lifetime.

Lauren flicked at the insect biting her earlobe, sighed and snuggled into her pillow. It returned, pulling her a little further from sleep.

'Wanna go for a walk and watch the sun rise?'

Whispered throaty seduction.

In an instant she was wide awake, catching at the hand whose fingernails were tickling her lobe. Matt lay beside her, fully dressed in jeans and warm jumper, eyes gleaming with mischief. The only light came from the open ensuite door.

How come he wanted to go hiking and her main desire was to drag him close for a repeat of last night? And later. And some time in the early hours of today. It would take only his touch to turn her languid muscles molten and rekindle the passion he'd ignited again and again.

'What time is it?' She stretched, and shivered as the cold morning air hit her arms, glared at him when he pulled the quilt off her. He sucked air between his teeth as she tried to drag them back.

'Early. I've got snacks, drinks and directions to the best lookout.' He was excited, eager like a puppy ready for his daily walk. 'You've got five minutes.'

'You asked for ten on Friday,' she muttered, pretending to be annoyed. Secretly she was thrilled he wanted to share this outing with her. His laughter followed her to the shower.

He took her hand as they left, guiding her down the back steps and over the lawn, his torch lighting their way. They followed the path through the trees, accompanied by only the sound of the breeze rustling the vegetation, the scuffling of animals in the undergrowth, and dried leaves crunching under their sneakers.

Lauren relished the chill on her face, the night hiding the factual mundane world and the warmth of his fingers linked with hers. This was more than special, this was super memorable. A never-to-be-forgotten occasion to be taken out and savoured in the future whenever she felt sad.

Matt stopped suddenly in the centre of a small clearing,

and bent to place his backpack on the ground. She heard a click and the beam disappeared, leaving them in complete darkness, surrounded by black velvet. Magical. Ethereal.

He drew her into his arms, and she wrapped hers around his neck. His lips were soft, his kiss firm yet holding a tenderness that touched her heart. No bells or fireworks. This was a moment of profound contentment. The moment she acknowledged the truth. She was in love with Matt Dalton.

With their lips a whisper apart Matt breathed out Lauren's name, too stunned to form any other words. He'd switched off the torch for effect, to heighten the ambiance when he'd kissed her in the dark. Hadn't expected to be so unsettled by his own emotions.

Only she could access his soul and revitalise the beliefs he'd long discarded, make him yearn for a better time when he'd had faith in for ever. She fitted him perfectly, her soft form to his hard muscle. He didn't want to—couldn't—let her leave until he…he wasn't sure what.

Keeping one arm around her as much for his comfort as hers, he bent to retrieve the torch, waved it round and led her to the gap in the trees. In the light's limited sphere there was a valley below and hills beyond, vague mysterious shapes. The wind was stronger here in the open, blowing up and over the edge, causing him to strengthen his stance.

His intention had been to give Lauren a weekend of pleasurable memories. Now he was storing them up for himself.

Taking the picnic rug from the rucksack, he laid it out between the trees near the edge of the cliff. Lying down on one elbow, he held out his hand. His already racing heartbeat hit rocket speed as, without hesitation, she joined him, eyes sparkling, lips parted. She stroked his cheek, and ran her fingers across his jaw, triggering reactions that blew his control.

Shy, exquisite Lauren was teasing him, playing havoc

with his libido. She tempted him with her inviting smile, her tongue-tip tracing her lips, and her feather-light finger touch. He bent over her, lowered his head and clicked off the torch.

The first small pink and orange rays shimmered on the horizon. Matt leant against a tree trunk, nestled Lauren's back onto his chest, and rested his chin on her shoulder as they stared across the valley. He breathed in her delicate scent, tinged with his cologne and their personal aromas.

This was an extraordinary moment, life changing. For those few incredible minutes, they'd been one entity, bound by a force he didn't understand. Knew he wanted to relive it again and again.

For ever? She wriggled, reigniting the desire. His body would willingly comply for as long as he lived. His resolute mind clung to the hard lessons he'd learnt. He refused to make false declarations to gain any advantage or to give false hope of any kind.

No deception. No lies. What they had was good, much better than good. There was no reason they couldn't continue to be together until she flew home. His arms tightened, reinforcing his hold, and she gave a cute gasp. He nuzzled her neck and she sighed. He nibbled her earlobe.

'Oh-h-h…' Her breath whooshed out as vibrant colours tinted the edges of emerging clouds and gradually spread across the sky. Dark shadowy shapes began to appear on the landscape, slowly taking recognisable form. Unforgettable. Unbelievably spectacular.

His own breath caught in his throat. His body stilled, his pulse raced. This was supposed to be a unique experience for Lauren to treasure, along with the other special occasions they'd shared. He hadn't expected to feel anything more than he did at fireworks displays or the like.

Instead nature at her finest tugged at his heartstrings,

ınd raised the hairs on the back of his neck. The adrena-
ıine rush was greater than when he'd skied the Swiss Alps
ınd white-water rafted in Wales, heightened by sharing it
with Lauren.

The sun's softer morning rays revealed the delicacy of
her skin, rapture in her wide-open eyes, and ecstasy on
her beautiful face. He burned it into his memory, to be recalled at will.

'Matt.' Husky with emotion. Crumbling what little composure he had left.

'Darling Lauren.' Rough, dragged over the constricting
lump in his throat.

'It's wonderful. Unbelievable. Thank you.'

He cradled her cheek, leant forward and kissed her,
wishing the earth would stop spinning and the magic would
never end. He laid his head next to hers and pretended it
hadn't.

Lauren wished she could reverse time, have the sun set
then rise again. In slow motion. With her senses already
heightened by his gentle loving only minutes before, she'd
been enthralled by the fluid change of colours. The pan-
orama in front of her, the solid wall of his chest behind
her, and his muscular arms enfolding her intensified the
sensation of being snugly cosseted in a vast open universe.

She loved the mystical atmosphere of night becoming
day, of small pockets of mist among the trees. Of feeling
they were alone in the cosmos. Even the nocturnal crea-
tures were silent in mutual reverence.

His kiss was magical, soft with an underlying hint of
yearning. A longing echoed in her heart. A craving for
this never to end.

Lights flickered in the distance, and the wind picked up,
bringing with it faint sounds of traffic. They ate the chocolate bars and drank the hot coffee he'd brought. Cuddled

close in their padded winter jackets, neither ready to leave and return to the real world.

Only when they heard the dogs barking did they stand and pack up.

'I think I need a bigger car,' Matt joked as he juggled the luggage into the boot for the late-afternoon return to the city.

'Don't whinge. I'm the one who'll be paying for excess weight on the plane.' Lauren's light retort masked the pain of knowing every moment brought her departure closer.

They'd have a few evenings, maybe part of the weekends together, and distant phone calls while she was driving around being a tourist. All too soon she'd have used up her ten days and they'd say goodbye.

There hadn't been, nor would there be, any promises or declarations of keeping in touch. And she'd never ask for them.

'It might be cheaper for me to drive you home.'

CHAPTER FIFTEEN

HER HEARTBEAT SPIKED. His tone was light but his eyes were grave, his lips firm and unsmiling. She couldn't have replied to save her life, and ached to have him add he meant it.

'Got room for more?' Clair came down the steps carrying a huge bunch of flowers. 'Duncan's bringing the fruit we promised.'

Lauren pressed her hands together, her index fingertips on her lips. How had she ever been daunted by this considerate, generous couple?

'They're beautiful, Clair. Thank you for a wonderful weekend. It's been unforgettable.'

She recognised roses and tiger lilies, others were unknown. When she reached up to kiss Clair's cheek as she accepted the stunning gift, she was drawn into an unexpected motherly hug.

'You'll always be welcome, Lauren,' Clair said, and gave her an extra squeeze.

'Even when she hasn't stuffed up on her computer.' Duncan laughed as he appeared behind her with a big cardboard box. 'Should last you a few days,' he added, handing it to Matt.

Lauren buried her face into the blooms and inhaled their perfume before placing them on the back seat alongside her overnight bag. Gently touched the petals, blinking back tears at the Fords' kindness.

She noticed Matt and Clair in close conversation, serious expressions on their faces. Was he also being given friendly advice? She walked over to Duncan to thank him and was pulled into a friendly embrace.

'I'll be eternally grateful to you for helping Clair and boosting her esteem. Other technicians made her feel inadequate though she hid it well.'

'It wasn't much compared to your company and hospitality. I've loved every moment.'

'Then come again—plan for a holiday in the spring or in December. Despite the heat, we always have a festive season, including long evening walks followed by hot or cold drinks on the veranda.'

'It sounds inviting.'

'Then be here.' He smiled down at her. 'Pity you're based in Sydney. It's such a long way away.'

The farewells lasted another ten minutes and included more hugs for Lauren as if they feared they wouldn't see her for a long time. Finally they were on the road, and she let her head fall back and closed her eyes.

'Tired, darling?'

Every cell in her body sprang to high alert at his endearment, the second time he'd used it. Was it an automatic name for the women he made love to?

'A little. It's been a full weekend.'

'Any regrets, Lauren?' Low, and slightly hesitant. Not like him at all.

'None, Matt.' She paused and grinned. 'Well, maybe the purchase of a T-shirt depicting a joey in its mother's pouch, waving an Australian flag. I'll give it to a friend with quirky taste.'

Matt chuckled. His mood lifted. The idea he'd been contemplating was the best option for both of them. All he had to do was find the words to convince her. In his usual competent way, he rehearsed the phrasing, while negotiating the bends and merging onto the freeway. Lauren was lost in her own thoughts.

Satisfied he was ready, he glanced across and forgot it all in a rush of affection when he saw her lovely features relaxed in peaceful sleep. He faced the road again, tightening his grip on the wheel to conquer the urge to caress her cheek.

He had the rest of the day for gentle persuasion. If she agreed they'd spend all their free time together for the two weeks she had left. Fourteen days, and he'd count down every one.

Moving into the left lane, he slowed down. There was no urgency, Lauren was peaceful and the hectic uncertainty had eased from his life. He didn't know exactly what he faced legally but he'd been totally honest and had good representation. He had no idea how bad the backlash might be if, more like when, his father's duplicity became public but was assured of Duncan's full support.

He had faith in his own ability to reform the company and keep it viable. And—he shot an affectionate look at his sleeping passenger—he had Lauren. Sweet, adorable Lauren, who hijacked his thoughts at inopportune moments and flipped his heart with a wisp of a smile. She even had him questioning his steadfast beliefs.

A semi-trailer whooshed past in the next lane, too close, causing him to veer to the left. Lauren stirred and stretched her back, blinked and gave him an apologetic smile.

'I fell asleep.'

'I noticed. Sweet dreams?'

'I can't remember. Why?'

'You sighed a couple of times, low and contented. Cancel the hotel booking, Lauren. Stay with me.' Blunt and rushed—not as he'd practised. 'Sorry, I had a persuasive speech planned. Logical reasons to…'

He stopped midsentence as she silently bent, took her mobile from her bag and scrolled for the number. He shook his head to clear his muddled brain and closed his open mouth. Elation zapped along his veins. She'd be there to welcome him in the evenings. They'd have quiet hours to talk and long nights to hold each other.

'Done. I can do one-day trips to the southern area or the hills.' She dropped her phone into the drinks holder.

They were approaching the turn-off sign and he checked his rear-vision mirror in preparation for switching lanes. Pulling up at the lights, he covered her hand and revelled in the heat surge that simple act generated.

'And be home for dinner?'

'Oh, if you're expecting meals like Clair served us, you'll be disappointed. I'm very basic, usually cook for one or have cold meat and salad.'

'You've seen my fridge. It's been takeaway or dine out since I arrived home. We'll improvise as we go. I have dinner with my parents on Mondays and call in after work whenever I can.'

'They need your support so that mustn't change. And you can't neglect your sister's family either.'

'I won't. They and Alan are the ones who've kept me grounded and sustained me through it all.'

'You're lucky to have them.'

He flicked her a quick glance. It was a genuine remark with no undertone of acrimony.

'We never tried that pub near the unit. Wanna give it a go tonight?'

Wednesday's dinner was crumbed lamb chops and salad, followed by bakery fruit pie and carton custard. As basic as you could get. Lauren thanked the stars for the local butcher whose selection of ready-to-cook meals was superb and included helpful advice.

She'd revised her plans, exploring Adelaide suburbs and southern coastal areas on alternate days to limit the long drives. Today she'd been to the museum and art gallery in the city, tomorrow's choice was the Fleurieu Peninsula's historic towns.

Their evenings were casual yet special to her. They'd have a quick run of the taped news followed by lively discussions as they watched a favourite programme or two.

The nights held mutually shared passion and deep, peaceful sleep.

They lived in the moment. The future was never discussed but she wondered if he thought about it as much as she did.

Anticipation thrummed through her at the sound of his car. Soon she'd have to learn to live without the tingles over her skin, the breathlessness and the tom-tom racing of her pulse.

'Lauren.' She loved his homecoming routine: the same raspy greeting, the same admiration in his midnight-blue eyes, and the deep loving kiss, lasting until the need for air broke them apart. Plus for her the same intense pang to her heart.

'Mmm…' He nuzzled her neck, then sniffed appreciatively. 'Dinner smells almost as good as you. Let's talk 'til it's ready.'

What had happened? Bad news about his father's actions or the company? Serious talking was for as they ate, then forgotten in the pleasures of the evening. The way he grasped her fingers as they sat on the sofa was different, and disturbed her. *He was nervous.*

'What do you have planned for Friday?'

'A tram ride and walk on the beach.'

'Without me?' His eyebrow quirk and sudden grin confused her even more.

'Drive in with me, process the work I need done then go for your walk.'

'And?'

He seemed loath to continue, his eyes dark and intense, trying to predict her reaction to his announcement.

'I've got tickets for the Crows' game in the evening.'

Relief had her sagging into the cushions. That was all? He didn't want to upset her by leaving her alone for a few hours?

'That fine, Matt. It'll do you good to let off steam and I can amuse myself.'

Matt knew damn well she could, how self-reliant she was. While relishing the times she'd depended on him, he also loved her independent spirit. She'd admitted to rethinking her relationship with her family. Now he was hoping Friday's outing would help her move on.

'Two for Alan and his date and one for me.' He paused, eyes on her face. 'The fourth is for you.'

Her reaction was everything he'd hoped for. Wide eyes, gold specks sparkling. Red lips parted and inviting. Index finger pointing at his chest.

'I told you I don't attend matches, only watch bits when I'm visiting friends who have the television on. Take someone else.'

She was magnificent, head high, chin jutted and eyes that flashed defiance. He stored the memory and prepared to counter.

He caught her finger in one hand, and cupped her chin with the other, stroking the silken underside of her stubborn jaw. Inhaled deeply as her eyes softened in response to his action. He so wanted to let her off the hook but it was more important to have her exorcise this demon.

'Lauren, you bound the whole concept of your perceived lack of parental attention with the sports your brothers played. Come and put it to the test. One game. Share a Crows win with me. Supper's on Alan.'

She looked down, bit her lip, and made a flimsy attempt to free her hand. It took little effort for him to hold on. She finally peered up at him and tilted her head.

'Do they still sell hot dogs?'

His heart swelled to bursting point. She was adorable.

'As many as you want, darling.' He pulled her into his arms and if the oven's timer hadn't rung, dinner would have been served a lot later.

* * *

Lauren liked Kaye at first sight when she arrived in the office with Alan and pizza. She was a trim, toned extrovert and an avid Crows fan, wearing all the club regalia and waving a beanie at a protesting Matt.

She also had a photo on her mobile screen showing a litter of squirming newborn puppies. A wriggling mixture of brown, white and black.

'You promised to wear it for the rest of the year if I found a suitable puppy for your nephews. These are a cross breed of black Labrador and German shepherd. They'll be gentle and protective, perfect for active children. You get first pick and they'll be ready to take home in five or six weeks.'

'They're adorable. Are you going to let the boys choose?' Lauren enthused, wishing she could have one too. Not practical with her profession or in an apartment.

'Under supervision, otherwise we'll end up with a car full,' Matt insisted, jamming on the hat. He'd cleared his desk for the meal and, when the others went to fetch chairs from Lauren's office, he muttered in her ear.

'She cheated, made the deal when our forward was lining up for a winning goal, sixty metres out and less than a minute on the clock.'

'If you agreed, it's binding.' She grinned at the usually stylishly dressed man—even in casual clothes on the weekend—now in well-worn jeans, football jumper and that distinctive beanie. And loved him even more.

'You siding with Kaye?' He gave her a hard, lip-smacking kiss. 'I can think of a few bets I'd willingly lose to you.'

She recalled hours of sitting rugged up on cold benches, being bumped and bruised by excited supporters. She thought of days wasted setting up stalls, being bored and trying to persuade people to buy merchandise or raffle tickets. Now she looked into hungry blue eyes and knew she'd go through all of that in a thunderstorm if he were beside her.

* * *

Matt kept a tight hold on her hand as they walked to the stadium, joining an ever-growing throng that bottlenecked at the bridge over the river. He kept telling himself this was for her but that excuse was wearing thin. It was he who wanted to share his enthusiasm for their national game, who wanted to see her lose her inhibitions and cheer with the mob. It was he who wanted her with him when they played in the finals.

It was a full house by the time they bounced the ball for the start and the noise was deafening. For the first time ever his concentration wasn't out there with the players. He watched Lauren, quite prepared to take her out if she became stressed. Instead he saw interest grow as her eyes darted from the field to the big screens and back.

His heart usually pounded at the fierce interaction between players, now it was because she leant forward as they ran, held her breath as they shot for goal and flopped back when they missed. By the fourth quarter, she was on her feet with Kaye every time the lead changed, face flushed and eyes shining. And he didn't care an iota that he missed most of the action on the field.

'A twenty-eight-point win. Our best this year.' Kaye danced up the steps, arms swaying with her scarf held high. 'You must be our lucky charm, Lauren.'

Matt hugged her close 'You are definitely mine.'

Lauren clung to him, treasuring his words. The excitement had been contagious. Her head spun, whether from the buzz of the crowd or the shock of discovering the thrill of the game overrode her inhibitions, she wasn't sure. As if tied to Kaye with invisible bonds, she'd found herself leaping to her feet and calling out phrases she'd never spoken, hadn't known she'd memorised.

Matt was grinning as if he'd been the star forward. Not a smug, I-told-you-so smile; he was genuinely happy for her.

Had she been wrong all her life or was she seeing everything through new eyes? And if she had changed because she loved him, why couldn't he love her for the person he was helping her to become?

Monday afternoon Matt decided to grab a chicken wrap on the way back from the bank. Funny how easily he'd adapted to healthier meals and salads. Not funny that in a week he'd be eating alone again.

Lauren. His pulse hiked up, and he quickened his pace as he saw her opening the door of a café across the street. He halted when she spoke to the dark-haired woman entering behind her. She hadn't mentioned meeting anyone.

By the time he'd crossed at the lights and walked along, they were seated at a table studying menus. An old friend she'd caught up with? He wouldn't disturb them; she'd tell him over dinner tonight.

She didn't. She was quiet and withdrawn, claiming fatigue and a headache. Concerned, he persuaded her to take a tablet and go to bed. In the morning he left her sleeping.

Tuesday was no different. She blamed it on the current autumn virus and he had to admit she looked unwell, though she didn't cough or sneeze. Was she depressed thinking of the shrinking time they had left? That he understood.

He'd never considered a cross-country romance. There'd never been a reason to. The idea of seeing Lauren only on weekends was gut-wrenching but better than not being with her at all. Would she be prepared to try?

Alan's text came through as he was driving to work Wednesday morning, and he read the short, concise message in the lift. Apprehensive, and with fingers tapping his desk, he accessed the online morning papers. The small article tucked away in one of the business sections sent his world crashing in flames.

Names weren't mentioned but anyone with determination and knowledge of the company or his father could identify them. Obscure hints were made of illness, legalities and the long-term viability of the business. His temper rose as he researched the reporter, found her profile and photo.

And his fragile faith was obliterated in a torrent of bitterness, far worse than all the other betrayals combined. This was the woman Lauren had been with on Monday, the reason for her reticence since.

She was one of the very few who had knowledge of his father's dementia *and* fraud. What reason could there be for meeting that woman? Why?

His chest heaved, and anger ruled as he reached for his keys. Threw them down, snatched up his mobile, and paced the floor until Lauren answered.

'Matt?'

Diffident and wary. Guilty?

'Who was the woman you were with on Monday?' Grated out without polite niceties.

Her quick gasp sharpened his pain. Her silence exacerbated his temper.

'She's a damn reporter. What did you tell her?'

'You… I'm…'

'Lost for words, Lauren. What am I? A magnet for cheats and liars? Dad, Christine, and now you? Do you have any idea what I…? No, you wouldn't. I can't bear to see you. Don't want to hear your voice.'

He hung up, tossed his phone on the coffee table and sank into a chair, burying his head into his hands. This was it. He'd never fully trust anyone again.

CHAPTER SIXTEEN

LAUREN CURLED UP on his settee, buried her head into his cushion and sobbed at his tirade. How could he believe she'd break her promise?

Idiot, stupid, stupid idiot. She hadn't realised the woman was a reporter until she'd begun to ask about Marcus. Fearing he might be annoyed that she'd been duped into the conversation, she hadn't told him. Things the woman had hinted she knew could only have come from one of the select few people he trusted implicitly.

He hadn't said what the reporter had claimed to know, only accused her of telling family secrets, and she had no way of proving her innocence. Maybe if she had been truthful with him he'd be looking for the real culprit. Instead he'd condemned her without even seeing her, proof his caring had been superficial.

She rubbed the tears from her cheeks, and went to wash her face with a cold flannel. The red-eyed wreck in the mirror gave her no choice.

She loved him so she'd make it easier for him. He didn't want to see her so she wouldn't be here when he came home. She booked a flight, packed her belongings and called a taxi.

Matt hadn't needed his cousin's harsh rebuke over the phone to know he'd been wrong to call her in anger. Personal confrontation when he could see her eyes and read her expression would have been better. Didn't change the reality. Or did it?

Alan had rung to say he'd done what Matt should have—checked and found out the reporter was ambitious, and not particularly scrupulous in her methods of obtaining information.

He couldn't postpone the morning's scheduled meeting though he came close to doing just that. It was crucial to the company's survival, especially after today's media article. With the prospect of legal proceedings giving him motivation, he blocked Lauren from his mind and went to the boardroom to fight for his and the company's future.

He deliberately stayed late at the office, arriving home to a dark and silent unit. Refusing to acknowledge the sour churning in his gut, he walked in.

I can't bear to see you. Don't want to hear your voice.

His words echoed in his head. He sagged against the door jamb leading to the kitchen area. The table was bare. The vase had gone. Lauren had gone.

Lauren had never felt more alone. She ached for Matt's smile, his spine-tingling touch, and his midnight-blue eyes that could make her pulse race from across a room. She even missed his cajoling her to reassess her relationship with her family.

Knowing he believed she'd betrayed him tore her apart. Knowing she had unconditional support from her friends held her together. Whatever they suspected, they'd never push, would give her all the time she needed until she was ready to confide in them.

On Wednesday night, she cried herself to sleep, reliving his caresses, his kisses. The passion they'd shared. On Thursday she wandered aimlessly for hours, stopping only for drinks and an occasional snack. On Friday morning she went to see her employer and resigned. When she got back to the units, Pete was home so she told him.

'You can't, Lauren. You're the best. You love digging out the solutions where others have failed. You…' Words failed him and his arms flailed in the air.

Lauren shrugged. She'd lost enthusiasm for her work, and her heart hurt every second of every day. Matt didn't

want her, didn't love her and had never really trusted her.
He hadn't bothered to ring but she'd have blocked the call
if he had. His throaty voice was implanted in her brain.
She heard it every night as she lay alone in her single bed.
Didn't need to hear the reality and have her heart ripped
apart even more.

'I'm going to teach.'

Pete made a scoffing sound, and dropped down beside
her on the sofa. 'You'll be bored and climbing the walls in
a week. And the salary's crap.'

'Private lessons to adults. One on one showing them
just the functions they want to use on their own personal
computers. I've done it for friends, and they all said they
knew people who'd pay for the service.'

'You've thought it through? It's really what you want?'

'For now it's what I need, Pete. Who knows what's
ahead?'

Nothing but memories and what-ifs for her. Her throat
tightened—it seemed to do that a lot lately—her breath
hitched, and she shivered.

In an instant she was wrapped in friendly arms, her head
was cradled to his shoulder and his hand made soothing
strokes over her back.

'I'd like to find the guy who hurt you and feed the most
destructive viruses I can find into his computer system.
And him.'

She choked up at the thought of polite, pacifist Pete
going into battle for her. She felt warm and cared for, knowing he meant it and that the others would back him up. They
might not have Matt's name or details of the breakup but
he was now the enemy.

Easing away, she stood up and brushed off the few tears
that had escaped.

'Save your knight-in-armour mode for Jenny. He wasn't

completely to blame. He'd been betrayed by someone he trusted and circumstances showed me in a suspicious light.'

'Loving means trusting.'

Which again proved Matt didn't love her.

'And the only way is forward. I'll take each day as it comes.'

And hide my torment in the dark nights.

All Matt wanted to do was to cower in a dark corner and lick his wounds. Nothing he'd suffered before had prepared him for the gut-wrenching pain whenever he thought of her, which was almost every minute of every day. He lay awake remembering the nights they'd spent together, reached out for her in his restless sleep on the couch.

The sun was rising as he drove into the city on Monday, an unneeded reminder of last weekend. Telling himself he was better off without her had no effect. His brain kept repeating one word over and over. Why?

Mid-morning he brewed another mug of strong coffee, couldn't bear to drink it in his office. Even with the connecting door shut, he kept glancing that way as if she'd suddenly appear. He walked to the boardroom because she'd never been in there but she came with him now, in his head and his heart. There was no escape.

On the way back, the lift doors opened as he went through Reception and Clair stepped out. Surprised by her tentative smile when she saw him, he walked over.

'I didn't expect to see you, Clair. You're always welcome, of course.'

'I had to come. Can we talk?'

Her apprehension triggered a kindred unease. That damn article? Duncan had already assured him the reporter's insinuations hadn't affected his opinion at all. There was nothing he wasn't aware of and their association wouldn't change. He was also convinced the people who mattered wouldn't equate Marcus's condition with Matt's aptitude to run the company.

'Of course, this way.' He guided her to his office, and over to the window seats.

'Coffee or tea?'

'Not now. Please, Matt, sit down. This is personal and it concerns you.'

His gut tightened as he obeyed. Lauren? He'd told Duncan she'd returned to Sydney. Not why.

She fiddled with the handle of her bag then dropped it onto the floor. He leant forward and took her hand, shocked to feel its trembling.

'What's wrong, Clair? If there's anything I can do, just ask.'

'It's the other way round, Matt. I came because I'm partly responsible for that reporter's knowledge, limited though it was.'

'You?' He shook his head, couldn't take it in. A chill seeped into his muscles and he dreaded hearing more.

'Your mother came to our group lunch two weeks ago, first time for ages. We were chatting in a quiet corner and she began to tell me about her problems with your father and his deterioration. I should have suggested we talk later somewhere more private but she was desperate to let it all out.'

The chill became icy. Every cell in his body seemed to shrink and close down. He had a vague awareness of letting go of her hand, of his shoulders slumping.

'She said your father kept telling her things she knew weren't true or dropping hints about special funding for his secret hideaway retirement. She didn't want to worry you or the family with his fantasies, just wanted someone to sympathise with her.'

His mother had confided in a friend because he'd built barriers between them. She'd been overheard and Lauren was innocent. The reporter had been trying to get confirmation or more details. It was as if he heard the facts but couldn't process them through the fog in his head.

'Duncan showed me the article, and this morning I found out the woman who wrote it had been at the venue. I noticed her hanging around, and assumed she was a guest. I'm so sorry, Matt.'

Oh, Lauren, what have I done?

Guilt and anguish raked him, his throat clogged, and his stomach heaved. Condemnation roared in his head. Sweat dripped down his back, and his fingers balled into fists.

'Matt. Matt, are you all right?'

His mind cleared. Clair was leaning forward, regarding him with deep concern. He shuddered back to reality.

He'd listened to her, heard what *she* said. He hadn't heard Lauren's explanation because he hadn't given her a chance to tell him.

'No. I think I've made the worst, stupidest mistake of my life and I'm not sure she'll ever forgive me.'

'Lauren?'

He nodded, too ashamed to speak.

Clair patted his knee. 'Go and tell her in those exact words. Lauren loves you, Matt, and we women in love can forgive our men almost anything if they love us too.'

Could they? Would Lauren, after his bitter accusations?

Lauren stared at the four family-sized pizza boxes and clutched her fingers in her lap. She'd always begged off the Monday pizza, footy and whatever-you-want-to-drink evenings in Pete and Jenny's unit. Why had she agreed to come tonight?

Because she wanted to prove she could watch an Aussie Rules game without breaking down. And she would as long as she didn't think of the crowded Adelaide oval and being crushed against a warm, muscular body in the crowd.

'So, did you keep that appointment with your boss, Lauren? Has he made an offer you can't refuse to get you to stay?' Jenny leant forward and opened the top box, the aroma evoking memories of the last time she'd been in Matt's office.

'We talked. He wants me to consider freelancing for him whenever he gets a job he thinks worthy of my talents. His expression. Soft soap and flattery. I think he's hoping I'll relent and come back full time after I've had a break.'

'Could happen.'

'I doubt it but the idea of a real challenge now and again is tempting.'

The last one had been and look how that ended. No chance of a repeat. She'd fallen in love and lost her heart to Matt Dalton, irretrievable and never to be reclaimed. The pain would subside and become a dull ache she'd learn to live with.

Matt needed someone to confess to, someone who'd listen, tell him what a drongo he'd been, and offer to help find her. The one person who'd shared all his dreams and aspirations, almost every failure and heartbreak. As soon as he'd finished essential work, he took a taxi to Alan's city apartment, picking up Chinese food on the way.

The food was hot and spicy, and the cold beer from the fridge slid smoothly down his throat giving him courage to begin. He lounged back, crossing his ankles.

'Lauren was my balcony girl.'

Alan stopped chewing and stared.

'You're kidding? I don't remember seeing her that night and she'd have been noticeable even then. *You* definitely never forgot her.'

'No, she was always there, even when I was contemplating marriage to someone else. I didn't realise who she was until I kissed her again.'

He almost lost it as the memory seared his brain. Closed his eyes, picturing hazel eyes full of passion, and a smile that always sent his pulse soaring.

'I'm an idiot, Alan. A blind, insensitive idiot who didn't have the nous to see the truth in front of me or the guts to claim the sweetest prize any man was ever offered.'

His cousin nodded. 'I agree. Now you tell me what happened and we'll work out how you find her, grovel like a lovesick fool—which you'll happily be—and win her back.'

Matt spilled his guts, taking all the blame. He'd cursed himself for not asking more about her life, her suburb, or the names of her friends. She wasn't in the phone directory and he hadn't been able to locate her on social media. Her employer had offered to forward any mail he sent, after justifiably refusing to divulge personal information. Apologetic words on paper could never convey his guilt and remorse. He needed to see her, hold her and beg for forgiveness.

'My last hope is to contact one of her brothers but they'd probably ask why and refuse if I tell the truth. All I know is she lives on the same floor as her friends, in a suburban block of units in Sydney. I didn't bother to ask her anything—'

He jerked upright, beer spraying onto his jeans and the floor.

'The form.' He sprang to his feet, dumping the can on the table. 'Come on—you drive.'

'What form? Where?

Matt was already halfway to the door.

'The personnel form I filed without bothering to read it. Her name and address, contact number in case of an emergency, et cetera.'

Ten minutes later Matt perched on *her* desk and read the form out loud.

'"Lauren Juliet Taylor", her address and mobile phone number. And—' the rush of joyful adrenaline almost tipped him off the desk '—"Peter Williams", her friend in the apartment opposite hers.' He punched the air in triumph. 'I've got where she lives. I've got her friend's number. And with his help, I've got a plan.'

Lauren fumbled in her shoulder bag for her keys as she took the last few steps to the third floor. Her first private lesson had been a success and her next three Tuesday afternoons were taken.

If even half her future clients were as good as feisty seventy-two-year-old Mary—or seventy-two years *young* as she'd claimed—her new occupation would be a pleasure. She'd listened intently, made copious notes in a neat legible hand, and was willing to give anything a go. She claimed making mistakes was part of living.

If that was the case, Lauren was certainly alive, so why did she feel numb inside? There was…

A large vase containing an incredible arrangement of orchids on the landing outside her door. Her foot caught on the last stair. She couldn't breathe, couldn't form a coherent thought.

Orchids: deep reds, yellow with leopard spots, and lilac ones of every shade imaginable. She stumbled forward and fell onto her knees, her trembling fingers reaching out to touch the soft petals, confirm they weren't her imagination.

Tears flooded her eyes. Her heart hammered into life, sending her blood racing to regenerate every pulse point. Orchids. Matt. Linked together in her mind for ever.

'Lauren?'

Broken, rasping voice. Trembling arms clasped her in a strong embrace. Warm lips pressed to her forehead. Disbelief scrambled her brain, and hope fluttered in her stomach.

'Don't cry, my love. Please, don't cry.'

My love. Matt's voice saying words she wouldn't dare to dream. Matt kneeling beside her, his body warm and solid, and his heart thudding under her hand. Matt's fingers lovingly stroking her cheek, and tilting her chin.

She barely had time to register dark shadows under his compassionate blue eyes before he kissed her. Not with the smooth arrogance of the youth, or the competent skill of the sophisticated man. Hesitant, unsure of her response.

She wanted the passionate lover who'd taken her to the moon and beyond, and refused to settle for less. Wrapping her arms around his neck, she tangled her fingers in his hair, binding him to her. She teased him with the tip of her tongue and nipped his lip with her teeth.

In an instant he crushed her against him, chased her tongue back inside with his, stroking and tangling, claiming his rights as her man. His hands caressed her, fuelling fires she'd believed extinguished. His breathing was as ragged as her own.

Voices echoed up the stairwell and he lifted his head, chest heaving, throat convulsing and eyes gleaming.

'Inside?' Rough and barely audible.

Unable to speak, she nodded, and looked round for the keys she'd dropped. Matt picked them up and helped her to her feet. Her fingers trembled too much to take them, and her heart flipped at his unsteady attempts to unlock the door.

He followed her in, stopped just inside gazing wide-eyed at her home.

Her home, where she'd spent six tortured nights berating the fool that she'd been to fall in love with him. Where she listlessly performed necessary chores, and agonised over a solitary future without him.

He stood there as if he were a returning hero carrying his gift like the spoils of war. And the anguish and heartache she'd suffered surged into a torrent of anger at his injustice.

'No.'

CHAPTER SEVENTEEN

HIS BODY JERKED, his brow furrowed, and his mouth fell open.

'You bring flowers and expect what you did to be wiped away and forgotten? You judged me guilty without proof, willingly believed I lied to you.' She retreated as she spoke, torn between aching for him and never wanting to suffer like this again.

'You never trusted me from the day we met. You were willing and eager to take me to bed but never prepared to give anything of yourself. Except your body for your own pleasure.'

'No. No, Lauren. I was...'

'Protecting yourself.'

His features contorted. He raised his hands, blinked as the orchids came into his view, and strode across the room to place them on her bookshelf. He turned to face her, his hands reaching out to her, and his dark beseeching eyes pleaded for understanding.

Her heart clamoured for her to run into his arms, surrender and forgive. But he'd disowned her over the phone, without giving her a chance to explain.

She straightened her shoulders and lifted her chin. When his hands fell then one rose to rake through his hair, her fingers itched to join it.

Flowers and kisses came easily to him. If he thought he could win her over by...

'How did you get into the building?'

He broke eye contact, and stared at her cream velour sofa with its colourful cushions. Typical Matt, plotting his reply instead of saying what he felt.

'Can we sit and talk? Please, Lauren. I know I've been a drongo and selfish as hell. And the dumbest prize idiot for not admitting even to myself that I love you.'

Her world slammed to a shuddering halt. The air rushed from her lungs, her legs trembled, threatening to buckle, and she leant on the breakfast bar for support.

'No, you don't.' Breathless. Distrustful.

The adoration in his eyes stirred the cold embers in her core, and she scrunched her fingers, wouldn't fold. He'd coerced her so many times. She'd need more than words to risk her heart again.

She moved to the sofa, determined to conceal the effect of the hot tendrils of desire weaving their way to every extremity as he joined her. Leaving space between them, he spread his arm along the back and hooked one ankle over the other knee—a simple, familiar habit that chipped at her resistance.

'Pete let me in.'

This wasn't going the way Matt had planned. He'd been wrong in so many ways, including persuading her to face her demons while fooling himself about his own.

He'd banked on her being thrilled with the flowers, and melting into his arms. Seeing her on her knees with tears streaming down her face had shattered him.

Her response to his kiss had been all he could have wished for. She cared. They'd talk and she'd forgive him. They'd make love and work out how they could be together.

Lauren had stunned him with her hostile stance and accusation, her flashing hazel eyes demanding he fight for her, and prove he was worthy of her love. Living without her had been hell. Together they could build their own heaven.

'You named Pete as your contact on the company's personnel form I'd filed without reading. I had completely forgotten about it until yesterday. He was tough to convince, but finally agreed to meet me with no guarantees of help. He also threatened to take me apart if I ever hurt you again.'

Her lips curved and he found himself grinning at the

image too. He had height and weight advantages but he had no doubt Pete's threat was sincere.

'I have…had trust issues. I never saw my parents kiss or be affectionate, and rarely heard them argue. Came home one evening and it was full on. He'd been having affairs for most of their married life. She put up with it because she wanted the lifestyle he provided. I was gutted at their hypocrisy.'

'That's why you left Australia.' She leant towards him. The tightness in his gut eased, and he ground out the rest.

'He used his business premises for rendezvous.'

'The bedroom?'

'I've never been in there. It's a tangible reminder of his adultery, and I swore I'd never be like him. That's what always stopped me from kissing you in the office.'

She shuffled a bit closer, and covered his outstretched hand with hers. As always with her touch, his heart beat faster, and his temperature rose. He needed to get the truth out, have no more secrets. Then he could hold her again.

'Apart from the woman in London, I knew others, male and female, who believed fidelity was outmoded. Faithful couples seemed to be a minority, or maybe my pride saw it that way as proof my father wasn't so contemptible. If I didn't believe in love their relationship wasn't abnormal.'

He took a chance and moved towards her. She stopped him with a hand on his chest, eyes wary and sceptical.

'You didn't want any of the photos.'

He caught her hand, raised it to his lips and kissed her palm. Rejoiced in her quivering reaction, and his own. Regaining her trust was paramount so he fought the craving to enfold her in arms and kiss her the way he had in the hall.

'*They* were for you. I ordered another set, which should have told me how special the evening with you was, and how much you already meant to me. It came the day after you left.'

His thumb began an automatic caress of her knuckles.

When she didn't pull free, he closed his eyes and took a long breath.

'I refused to believe in love even though I knew couples who proved me wrong. My experiences, including suspicion of my father's computer deception, gave me little reason to trust in any sphere of life.

'Then you walked into my office and all my resolutions collapsed. I fell in love, probably had ten years ago and hadn't been mature enough to recognise it. I stubbornly ignored the reality when we met again.'

Her smile grew as he spoke, her beautiful hazel eyes glowed, and his resolve crashed. He gathered her into his arms where she belonged, setting his world right. A different aroma, as alluring as the other, filled his nostrils. He brushed his lips across her forehead, and if his heart beat any faster, he'd short circuit.

'Matt?' She raised her head, a tiny furrow creasing her brow. 'That reporter…'

'She overheard my mother talking at a luncheon and started digging. I should have come home and talked to you. Instead I let my past rule my head. I couldn't admit, even to myself, that only you had the power to break my heart. My stupid pride almost destroyed us both.'

'She said she knew Clair, implied things about your father. I swear I told her I didn't know what she was talking about.'

'I believe you. I'll never doubt you again, my darling. I love you. With all my heart and all that I am.'

He kissed her deeply, lovingly with no reservations. Cradled her as close as humanly possible, only breaking away to breathe. Found the air clogged his throat at the love shining in her eyes.

'I love you too, Matt.'

He slipped from the sofa onto his knees in front of her and held her hands in his.

'Lauren Taylor, you are sweet and courageous, and I'll love you 'til my last breath and beyond. I'm yours, only yours, for ever. Marry me?'

Lauren couldn't speak. Her head spun as if she'd drunk too much champagne; the electrical zing from his fingers through hers was zapping along her veins at airship speed. Her already pounding heart threatened to burst from her ribcage.

The love in Matt's eyes wrapped her in an aura of soft warmth, a haven where there were only gentle caresses and love. A special place of devotion and commitment. For two.

'Yes. Oh, yes, please. I love you, Matt. I'm yours, now and for ever.'

He let out a roar of triumph, scooped her up and swung her round. She clung to him as her joyous laughter mingled with his. When he stopped, his kiss was gentle, reverent. He laid his forehead to hers.

'I ache to make love to you, darling, but I promised Pete and Jenny we'd go and tell them the good news.'

'Confident, huh?' She tried to sound stern; it came out husky and adoring.

'Optimistically hoping I hadn't misread the signs when we were together, the passion when we made love. No way was I going to walk away unless you looked me in the eyes and swore you never wanted to see me again.'

He kissed her again then set her on her feet and nuzzled her neck.

'We'll still have all night.'

Matt missed the earliest flight home in the morning, caught the next and went straight to the office. He stood in the doorway, taking in the expensive décor, the stunning views and his father's top-of-the-range desk. He didn't need all this to define himself, never had.

Knowing Lauren loved him gave him a goal to be better than he was. It was time to lay the first ghost to rest. He strode purposefully across the deluxe tiles, through the first door and into the bedroom.

It was neat, tidy and impersonal. Overwhelming sorrow shook him as he thought of how much his father had risked for the brief encounters in this cold place. He thought of his mother knowing the truth and living a lie.

Closing his eyes, he conjured up Lauren's lovely face as he'd kissed her goodbye, hair tousled, eyes shining. Together they'd face the uncertainties ahead. Together—a couple united by a vow to share life's fears and sorrows, its triumphs and joys.

Leaving youth's judgement and bitterness behind, he scrolled for his mother's number. From today he'd make up for the years of estrangement.

That evening, Matt held his mother close without censure and, for the first time in nine years, embraced his father. The hug he received in return filled his heart with love and relief.

Marcus was almost his old self and pleased with the gift of his favourite wine. As Matt opened it he regretted missed opportunities like this, reflected on his culpability then let it go. The past couldn't be changed but it could be left behind if they were all willing to face the future.

'I'm in love with a very special lady and she's agreed to marry me.' He couldn't keep it in any longer, and was elated at how good the words sounded out loud. Even more so when his mother hugged and kissed him and his father shook his hand.

'She's flying in from Sydney on Friday and I'd like Lena, Mark and the boys to join us here for lunch on Saturday to meet her.'

Before he left he had a private talk with his mother, pledging his and Lauren's support in caring for his father.

They'd sworn together to keep their knowledge of his father's infidelity a secret from her, saving her any more pain.

Finally acknowledging that loving someone meant accepting their faults and weaknesses, he put his arm around her. Holding her close, he regretted the years they'd lost.

'I was young, arrogant and so very wrong to keep distance between us for so long. If I hadn't you'd have been able to confide in *me* and that reporter would never have had a story to write.'

'You have your father's pride, Matthew. Promise me you won't let it come between you and Lauren.'

'I promise. She's more than I deserve, and is willing to help us keep Dad at home with you as long as possible.'

She wrapped her arms around him and he clung tight, grateful that he had the chance to make amends and heal the rift between them.

Mid-winter, the twenty-third of June. Lauren woke before the alarm, stretched and smiled at the blue skies behind the treetops outside. Sunshine as predicted for her winter wedding day, though not even a cyclone could mar the occasion. Tonight she'd be Mrs Matthew Dalton.

She threw back the covers, and ran to the shower, leaving the door open in case he rang early. He did, but by then she was perched on the side of the bed, wearing her dressing gown, and combing her towel-dry hair.

'Happy wedding day, my love. I missed you.' The sound of his voice, gravel rough from sleep, was her favourite way of starting each day.

'Me too, Matt. I'm lost in this bed without you.' She lay back into the pillows, wishing he were here beside her in the Fords' guest suite.

'Wasn't my idea to spend the night apart. Clair and our mothers ganged up on me. Never going to happen again if I can prevent it.' The low growl in his voice skittled up and down her spine. He'd only begrudgingly agreed after she'd said it would please the older women.

'I'll make it up to you.' She dropped her tone, trying for seductive, laughed when he growled again.

'You will, my love. I kept myself awake compiling a list.'

She quivered with delight, imagined ticking off each item. 'I love you, Matt. Four o'clock is a long time away.'

'Longer until we're alone. Then we have two weeks, just you and me where no one can find us.'

Someone tapped on her door.

'I have to go. I've got company.'

'Look in the bottom drawer on my side of the bed, darling. I'll see you at four. I love you, Lauren.'

Her mother peeped in as she ended the call. Along with thrilling Matt and Lauren with the offer of their home and grounds for the wedding, Duncan and Clair had invited her parents to stay with them for the event.

Accepting there would always be differences between herself and her family had allowed her to form a real bond with them. Matt had ensured no one on her guest list was absent, and hotels and guest houses in neighbouring towns were filled with relatives and friends from interstate.

'You're awake. Happy wedding day, darling.' Her mother hugged and kissed her, and sat on the edge of the bed.

Do you want to come for a walk with me, Clair and the dogs after a quick breakfast? It's going to be chaotic once the trucks start arriving with the marquee, and everything.'

'Give me ten minutes and I'll see you on the veranda.'

As soon as her mother left Lauren dived over the bed, pulled the drawer open, and took out a small black box. She gasped with joy at the delicate yellow pendant and earrings. A real full orchid and two orchid centres preserved in resin with their true colours.

Matt's message, handwritten on the small white card,

was memorised, never to be forgotten. Every word of the
text she sent him came from her heart.

It didn't turn out to be so long after all when the hours were
filled with the walk, meals and watching the lawn areas
being transformed into a perfect venue for her dream wedding. She agreed to a hair stylist but did her own make-up,
her hand as steady as her heartbeat. And every two hours
she slipped away to be alone when Matt called, their secret
pact to keep in touch throughout their special day.

Marcus and Rosalind arrived and she shared a quiet time
with the two sets of parents. Her future father-in-law had
no idea he'd been spared prosecution because of his dete-
riorating condition and the fact that no withdrawals had
been made from the secret accounts. Everything had been
transferred into the company files and all due taxes paid
with interest for late submission.

Dalton Corporation had a new direction, the contracts
for the new project had been signed last month, and Matt
was the official CEO. He and his colleague in London were
negotiating the sale of his flat and his shares in the consultancy firm.

The way everything fell into place, and ran smoothly
to favourable solutions, sometimes scared her. Then she'd
look into Matt's eyes, and know that, whatever troubles
they encountered, he'd be there to love and support her,
and smooth their way forward.

It was ten minutes to four. There was a chill in the air, and
all areas were dotted with outdoor heaters. Somewhere in
the garden Matt was waiting for her, as impatient as she
was to make the vows that would join them for life.

She saw the rows of seated people waiting as her father
escorted her across the veranda, looked beyond them to the
decorated arch where the celebrant stood with…

Everything bar the man who'd turned towards her became lost in a haze that surrounded her. Matt, who'd taught her to let her true self shine, and showed her she was worthy of being loved. There was only Matt and his irresistible smile, his electric touch and those oh-so-persuasive lips drawing her closer. Only his midnight-blue eyes growing misty as she reached him. Only him, his gentle kiss and whispered words as he embraced her.

Matt would never find the words to express the emotions that rippled through his body when he turned to see Lauren at the top of the veranda steps. A vision in white was inadequate. She was gorgeous, stunning, and wearing his wedding gift.

This beautiful woman who'd captured his heart and soul as she helped him save his father's company and reputation. His own special angel who filled his days and nights with love and laughter.

Their eyes locked and the world disappeared as he willed her to his side. He acknowledged her father's traditional greeting automatically, his focus on Lauren's dazzling smile. Drawing her into his arms, he kissed her soft lips and whispered how much she meant to him.

They stood face to face, hands joined. Ten years ago he'd asked for a prize and claimed a kiss. He might not deserve her, but today he was claiming the best, the sweetest, the most loving woman as his for ever.

* * * * *

COMING SOON!

We really hope you enjoyed reading this book. If you're looking for more romance, be sure to head to the shops when new books are available on

Thursday 16th May

To see which titles are coming soon, please visit

millsandboon.co.uk/nextmonth

LET'S TALK

Romance

For exclusive extracts, competitions and special offers, find us online:

 facebook.com/millsandboon

@MillsandBoon

@MillsandBoonUK

Get in touch on 01413 063232